PRAISE FOR THE NOVELS OF SUSAN ANDERSEN

"Susan Andersen pens bright, smart, sexy, thoroughly entertaining Romantic Suspense—the kind of stuff I love to read."

Jayne Ann Krentz

"A smart, arousing, spirited escapade this is graced with a gentle mystery, a vulnerable, resilient heroine, and a worthy, wounded hero and served up with empathy and a humorous flair."

Library Journal on Burning Up

"Andersen again injects magic into a story that would be clichéd in another's hands, delivering warm, vulnerable characters in a touching, yet suspenseful read."

Publishers Weekly on Skintight, starred review.

"For a fun, sexy, unputdownable read, Susan Andersen is my go-to girl."

#1 New York Times bestselling author, Robyn Carr

"You always enjoy the ride!"

Oakland Press

Other Books from Susan Andersen

Running Wild
No Strings Attached
Some Like It Hot
That Thing Called Love
Burning Up
Playing Dirty
Bending The Rules
Cutting Loose
Just For kicks
Skintight
Coming Undone
Hot & Bothered
Head Over Heels
Getting Lucky
All Shook Up
Baby, Don't Go
Be My Baby
Exposure
On Thin Ice
Obsessed
Present Danger
Shadow Dance

To read excerpts visit www.susanandersen.com

NOTORIOUS

SUSAN ANDERSEN

Cover Art by Grifone Sky, Inc   Thanks, Chery. This is my favorite cover ever!

ISBN: 97809974412-1-5

This is dedicated,
with a whole lotta love,
to my critique group:
Lois Dyer, Rose Marie Harris and Krysteen Seelen.
And to my editor Ellen Price.
Each of you taught me something new
and it doesn't get better than that.
This is also for
Victoria Alexander. You are the cleverest of the clever,
girl! Thank you from the bottom of my heart for my best
ever cover.

Hugs and smoochies and thanks to you all
I so appreciate your generously
Given time and effort.

You guys
rock!
~Susan

Prologue

CONCORD DAILY STAR

Elusive Widow's Silence Sparks New Dialog on Capital Punishment

First in a four-part series
March 11, 2016

Lawrence Wilson, 21, of Concord, New Hampshire, robbed a clerk at gunpoint in a local 7-11 on June 17, 2012. A customer, Dennis Prescott, disarmed him, wrestled him to the ground, and held him until police arrived.

Wilson had no priors and as his gun proved to be a toy, he was sentenced to three years for aggravated robbery. He was paroled for good behavior on April 25, 2014, after serving a year and a half.

That evening he murdered Dennis Prescott in cold blood.

The victim's wife Hayley Prescott identified Wilson as the man she saw exiting her house when she arrived home. Inside, she found her husband bleeding on the floor. He was rushed to Concord Hospital Trauma Center, where he remained in a coma before succumbing to his injuries on August 29, 2014.

In early 2015, Wilson was convicted of first degree murder, and after two failed appeals is scheduled to be executed on August first. Unless granted a stay of execution, Wilson will be the first New Hampshire inmate put to death since Huey Long was hanged in 1939.

The Widow's testimony played a large part in placing Wilson on Death Row, yet she shuns all media contact. Her refusal to comment on the death penalty has renewed debate on the subject. Attention shown this case from news outlets far outside New Hampshire indicates it is a topic with wide reach.

2nd Installment 2 Next Friday

By: Joshua Kapler
Concord Daily Star staff reporter

Elusive Widow's Silence Sparks New Dialog on Capital Punishment

First in a four-part series

Lawrence Wilson, 21, of Concord, New Hampshire, robbed a clerk at gunpoint in a local 7-11 on June 17, 2012. Customer Dennis Prescott disarmed him, wrestled him to the ground, and held him until police arrived.

Wilson had no priors, and as his gun proved to be a toy, he was sentenced to three years for aggravated robbery. He was paroled for good behavior on April 25, 2014, after serving a year and a half.

That evening he murdered Dennis Prescott in cold blood.

The victim's wife Hayley Prescott identified Wilson as the man she saw exiting her house when she arrived home. Inside, she found her husband bleeding on the floor. He was rushed to Concord Hospital Trauma Center, where he remained in a coma before succumbing to his injuries on August 29, 2014

In early 2015, Wilson was convicted of first degree murder and after two failed appeals is scheduled to be executed on August first. Unless granted a stay of execution, Wilson will be the first New Hampshire inmate put to death since Huey Long was hanged in 1939.

The Widow's testimony played a large part in placing Wilson on Death Row, yet she shuns all media contact. Her refusal to comment on the death penalty has renewed debate on the subject. Attention shown this case from news outlets far outside New Hampshire indicates it is a topic with wide reach.   **By: Joshua Kepler, staff reporter**

CHAPTER 1

The sun set late mid-June in the Pacific Northwest. Ordinarily going on eight in the evening looked more like five p.m. did back in Concord, New Hampshire, where Hayley Prescott had lived since college. But in the final seven miles before the turnoff to her hometown of Gravers Bend, Washington, branches from the immense evergreens lining the highway met in a tangle overhead to form a tunnel-like effect that created a false dusk. She drove through the long dim stretch with the top down, greedily inhaling the Douglas fir and pine scenting the cool air blowing her hair around her head.

Her final year in Gravers Bend had totally sucked, but she never denied it was a beautiful, beautiful little corner of the world that sometimes smelled so divine it could bring tears to your eyes. The notoriety that hounded her back then had kept her from coming back for anything lengthier than a flying visit. The last time was three years ago in the wake of her mom's unexpected death. But more than twelve years had passed since high school and she'd discovered in that time *real* trouble was having your husband murdered and finding yourself the center of a media circus.

Anticipation began to build in her chest, because she would soon see Kurstin McAlvey nee Olivet. Kurstie was the closest thing to family she had left, and she needed her right now. Quite desperately, she needed her.

The old Pontiac's engine faltered and choked as she took a left off the highway. It hesitated on the edge of a stall, and she held her breath. Then the engine smoothed itself out and she exhaled in relief. *Hang in there,* she exhorted silently, sparing a quick glance at the odometer. *Only five and a half miles to go.*

The lake road's winding length was less thickly forested, and shafts of sunshine speared through gaps in the branches overhead, dappling the hood of her car and the asphalt beneath her wheels. Then, as she rounded Devil's Outcrop, the forest dropped away on the shore side and there, spread out in all its glory, was Lake Meredith.

On impulse she cranked the wheel and the car swerved off the road onto the scenic overlook. Before the car quit rocking on its shocks, she had begun double guessing herself. What on earth was she doing? Time was getting on and there wasn't much point in stopping here—she didn't even dare turn off the engine for fear it would refuse to start again.

Then she shrugged and switched off the Oldies station that had been fading in and out for the past several miles. The Cowboy Junkies died in mid-static crackle.

Immediately, the peaceful hush of her surroundings, the quiet lap of water against the pebbled shore below, seeped into her soul, soothing her. So, big deal, she wouldn't turn the engine off. And why not take a moment? This lake held a lot of personal history for her.

Hunched over forearms crossed atop the steering wheel, she propped her chin on her uppermost one and narrowed her eyes against the glare coming off the water. Buttery sunlight flooded the lookout, shining unimpeded from over the treetops across the lake and glittering off the myriad wavelets feathering the water's surface. Its heat baked her through the windshield while the shade at her back chilled her shoulders.

A tourist would look at Lake Meredith and see spectacular scenery with the added potential for a photo op or two. Hayley looked at it and saw the first eighteen years of her life. She had rowed boats and water skied on this lake. Gone skinny dipping with Kurstin. She'd traversed the train trestle across Big Bear Gap with her best friend and drunk beer at illicit bonfire-lit keggers with Kurstie and assorted schoolmates.

Lost her virginity on a blanket in the woods with Jon-Michael Olivet.

Heart inexplicably pounding, she stuffed her memories back into a compartment in the rear of her mind and determinedly sealed it. The Pontiac's engine throbbed warningly and she pressed her foot against the accelerator to feed it the measure of fuel she had learned through trial and error would stop it from stalling. Easing the gearshift cautiously into reverse, she backed onto the lake road again, and pointed the hood toward Kurstin's. *Just an other mile or so*, she mentally assured her clunker of a car, reaching to pat its cracked, imitation-leather dashboard. *Do not die on me now.*

Everything she owned was packed in the trunk or thrown on the back seat of her car. If worse came to worst, she was now at least within walking distance of Kurstin's house. She would rather forego the pleasure of finishing her journey on foot, though. Coming home again after twelve and a half years of keeping her distance had been a tough enough decision as it was. She preferred not to arrive on Kurstin's doorstep like some ragtag Gypsy queen, her ratty little pile of belongings piled at her feet.

Easing the Pontiac along the twisting shore road on the final leg of her journey, she noted the development that had taken place along Lake Meredith since her last visit. It was surprisingly minor given the growth rate of other areas she'd seen along the way. She'd give decent odds, however, that it chapped the bejesus out of Kurstin's father's hide. Richard had always felt rather proprietary about the area.

Hayley swallowed a snicker. *Rather* proprietary...that was good. Renaming it Lake Olivet would have seemed reasonable to Richard.

The Olivet estate hadn't changed in the least. Hayley brought the Pontiac to a full stop at the apex of the circular drive, rammed the gearshift into park, then simply sat a moment looking up at the back of the rose-brick mansion.

Everything was precisely as she remembered. The lushly manicured, fully landscaped grounds still rolled between stands of trees down to the lake. The same black shutters framed sparkling windows, and oversized terracotta pots of flowers still flanked the kitchen door painted the same black enamel. Slowly, Hayley reached for the ignition key and turned it off, rolling her eyes in disgust when the engine continued to cough and chug and struggle to shut itself down.

Nothing like making a memorable entrance.

The back door banged open and her oldest and dearest friend came running across the brick patio. "Oh God, Oh God, you're *here!*" Kurstin screamed.

A laugh exploded out of Hayley's throat and she threw her door open, clambering out of the car. She didn't get two steps before she was engulfed in the welcome warmth of her best friend's arms.

They clung to each other for a long moment before Kurstin finally stepped back. Holding Hayley at arm's length, she inspected her from head to toe. "I thought you'd *never* get here," she exclaimed. "I left work at noon because I just knew you'd arrive early."

"I told you it would probably be around eight."

"I know, I know. But I was so excited to see you I convinced myself you'd be premature."

"I'm often immature—does that count?"

Kurstin laughed. "Oh God, I am so glad to see you, Hayley. I've *missed* you. Who else would say something so completely asinine to me?"

"Well, please, *premature*? You still haven't figured out real people don't talk like that. And look at you!" She reached out both hands to muss Kurstin's immaculate blonde hair and then leaned back to eyeball her friend's sleek shantung silk capris. "Don't you own a pair of jeans these days?"

"'Course I do. They're at the cleaners."

Hayley laughed. This was the reason she had returned.

Unlike Kurstin, she was from a strictly middle class family, but they had been best friends since the first grade. When Hayley's dad abandoned her and her mother a couple of weeks after her twelfth birthday, it was to Kurstin she'd run. Her bestie had soothed her with unconditional love, assuring her it wasn't Hayley's fault he had left, as she had feared. A couple years later, she had done her best to return the comfort and support Kurstin when her friend's sweet, warm-hearted mother died of an aneurism. And, of course, continued to do so whenever Kurstin's father let her down.

Which, unfortunately, had been far too often.

The Pontiac chose that moment to give its final attenuated rattle and die an undignified, wheezing death. Open-mouthed, Kurstin watched its antics. Turning back, she cocked a brow. "Nice car."

Hayley gave her a crooked smile. "I'm so glad you like it. I thought I'd sign over the title to your father as a thank you gift for letting me stay here a while. What do you think about just leaving it where it is and planting it full of flowers? We could tell him it's the latest arrangement from FTD."

"I think we'd better push it down to the garage before he shows up. My God, Hayley." She walked around the car to view it from every angle. "This gives a whole new dimension to the term lemon." She prodded a tire with the toe of her pristine Gucci flat. "Where did you get the thing anyhow?"

"Happy Hal's Auto Barn in Manchester." Seeing Kurstie's eyebrows furrow, she added, "The New Hampshire city, sweetie, not the little town in Washington."

Kurstin grinned. "Okay, that makes more sense. I

wondered why you'd go though the hassle of buying a used car when you were only an hour or so from us."

Hayley unlocked the trunk and reached in for one of her boxes. She hauled it out, boosted it into position with her knee, and secured her grip on it before pinning Kurstin in her sights over its top. "This puppy is pretty much a case of you get what you pay for. Don't knock it, though; it brought me from one coast to the other. I'm satisfied I got my money's worth."

Kurstin shot her friend a look as she reached in the trunk to grab out two suitcases. "I guess it's been pretty abysmal for you financially."

Ignoring the urge to razz her friend over her ten-dollar adjective, Hayley simply answered the concern she heard. "We were wiped out by the time Dennis died," she agreed. "We hadn't much of a savings, I was still paying off the remainder of my student loans that Mom's little inheritance didn't cover, and our insurance had a ceiling that maxed out in no time."

She adjusted her grip on the box. "But I talked to the financial people at the hospital, who forgave a good sized chunk of the debt. And when I decided to come back here, I sold everything I still owned to pay off what was left. But, hey." Deliberately lightening the mood, she smiled crookedly and shrugged. "I'm free and clear now. Dead broke, maybe, but I can truthfully say I am no longer in debt."

Kurstin dropped a suitcase to give Hayley a fierce one armed hug. "I'm so glad you decided to come home. You won't regret it, Hayley; I promise you." Turning her loose, she picked up the abandoned piece of luggage again and led the way indoors. "You know I've missed you like crazy." She glanced over her shoulder at her bestie as they climbed the back staircase to the second story. "And I've worried about you since all this shit with Lawrence Wilson began. I am so sorry you had to go through so much of it alone."

"I know you are. I was grateful for the times you were able to get back there. Your phone calls and letters really helped, too."

"It hardly seems sufficient." Opening a door midway down the hall, Kurstin made a sweeping gesture, inviting Hayley to step past her into the room. "I hope this will do," she said.

"Oh, Kurstin, it's wonderful." Hayley carried her box in, dumped it on the bed, and looked around with appreciation at the spacious, beautifully appointed room. She turned back to her friend to assure her earnestly, "I won't overstay my welcome here, I promise. I have an interview tomorrow, so once I get a few paychecks under my belt—"

"Don't be absurd," Kurstin interrupted her impatiently. "You stay as long as you need. My house is your house."

"Yeah, well, frankly I was surprised *you* moved back here after your divorce. Don't you find it a tad awkward living with Daddy again?" Especially when one's father was the cold and controlling Richard Olivet.

Kurstin flashed her warm, charming smile, clearly not offended by Hayley's blunt question. "Nope. Father doesn't spend any more time here now than he did when we were in high school." Both women remembered high school events that Richard had never attended and the two of them arriving home late at night to find this huge, isolated house dark and unwelcoming. Hayley had spent many an unplanned sleep-over on Friday and Saturday nights so Kurstin wouldn't have to stay alone except for the gardener and housekeeper/cook, whose apartment was over the garage, and who still kept the house and grounds running impeccably. Her brother had generally arrived home even later than she did.

Kurstin shrugged now and added, "If he's not working, he is at the club, and he still has that apartment on the other side of town. Which is a long way of saying I have the place pretty much to myself. Living here is convenient."

"Well, blow me away." Hayley studied her friend as they left the room for a last trip to the car. "I'm still trying to get used to the fact that you went to work in the family biz." Kurstin had once harbored a great deal of resentment toward her father's workaholic tendencies and the family-owned business that made him the richest man in Gravers Bend. So it had caught Hayley flat-footed last year when, via one of their two-hour long phone conversations, her friend had announced she was the newest hire at Olivet Manufacturing. Hayley was freshly amazed every time she thought of it and never failed to say so.

"Yeah, well, get over it," Kurstin advised. "I told you I had no desire to remain in the city after Marcus and I split. Where else in this burg am I going to make enough money to support me in the style to which I am accustomed?"

"You got me there. What's it like to work with Richard?"

"Not bad. I know it's difficult to believe, but he actually leaves me to run Human Resources my own way. Jon-Michael's the one who butts heads with him all the time."

Even after all these years Hayley could feel her features stiffen at the mention of Kurstin's brother. Considering the events of the past few years, a more-than-decade-old humiliation she had suffered at Jon-Michael's hands should be a minor snag in the overall tapestry of her life. And for the most part it was. But perhaps because it was a humiliation dealt her during her impressionable teenage years she had never been able to completely shrug it off. The face she turned toward her friend now did not encourage a conversation that featured Jon-Michael as its primary subject.

Kurstin gave her the Big Sigh. But she let it pass.

It was Hayley who had trouble switching gears when her friend graciously changed the subject. The truth was, if she'd been surprised when Kurstin went into the family business, she had been downright astounded to learn Jon-

Michael had done so as well. And that, by all reports, he was every bit as dedicated to the work ethic as his father had ever been. The concept was so foreign that Hayley simply couldn't picture it. Much as she hated to admit it, she had tried. The visual refused to gel in her mind's eye.

Jon-Michael, who had valued adaptability and innovation above all else, who from the day he could first string two words together had questioned every established truth and norm, working with Richard? Jon-Michael, whose bitterness in the old days regarding their father's neglect had made his sister's look pale in comparison? The mind boggled.

Richard had fully expected his only son to join the family enterprise—a prospect she recalled consistently prompting, *"Yeah, that'll never fucking happen,"* from Jon-Michael. She itched to grill Kurstin about his reasons for such an about-face. She wanted to know specifically what he and Richard butted heads over.

Instead she bit her tongue and filled Kurstin in on the upcoming interview she had scheduled for tomorrow at Lincoln High School.

* * *

Jon-Michael lifted his upper body out from under the hood of Hayley's Pontiac the next morning and wiped his hands on the rag he had stuffed in his back pocket.

The car was a piece of shit and he didn't know what the hell he was doing working on it. Not that he couldn't get it running again, of course, because he could. It would never be a piece of precision machinery and it sure as hell wouldn't carry her back to New Hampshire if she developed a sudden urge to return there. But he could have it running sweet enough to get her around Gravers Bend on a fairly reliable basis. His aptitude with machinery was not the issue. The problem was how he'd allowed himself to be talked into working on the damn thing in the first place.

Okay, Kurstin was persuasive and could probably sweet talk the devil out of his cloven hooves. *He* sure as hell hadn't presented much of a challenge when she rousted him out of bed an hour ago to do this. Besides–he admitted it—he was curious.

Hayley had hardly said a word to him in nearly thirteen years and he was…interested in seeing how those years had treated her. In the past two/three years in particular a whole a lot of shit had rained down on her and he just wondered: had the events aged her?

Not so you would notice, he decided a short while later when the garage door opener whirred, the doors lifted, and she drove one of his father's spare cars in. He didn't plan pulling back into the shadows; he simply followed through on a split-second, subconscious decision to observe before they interacted. Barring an unlikely sudden craving on her part to hang around the garage, his presence here would pass undetected. Her vision would still be adjusting from bright daylight to the garage's dim interior. Standing in the shadows, he watched as she climbed out of the car and slammed the door.

Damn. He thought he was prepared. He wasn't.

She still had the same thick, so-dark-brown-it-was-nearly- black hair he remembered. It was all twisted up into one of those girly, vaguely French-looking do's, but nothing could tame the myriad flyaway tendrils that escaped around her forehead, temples, and nape. She still had the same long nose, same curvy lips, the same poreless skin, unlined as far as he could see.

A silent breath of mirthless laughter slid up his throat. Yeah, big surprise. She was Kurstie's age, thirty to his thirty-one. Not exactly a senior citizen. And running his gaze over her, he did not fail to notice her little cupcake breasts were exactly the way he remembered them in the little bikinis she had run around in with his sister, as was the ass that was surprisingly round on a woman built along such lean lines. *Gimme*, his body whispered.

His body could be a mindless testosterone-driven animal, however, so he sternly ignored it.

She punched the button to activate the garage door. Watching her skirt swish around her calves as she ducked beneath it, leaving the garage and him behind, he tried to visualize her naked and wondered if that view remained unchanged as well.

Not that he would know the difference. He couldn't remember a goddamn thing about what it had looked like before.

That was where the curiosity stemmed from, of course. Hell, it was so obvious it was damn near Freudian. He'd made love to girls before Hayley and to women after, and most of their faces had long ago faded from his memory. But he had never slept with anyone else where he'd been unable to recall a single detail of the encounter afterward. It was bound to make the woman involved stand out in his mind. Who would *not* be curious about the female who had featured in the one night of his life to which he hadn't the slightest recollection?

And that was aside from the sick knowledge that before the night was through, he had done something that shamed him to the bone once he'd sobered up.

Jon-Michael thrust the memory aside, rolling his shoulders impatiently. What the hell—*forget* it. It was a long time ago and he was a different man than he had been then. Hayley had moved on and so had he. There was no point in beating himself up over an action so ancient it creaked, regardless how piss-poor it had been. No point at all.

Picking up a five-eighths ratchet, he bent back over the Pontiac's engine.

"Congratulate me," Hayley demanded.

Kurstin looked up to see her friend sliding into a chair

across the dinner table. "For?"

"I am now officially among the employed."

"Congratulations! The interview went well, I take it?"

"Aside from the principal's curiosity about my husband's murder, yes, pretty well. I got the job, anyhow. That's the good news."

"Aw, I'm so sorry, Hayles." She looked up from snapping out and placing her linen napkin in her lap. "That must have been rough."

"I'll live." But she looked weary.

So Kurstin stretched a leg under the table to poke her friend with her toes. "You said that was the good news. That sounds ominously as if there's bad news to go along with it."

"Well, I'm officially hired as Lincoln High's brand new student counselor. But school doesn't start until September." Her shoulders twitched in a tiny shrug that could not quite pull off a sense of nonchalance. "The bottom line is I'm employed but I still don't have a job. I need to find summer work so I can start bringing in a paycheck."

Kurstin considered her friend for a moment. Then slowly, reluctantly, she asked, "Do you still know how to mix a Tequila Sunrise?"

"Sure. I bartended all through college—which you well know." Hayley sat up straighter. "Why? Do you know of a bar here in need of one?"

"As a matter of fact, I do." Kurstin bit her lip. Oh, she was bad, so bad, to be doing this. On the other hand— "Remember Bluey's down on Eighth Street?" It was for a good cause after all. That was the thing to remember.

"I'm hardly likely to forget it," Hayley replied dryly. Her mouth curled up at one corner. "You and I got kicked out of there in, what? Our senior year?"

"Summer after senior year," Kurstin agreed sadly. "They even stripped us of our fake ID, the bastards."

"After it took us the better part of the summer to lay our

hands on them, too." Hayley grinned at the memory. "My God, I haven't thought about that in years. Do they still offer up the hottest blues and jazz in three counties?"

"They do." Kurstin shifted uneasily in her seat, feeling guilty. She couldn't do this; Hayley would never understand. "On second thought, maybe it's not such a superlative idea," she said.

Hayley looked at her in patent surprise. "Are you kidding? For once one of your adjectives is right on the money. It is an *excellent* idea!"

"No, trust me; it's not for you," she insisted. "I know they need a bartender, but now that I think of it, it's a bit of a step down from school psychologist, yeah? I mean, you didn't go to school all those years for this. Forget I mentioned it." She waved a hand. "We'll find you something worthier of your education."

"Okay, you're scaring me here. It's not like you to be such an elitist. So tell you what." Hayley gave her a look. "I'll be a snob about it next summer. *This* summer I only have forty-seven dollars to my name. And chances are I can make more in tips tending bar than I'd make in salary at any office job I'd qualify for."

"Are you sure?"

"Absopositively."

Hey, I tried, Kurstin assured herself righteously. Truly, a woman could not do more than that. "Well, if you're certain. I'll call the owner and set up an interview."

"I can't get over this." Hayley planted her elbow on the table and her chin in her palm and smiled across the table at her. "I cannot reconcile my old trouble-making buddy with the respectable wheeler dealer, mover and shaker you've turned into. Omigawd!" she straightened in her chair. "Have you become a Gravers Bend *Junior Leaguer*?"

"Hardly."

"Thank God. Still, you are a very big fish."

"In an exceedingly small pond." She slanted Hayley a look. "You're giving me infinitely more credit than I deserve. It happens I hired the granddaughter of Harve Moser, the guy who owns Bluey's, for a summer filing job at the factory. And I heard through one of the regular band musicians his bartender quit without notice last week." She shrugged and tried not to look as guilty as she felt when she thought about who that musician was. Well, what the hell. Hayley had said it herself: she needed a decent paying job and she needed it now.

Kurstin nevertheless hastily changed the subject. "I had somebody over to look at your car," she said and picked up the little hand bell to the right of her plate, giving it a brief ring. The door swished open a moment later and Kurstin's cook and housekeeper Ruth, carrying two salad plates, entered the room. She smiled at Hayley as she set hers in front of her, gave her a quiet, "Welcome home," then exited as quietly as she had entered.

Hayley felt as if she had stepped onto a movie set. "This is too spooky. Last week I was slapping together tuna sandwiches for lunch. Now I'm being waited on like visiting royalty. I can't get used to it."

"Never mind that," Kurstin advised with the carelessness of someone accustomed to a lifetime of being served. "About your car—"

"I wish you hadn't done it. You know the shape my finances are in. I don't have any idea when I'll have enough money to pay a mechanic."

"*Forget* paying. It was done as a favor to me."

Bitterness surged up Hayley's throat. "How very grand for you," she said flatly. "Must be nice." The words echoed in her head in the wake of the sudden silence following them, and she set down her fork. "I'm sorry," she said in stricken contrition. "That was so uncalled for."

"No, I'm the one who should be sorry," Kurstin said. "I'm trying to take over, just like I always do. I want everyone to be happy, so I bulldoze situations into whatever configuration I think works best to accomplish my ends." She pushed salad around the plate with her fork for a second then set her silverware aside as well. "Regarding which, I suppose I had better make a clean breast of it and tell you the truth about..."

The doorbell rang and Kurstin cast her a beleaguered glance across the table. "Oh, for God's sake," she said impatiently, rising to her feet. "*Now* what?"

"Never say you're going to answer that yourself?" Hayley demanded in faux shock. "Is it the butler's night off?"

"You're so droll. We still make do with Ruth and Ernesto."

Hayley raised her eyebrows at her and Kurstin flashed her a sheepish smile. "Okay, and a cleaning company that comes in once a week."

The doorbell rang again and breathing, "I'm *coming* all ready," Kurstin whirled away to answer it.

Chapter 2

"Hi, Kurstin, it's that time of year again!" a female voice exclaimed. "I hope you have the decorations all ready to go, because you are on my To-Do list and I need to cross you off."

Hayley briefly closed her eyes. It had been a long time since she'd last heard that voice, but she recognized the cheerful, determined tones greeting Kurstin when her friend opened the front door. *Oh, please, Kurstie, not tonight,* she prayed. *Get rid of her. Please, please. I don't care how you do it; just get rid of her.* She also didn't care if it was selfish. She simply was not up to making catch-up chat tonight.

"Consider me crossed," she heard Kurstin say. "They're in a box up in the attic and I will have Ernesto bring them down in the morning so I can drop them off at the country club on my way to work."

"Oh, let's not put off until tomorrow," the voice insisted. "I am here now, so if you will just have him run up and fetch them, I'll take them with me and you will not have to bother any further."

"Ernesto's off the clock, Patsy, and I am not rousting him out of his cozy apartment after the long day he's put in on the grounds," Kurstin said firmly. "Plus, I have company. So, I'm afraid tomorrow will simply have to do."

"Is *Hayley* here? Oh, I must say hello!"

"Tonight isn't a good time," Kurstin demurred. "We're in the middle of dinner and Hayley is very tired—"

"For heaven's sake, Kurstin," the voice said, coming closer, "I will only take a moment. I am sure she wants to see her old friend."

"Hayley, look who's here," Kurstin said seconds later as she all but trod on the heels of the woman striding into the dining room. Shrugging helplessly, she flashed a grimace of apology. "It's Patsy Dutton."

"*Beal*, Kurstin," Patsy corrected her. "It has been Beal for seven years now."

"Yes, of course it has, my apologies. Patsy Beal, Hayles."

Hayley offered a weak smile. "How…nice to see you again. It's been a long time." Rising to her feet, she offered her hand.

Patsy ignored it, reaching out instead to grasp her to her breast in a fierce hug.

Hayley gave a start of surprise but she returned the embrace gamely. The Patsy she remembered had been almost painfully reticent about physical contact.

"It is so good to see you," the other woman whispered fiercely in her ear, then pulled back and held Hayley at arm's length, giving her a thorough inspection. She was so enthusiastic Hayley felt like a bitch for wishing she would simply go away and let them put this off for another day.

Looking into Patsy's face, she saw little had changed over the years. The other woman still wore her more-brown-than-blond hair in the same blunt-cut bob, still had those pale blue eyes that transmitted the same contradictory message made up in equal parts of vulnerability and aggression. Observing Patsy's eagerness, Hayley felt guilty.

Patsy had been a friend back in high school, but they'd drifted apart once Hayley left Gravers Bend. And even in their closest days, the dynamics between the three of them had always left Patsy lagging several steps behind.

Where she and Kurstin had always taken a certain joy in seeing how many rules they could bend and routines they could alter, Patsy had been all about the regulations and staying within her comfortable old habits. Where they had laughed themselves sick over the joke of the moment, Patsy had never quite grasped the point of their humor or, worse, had gotten it ten minutes after they had moved on to the next funny thing.

Hayley swallowed a sigh. Ah, well. Patsy's heart had always been in the right place and it surely wasn't her fault that *she* felt emotionally wrung out tonight. She smiled gently. "Sit down," she invited to atone for her lack of enthusiasm. "Would you like a cup of coffee?"

Kurstin bared her teeth at her behind Patsy's back but when Hayley just gave her the slightest of lopsided smiles, she cast her gaze to the ceiling and reached for the hand bell, giving it a little jingle.

The door swished open and Kurstin addressed the woman who poked her head out. "Ruth, would you bring Mrs. Beal a cup of coffee, please?"

Ruth nodded and the door swished shut again.

Hayley turned her attention back to Patsy. "I heard you say something about decorations for "that time of year". Don't tell me you head up the big Fourth of July dance at the club!"

Patsy smiled proudly. "I do. They seem to like my work."

"I guess so! But why are the decorations here? Surely the country club has its own storage."

"They had a flood in the basement this winter," Kurstin explained. "So a few of us volunteered to store the supplies until the problem could be rectified. Little by little everything is being returned. Oh, good, here's your coffee, Patsy," she said as Ruth came through the door. "Hayley, eat your salad before it wilts," she commanded next. "Ruth, please hold the main course an extra ten minutes."

"I was so sorry to hear about your husband, Hayley," Patsy murmured. She picked up her eggshell porcelain cup and blew gently across the top of the steaming surface before taking a cautious sip.

"Yes, I received your condolence card at the time. That

was so thoughtful." *But I really don't want to talk about it now.* She willed the other woman to read the nuances in her tone and let it drop.

No such luck, naturally. It had been that kind of day.

Who was she kidding? It had been that kind of *year.* She could not go anywhere without people wanting to talk about Dennis.

"And here you are, back home and notorious again," Patsy continued avidly. When Hayley and Kurstin stared at her in disbelief that she dared bring up...*that,* Patsy cleared her throat. "That is, your husband was so heroic", she amended. "You must have been immensely proud of him."

Hayley murmured an appropriate response but something in her expression or voice must have given her away, because later, after Patsy finally took her leave, Kurstin silently studied her face feature by feature.

"Whoops," she said when her friend continued to scrutinize her without saying a word. She raised her linen napkin to her lips, dabbing them self-consciously. "Do I have spinach in my teeth?"

"No, I was just wondering..."

Kurstin's voice trailed away, and when she showed no sign of picking up the conversation Hayley rapped her knuckles on the tabletop. "Hel-lo! You plan to spit out *what* you're wondering about sometime tonight?"

Kurstin looked up from the table, meeting Hayley's gaze squarely. "Why did you look like you were crossing your fingers behind your back when you told Patsy how proud you were of your husband?"

"Ouch." Hayley flinched but then gave her friend a look of admiration. "Damn. I forgot how good you are at slipping in the knife where it's least expected."

"Yes, it's a talent of mine." Her friend's level look made it clear she would not be sidetracked. "So tell me about Dennis."

Hayley pushed her plate away and reached for her

wine. "There isn't much to tell. What he did to disarm Lawrence Wilson was every bit as heroic as Patsy implied. And, God, I was so furious with him for doing it!" She took a sip of wine and leaned back, cradling the goblet to her chest. "We'd only been married three years and he just as easily could've gotten his head blown off. It wasn't as if he took time to evaluate the situation before he reacted."

"But in the end it worked out fine," Kurstin argued. Then she blanched. "Oh, God, Hayley, I'm sorry. I cannot believe I said something so moronic. The end result wasn't at *all* ri—"

"Don't," she said. "I know what you meant. And you're right. At the time it appeared it had worked out fine. Wilson went to jail and Dennis was hailed a hero by the local media. I'm not trying to detract from his accomplishment, because he *was* courageous. Without a thought for his own personal safety, he single-handedly foiled what he believed was an armed robber and saved the day. The problems—*our* problems—began when he started believing his own press and thought he had to live up to his shiny new image."

She drained her glass and set it on the table. Caught up in her thoughts, she stared at it for a few silent moments, then reached out to give the goblet an impulsive flick of her fingernail. It chimed with the round tones of good crystal until she pressed her fingertip against the rim to still the vibrations. In the ensuing silence, she looked up to meet her best friend's gaze across the table. And confessed, "We were talking divorce when Wilson murdered him."

Kurstin straightened in her seat. "*Divorce*?" she asked. "Hayley, why on earth—?"

Chin elevated to a pugnacious degree, she interrupted with stiff pride, "Because Dennis started partying hard and messing around with other women." And, oh, dear God, regardless how much time had passed, it remained painful to admit out loud.

"That isn't what I was going to ask." Kurstin reached

across the table to give her hand a squeeze. "God knows I'm in no position to judge the dissolution of someone else's marriage when my own was so screwed up toward the end. And you should know me well enough to realize the last thing I would ask for is details of that sort. What I really want to know is why you kept this to yourself all this time. You were there for me when I went through my divorce. Why didn't you let me be there for you?"

Hayley expelled a laugh that even to her own ears sounded more bitter than amused. "I guess I take rejection kind of personally. I'm funny that way."

Kurstin's hand on hers squeezed harder and Hayley looked up to meet her friend's gaze with a vestige of the uncertainty she had felt during those last months of her failing marriage. "Face it, when your husband starts prowling around, it must mean you're the one lacking some necessary attribute. I wasn't exactly anxious to share the news."

"Oh, sweetheart, you do pull inward when you're hurting, don't you? Just like when Jon-Mi—"

Her look must have warned Kurstin not to pursue that subject, for her friend changed direction. "But you are dead *wrong*, Hayley, if you think Dennis' catting around is a reflection of your desirability," she said fiercely. "You are so bright and beautiful and funny."

Her brief bark of laughter was brittle. "You think I haven't assured myself of that a gazillion times? But personal experience doesn't seem to bear that out. Not back in high school, and not now, either."

She waved a forestalling hand when Kurstin opened her mouth to argue. "I'm not stupid," she said. "On an intellectual level I understand Dennis simply got caught up in the attention focused on him by all the publicity following the robbery. But *intellect* wasn't uppermost all the nights he came home in the wee small hours stinking of whiskey and another woman's perfume."

"The son of a bitch."

"Yeah. My emotions tended to eclipse anything my brain had to say, but even those were just about worn to a nub by the time I found him bleeding all over the kitchen. We were still living together in the same house, but mentally I was halfway out the door." She rammed her fingers through her hair and looked at her friend. "Which makes all the media hype doubly difficult. *Grieving Widow Testifies at Wilson Trial*," she mimicked bitterly. *"Grieving Widow Attends Appeal."* She swore softly. "I feel like such a hypocrite."

"Why, because you didn't grieve?"

"Of course I did! You don't live with a man for five years and just get over his brutal murder with a snap of your fingers. He was a great guy before all this happened and the first years of our marriage were wonderful. He didn't deserve to die that way. *Nobody* deserves to—" Comprehension dawned and she broke off mid-tirade. "Oh. Very tricky, Olivet, McAlvey—whatever." She scrutinized Kurstin. "Let me ask you something. How did *you* feel when you and Marcus realized your marriage wasn't going to work?"

Kurstin made a face. "Like a failure."

"Exactly. Divorce isn't an easy decision even when you know it's your only true option, and I doubt many people get through one with no regrets. But try to imagine that in addition to feeling like a failure as a wife, you have the media doing their best to turn you into THE WIDOW, this tragic public figure who exists in bold font caps. Whom, believe me, they do not wanna know was in the initial stage of divorcing their cheating shit of a hero. Maybe then you can get a feel for why *I* feel like a damned impostor."

"Well, it will all be resolved one way or another soon," Kurstin assured her comfortingly. "Then your life can finally get back to normal."

"Whatever the hell that is." *Oh, bitch, whine, complain!* Summoning a silver lining, she shot Kurstin a wry smile. "Other scandals came along and pushed Den's heroics out of the limelight for almost a year before Wilson was let out on parole. The murder, of course. turned everything into a total feeding frenzy. But even that had begun to be treated as old news, until the debate over whether Wilson should be the first felon executed in the state since forever heated up again. Then the press came out of the woodwork like an army of carpenter ants. So Patsy had it right—I am notorious again."

"Ignore her."

"She seems...*needier* than she used to be."

"She's become so over the past couple of years. We've drifted apart. Still, I cannot believe she said that!"

"I can. Not much surprises me anymore. Even with breaks of relative quiet, I've been living with this notoriety for so long I barely remember what normal feels like."

Then she perked up. "But at least here I have a chance of finding out without the press breathing down my neck and poking inquisitive fingers into every corner of my life. They're relentless and so damn intrusive, you cannot begin to imagine. But, hey, what do journalists in the state of Washington care about a New Hampshire execution? And face it, with me out of the picture the East Coast media will lose interest and move on to the next poor sucker to provide them with an interesting sound bite or a few paragraphs above the fold."

Or so she fervently hoped.

***

Ty Holloway re-seated the telephone receiver with a bang and swore. Fuck it to hell. Where was Hayley Prescott?

With Lawrence Wilson's execution back on the table, she was supposed to be his ticket out of this podunk New Hampshire daily. Okay, so it was not the smallest newspaper in the land. But it was light years from New York or DC, so find her and he could practically write his own contract at the Times or Washington Post. Then it would be *So long Manchester; Hello, Big Time.*

Fail to find her, however, and he'd probably be stuck here forever.

She had been MIA for over a week now. You could find anything on the Internet these days, so he had managed to locate her home town. So far, however, his discreet inquiries into whether she'd shown up there produced squat.

He leaned back in his chair. "Marie," he called out. A young woman across the room looked up from her computer screen. "Fetch me a cup of coffee, will ya, hon?" he asked the minute he had her attention.

It was an inappropriate use of the intern's time, but he knew she had a crush on him and shamelessly took advantage. His mouth tipped up in sardonic amusement as he watched her hop up to do his bidding.

Moments later, with a smile that dimpled her full cheeks she handed him a mug. "Here you go, Ty," she said breathlessly.

"Thanks." He brushed his fingers over hers as he accepted the cup. "You're a doll and a half." Blushing, she turned away and missed seeing him raise an ironic eyebrow at Cal Duncan, to whom he'd queried just the other day, "Where do you suppose Marie buys her dresses, Manchester Tent and Awning?"

Then Ty dismissed her, dismissed Duncan, and swiveled back to re-apply himself to his problem. He picked up the phone and punched the extension for the newsroom morgue. Once connected, he requested every bit of available information on Hayley Granger Prescott be delivered to him ASAP. Reseating the receiver, he thrust the fingers of both hands through his hair.

He had to find her, and find her fast.

* * *

A narrow tunnel of sunshine flooded the dark cave of Bluey's bar when Hayley shoved opened the entrance door late the next afternoon. "Shut the goddamn door," a belligerent male voice demanded. "Whataya tryin' to do, blind me?"

"Sorry," she murmured and stepped into the bar, closing the door at her back. Her own vision vanished and she stood blinking in the dark for a second. The cool, dark cavern smelled of worn leather and liquor and a hint of stale tobacco even though smoking in public buildings was outlawed years ago in Washington. From invisible speakers Bobby Blue Bland crooned it was a stormy Monday. He was lamenting that Wednesday he went to work and Thursday was "oh, so sad" when her eyes adjusted enough see the dim outlines of tables and the chairs tipped upside down atop them.

"You Hayley Prescott?" the voice demanded and she turned a fraction to the right. Hunched over the end of the bar was the silhouette of a man. A barstool creaked as he swung around to stare at her and the end of a cigarette glowed crimson for a moment as he took a drag.

Well, that explains it.

The smoke he exhaled was a gray wraith slowly drifting up past his head to be pulled out of the room by the efficient ventilation system installed in the ceiling. "Well?" he prompted impatiently. "It's not that hard a question. Either you are, or you ain't." The end of his smoke glowed brightly once again as he drew in another deep drag.

"Yes, I am," she said, stepping forward and extending her hand. "Harve Moser, I presume?"

"Call me Bluey." A large hand emerged out of the gloom to swallow hers up. It pumped once and then slid away. "Hang on a sec," he commanded and swiveled back to face the bar. He rose to lean over it. Fumbling around with something on the other side, he swore, but soon emitted a small grunt of satisfaction. A switch clicked and lights sprang on behind the bar. He turned back to Hayley. "All right then," he said gruffly. "Let's get a look at you."

Hayley stood patiently as he inspected her, using the time to examine him in return.

Bluey Moser was a big man. He had a full head of white hair, a Roman nose and pugnacious pale blue eyes. Around sixty-five, he still had shoulders and arms like a stevedore. And despite the hint of softness that padded his middle, Hayley would bet he could bounce the meanest drunk out the front door in the blink of an eye should the occasion warrant it.

"Well, you're a looker," he conceded and swiveled back to the bar to crush out his cigarette. "It's not a job requirement but it never hurts for pulling in business." Turning back, he exhaled his last lungful of smoke and gave her another swift once-over. "A little more elegant than my regulars are used to seeing around here, maybe, but the little outfit should take care of that. No doubt they'll think you're cuter 'n a button once we get you rigged out."

Little outfit? Kurstin hadn't mentioned anything about a little outfit. Unpleasant visions of fishnet stockings and flounced, butt-length skirts flirted disagreeably on the fringes of her mind. Hayley opened her mouth to ask about it, but the thought of her nonexistent bank account closed it again. Then visions of some male-fantasy X-rated Parisian-maid getup bloomed in her mind and she once again considered asking exactly what sort of 'little outfit' they were talking about. Before she had a chance to say a word, however, Bluey clamped a hand around her wrist and dragged her behind the bar, where he turned her loose.

"Let's see what you can do," he commanded. "Make me a tall water."

Hayley grabbed a glass. Flipping up the cover on the built-in ice bin, she scooped out ice and dumped some in. She selected a bottle of bourbon and measured a jigger over the glass. She allowed the bottle's pour spout to continue dribbling bourbon into the glass while she emptied the shot over the ice. Returning the bottle back to its spot on the shelf, she reached for the soda gun, found the W button and pushed it, adding water to the top of the glass. She placed a napkin on the bar in front of Bluey and set the drink on top of it. "Your tall water, sir," she said with a slight smile.

"Pretty damn generous with my bourbon, ain't ya?" Bluey demanded. He took a sip and scowled.

Hayley flashed a spontaneous grin and he paused, the glass suspended halfway to his mouth, an arrested expression in his eyes.

She shrugged. "I learned to tend bar in a Chinese restaurant."

"That explains it then," he agreed sourly, taking another sip with palpable appreciation before setting the glass down on its coaster. "The Chinese believe in serving a strong drink."

"They do. It's the only way I have ever made one."

"Well, you wanna work for me, girl, you're gonna have to get over it. I believe in one jigger per drink and no more. On the other hand, if you can curb your heavy hand with my liquor then you've got yourself a job." He named an hourly wage. "Plus tips. Tuesday through Saturday, seven to two. If you need an occasional weekend night off, it can be arranged as long as you request it ahead of time." He pulled another Marlboro out of his shirt pocket and fired up. Then he scowled down at her. "So, you want the goddamn job, or not?"

"Yes, I'll take it. When do you want me to start?"

"Tonight."

"Okay." She hesitated. He wasn't exactly a small talk kind of guy, but what the hell. She didn't plan to start monitoring every word that left her mouth at this stage in her life. She had come home to make her life less complicated, not more so, and worrying that a simple statement might trigger a grouchy old man's impatience was definitely more complicated. If he didn't want to indulge in small talk, that was too damn bad. "I hear you still bring in some of the best blues players around," she said. "I'm looking forward to hearing what you have to offer."

And concluded Harve 'Bluey' Moser must not consider blues small talk when he almost smiled at her.

"You like blues and jazz, girl, you're gonna like the bands we've got playin' here. Hell, come to think of it, I guess you already know the sax player who plays with Ragged Edge. Guy named—"

The front door banged open and in spite of the light on behind the bar, Bluey's arm flew up and he hissed like a vampire caught by dawn's early light. Then he swore roundly, ending with, "Son of a bitch, I forgot this is Wednesday. That's delivery day," he added unnecessarily as a young man wheeled in a hand truck stacked with boxes. He turned to her. "Listen, you come on back at seven and we'll get you set up. Oh, wait. I better get you your little outfit."

Now it was Hayley's turn to swear, if only mentally. She followed him to a closet behind the bar, trying to marshal a good solid reason why she should not have to wear his stupid costume. Before she could dredge one up, however, he had already opened the closet door, rattled through some hangers, and whipped something out.

"Here," he said, thrusting a little turquoise vest at her. "Try this one on, I think it should fit you. You can wear a tank top underneath it if you want to, though you'll probably pull in more tips without it. Pair it up with a black skirt or pants-- your choice. And don't forget the bow tie. For some damn reason men really go for that. Idiots probably think they're being served by a goddamn Playboy bunny or something."

Hayley sagged back against the bar and nearly laughed in relief. She stared down at the scrap of material in her hands for a second, then slid it on atop a taupe silk shirt that was left over from more prosperous times and fastened the vest's two buttons. *This* was the little outfit? Not tacky stockings or an obscenely short skirt that would show her butt for all the world to ogle if she was not super cautious? Well, alrighty then. This, she could live with.

Her attitude wasn't quite as insouciant that evening when she donned the garment sans the elegant silk blouse. She was standing in her panties and bra in front of the full length mirror when Kurstin knocked on her bedroom door. Quickly whipping the vest on to prevent her friend from seeing the safety pin holding her bra strap together, she called out an invitation to enter. First paycheck she received, she was buying some decent underwear.

Buttoning the vest automatically, she turned back from smiling a greeting over her shoulder to check its fit in the mirror. Her jaw dropped.

Sweet Mary, Mother of God. A slice of her worn bra's lace cups showed in the vest's V neckline, and entire stretches of the shot elastic that formed the brassiere's sides were exposed in the deeply cut arm holes. She scowled at her image. She looked ridiculous. She—

"I look like a damn rag picker," she groused, reaching up to pinch the shoulder seams until everything was properly covered. Her gaze sought Kurstin's in the mirror. "How are you with a needle and thread?"

"About as proficient as you." Kurstin dropped onto Hayley's bed and rolled onto her side, propping her head in her palm as she observed the dilemma.

"Shit." Hayley blew a strand of hair out of her eyes. "Okay, tank top," she muttered, and letting the seams go, turned away from the mirror to rummage through her dresser. "I planned to go for the tips, but I'll just have to wear one of these babies underneath instead." She held up two for Kurstin's inspection. "What do you think, black? Or this little ecru number with the lace?"

"Take off your bra."

"Huh?"

"Let's see what the vest looks like without a bra."

"Are you crazy? I'll spill out all over the damn place."

Kurstin snorted. "Have you had a boob job since the last time I saw you?"

"Well…no. But how rude of you to mention I'm not very busty. Okay, okay," she said in response to her friend's sardonically arched eyebrow and unbuttoned the vest. Pulling it off, she tossed it on the bed next to where Kurstin lounged. "I was hoping to avoid displaying the ratty condition of my underwear in front of the Olivet heiress, but I can see that's a futile wish." The bra was flung after the vest and Hayley snapped her fingers at her friend. "C'mon, c'mon, don't just lie there. Pass me the damn thing." She pulled the proffered vest on over her bare skin, buttoned up and turned to face her reflection. "Oh," she said weakly. "My. I don't know about this."

"I do. Now *that* is a look guaranteed to bring in tips."

Hayley turned left and right to inspect her image. Her gaze kept returning to the exposed side curves where her breasts lifted away from her ribcage and were revealed above the armholes. The vest's lapels decently covered the rest of her small boobs except for the subtle hint of her inner curves revealed in the V neckline.

"Sweet suffering Mother Mary. Could it be any more obvious I'm naked under here?" She tweaked up the shoulder seams again, trying to make the fit more conventional.

"That's the beauty of it," Kurstin said. "Basically, you are all covered up; yet there's that hint of bare skin that's so sexy. It's rather interesting, really, if you stop to analyze it. Who would've guessed the tiny bit of boob you're showing would be ten times sexier than a push up bra could ever be? No acres of cleavage. Just a suggestion here and there of unfettered boobage. It's subtle…like you. Quit messing with it," she ordered and indicated the pair of black skinny jeans and the long black Indian gauze skirt neatly laid out next to her on the coverlet. "Which will you wear with it?"

"I don't know. Hand me the skirt and I'll see how it looks." She tried it on first and then modeled the jeans. A few moments later she turned to her friend. "What do you think?"

"The pants. The skirt looks good—it's pretty—but pants are loads more practical. Well, either those or a straight skirt. All that material is just going to get in your way."

"Yeah, you're probably right."

"Of course I am."

Rolling her eyes, Hayley scooped her flyaway hair away from her face with both hands. She gave it a side part, sectioned out three hanks and deftly assembled a waterfall braid. She leaned into the mirror to check her makeup, stood back to assess the overall effect and then turned to her friend. "Whataya think? Do I look all right?"

"You look great. I like your hair like that," Kurstin said, indicating the French-type braid starting near the side part and looping around the back of her head to her opposite ear—and the cloud of dark waves and "waterfall" sections below it made by dropping some of the braid sections. Then her friend raised her eyes to study Hayley's expression. "You're nervous, aren't you?"

"A little." She blew out a breath. "I had better get going. I want to arrive a few minutes early to go over Bluey's pricing policies and be checked out on the cash register."

Kurstin climbed off the bed. "Knock 'em dead, toots."

"Oh, I intend to." She sent a cocky smile winging her friend's way. Then, picking up her purse, she sailed out of the bedroom.

The smile faded before she reached the kitchen door and was barely a memory by the time she parked the Pontiac in the gravel lot fronting Bluey's.

She knew what happened in this burg when new meat hit the street. Word got around fast and small town folk assumed they had the right to know all your business. If there were two people in the bar tonight who remembered her past history or knew of her current woes, word would spread like wildfire.

Not that she gave a great big rip what people said about her.

But she sure was tired of having her every breath dissected for people's entertainment.

Mouth arid, heart thudding against her rib cage, she sat in the car for a few tense moments, staring up at the cobalt neon sign blinking the establishment's name.

Then she straightened. What the hell. It was what it was. She had known what she was in for the moment she'd decided to come back here. She'd get through it just like she did her First Day stage fright every new school year. She drew a deep, calming breath. Hey, she had her moments of being engaged in the world. Sometimes she was even downright gregarious. But at heart she was private and a bit introverted, so she had to work at new situations involving crowds. It was just a fact of life.

But she could do this. With another calming breath, she shook out her hands, climbed from the car and exhaled gustily.

Show time.

Chapter 3

The lighting inside Bluey's was the first thing Hayley noticed when she pushed through the doors. It was geared toward dim and atmospheric with recessed spotlights that reflected off the bottles behind the bar. Candles flickered in red glass votives on the tables and a few strategically placed neon signs cast a tinted glow down the walls. A blue spot was trained on the small stage, which held instruments but no performers.

The singer on the jukebox crooned that she got her whiskey from a bottle and some cocaine from a friend as Hayley crossed the room. Bluey was behind the bar, an unlit, drooping cigarette glued to the corner of his lip as he lined up glasses. Perched on stools in front of the bar owner, two women sipped drinks.

They wore turquoise vests identical to Hayley's.

The plump brunette wore hers over a white cotton tank top paired with black polyester pants and sensible shoes. The blonde next to her had dyed the bottom third of her hair jet black. She'd combined her vest with a black lace push-up bra, a long, slim, black skirt slit to mid thigh, black lace-patterned stockings and black motorcycle boots. Plus an onyx nose stud, Hayley noted as she approached the bar. Her own self consciousness at the tiny bit of flesh she displayed dropped several notches.

Bluey looked up as she drew near, squinting at her through the column of grey vapor he exhaled from what she saw was an e-cigarette. "Good. You're early," he commented gruffly. "I can show you what you need to know before your shift starts. Meet Marsha," he said, indicating the mild-featured brunette. He jerked his head toward the two-tone blonde. "And that's Lucy. Hayley is the new bartender I told you we were getting'."

"Well, thank God for small favors," Lucy said and flashed Hayley a cheerful smile. "Getting the grump out from behind the bar can only improve our tips."

"Go touch up your roots," Bluey suggested in a tone both abrupt and rude. "Damn smart-mouthed brat," he muttered. But Hayley was beginning to understand his actions were not as unkind as his speech suggested. He looked up to catch her watching him speculatively and impatiently waved her around the bar. "Well, c'mon; I ain't got all night," he groused. Rattling off the price list, he showed her how to use the cash register and then tested her on how well she had absorbed the knowledge.

"Waitresses get comped two well drinks a night," he informed her with his habitual brusqueness. "One at the beginning of their shift and another at the end. The same goes for you. Band members pay for their own liquor but can have all the free soft drinks they can handle."

He showed her where everything was stocked behind the bar. "We get a pretty decent crowd in here as a rule," he informed her. "But if anyone gets too loaded, cut 'em off, no excuses. If they give you trouble, call for me. If I'm not available, call the sheriff. And if you're ever threatened and none of those options seem viable, lay 'em out with this." He reached under the bar and pulled out a sawed-off wooden oar handle. He eyed her slender-boned, medium-height frame. "Just give 'em a good hard rap upside the head," was his ultimate recommendation. "You ready to get started?"

"Yes."

He grunted. "Then make me a tall water."

She reached for a glass but he stopped her. "Wait a minute. Where the hell's your bow tie?"

Hayley's hand went to her throat and she whispered a

swear word that would have rolled her mother over in her grave had Mom heard it coming from her lips. "On my dresser at home," she admitted contritely. "I'm sorry, Bluey."

He grunted again. "Go get another one out of the closet," he ordered. *You silly bitch* seemed to be the unspoken subtext. Yet when she set his drink on a coaster in front of him a moment later, he stuffed the first dollar bill into the brandy snifter set on the bar for her tips.

People started drifting in, and by nine o'clock, when the band was due to begin their first set, Hayley was elbow deep in orders. She could hear the musicians noodling and tuning up their various instruments but was too busy to spare them more than a distracted glance. She'd seen more than one customer stare at her before leaning over to talk furiously to the person next to them. She would take a wild stab here and guess the word was out. The only question was whether it was regarding her past history or her current woes.

She looked up when Lucy came to the end of the bar. The waitress slapped her tray down on the polished wooden surface and said, "I need a Lemon Drop, a Vodka Collins, a Cutty's on the rocks, two house wines—one white, one red—and a Bud Light." Straightening the bills in her cash box, she absentmindedly rubbed her cheek against her hunched up shoulder to smooth back a blonde and black strand of hair. She blew out a weary breath and watched Hayley for a moment as she efficiently poured the wine and grabbed a cold beer from one of the refrigerated units under the mirrored shelves of bottles. Hayley popped the top off the beer, set it on the tray next to the glasses of wine, and reached for a hi-ball glass.

With a little sound of contentment Lucy eased her butt onto a newly vacated bar stool. "Oh that's nice." She looked at Hayley again. "Band's about to start up," she commented. "It'll quiet down a bit then and you can take a break."

Hayley looked up from her work and smiled. Stabbing a lime wedge and a maraschino cherry with the little plastic spear, she added it to the vodka Collins. She placed the drink on Lucy's tray and reached for a martini glass.

"I love this band," Lucy said. "Ragged Edge, they play here week nights, then Bluey has out-of-town bands most Fridays and Saturdays. You ever heard 'em play?"

"No, I've only been in town for a couple of days and he said they were local talent."

"Yeah, they are. But he told me you knew one of the musicians."

Hayley shot her a puzzled glance and Lucy's brows elevated. "No?"

"No, I had never even heard the name until Bluey mentioned it this afternoon."

Lucy shrugged. "Huh. I suppose I could have misunderstood." Her expression said she doubted it, though. Eyebrows scrunching delicately above her nose, she scrutinized Hayley for a moment. "You are from Gravers Bend originally, aren't you?"

Marsha squeezed in next to her. "I need a pitcher, Hayley."

Hayley cocked an eyebrow at Lucy.

"Go ahead. I can use another moment off my feet."

Hayley set down the Martini glass and grabbed a pitcher, sliding it into place and pulling the tap, pouring beer in a careful cascade down its side. She glanced up at Lucy. "I was born and raised over on Oakley Street, but it's been a long time since I've lived here," she said.

"You graduated from Lincoln High, though, right?"

"Um hmm."

"What year?"

Hayley told her and released the tap, angling the pitcher out from beneath it and sliding it across the bar to Marsha. She reached for the abandoned glass to complete Lucy's order.

"Then you probably do know a couple of the band

members, by name if nothing else. Brian Dorsey?"

"Oh sure. He was a year ahead of me but I remember him." Hayley's voice was light, but her stomach tensed up. Brian was once a friend of…

"He's the band's singer, plays guitar. He's a pretty good lookin' guy. But my personal favorite is the saxophone player. Yummy build; the guy's got a stomach on him like corrugated steel."

The image her description conjured up was so vivid that Hayley flashed a big spontaneous grin, and Lucy blinked at her owlishly.

"Jeez, killer smile," she commented. "You oughtta do that more often."

"So, the guy with the washboard abs…is he by chance a close personal friend of yours?"

"I wish. Nah, he just sweats under the lights and has this tendency to use whatever shirt he's wearing to wipe it away. I try to be there to catch the show. As a matter of fact he's the musician Bluey thought you knew…graduated the same year as Brian. Jon-Michael Olivet's his name. Sound familiar?"

The martini glass in Hayley's hand slipped through her fingers and bounced into the stainless steel sink.

* * *

Another package was at the post office box today and I'm going to explode if I cannot open it soon. I picked the damn thing up at noon. But it has been one of those days when everything that can go wrong has. It has taken me nine long hours to get to the point where I can almost, *almost,* satisfy my curiosity about what the service sent this time.

But not quite. Because I am not alone.

Lately the spouse never seems to be at home. So doesn't it figure that tonight when a smidgen of solitude would be appreciated, it is the one evening the better half took forever getting ready to go out?

But the spouse finally leaves and immediately I retrieve my package from its hiding place. I rip it open with a few efficient flicks of my hands and carefully bury the wrappings deep in the garbage where they won't be noticed.

Then I skim the enclosed clippings while still standing in the middle of the kitchen. Impatience I know better than to show even when I'm alone simmers deep in my gut as I take the stairs two at a time up to the rarely used third floor room.

I pore over the articles a second time with avid thoroughness. Then I unlock the secret closet, remove the cap from the tube of acid free paper cement and painstakingly brush the backs of the articles with it. It only takes a moment to add them to the existing collage lining the closet's interior. Then I pop the DVD included with the clippings into the player. Anticipation building, I sit back to view the results.

The screen turns blue for a second, then opens to a man on a talk-show set. "Good evening and welcome to *Inside Forum*," he says. "I am your host Graham Sturgis and tonight's subject is capital punishment in the state of New Hampshire."

He makes a subtle adjustment that leaves him facing the camera more fully and recaps everything I already know about Lawrence Wilson: brutal murder of Dennis Prescott, slated to be executed, first since 1939, yadda, yadda.

I tune back in when he says, "And once again the capital punishment controversy is heating up.

"The question, abolitionists contend, should not be whether Wilson will die by hanging or lethal injection. They argue that both the specific method of execution and capital punishment by its very nature are cruel and unusual punishment and are therefore prohibited by the Eighth Amendment.

"On the opposite side of the issue are families of victims

and victims advocate groups. They argue that putting offenders to death is the only way to ensure that these heinous crimes are not allowed to become habitual. Join our guests David Sparks of Amnesty International and Marian Berg of Advocacy For A Safer America after these commercial messages—and *you* be the judge."

I feel vaguely cheated after watching the entire program. It dealt with Hayley Prescott but Hayley herself wasn't on it. And it is she, after all, I tuned in to see.

Not that she has ever voluntarily participated. But, still.

I didn't realize my teeth were clenched until I heard my impatient exhale. Sucking in a calming breath I reach for one of the older DVDs. I substitute it in place of the newly received selection and sit back once more, fast-forwarding the news clip filmed outside a courtroom until Hayley's face appears. My small grunt of satisfaction sounds loud in the otherwise silent room.

Now *there is* the face of a person who understands life can get screwed up through no fault of one's own. That is the face of a survivor, a *savior*, someone infinitely kind and compassionate.

* * *

"I'll kill her," Hayley said between her teeth as she reached for a clean glass. Her hands, she noticed with furious self-disgust, were trembling slightly. Perfect. That was. Just. Freaking. Perfect. "I will personally put my hands around her throat and *squeeeeze* the life out of her." She scooped fresh ice into the glass and reached for the bottle of Cutty Sark.

"Who?" Lucy wanted to know, fascinated by the calm delivery of violent words.

Hayley hesitated, but, really, what was the point in keeping her own council, even if she and Lucy didn't know each other? "My good and great friend," she said. "Kurstin McAlvey."

"Kurstin *Olivet* McAlvey?"

"Oh, yeah. The one and only."

"Ooh." Lucy's mouth stretched into a slow grimace of comprehension. "You, uh, *do* know Jon-Michael then, I take it."

"Yes, indeed," she agreed. "In the Biblical sense, you might say," If the looks she had noticed earlier were anything to go by, the entire town would have her every move from cradle to the current moment chewed up and spit out before she got off shift tonight. Seeing no reason to try keeping the unkeepable a secret, she informed the barmaid flatly, "Jon-Michael Olivet relieved me of my virginity when I was seventeen years old." The story was bound to be resurrected and make the rounds again anyway, given their close working proximity. Which would supply yet another reason to keep her notoriety alive and well and at the forefront of everyone's minds.

She was going to kill Kurstin, pure and simple.

Lucy's jaw dropped open. "He *raped* you?"

"No, no, Lucy, that is *not* what I said." Had anything been capable of amusing her in that moment, that would have been it. She wasn't sure how Lucy's take on her words had made the leap to that particular conclusion, but wouldn't it just serve Jon-Michael right if he were on the receiving end of a rumor for a change?

She was, unfortunately, still much too furious at Kurstin's duplicity to see any real humor in the situation. "There was always a boatload of chemistry between Jon-Michael and me, and both parties fully consented to the act," she clarified. "Of course, he was too drunk to *remember* any of it the following day—"

"Oh boy."

"But not so drunk he failed to divulge all the sordid details to the entire soccer team before he blacked out."

"Shit, oh, shit. That must have made life at school fun."

"Yes, ma'am. It was a laugh a minute. He graduated and went off to college. *I* was the sweetheart of Lincoln

High for another year and then some. But, hey, looking on the bright side, I never lacked for dating opportunities." She placed the drink that completed Lucy's order on the tray.

Lucy slid off her stool and picked it up. But she lingered for a moment to contemplate Hayley. "So what are you going to do?"

"Nothing." Hayley shrugged. "Not a damn thing. Well, except maybe smack Kurstie around a little for allowing me to walk into the situation blind." She shook her head, blowing out the calming breath she had drawn. "No, really, it was all a very long time ago, and too much has happened in the years since to make it that important anymore. It's an annoyance, is all." She shrugged a bare shoulder. "But what the hell. I'll pretend I'm an adult and just handle the situation as it arises. I am sure Jon-Michael will, too."

Very mature, she congratulated herself when Lucy walked away. But what was he doing here? She could not help but gnaw on the question during the band's set like a puppy with a knotted rag. The last place she had expected to run into him again was Bluey's bar on Eighth Street. Not that she had run into him yet, of course—and she assiduously avoided so much as glancing in the stage's direction precisely so she would not *have* to see him. Still, it was only a matter of time.

Too little, her oh-so-adult words to Lucy notwithstanding, than she might have hoped for. She could have used a bit more time to prepare herself, she discovered during the band's first break.

Could have used a helluva lot more time.

She saw him before he saw her. A redhead sitting at the far end of the counter stopped him as he made his way to the bar, detaining him with a soft grip on his forearm and an admiring smile. Jon-Michael didn't hesitate. In the inimitable style Hayley remembered, he draped himself against the corner of the bar and plunged feet first into a full blown flirtation. Sneaking covert glances while she hustled to fill the sudden deluge of orders, Hayley inventoried the changes that time had wrought.

His face was leaner, more mature, these days, which, okay, was hardly a huge surprise considering over a decade had passed since she had last seen him. He still had the same over-long dirty-blond hair she remembered, darkened a bit now with sweat, and the same Hershey Kisses-colored eyes with thick lashes that slanted the lids down so heavily in the outside corners he always appeared sleepy. Bedroom eyes, the girls back in high school had called them.

The dark stubble was new. From his upper lip, it angled down just inside the creases bracketing his mouth and joined its brothers on his strong chin and lean jaw. It was almost long enough to be an honest-to-god beard or goatee, or whatever, but was just the other side of that. Hayley smiled politely at a customer as she counted back change and handed over his drink. She had never cared much for stubble.

She sneaked another glance at Jon-Michael as she poured two pitchers for Marsha. Okay. As much as she hated to admit it, the style looked pretty good on him. It complemented the long, lean bones of his face.

She noticed he still had the same old habit of leaning against the nearest piece of furniture. Jon-Michael never had stood if he could sit or sat if he could lie down. He had always moved so slow and easy it could fool the unobservant into thinking he was lazy.

In truth, he could cover more territory and accomplish more business giving the appearance of standing still than most people could in a flat-out sprint.

"Rum and coke," a quiet voice said, pulling her attention back to the job at hand, and Hayley looked up at a man about her own age. He was smiling at her and she responded automatically with her own polite version, but there was an expectancy in his eyes that caused her to study him more closely as she poured ice into a glass, added a shot of rum, and reached for the soda gun. Pushing the cola button, she divided her attention between the glass she was filling and the man's face.

He looked familiar somehow. He was nice looking, with blue eyes and straight brown hair that had receded only to the point of giving him an intellectual look. Her gaze was drawn back to the expression in his eyes. "Do I know—?" Eyebrows furrowing, she passed him his drink. "Joe?" she queried uncertainly. "Joe Beal?"

"The same." He grinned at her. "It's been a long time, Hayley."

"Yes, it's been over a dozen years. That will be eight dollars, please." She took his money and rang it up. When she turned back it was to a temporary lull in the activity.

"You look exactly the same," Joe said and took a large sip of his drink, staring at her as Hayley's pleasure manifested in a grin.

"Well aren't you the sweet talker," she said. "Full of blarney right up to your pretty brown eyebrows, but sweet, no doubt about it."

"No, I'm serious. You haven't changed a bit. No one would ever know to look at you all the crap you've been through these past several years." Dull color climbed his throat. "I'm sorry. That was incredibly tactless of me."

She bit back a sigh. "Don't worry about it, Joe. I have waded through a lot of crap, and pretending otherwise doesn't change the facts." At least he hadn't asked for particulars. That happened to her frequently. Due to the massive publicity surrounding Dennis's death and the sensationalized trial that had followed, people didn't seem to comprehend it was insensitive to demand the details of a matter that was, to her, extremely private and painful.

He leaned in and lowered his voice so the two men loudly dissecting a call on last night's Mariners game wouldn't hear. "You were the sole witness to your husband's murder?"

Well, there went his points for being more understanding than most. And the kicker was, she couldn't simply ignore the question. As much as she might love to tell Joe that the details of Dennis's death were truly none of his business, she knew she would not. She had become a realist over the past several years. And realistically, she could not afford to offend a client a mere three hours into her first shift.

"I didn't see Wilson commit the actual murder," she replied without inflection. "I saw him leaving our house." Which had scared her to the marrow and she'd pulled back against the siding, in the dense shadow of a maple tree, until he had climbed into a car and driven away. Then she had run inside to find Dennis on the kitchen floor.

God. There had been so much blood. All over the place: on the floor, on the walls, smeared across the counter and the cupboards. Pooled under Dennis's body.

Hayley swallowed dryly but managed to say levelly, "My testimony placed him at the scene of the crime, which turned out to be fairly crucial as all the rest of the evidence presented by the Prosecuting Attorney was strictly circumstantial."

Fairly crucial. The words mocked her. It was, in fact, her testimony that was most likely responsible for Wilson's death sentence. Not a soul in the world knew how she felt about that. In all honesty, *she* wasn't certain how she felt half the time.

Joe looked at her across the bar and must have noted her rigid posture, her white knuckles and what she feared was a sudden pallor, given the way she felt, because he proved to be less insensitive than many Hayley had encountered.

"I'm sorry," he said with sincere contrition. "I really am tactless. To me it's like having an opportunity to talk to the author of one of those true crime novels. I forgot for a moment that for you it is all too real. You didn't write it, you lived it. Please accept my apologies. What I should have said is I'm sorry for your loss."

"Thank you. That's why I came back: I could not seem to put it behind me in New Hampshire and I'm hoping to do a better job of it here." She gazed past him into the crowd and then looked back at his face. "Speaking of people who haven't changed much, I saw Patsy last night. Is she here with you?" She gave him a crooked smile. "I heard you two got married."

His expression seemed to cool somewhat, but his tone was so equitable when he said, "She didn't come with me tonight," Hayley decided she must have imagined the slight change in his attitude.

Lucy elbowed up to the bar and rattled off her order. Hayley gave Joe another watered down version of her smile. "I better get back to work," she murmured. "It was nice seeing you again." She turned away to fill the new order.

He stuffed a dollar into her tip glass and backed away from the bar. "Thanks, Hayley," he raised his voice to call over the din. "Hope I see you around real soon."

Jon-Michael's head snapped up. Here? Hayley was here? His eyes scanned the dimly lighted lounge but he didn't see her.

"Well, listen, I hate to cut this short but I gotta go," he interrupted the redhead's discourse on this year's fashions and straightened from his indolent slouch against the bar.

"Oh, don't go, Jon-Michael."

"Gotta." But her hand on his arm kept him in place and, propping his elbows behind him on the bar, he leaned against it for a moment's support while he explained, "I need something to drink before the next set begins and then I have—"

She called down the bar for the bartender.

"—a few things I need to attend to," he trailed off lamely. Shit. She was already raising her glass to indicate another of the same to the bartender. Turning to him, she inquired, "What will you have?"

"I'll take my usual, Bluey," he said absently while his mind raced for a way to gracefully ease himself away before the break ended. He continued to scan the crowd for Hayley but couldn't find her.

"Well let's see now, you have all of five minutes before the next set is scheduled to begin," a feminine voice replied sarcastically from behind the bar. "So does that mean I pour you a single shot of Black Velvet or just bring you the bottle?"

He swiveled around, feeling his cheeks creasing in a big smile. "Hayley Prescott!"

Without returning his smile, she gave him a subtle, so-what-is-it-gonna-be look, and he said, "How have you been, darlin'? I see you still have a mouth on you." He had always liked that about her. "Just bring me a club soda, please."

Eyebrows elevating in unspoken amazement, she turned away. Grinning, he leaned forward on his forearms to keep her butt in view as she walked the length of the bar.

He was still draped over the corner of the bar when she returned with the drinks a moment later. She set them down in front of them. "That will be eight fifty for the Collins."

The redhead waited expectantly for Jon-Michael to pay for her drink, but he merely sipped at his club soda and smiled lazily at Hayley. With a little huff of impatience, she reached in her purse for her wallet.

"Suave as ever, I see," Hayley murmured as she accepted money from the redhead. Jon-Michael looked up from contemplating the modest cleavage exposed by her turquoise vest to give her a sleepy smile. Then slowly, he pushed himself upright.

"Guess I had better get back to work," he said, drank down the rest of his club soda in one long swallow, and set the glass on the bar. He said, "See ya," to the redhead, winked at Hayley, and ambled away.

Behind him he heard Hayley make a rude noise, then walk away in response to the summons of a patron down the bar.

Climbing up on the stage, Jon-Michael picked up his alto sax and licked the reed. He started to wrap his lips around it but was interrupted by Brian.

"Was that Hayley Granger I saw you talking to?"

Jon-Michael's gaze located her behind the bar and he nodded. Lowering the sax, he corrected, "Prescott. It's Prescott now."

"But it's still Hayley of the 'skin like velvet, pussy sweeter 'n wine,' right?"

His eyes narrowed. He wished to hell he could remember that night. An entire high school soccer team from back in the day knew more about it than he did...to his eternal shame. He'd heard his words repeated back to him over the years but could not recall a thing about the event leading up to his having uttered them.

He really wished he could remember why she'd agreed to sleep with him at all. He had been so full of himself in those days, and where other girls had stroked his ego and told him what a super special guy he was, Hayley Granger had poked little sharp sticks at his ego and enticed him not to take himself so seriously. But she had lain on a blanket with him one night in the woods off Lake Meredith and surrendered up her virginity.

"Yeah," he replied and then pinned Brian in place with his gaze. "But bring it up again and I will knock your teeth down your throat. We aren't in high school anymore and it is way past time to let that shit go. If anyone else says something about her tell them to shut the fuck up."

"No problem." Brian shrugged. "So, what is she doin' back in town?"

"Avoiding the press." The look Brian gave him was blank and Jon-Michael rolled his shoulders impatiently.

"Don't you ever pick up a newspaper or turn on the news?"

"Nah. It's got nothing much to do with my life." He showed signs of interest. "Why, she ice somebody or something?"

"She fingered the guy who killed her husband and he's scheduled to be executed the beginning of August."

"No shit. They gonna fry him?"

"Lethal injection. It's still being fought out in the courts." And reported faithfully on national television and in the press on slow days.

"No shit," Brian repeated. "Cool."

"Jesus, Brian, you're hopeless." Jon-Michael was grateful when the piano player suggested they get back to work.

His gaze, during their second set, kept getting pulled back to where Hayley was working behind the bar. Her position as the new bartender was going to throw them together a lot. Unsure what he wanted from her, he didn't have the vaguest idea how he would handle the interaction that was bound to crop up between them.

He knew what he wasn't going to do, though. He was not going to apologize again for that night at Lake Meredith. For an entire *year* after the event, every time their paths crossed he had tried to talk to her about it, to tell her he was sorry. She had refused to have anything to do with him.

Well, so be it. More than a decade had passed and the episode was a dry skeleton without an ounce of flesh left to lash. The best thing was probably to just give her as wide a berth as possible. Be polite when their paths crossed but do his damnedest to otherwise stay out of her way.

He headed straight for the bar at the next break.

"Club soda," he ordered, sliding his butt onto a stool and leaning his forearms on the bar, collapsing from the waist to prop his chin on his fists.

She plopped some ice in a glass, filled it to the rim from

the soda gun and slid it across the bar to him. Then she turned away, busying herself with an order for Marsha.

"So, how is the car holding up, darlin'?" he asked when she orbited back down to his part of the bar. He swirled ice around in his glass.

"My Pontiac?" she asked him. "It's fine. Why do you ask?"

"Not stalling out on you any more?"

She stopped what she was doing and stared at him. "Oh, don't tell me. It was you, wasn't it?" When he merely looked at her from between his lashes, she huffed out an exasperated breath. "It was *you* Kurstin got to work on my car?"

He killed off the soda, smiled at her lazily, and held the glass up for a refill. She snatched it out of his hand.

"Great. That is just perfect. Out of all the people in the world, you are the *last* I would choose to be beholden to."

"Don't owe me a thing, cupcake."

"You have that right, Olivet." She stormed off to make a customer a drink.

Minutes later she was back. "I'll give you some money to cover your expenses as soon as I get paid," she informed him tightly.

He sat up. "The hell you will. I just used some odds and ends that were lying around the garage. My old man's never going to miss the stuff." His eyes went hard. "He can sure as hell afford it."

"I'll pay for your time then."

"No."

"*Yes.*"

Jon-Michael picked up his glass and slid off his stool. Moving slowly, he reached across the bar, caught her pointed little chin in one hand, and leaned in close. "No," he said with firm finality. Then he turned her loose and sauntered away.

He could hear her behind him, growling with frustration, and it made him grin. Oh, this was gonna be good. He had forgotten how much fun it was to piss her off.

And how about that anyway? Surprise, surprise. The old dark chemistry between them was still alive and kicking...at least on his part. It wasn't something he had expected. It was sure as shit not something he had planned.

But he could not in all honesty say it was something he minded.

Chapter 4

"You have to be here for Sunday dinner." Kurstin declared, hoping if she stated it as if Hayley could not possibly refuse, she wouldn't.

That worked about as well as usual with her best friend. "I don't have to do a damn thing I don't want to do," Hayley disagreed coolly.

"Oh, come on," she protested. "Are you still sulking over my one tiny failure to disclose everything I know? I can't be expected to remember everything. It was an oversight."

"Oversight, my ass. And I do *not*—"

"So, fine," she interrupted. "I neglected to tell you Jon-Michael has a gig at Bluey's—"

"—sulk. And you purposefully failed to tell me about Jon-Michael's gig because you knew damn good and well—"

"You wouldn't take the damn job if I did! Yes. All right! I am guilty as charged. So, shoot me. You would have cut off your skinny little nose to spite your face, and after you'd told me yourself you needed a job *now*." She flopped back on her elbows on the beach towel and looked up at Hayley.

Standing over her with her arms crossed militantly beneath her breasts, Haley returned a cool stare. One, unfortunately, that did not completely hide the sense of betrayal at its core.

Kurstin drew in a deep breath, then blew it out in a gusty sigh. And shed her posturing. "Okay," she said. "I truly am sorry. I knew it was underhanded, but the job seemed tailor-made for your needs. So I just...went ahead and did it anyway."

Hayley sank to sit cross legged on the corner of the towel. "Move your butt," she commanded. When Kurstin promptly made room for her, her life-long BFF made herself more comfortable.

And conceded, "It's a good job. I made a killing on tips last night."

"Does that mean I'm forgiven?"

"I suppose. But do *not* get in the habit of manipulating me, Kurstie, or we will have an issue."

"I won't. I swear I was not proud of how I handled the situation and, honest-to-God, I must have started to 'fess up a dozen times." Water lapped against the pilings beneath them as she watched Hayley wrap her hands around her ankles and slowly butterfly her knees up and down. She hated that her bestie's face was averted, but Hayley determinedly kept her gaze on the lake. "So, will you come to Sunday dinner?" Kurstin finally asked again. "Please?"

Hayley groaned deep in her throat, undoubtedly remembering the formal, stifled affairs of the past.

"Please," she reiterated. "I invited Patsy and Joe Beal. I know I should have cleared it with you first, but Patsy has been bugging the hell out of me. I have no idea why she seems to think you're her best bud all of sudden, but since your schedule precludes most evenings it seemed like a good time to get everyone together. Not to mention that if enough people are there, perhaps my dad and brother will be on their best behavior for a change instead of trying to rip out each other's throat."

Okay, Hayley admitted it: she could not resist the chance to find out what was going on there. She swiveled to face Kurstin, bringing her knees in toward her chest. Hugging her shins, she propped her chin atop her kneecaps.

"What's the story with those two?" she demanded. "Being at each other's throat is not exactly hot-breaking news, but I thought things between them were all hunky dory these days. Last I heard, Jon-Michael joined the fold when he went into the business, which I gotta tell you, Kurst, knocked me for a loop. Now I find him playing his sax in a lounge on Eighth Street."

"Jon was great at his job," Kurstin retorted as if she had somehow implied otherwise. "He was innovative and had a versatile, enterprising approach to work. But he resists anything that smacks of hierarchy."

"And hierarchy is Richard's middle name."

"Precisely." Kurstin sighed. "Some things never change. Put those two together and they are still like vinegar and baking soda. Dad just can't resist micro-managing every aspect of the business. It doesn't matter that Jon-Michael gets results with his methods; they are not *Father's* methods. Dad is extremely task oriented and he wants things done a certain way. Jon-Michael's way is more fluid and he questions everything. They butted heads at every turn."

"They must have known going in that was a distinct possibility."

"You would think so, right? And for all their clashes it actually worked for a while. Then all of a sudden it fell apart. Jon-Michael left in a huff and Dad has been unrelentingly furious ever since that an Olivet has been—and I quote—'throwing his life away in that *iniquitous* dive.'" She smiled slightly. "Good word, iniquitous. I will give him points for that."

Clearly, something specific had occurred to bring the situation to the flash point and Hayley wondered what it was. Jon-Michael was outspoken and strategy minded, and she could see him fighting tooth and nail to stave off Richard's attempts at imposing a bureaucratic structure to his methods and relishing every minute of it. So what had

---

made him stomp off in anger? Not only did Kurstin not seem to know, she apparently didn't even suspect a deeper motive for the split.

Hayley suspected like crazy and privately acknowledged that her cynicism had been honed to a fine finish over the past couple years. Maybe she would snoop around in someone else's life for a change and see what it was like from the other side.

"But you are not getting me off subject." Kurstin said, waving the current topic away with an impatient flip of her hand. "Are you going to be here for dinner or not?"

"You bet. I wouldn't miss it for the world."

* * *

"Sherry?" Richard Olivet asked the following Sunday as long fingers of early evening sunshine crept across the parlor's hardwood floors.

"Chablis, please," Hayley responded. "I've never really cared for sherry." As he turned away, however, she had the distinct impression he hadn't listened to her reply. He had given her a brief critical inspection, then dismissed her. The practiced tactic left Hayley feeling as if she should be the one serving the drinks. Richard had always had that effect on her.

She discreetly checked her hem to make sure it wasn't sagging anywhere and plucked a loose thread from the bodice of her sundress and rolled it into a little ball she surreptitiously tucked beneath a Limoge dish of chocolate truffles. She smiled politely when Richard returned and handed her a glass. Lifting it to her lips, she took a tiny sip and hid her grimace. Sherry.

She inspected him for the odd wrinkle, unsurprised to find him as impeccably groomed as ever. It was not particularly warm this late June day, but Hayley had no fear her bare arms and legs might court goosebumps within the lavishly appointed, temperature controlled room. So, if she were comfortable in a skimpy sundress, she could only believe Richard, dressed in a summer-weight wool, must feel downright stuffy.

But then stuffy was his default mode. He was all tricked out in an exquisitely cut suit and London tailored shirt and tie, with his crisply laundered pocket handkerchief arranged just so and not a silver hair on his expensively barbered head out of place. No weekend Dockers and casual, rolled shirt sleeves for this man.

This was the first time their paths had crossed since she moved in, and she dragged out her manners. "I have not had the opportunity to thank you for opening up your home to me." Her mother may have been an assembly worker in Richard Olivet's factory, but she hadn't failed to teach her daughter etiquette.

And she had been ten times the parent Richard Olivet would ever be.

He responded with impersonal civility, leaving her with the impression, as he always had, that his mind was on weightier, more important considerations than conversing with a friend of his daughter's. Then he bestirred himself to say, "I understand you have a Master's degree and you have been hired by the high school. As a psychologist-counselor, Kurstin said?"

"Is that the story you're spinning these days, Hayley, honey?" a lazy voice inquired.

Hayley and Richard stiffened and turned as one to stare at Jon-Michael, who was indolently propped against the doorjamb. *He*, Hayley noticed, wore weekend Dockers and a rolled sleeve yellow shirt of richly textured cotton.

"It's not a story, Olivet—it is fact. My job at Lincoln High starts the last week in August." Her chin elevated proudly and her gaze was level when it met his. "Unlike you, rich boy, I don't have a trust fund to fall back on until then."

Turning to Richard, she explained coolly, "What Jon-Michael is obviously dying to tell you is that I took an additional job at Bluey's over on Eighth Street, tending bar. It's how I made my living while I worked toward my Masters." She graced the two men with an impartial, polite stretch of her lips. "Now, if you will excuse me," she said distantly, "I really do not care for sherry. I believe I'll get myself a glass of Chablis."

Kurstin joined her at the antique tea caddy doubling as a portable bar. "Big help you're going to be," she murmured as she plucked ice cubes out of the silver bucket with a pair of tongs and dropped them in her crystal tumbler.

"Yes, I can tell already this is going to be monstrous fun." Hayley gave her friend a sidelong look. "Tell me again how I let you talk me into it."

"I think the turning point was when I said that for all their clashes Dad and Jon-Michael's working relationship seemed to be working out for them...right up until some inexplicable thing happened to destroy it."

Hayley turned to stare at her. "Oh. You are good. So much for your vow not to manipulate me, but you are clever, I'll give you that."

"That wasn't manipulation," Kurstin disagreed. "That would be if I knew something you don't and used it to my own advantage. But I really do not know what happened between Dad and Jon-Michael. I wish I did." She raised her eyebrow at Hayley. "Being clueless exonerates me of all charges. All I did in this case was appeal to your love of solving puzzles."

"To get your own way," Hayley interjected.

"Well...*yeah*. What's your point?" She grinned and gave Hayley a nudge. "Come on, admit it. It was the perfect ploy. Tell me the truth. I'm the ultimate wit, yes?"

"You're half right." Hayley looked at her friend, who was so clearly and thoroughly tickled with herself she could not help but smile wryly. "How did you get to be such a big hotshot personnel director, Kurstie, when you still cannot resist going *na-na-na-na-na* when you think you've pulled a fast one?"

"Oh, sugar, that's simple. My daddy owns the company."

Patsy and Joe Beal arrived and shortly afterward everyone was called into the dining room for dinner. Hayley hoped to get through the meal without a rehash of Dennis's murder or Lawrence Wilson's upcoming execution. It would make such a pleasant change from the social events she had attended in the recent past.

She was not that lucky, of course. She hadn't really expected to be.

It was Patsy who first brought it up. She turned to Hayley during the salad course and said with heavy-handed sympathy, "I imagine this is a very trying time for you."

Hayley smiled politely in return but failed to comment, knowing where the conversation was headed. She'd had plenty of time to construct stock answers for these situations, but had kind of hoped they would not be necessary back here in Gravers Bend. Naïve of her, she knew. But hope truly did spring eternal.

Patsy studied her for a moment and when it became apparent she was not going to respond, elaborated, "What with the execution date drawing near and all."

"For God's sake, Patsy," Joe snapped and watched without visible sympathy when his wife flushed at being reprimanded in public.

Hayley blinked at Joe's impatience. It was a marked contrast with the low-key friendliness he had displayed at the bar.

Kurstin smoothed over the awkward moment. "The reason Hayley moved back to Gravers Bend," she explained in an attempt to lead Patsy into other conversational waters, "was to get away from all the speculation and constant reminders of the ordeal she has been through."

"Well, of course it was," Patsy agreed. "But we are not

just anybody. We are like family and Hayley surely needs her family around her. Especially now. I am just trying to understand what it must be like for her." She turned to Hayley and appealed, "You understand, I am sure."

Family? Her face felt stiff but otherwise composed and noncommittal. Mentally, however, her jaw was sagging. Luckily, she was saved from having to scramble for a reply by Jon-Michael.

Lounging back in his chair, he pinned Patsy in place with his dark-eyed gaze. "When was the last time you saw Hayley, Patsy?" he inquired conversationally.

She turned to him, pert as a robin. "Why, the day after she arrived in town, I believe it was."

"Uh huh. And before that?"

"Well, let me see." She looked thoughtful. "It must have been right before she left Gravers Bend for college."

"So going on thirteen years ago. How many emails or letters or whatnot did you two exchange during that time."

Patsy squirmed slightly. "I do not see what the point of your question is, Jon-Michael. But one."

Which would have been the sympathy card Patsy had sent when Dennis died and her own reply.

"Then how the fuck," Jon-Michael wanted to know, "does that make you family?"

"Jon-Michael!" Richard rapped out coldly. "That is quite enough. Patsy is a guest in our home—"

"And as such I apologize for my language," Jon-Michael said smoothly. It was clear to everyone present his language was the only thing he apologized for.

"—and an Olivet does not—"

Jon-Michael cut his father's comment in two. "This Olivet does," he said in a hard tone. "You just don't get it, do you, Dad? I don't care how that might make me appear in another's eyes. Neither do I give a flying...flick about preserving the sanctity of the precious Olivet name. That is the major difference between you and me. My only real concern is if *I* feel I have behaved honorably."

Hayley choked on her sip of wine and Jon-Michael turned to look at her. Studying her in silence for a moment, he ultimately gave her a wry, one-sided smile. "Yeah, I suppose that does sound like a load of horseshit, coming from me," he said and waved his father aside when he once again took exception to Jon-Michael's language in front of their guests. Softly slapping his hands down on the table's highly polished surface on either side of his place setting, he leaned forward to stare intently at Hayley. "You and I really will have to have a long talk about that night sometime, Hayley. And all the ways I have changed since then."

"Ooh," she said, deadpan. "I can hardly wait. Of course, the conversation will be a little one-sided, won't it Jon-Michael? Considering I am the only one who can *remember* that night." She had the satisfaction of seeing a dull red flush climb his throat.

And as a diversionary tactic, it proved to be brilliant, leaving Richard confused and luring Patsy away from her pique at being publicly rebuked. Her gaze ping-ponged between Jon-Michael and Hayley, studying their expressions with avid curiosity.

Kurstin, who must be feeling the afternoon disintegrate right before her eyes, turned to Joe. "So!" she said with slightly desperate cheer, "I understand you are an ardent bow and arrow hunter."

"Yes," he agreed. "I've hunted deer since my father gave me my first rifle for my twelfth birthday. I discovered bow and arrow hunting about eight years ago."

"No kidding?" Jerking her gaze away from Jon-Michael's, Hayley leaned forward, her interest sparked. "You hunt with bow and arrows like the American Indians used to use?"

"Well, not exactly," he replied, turning to her. "People do hunt with traditional long bows but I prefer the compound bow."

"How are they different?"

"The compound bow is configured differently and rigged with pulleys. Drawing back the arrow is most difficult at the beginning of the pull when the bow's limbs are at their straightest. The further back you draw it, the more the bow's limbs curve, and the easier it becomes."

She looked at him with interest. "I suppose then a person would need a lot of upper body strength to use one, huh?"

"Not necessarily. Patsy hunts, but her bow compensates for her lack of arm power with a lesser draw length and weight." Shifting, he shot his wife an indecipherable look before adding almost perfunctorily, "Not that she's not in good shape, of course."

"Patsy! You dark horse!" Hayley studied her former schoolmate with surprised curiosity. "You hunt deer?" She remembered how adamantly opposed Patsy had once been to what she'd stridently termed 'Bambi killers'. Yet giving it a moment's further consideration, she also recalled Patsy had been going with a boy at the time whose politics she had adopted. She tended to do that a lot back then: be interested in whatever her boyfriend was interested in. "Is that how you guys got together, through a bow and arrow club or something?"

"No." Patsy shook her head. "Joe was just getting into it when we first became reacquainted, and he described it so enthusiastically I simply had to see for myself what all the fuss was about."

Hayley hid a smile. Some things never changed, apparently.

"She's pretty good, too," Joe said. "Last fall she brought down a four-point buck."

A train whistle blew mournfully out on the other side of the highway, and Hayley's head snapped up, her attention arrested. She glanced down at her watch. It was five forty-five. "Oh, my God," she said. "I don't believe it. Is that...? No, it can't possibly be." She turned to Kurstin and found her grinning at her. She grinned back. "It is, isn't it? That *is* the five o'clock! And darned if it isn't—"

"Right on time!" Kurstin and Jon-Michael chimed in, finishing the sentence with her. Hayley laughed a deep, genuine, from-the-heart laugh.

"Who would have thought?" she said once she regained control. Looking around, taking note of the expressions of the table's other occupants, she smiled ruefully. "Sorry."

Richard was regarding the three of them with impatient disdain, as if they had held a farting competition in public and he could not for the life of him understand how Olivets could have participated. Joe cocked inquiring eyebrows but looked amused and Patsy was all but rolling her eyes. But then Patsy never had gotten the point of most of their humor.

"You must think we're crazy," she said. "I just didn't expect that train to still be running through Gravers Bend."

"It doesn't actually stop here anymore," Jon-Michael said, and their eyes met. "It just passes through." Then he grinned, his cheeks creasing into raised parentheses framing his omnipresent stubble. "But as you can see, it passes through on its long-held schedule."

Gaze tangled with his, Hayley confronted a truth for the first time in a long, long while. She had determinedly shoved into a far corner of her mind the fact that Jon-Michael was more than just the conceited son of the town's richest man and a boy who had always drank too much. Even then he had also been humorous and inventive, clever and vulnerable. Those very qualities had led her to a blanket alongside Lake Meredith one long-ago night.

But that was neither the subject under discussion nor one she cared to pursue. She gave herself a brisk mental shake. "It was a standing joke with us," she explained to Joe, whose expression was most receptive. "Hasn't Patsy ever mentioned it?"

He shook his head and Hayley had to admit that, no, Patsy probably would not.

"You see, according to the schedule, the train's arrival

time was supposed to be five p.m. But we always heard its whistle blow, day after day, year after year, at five forty-five. On the dot."

"How amusing," Richard commented flatly, his tone suggesting it was anything but.

"Not really, I suppose." Hayley's gaze met his and her shrug held no apology. "But it seemed hilarious enough when we were twelve, fifteen, seventeen years old. Nostalgia alone tends to lend it amusement value now."

"Save your breath, darlin'," Jon-Michael advised. "He will never in a million years get it. Dad fails to see the humor in anything not equipped with a dollar sign. Right Pop?"

Richard neatly folded his cloth napkin and set it on the table, then rose and stalked out of the room.

Picking up her butter knife, Kurstin slapped her free hand to her forehead and tipped her head back in one smooth motion, exposing her throat. She drew the knife across her bared neck from ear to ear.

Jon-Michael laughed. "Sorry, Kurst. I'll be good from now on, I promise."

"Sure you will," she muttered. "Observe me holding my breath."

Hayley shot her friend a knowing gaze across the table and Kurstin shrugged.

"Okay, so I should have seen it coming," she said. "Just shoot me if I ever suggest holding one of these damn family dinners again."

"You got it." But she watched Kurstin resolutely stiffen her spine, set down the knife and apply herself to smoothing over the rifts.

And pitched in to help salvage the rest of the meal.

Chapter 5

The following Tuesday Hayley's gaze lingered in dazed admiration on the changes wrought in Lucy's appearance as the cocktail waitress set her tray on the bar. Sometime since last night's shift, the other woman had turned the blonde portion of her two-tone hair pink. She had coordinated with matching hose and satin push-up bra beneath her turquoise vest, pairing all that rose-pink with a long black skirt that flirted with her Doc Martens. Her nose stud tonight was a garnet.

"You know how to make a Pink Lady?" the waitress inquired over the moody licks of a blues guitar and the soft wail of a saxophone.

"Yes. It's old school but I do."

"Good, 'cause that's a new one for me. Give me one of those, a Beefeater martini straight up with two olives, a Diet Coke, and two non-alcoholic St. Paulie Girls."

"Coming up—provided Bluey keeps any eggs in here." Hayley stooped to open the small fridge under the bar and breathed an appreciative "thank you," when she found a half dozen. She pulled out one and popped a martini glass in to chill. Setting the egg aside, she assembled the rest of Lucy's order, then measured the liquor and grenadine for the Pink Lady into a shaker and squeezed in the juice from half a lemon. After separating the yolk from the egg white, she added half of the latter to the rest of the mixture. She gave the shaker a good long, hard shake to emulsify the egg white. Adding ice, she shook it hard again, then retrieved the chilled glass from the fridge. As she strained the mixture into the glass, she said, "Have you met my friend Kurstin, Lucy?" With a small gesture of her little finger, she indicated the woman sitting across the bar from her. "Lucy, Kurstin McAlvey. Kurstin, meet Lucy."

"Hey," Lucy said around the gum she was chewing, looking up from straightening her cash drawer.

"Hello," Kurstin replied with a smile. "Nice to meet you."

"I like your brother's music," Lucy told her. A tiny smile curved up one corner of her mouth. "Not to mention his abs."

Kurstin blinked. "His abs? Jon-Michael's?"

Assembling the rest of the order, Hayley slid the tray back to Lucy. "Here you go."

Lucy cracked her gum. "Thanks. You're a doll." She picked up the tray and walked away.

Kurstin swiveled around on her stool to watch her go. Turning back to Hayley, she grinned. "I must say, things are much more interesting around your work place than they are in the stodgy old HR department at Olivet's. What did she mean about Jon-Michael's abs, though?"

"She claims they're ripped." Hayley glanced toward the bandstand and felt her mouth go dry at the sight scorching her eyes. Reaching over, she nudged Kurstin to direct her attention. As if he had been privy to the conversation, Jon-Michael dropped his sax to hang from the strap around his neck and swiped the sweat off his face with the tails of his shirt. "Jeez-Marie," she breathed. "She wasn't kidding."

"No fooling," Kurstin agreed, blinking. "How have I never noticed that before?"

"You're his sister." Hayley tried her damnedest to look away in order to meet her friend's gaze, but her eyes refused to obey until the shirt fluttered back into place and he had raised the sax back to his lips. "There is no, um, reason you should have." Holy Mary, Mother of God. She felt flushed all over and had to concentrate like the devil to bring her focus back to Kurstin.

"I'm glad you came by tonight," she finally said. "I've missed you."

"Yeah, I have missed you, too. It's the main reason I decided to stop by. Between the demands of our schedules, we've seen darn little of each other and I wondered if on Sunday you would like to go—"

"Could I have a rum and coke please?"

Both women looked up. Joe Beal was standing there, smiling at Hayley. "Hi," he said softly when she turned her attention to him.

"Hi, yourself," she said briskly. "One rum and coke, coming up." She reached for a glass.

Kurstin leaned back to contemplate Joe as he watched Hayley assemble his drink. "So where is Patsy tonight?"

"Oh, hi, Kurstin." He spared her a brief glance. "Home."

"Attending to all those last minute details for the big Fourth of July dance, huh?"

"Yeah, I guess. She gets off on all that stuff."

"Here you go, Joe." Hayley handed him his drink.

He tried to engage her in small talk while she made change from the twenty he had handed her, but she kept her replies polite, brief and impersonal. After a few moments spent hanging around the end of the bar watching her fill orders, he stuffed a dollar in the tip snifter and walked away.

Picking up Kurstin's drink to wipe away a tiny pool of condensation from beneath it, Hayley glanced up to watch him go, her eyebrows pleated. Then she looked at her friend. "What's the story with his and Patsy's marriage?"

Kurstin swiveled to watch him as well then turned back to the bar. "Beat's me," she admitted. "I would have said it's solid, but there was something on Sunday I could not put my finger on. Perhaps because he hardly ever looked directly at her." Her gaze nailed Hayley's feet to the floor. "He certainly seems to think you're cuter 'n a button, though."

Hayley whispered a curse. "He's been here without his

wife twice this week already, kind of hanging around trying to chat me up while I work. I realize I have become a bit cynical these days, so I was sort of hoping it was just a case of my suspicious little mind overreacting."

"Wasn't he one of the guys who asked you out in our senior year?"

A derisive noise detonated softly in her throat. "Can you think of anyone who did not? Jon-Michael's public relations job made me sound extremely talented." She indicated her friend's glass. "You care for a refill on that?"

"Please."

"To be fair," she continued as she freshened Kurstin's drink, "Joe was kind of shy back then and I suspected he might be one of the few who was actually more interested in me than in my red-hot reputation."

"But you never dated him."

"No. I was beyond gun-shy by the time he got around to asking me out and unwilling to risk being wrong." She wanted to change the subject and did not bother to be subtle about it. "What did you start to ask me earlier?"

"Hmmm?"

"Just before Joe showed up and interrupted? You were asking if on Sunday I wanted to go—" She leaned into the bar, twirling a hand to encourage her friend to complete the sentence. "Fill in the blanks here, Kurst."

"Oh, exploring!" Kurstin laughed. "I wanted to know if you'd like to take a little trip down Memory Lane on Sunday to go check out some of our old haunts."

"Just the two of us?"

"Ab-so-tootly. Just you and me. Like the old days."

"I would so like that." And foregoing involved plans, they agreed to meet in the kitchen, at noon, on Sunday.

At closing time, instead of promptly packing up his saxophone and leaving the minute his last set was through as he usually did, Jon-Michael hung around, watching

Hayley cash out the till. Hips propped against a stool, legs sprawled out and his upper body draped over the bar, he rested his chin on his stacked fists and observed silently as, one by one, the waitresses finished their drinks and said good night.

The smell of snuffed candles hung heavily in the air for a few moments before the ever efficient ventilation system pulled it up through the ceiling vents. The neon lights' timers turned off one by one, making the room grow dimmer and dimmer until the only illumination was the mirrored wall of liquor bottles behind the bar.

Jon-Michael watched its reflected light filter through Hayley's flyaway curls, picking highlights from the rich brown and turning them into a red-streaked nimbus around her head.

"So, hey," he inquired lazily, "what time are we goin' exploring on Sunday?"

"Excuse me?" She stiffened a moment and he could practically see the wheels turning in her head. Then she relaxed. "What we, Jon-Michael? There is no we...get that through your pointy little head. Kurstie and I are going exploring. You are not invited."

He gave her his best imitation of hurt bafflement. "But I have such nice, muscular abs. That equates to a strong back. I can carry lunch."

"So Lucy claims," Hayley responded, thinking Kurstin had been mighty damn chatty tonight. But she shrugged a shoulder and even managed to look Jon-Michael squarely in the eye as she lied through her teeth. "Personally, I've seen better."

Okay, challenging a man's ego was never wise. Sometimes the temptation proved irresistible, but it was not smart; she knew that.

She may have remembered it too late in this instance, but she did know it.

Jon-Michael could move like the wind when he wanted. He was around the bar in seconds flat, crowding her. Yanking his shirt out of his waistband, he grasped her hand and, ignoring her resistance, pushed it up under the cloth to splay against the warm, hard muscles of his stomach. "Seen better, huh? And whose might that have been, petunia? Your husband's maybe?"

"Among others."

He rubbed her hand in little circles. She told herself it was merely friction that so promptly heated her skin--that made it tingle. She tugged against his grip. "Let go, Jon-Michael."

"Not...just...yet." His shirt bunched over the bend of her elbow as he moved her captured hand up his diaphragm to his chest. Rubbing it in slow circles over the hair roughened muscles there, he exhaled a quiet sigh and closed his eyes.

Hayley's eyes closed as well and she groped behind her with her free hand for support. Her fingers curled over the lip of the counter beneath the bar, and the heel of her palm brushed against the sawed-off oar handle.

Eyes popping back open, her palm stroked the smooth wooden spindle as she stared at him...And considered using it.

"So." He pressed her hand hard against his chest and took a deep, uneven breath. Heavy-lidded dark eyes opened and he gazed down at her. "Have you slept with a lot of guys then?"

"Oh, dozens," she lied without compunction. "Every one of whom was better than—"

"Don't say it, Hayley," he warned and for an instant his habitual lazy humor was nowhere to be seen. Then he relaxed, giving her the patented Olivet grin. "Come on, admit it," he coaxed. "I'm the best you've ever had."

"Sure, Jon-Michael, whatever you say. I surrendered my virginity to an eighteen-year-old drunk on a lumpy blanket in the woods." She shrugged. "It was a memory to treasure."

"Did I hurt you that night?" he demanded. "Jesus, I

wish I could remember."

Everything inside her stilled at the flash of anguish in his voice and her expression must have changed because his grew bitter. "Stupid question. As you said, you were a virgin and I was drunk. Of course I hurt you."

Actually, there had not been much physical pain. He had been slow and inventive even back then. Hayley saw no reason to let him off the hook by telling him so, however. Because emotionally he had devastated her. Not to mention humiliated her in front of what had felt at the time like the entire town. And it had taken her a long, long time to get over it.

He slid her hand back down to his stomach and Hayley exhaled a silent breath of relief, thinking he was going to release her. He did not. Slipping his free hand beneath the thick fall of hair at her nape, he used his thumb to tilt her chin up. "I don't drink any more, Hayley," he informed her in a deep, hoarse voice. "And I am no longer eighteen. I would take my time now, make it real good for you."

Holy cannoli. The man could probably convince the devil to take up saving souls. Hayley had known him at his worst and still she had her work cut out simply dredging up enough moisture to swallow.

"Um hmm," she agreed. "You probably could." She felt him startle against her, felt his fingers clench at her neck and over her hand. Watching his eyelids grow heavier yet and his head descend, knowing he believed she was going to allow him to kiss her, she took a savage satisfaction in bursting his bubble. "Of course then," she said coolly, "every night before I left Bluey's to go home, I would have to check the men's room walls to be sure my name and number are not up there under the recommendation For a good time, call..."

"Damn it, Hayley, I've changed." He stared at her mouth, slicking his tongue over his lower lip.

"Well, good for you. Go tell it to the mountain."

"I would rather tell you. Or better yet, show you. Kiss

me."

"No."

"C'mon. You know how bad I wanna kiss you."

She forced a rude noise through lips gone dry.

"Kiss me, Hayley." Without waiting to see if she would decline a third time, he lowered his head and rocked his mouth over hers.

And Holy effing—all thought shut down and she could only feel.

Strong lips.

Hot tongue.

Supple moves.

Damn him! He still had that old magic in spades. He wrapped her in the warmth of his body, the scent of his skin, and to her shame, she immediately grew wet. It left her with only one recourse.

Fingers curling around the oar handle, she slid it off the shelf, brought it up, and rapped him upside his head.

Chapter 6

Our family car suddenly swerves onto the scenic overlook at Devil's Outcrop and I grab for the dashboard. "What the—?"

My spouse, in the driver's seat, is not ordinarily given to impulse so this is way out of character. And I admit it kind of shakes me up. It is not until the car comes to a full stop and the gear shift is shoved into Park that I suck in a breath. My fingers nearly leave prints as I unclench them from the dash and I have to bite my tongue to keep from saying something I might regret. Sitting back in my seat, I follow the spouse's intent stare to its source.

And almost lose my breath all over again.

The train trestle above Big Bear Gap, suspended between two points of land a hundred and sixty feet above the lake, has the spouse's attention. Or rather the two women strolling across it as casually as they might the streets of Gravers Bend.

One is a blonde and the other has an abundance of deep brown hair. The distance is too great to see individual features but who needs to? "Isn't that—?"

The spouse nods before I can say more and continues to stare. There are only two females in all of Gravers Bend who used to take on the trestle with regularity.

Well, actually, once there had been three. I shoot another glance at the driver. Not that the third really counted, because she had done so timidly, reluctantly. I would have discounted her as one of the two up there now even if I didn't know exactly where she was at the moment.

Heaven knew, *she* had never possessed the guts these women displayed.

I appreciate their daring for a few silent moments, but begin to grow disturbed. This transmutes into anger, which I just as quickly suppress. Anger is never an acceptable solution. "Come on, let's go. We still have a lot to do today."

But for God's sake. Hayley and Kurstin are no longer high school girls. They have responsibilities now, to themselves, to others. Dangerous stunts like this are juvenile and it is past time they are left behind. Anger threatens to surface once again and the effort to keep it buried leaves me with a sense of pressure almost too large to contain. Accidents happen in a matter of *seconds*. A tragedy could so easily befall them.

And if something happens to Hayley--I glance back one last time as the spouse pulls onto the lake road once again--*what the hell am I supposed to do then?*

***

When Hayley and Kurstin were down on the lake earlier in the day it had a slight chop to it. The breeze had since died, however, as it did most evenings around this time. The surface far below, which Hayley eyed now between the slats of the trestle, was mirror-flat. Enjoying the heat of the sun on her hair and shoulders, she glanced up at Kurstin, picking her way across the trestle in front of her. "You have anything left to eat?"

Her friend glanced at her over her shoulder. "An apple and a box of raisins."

"Oh yummy," she said glumly. "*Good*-for-you food. I was thinking more along the lines of a chocolate bar."

"You ate that an hour ago."

"Fine, toss me the apple. The raisins are all yours."

"You mind if we get off the trestle first? It's getting close to five forty."

"What a chicken! Don't you want to see me do my famous death-defying Granger hand-stand?"

"Tomorrow, okay? Feel the vibrations? The five o'clock is right on schedule." Kurstin reached the end of the trestle and followed the tracks a few feet further onto solid ground, where she jumped off into the woods.

"Well, okay," Hayley said in a her best you-don't-know-what-you're-missing tone as she trailed behind, "but *Patsy* would have waited around to watch me do my trick." The vibrations underfoot had grown stronger by the time she, too, leaped clear of the tracks and she stood without unblinking until her eyes had a chance to adjust to the sudden gloom of the forest.

Catching Kurstie's glance, she grinned crookedly and her best friend grinned back. Patsy's fear of the trestle was an ancient standing joke. She had crossed it with them in the old days, but she'd done so inch by creeping inch, fretting about it every step of the way.

They had always allowed extra time when she was along to avoid being mowed down by the five o'clock.

It came hurtling out of the woods across the gap now, hitting the trestle with a horrendous rattle of wooden struts and iron rails. A moment later it thundered past the spot where they stood in the woods. Then it was gone, roaring beyond the lake to the other side of the highway, its whistle trailing a mournful wail.

Hayley shouted with laughter and threw an arm around Kurstin's shoulder. Her friend rotated her arm so Hayley could see her wrist watch.

"Five forty-five," Hayley said complacently. Then the two of them completed the old refrain together. "Right on time."

They smiled at each other in satisfaction. No one else ever found it as funny as they did, but there was comfort and amusement in the shared history of an old joke.

She sighed. "This is great," she said. "Thanks, Kurstie. I really needed a day like today." They climbed back up on the track and, looking at her friend, she debated her options as she made minor adjustments to her balancing act atop one of the rails. Should she tell her about last night with Jon-Michael or not?

"Is it starting to worry you, Hayley, that the date of Wilson's execution is growing nearer?"

With her mind elsewhere, the question caught her off guard. "No," she said. "Well, yes." She looked at her friend helplessly. "That is, sort of."

Kurstin 's smile was wry. "Your decisiveness is a trait I have always admired about you."

"I used to be decisive," she replied seriously. "Once upon a time I knew know exactly what I believed in."

"Like when you believed that capital punishment was wrong?"

Hayley jerked. "Oh, God. You remember that?"

"Of course I remember. Oh, I never expected to see you on the eleven o'clock news picketing a penitentiary on execution night. But you had strong feelings on the subject." She shot a glance at Hayley as they picked their way down the tracks. "What I don't know is how you feel about it now."

Stomach rolling queasily, Hayley tore her gaze away from the compassion in Kurstin's eyes. "I don't want to talk about it," she said flatly.

"Hayley, for Cri'sake! I've been waiting nearly two years for you to introduce the subject."

"And the fact that I never did wasn't your first clue?"

She knew she wasn't being fair. But she simply could not talk about all the mixed messages the Capital punishment topic raised—and the many ways in which they messed with her head.

"Fine." Kurstin rammed her hands deep inside her pockets to keep from reaching for a fistful of Hayley's hair, which she would love to give a satisfyingly hard yank. She felt rebuffed and angry. More than that, however, she felt massively frustrated, because she knew her friend.

Hayley did not bare her soul easily. She retreated deep inside with the problems that mattered to her most and refused to let anyone follow. Kurstin had faith that sooner or later she could beat down the wall her bestie had constructed around this particular dilemma. Seeing the stubborn set of Hayley's pointy little chin, however, she had to accept it would not be today. So for a while she simply observed her lifelong friend in silence.

Then finally asked, "What is bothering you, then, if it isn't the execution?"

Hayley's head shot up. "Who said anything was?"

"Your heartfelt tone when you said you really needed a day like today."

"Oh." For a couple heartbeats, Hayley considered trying to hold it in. Then she blurted, "This is embarrassing." Still, it was easier to talk about last night than the other, and God knew she had been thinking about it before Kurstin blindsided her with the Capital Punishment thing. Her feelings about the upcoming execution always hovered in the back of her mind, knocking to make their presence felt. At this moment, however, last night's debacle was a fresher issue.

"No kidding? Now you *really* have my attention. Dish. What's embarrassing and why?"

"Well it's pretty shallow, for one thing, compared to the issues of life and death. And it's something I shouldn't even allow to bother me."

"Allow, schmow, babe. Feelings are what feelings are. Tell mama what the story is with yours."

Hayley skinned her hair off her forehead with both hands and held it there while she stared at her best friend. "Your brother slapped the moves on me last night."

Kurstin 's eyebrow elevated. "Yeah? Well, golly gee whiz. Shocker." She gave Hayley a poke. "The million-dollar question is: how did you respond?"

"Uh, you're not going to like this, Kurst. I hit him in the head with an oar handle."

She could still see him falling back, clutching his temple. "Jesus, Hayley," he had growled. "A simple 'no' would have sufficed."

"I *said* no!"

"One that you meant, I mean."

Angry and rattled, she had been tempted to give him another rap. But Bluey had emerged from his office, demanding to know what the hell was going on, and she'd taken a large step back instead.

"Do not think this is the end of the discussion," Jon-Michael had warned in a low voice that had licked its way down her nerves. Then he had picked up his instrument case and faded away, leaving her to make a lame excuse to Bluey while he disappeared through the darkened lounge.

The coward.

Kurstin regarded her now with obvious relish. "He really got to you, huh?"

"Please. I succumbed to a moment of panic, is all." She tried to disguise her knee-jerk defensiveness with an indifference she was far from feeling. "I haven't attracted male attention in a long time, and it spooked me. I overreacted."

"Yeah, it probably spooked the hell out of you to discover you liked it."

"Who said anything about liking it!"

"Oh, come on, Hays, this is me you're talking to. Why else would you strike out at him?"

She bristled and Kurstin hastened to say, "Now, I am not saying you wouldn't have smacked the man silly if he were harassing you. But I've known you forever and if that were the case, you would have screamed bloody murder while you were beating him black and blue, and I'd be bailing him out of jail today." Kurstin gave her a stern look. "So, please back atcha. He kissed you or felt you up, or something, and you liked it. But—and this is the real issue—he has already messed up your life once so you didn't *want* to like it and you cracked him upside the head to make him stop. How am I doing so far?"

"Shit."

Kurstin grinned. "That's what I thought. So when is the wedding? I'm warning you, put me in pink flounces and I will make your life a living hell."

"Good God, you're a smartass. We have *got* to get you out more often."

"Well, lighten up. You're not seventeen any more. What could Jon possibly do to you now that is worse than what you have gone through the past few years?"

Hayley dropped her hands to her sides and blew out a breath. "Not a damn thing. Okay, you're right," she admitted and flashed Kurstin a crooked smile. "Crap, I spend nine months out of the year counseling teenagers to get in touch with their own truths, to learn not to lie to themselves, no matter how many lies they feel compelled to tell others to get through their days. Pretty good advice, don't you think?"

"Yeah, you should take it."

"I really should." She scooped her hair behind her ears. "Here's the thing though, Kurst. . . dealing with Jon-Michael sometimes? It makes me regress right back to seventeen. I forget I am an adult now with much bigger problems to handle. Instead I feel like those PTSD vets you hear about who get flashbacks. I get hit by all the old feelings of impotence and rage I had to deal with every time some thick-necked jock invited me out and I *knew* he thought he was gonna get a red-hot roll in the hay at the end of the evening for the small cash outlay of a burger and a shake. So, no. You are absolutely right." She expelled a harsh breath through her nose. "I don't want to like it when Jon-Michael kisses me."

Kurstin glanced over at her friend as they started walking again. Hayley's head was down, her hands stuffed in her pockets. "I'm not denying you have cause not to believe a word he says to you," she said. "But he truly has changed, you know. He is not the same self-absorbed eighteen-year-old anymore."

Hayley glanced up at Kurstin. She hesitated but asked, "When did he quit drinking?"

Her patent reluctance to even ask tempted Kurstin to jump right in and answer her. Except...

"I think you really should discuss that with Jon-Michael," she said with reluctance. Ooh, God, that hurt. She yearned to tidy up everyone's problems; it was her nature to do so. But in this instance it really was not her place.

"Fine." The flatness of Hayley's voice made Kurstin wince, for she was familiar with the tone and her friend's innate stubbornness. Hayley would choke before she'd ask Jon-Michael. Hell, Kurstin could practically see her nailing the lid on a curiosity she probably already regretted voicing.

"You know," she said slowly, thinking aloud. "You and Jon-Michael used to talk."

Hayley made a rude noise. "We used to spar."

She smiled. "Well, yeah, that too. Intellectual foreplay, I always thought. But if you are honest with yourself, you'll admit there was a lot more to it. You two really *talked* to each other. Except for me, you were probably the only person in the world for whom he didn't constantly put on a front." Watching her friend start to poker up, Kurstin acknowledged, " I know he broke faith with you in a big way. Sometimes, though, I think you tend to forget everything except that."

"So, what you're basically saying is I don't have a right to feel the way I do?" Hayley smiled bitterly. "So much for feelings are what feelings are."

Kurstin stopped dead in the path and glared at her friend. "Oh, quit being so goddamn obtuse!" She took a deep breath, drawing calmness in with the scent of the evergreens, before continuing more quietly, "I would just like it if you'd consider the earlier parts of your relationship with Jon...the good ones. Don't let one night poison all your memories."

"Since I have more or less told myself the same thing—" Hayley blew out a breath "—I'll consider it, okay? Then she unapologetically changed the subject. "So, you have anything left to eat besides those stupid raisins?"

***

"Mr. Olivet will see you shortly, Mr. Olivet." The secretary smiled self-consciously at the duplicated use of his name. She was new, and Jon-Michael studied her from where he sprawled in the hard-backed, hard-armed visitor's chair. His father was a difficult employer, demanding and gruff, and his secretaries generally only lasted somewhere between six and ten months.

The telephone rang and he felt no compunction about eavesdropping on the secretary's end of the conversation when she picked it up. "Richard Olivet's office," she said with professional pleasantness. "I'm sorry, sir, he is not available at the moment. May I take a message? Ben Thorton?" She scribbled on the pink phone-message pad. "I'm sorry, Mr. Thorton, would you repeat that? I didn't get the name of your company." She blinked at the receiver. "Mr. Thorton? Hello, Mr. Thor—*darn* it." Flustered, she reseated the receiver.

Jon-Michael hesitated, then supplied, "Thorton-Byer Machinery." He was familiar with old Ben's habit of barking out barely intelligible orders. "Phone number's in Contacts."

The secretary shot him a grateful glance and located the information she needed to finish filling in the slip.

It must have been she who had called to set up this meeting. Usually his dad's summons were peremptory demands, but she had presented it as a request, saying his father wanted to discuss something with him. And he had gotten his hopes up.

He contemplated his feet. Could the old man have had a change of heart concerning the Ben Thorton situation? Thorton's bidding practices had been an on-going battle between Jon-Michael and his father the entire time he had worked in the family business. Thorton-Byer consistently submitted competitive bids, but the actual work was rarely done on time and Jon-Michael had argued for years that awarding them the job ended up costing Olivet's more in the long run than if they had simply accepted a higher bid from a competitor to begin with. Sitting outside his father's office, it surprised him how badly he itched to get hold of the most recent bid and check it against the specs to see if Richard had forced Ben to toe the line this time. Surprised and irritated him.

He did not regret having walked out on the company, dammit. It was the only choice Richard left him. He had more drive, more plans and just plain *more* to offer than the old man seemed willing to entertain.

Yet if Dad is ready to bend a little on the Thorton issue, then maybe... Eyes narrowing, he looked up at the secretary.

"Inform my father he has exactly one minute, then I am out the door," he snarled, then felt like a real prince when she jumped, flushed a deep red, and reached for the intercom, shooting him an agonized glance when she fumbled it. *Way to go, Olivet—you're a regular chip off the old block.*

This was such a typical ploy of Richard's—calling a meeting and then leaving him to cool his jets. A moment ago Jon-Michael had been rather amused by it and than willing to play the game. Now he was no longer in the mood. He shoved to his feet.

The door to his father's office opened at that moment and Richard stood in the doorway, staring at his son with disapproval. "Come in, Jon-Michael," he ordered.

Everything in Jon-Michael stilled as his patently

uncalled-for hope deflated. His face stiffening into the blank expression he had perfected as an adolescent, hands stuffed negligently in his pockets, he ambled across the outer office and through the doorway. "Hey, Dad," he murmured as his father stood back to allow him by. He collapsed into the nearest chair and propped his feet up on the corner of his grandfather's mahogany partners desk. Giving Richard a lazy smile guaranteed to drive the old man crazy, he held his silence, awaiting his father's opening salvo.

Richard regarded his only son coldly. "When are you going to quit dragging the Olivet name through the mud and come back to work where you belong?" he demanded with icy displeasure.

Well, *there you go*, Jon-Michael thought derisively. *Did you really expect he would admit he was wrong?* "Chasing after fourteen-year-old girls would be a case of dragging the Olivet name through the mud," he said flatly. "Playing my sax in a well respected blues bar hardly qualifies as a blemish on our exalted family. As for where I belong, it is sure as hell not in a company that does not value my ideas, education, technical and business expertise or opinions."

"Olivet's has always done perfectly well the way I have run it and the way my father before me ran it!"

"Yes, it has. But times are changing, Dad. And if we want to keep up we have to be prepared to change with it."

"We do not need to diversify," Richard categorically stated. It was an old argument.

"The hell we don't!" Jon-Michael's feet thumped to the floor as he sat up. He leaned forward. "That is exactly what we need to do. Look at the industry, dammit. It's not improving. If anything it has grown weaker. Boeing laid off forty-three hundred people last month. They've lost contracts, which means we've lost opportunities. And, hell, who is to say they won't decide to expand into the production of our part themselves, if it comes to that? I would if I ran the place. I would look into manufacturing the part in-house. It would have the two-fold benefit of eliminating one more middleman from the process and keeping some of the company's own people on the payroll." He looked his father in the eye. "Boeing comprises—what?—forty-one percent of our business? Or is it still even that much, given how many plants they've moved out of state? We need to diversify now. It is never smart to depend on one enterprise for the majority of our income, especially if the income we receive from them is shrinking."

"Our profits were up this quarter."

"And they could hit the skids next quarter."

"If you have so much faith in your ideas' viability, why don't you present them to the board?"

Jon-Michael's smile turned bitter. "I learned a long time ago not to smack my head against brick walls."

"No," Richard disagreed with flat condemnation. "What you learned, Jon-Michael, was to walk away instead of sticking around long enough to face a problem head on."

"You sanctimonious son of a bitch," Jon-Michael said as ice lined his stomach. "You're goddamn right I learned to walk away. I got tired of being disregarded, and I finally learned to recognize a futile proposition when I saw one." He rose to his feet. "You know good and well that presenting my ideas to the board is the most futile proposition of all. I am nothing if not a fast learner. You have the board in your pocket." Shoving his hands in his own pockets he looked his father in the eye. "Well, I hope you're all very cozy together. But do yourself a favor and put a little something aside for when the company goes down the tubes. Because it will if you don't diversify pretty damn soon."

Richard smiled coldly. "Leave the worrying to the grownups, son. You can run along now. Go toot your little horn."

Jon-Michael had to consciously brace himself against

reacting to his father's ridicule. He could import a few home truths about how productive he had been each day before going to Bluey's and how capable he was of starting a company that would put his father's out of business. But why bother? Keeping his expression bland, he said coolly, "Yeah, why don't I do that. At least I'll have steady employment when you drive the company into the ground."

Then, stomach churning, he turned and walked out of the office, pulling the door closed behind him with the greatest of care. Gazing stonily straight ahead, he strode through the reception area, the barely heard secretary's farewell going unacknowledged.

Dammit. Why did he keep setting himself up to expect something different?

Chapter 7

"Yes!" Ignoring the startled looks around him, Ty Holloway hung up the phone and flipped his notebook onto the desk.

Leaning back in his chair, he grinned up at the ceiling. His persistence had finally hit pay dirt.

"Marie!" he called out and looked up in time to catch the intern staring at him from three desks over. He grinned and cocked an eyebrow, making her blush. "See what you can do about getting me a flight to Seattle, will you, doll? Oh, and take care of the car rental, too. I will definitely need a car once I get there."

"When do you want to go?" She reached for the phone on her desk with one hand and cyber-twirled an old-school rolodex app with the other until she came to the appropriate card.

"As soon as possible. Leave the return open-ended. I'm not sure when I'll be back." He pushed away from the desk and went to talk to his editor.

Twenty minutes later Ty was back at his desk, going through his notes again, meticulously harvesting all the minutia he could find.

Experience had taught him paying attention to detail nailed a story every time.

His concentration kept getting fractured, however, by one of the photographs included in the info the little weekly in Gravers Bend emailed him. Finally, he set everything else aside and reached for it, turning it up to the light.

Flipping it over he read the name penciled on the back. Kurstin Olivet McAlvey. He went back to studying the photo. Put together with the facts supplied in the accompanying report, it did not take a genius to see what he had here. Hayley Prescott's best friend.

Ty found himself smiling in bemusement at the black and white printout in his hand. There was something about the face gazing back up at him. She was blonde, she was beautiful, and she had a little half smile that spoke directly to his hormones. As an extra added bonus she looked...trusting. Tracing the outline of her jaw with the edge of his thumb, he smiled tenderly.

Elementary, dude. Simple as one-two-three.

***

It was the band's final break of the night—and it took every ounce of effort Hayley could summon to hang in there to the end of her shift. Her feet hurt, her breasts ached and a band of cramps squeezed her stomach and lower back.

"So, hey," Brian Dorsey addressed her genially as he accepted his drink across the bar. "I imagine you're prob'ly looking forward to them icing the guy who did your old man, huh?"

The splinter of pain stabbing her stomach suddenly had nothing to do with the imminent onset of her period. "You would think so, wouldn't you?" she managed to say in reasonably neutral tones. She picked up the ten he had set on the bar. "Let me get you your change." Good God, would this night never end? She felt like she had been here a week.

Jon-Michael materialized behind the guitar player and his eyes briefly met hers. "I'll have my usual, Hayley," he said, reaching out with the flat of his fingers to smack his fellow band member on the back of his head.

Brian's bourbon and seven sloshed onto the bar.

Swearing, he slammed the glass down and flicked the liquid from his fingers. "Christ almighty, Olivet!" He twisted around. "Why'd you go and do that for?"

"Because sometimes you are too dumb to live," Jon-Michael replied through his teeth. He had been tense all night in the wake of his cozy little chat with the old man, and he was just itching for a fight, any fight. The guitar player's lack of sensitivity was just the opening he was looking for.

Brian, however, apparently had too much weed floating through his system to take offense and before Jon-Michael could goad him into doing something rash, Hayley intervened.

"Here," she said, shoving his club soda at him with one hand as she wiped up the spilled bourbon from the bar with the other. "Give me that, Brian," she said, indicating his drink. "I'll freshen it for you. And you," she said sternly, tossing the wet bar towel aside and raising her hazel-eyed gaze to pin him in place. "Either take it outside or drop it."

"Hey, no skin off my teeth. Just trying to lend a hand."

"Well, thanks heaps, but don't do me any more favors, okay? Help like yours could end up getting the joint closed down." Her hands suddenly stilled in the middle of rebuilding Brian's drink, and her eyes narrowed as she considered him across the bar. "Or maybe that is what you're aiming for," she said slowly. "Ooh. Yeah. I bet you'd like that, wouldn't you, Johnny?"

"Don't call me Johnny, Granger."

"It's Prescott, remember?" Brian said, but they were too focused on each other to pay him any attention.

"Omigawd, I bet you would love that," she reiterated, "since any fight involving you would be good for a headline or two in the Chronicle." She studied him through dense narrowed lashes. "I can see it now. Olivet Heir Involved in Brawl in Eighth Street Blues Bar." Then her gaze locked on his. "What an absolute, perfect opportunity to piss off dear old dad."

Jon-Michael looked at Brian. "My apologies for jumping down your throat, dude," he said. "Mood she's in tonight, the state of New Hampshire oughtta just let her ice Wilson herself and save the taxpayers some money. She'd probably enjoy it."

Hayley sucked in a sharp breath, recoiling from a deep, ice pick stab of inner pain. Jon-Michael looked her up and down with analytical eyes before taking his club soda down to the opposite end of the bar where he fell into an immediate flirtation with a pretty brunette. Hayley watched him for a minute, then turned away.

God, what a night. If things got any damn cheerier around here, she just might open a vein.

She hated it when she got like this. Putting up with a period every month was bad enough, but while never a laugh a minute it was a fact of life women had to live with. But she sure as hell had not signed on for the shit that occasionally came her way before one even began, when for no better reason than crashing or spiking hormones, she got a case of PMS so severe she could not decide whether to kill or be killed.

So sue her if tonight she was depressed and testy and unwilling to take crap off anyone.

It had nothing to do with Jon-Michael's parting shot, she assured herself. *Nothing.* She was simply furious with herself because she had no real excuse for turning into the psycho bitch from hell. She detested that she couldn't control her moods, that she itched to take it out on someone else…and all because of a lousy monthly cycle. It made her the worst sort of cliché.

Well buck up, she ordered herself bracingly. It could be worse. At least she had been spared the weeps. Now, those were truly horrifying.

"Oh, damn it to hell," she whispered fifteen minutes later when Jon-Michael raised his sax to his lips for the last song of the evening and began to play Harlem Nocturne. Evocative of film noir movies of the Forties, the sinuous, haunting melody wove its way beneath her defenses and wreaked havoc with the few remaining emotions she had managed to keep under control. A crushing sadness settled heavy as stone on her chest. Staring at Jon-Michael across the room, thinking—oh, any number of unacceptable thoughts—she could not quite drag enough air into her lungs.

Tears pooled in her eyes, scalding and viscous, blinding her for brief moments until she blinked and sent them spilling over her lower lids. Immediately, they refilled. "Perfect," she whispered. "Now I've just got it all." Scrubbing furiously at her cheeks, she tried for several unsuccessful minutes to pull herself together.

Conceding defeat when a male patron approached the bar, took one horrified look at her face and veered away, she flagged Lucy over to take charge. She headed directly to Bluey's office.

Roughly scrubbing her fingers over her cheeks, she sniffed, took a deep breath, and pushed open the door. "Bluey," she croaked. "I gotta take off early."

"There's only fifteen lousy minutes to go," he snarled at her. "What's so goddamn important that—" Looking up, he caught sight of the steady stream of tears trickling down her cheeks and charged to his feet. "What is it?" he demanded. "Somebody out there givin' you a bad time? 'Cause I don't stand for nobody giving my girls shit."

"No." Hayley waved her hand. The tears ran faster. "Oh, crap. I feel like such an idiot." She swiped at her cheeks and then met the older man's concerned gaze. "I got the weeps, Bluey."

"I can see that for myself. C'mon now, enough of that," he ordered brusquely. "Pull yourself together." He patted her shoulder awkwardly and she cried harder. "What the hell's the matter with you?"

"PMS," she sobbed. It was such a catch phrase for every stray female vagary that she was loath to even admit it.

"Oh." A ruddy flush climbed his cheeks.

Hayley laughed shakily. "Nothing quite like a murderous premenstrual woman who can't stop crying, huh?" She knuckled her nose and sniffed.

Again he patted her and then guided her to the door. "Go on, get out of here," he said gruffly. "I'll close down the bar."

Hayley swiped at her cheeks again. "Thank you," she said, blinking up at him. "I'm sorry. God. I'm a damn cliché."

She sat out in the parking lot for several minutes, gasping in breaths of air and trying like hell to pull herself together. It was not until patrons began trickling out the front door that she fired up the Pontiac's engine and drove carefully onto the road.

Pulling into the garage on the Olivet estate a short while later, she climbed from the car, slammed the door, and dodged the lowering garage door as she stepped out onto the apron. Her tears had finally dried, but she took one look at the darkened house and turned toward the shore. No way in hell was this going to be one of those drift-right-off-to-sleep nights.

Dropping her purse on the dock's weathered planking, she stripped off all her clothes, stepped out of her shoes, and dove into the lake. A shock of cold water closed over her head and she strenuously frog-kicked underwater to propel herself as fast and far from shore as she could get.

Oxygen-deprived lungs finally drove her to the surface and shooting out of the lake with enough force to expose her to the night air clear down to her waist, she flung her hair out of her eyes and sank gently back into the water until only her neck and face rose above the dark surface. Treading water, she sucked in a noisy inhalation, blew it out, then struck out for the center of the lake in an efficient crawl stroke.

She had only swum about a hundred feet before it occurred to her that while exercise helped alleviate both the mood swings and her pre-period cramps, heading for the middle of the lake all alone at two o'clock in the morning might not be the mark of a mature, responsible adult. She turned and swam back to within a yard of the dock where she could touch bottom if she ran into trouble. She swam back and forth parallel to the shore.

After innumerable laps she finally decided she was too tired to feel sorry for herself any longer and was probably now weary enough to fall sleep. She swam back to the dock and pulled herself up the ladder.

Slowly straightening, she thrust her hands through her hair and gathered its mass to one side in a thick ponytail. She leaned forward and wrung water from it onto the bleached planks beneath her bare feet. Releasing it, she tossed it behind her shoulder and slicked her hands down her arms, her chest, her breasts and stomach, sluicing away what excess lake water she could. Then, feeling relaxed and almost content for the first time since she had rolled out of bed early that afternoon, she folded at the waist to give her legs the same treatment.

And nearly had heart failure when, out of the darkness, a voice commented dryly, "I am glad to see suicide wasn't on the agenda here."

CHAPTER 8

A short while earlier.

Three separate people went out of their way to tell Jon-Michael Hayley had left the bar in tears. He put the same effort into insisting to himself that was her tough luck. There was no good reason why he should get involved.

But the minute the band finished its last set he climbed on his Harley Softail and burned up the road between Bluey's and the old man's estate.

Remembering over and over again the devastated look in her eyes when he tossed off that thoughtless, smart-ass remark about saving the state money by killing Wilson herself.

At the turnoff, he killed the lights and the engine and coasted the bike down the driveway. No sense in waking the entire household if he could avoid it. Rolling to a stop at the apex of the circular drive, he straddled the bike's seat and stared up at the guest room where his sister had installed her best friend.

Not that there was a damn thing to see beyond a dark window.

Assuring himself he had done his Boy Scout best, he was about to push his bike back up to the road when he heard the tell-tale creak of the dock's old timbers and a splash in the lake. He rocked the bike back onto its kick stand, climbed free and sprinted down the manicured lawn to the water.

Rounding the stand of ancient Douglas firs, he arrived at the dock in time to see Hayley shoot up out of the depths of the lake like some mythic Siren, flashing pretty shoulders and a long, sleek naked back. She tossed her hair, sending an arc of crystal droplets flying before the soaked mass slapped against her back.

A nanosecond later, she sank to her neck again in the stygian water and that dark mane floated around her. She bobbed gently in place for a moment, then started swimming with strong, determined strokes away from shore. For one panicky minute, he actually thought she was about to drown herself.

He had his shoes off and his jeans down around his ankles by the time she turned around and started stroking her leisurely way back to shore. Feeling like the world's biggest dumb shit, he simply watched her. Then, whispering curses, he yanked his pants back up. Christ, what the hell was he thinking? Hayley was a fighter; she always had been. If she'd been the type to opt out of life's problems when the going got rough, she sure as hell would have done so long before tonight.

And over something a lot more important than a single thoughtless remark out of his mouth. He started to turn away.

But something stopped him. Because on the other hand, neither was she the weeping type. Try as Jon-Michael might, he could not recall a single time he had ever seen her cry.

He parked himself in the shadows and watched her swim vigorous laps up and down the shoreline.

It took her twenty minutes before she finally climbed up the ladder. And looking at her as she rose out of the lake to stand on the dock facing him, Jon-Michael forgot for several long seconds how to breathe.

He knew damn well he should alert her to his presence. Instead he just sat there paralyzed, taking a dazed voyeuristic pleasure in watching the progress her hands made squeezing the water from her hair. Stroking it from the surface of her skin.

Damn. He really needed to say something. But, oh, Jesus, he had tortured himself for more than a decade now wondering what her body looked like, thinking of all the possibilities given what he remembered from seeing her in various bathing suits over the years.

Now here she was, gloriously naked but for transparent panties and a bedraggled, sopping wet bow tie. Finally, he had an image to connect to all those vague imaginings.

And, Lord have mercy. What an image it was.

Hayley's turquoise work vest was low-cut on the sides. For over a week he had watched Bluey's customers give themselves eyestrain watching the point where the armholes teasingly bisected the soft outer curves of her tits. Watched idiots who had done everything but stand on their heads to score themselves a more revealing glimpse. One guy, a longtime regular, had started drinking the damnedest concoctions in order to make her reach for a bottle on the top shelf. Another, a man Jon-Michael knew for a fact did not even like beer, consistently ordered a bottle of imported for the sheer enjoyment of discovering if this would be the time she bent to retrieve it from the refrigerator unit instead of her usual habit of stooping.

The breasts everyone was so curious about were small and round and set way up high on her chest. Her skin was colorless in the moonlight and looked smooth as whipping cream. Pale nipples had drawn up into tight little beads aimed like miniature bullets straight at his heart.

The rest of her was slight. Her ribcage flowed into a narrow waist. Her stomach muscles were long and firm, her navel deep, and her hips had a curve so delicate as to be damn near nonexistent. But it was the apex of her long, firm thighs that drew his gaze. She had a soft little mons with a downy swirl of hair above plump denuded lips. Jon-Michael stared. And stared.

And could not look away. Every single oft-repeated word he had spoken that long-ago night rose up to haunt him anew.

Licking lips gone dry, he drew in a deep breath, eased it out, and managed to say in a reasonably wry tone, "I am glad to see suicide wasn't the agenda here."

A startled scream tried to rip Hayley's throat in two, and she danced in place for an interminable moment. Then the identity of the man in the shadows made its way to her blood-deprived brain.

She launched herself at him to do—she wasn't sure what. Before she could attain her nebulous objective, however, his hands reached out to grip her biceps. Holding her at arm's length, he stepped out of the darkness cast by the evergreen trees.

"I don't *believe* you!" She tried to kick him but he nimbly dodged her bare foot. "You scared the shit out of me, Jon-Michael! My God, I would have wet my pants if I had any pants on to wet." Abruptly she quit struggling. She felt her eyes go wide. Oh, perfect. How utterly...blooming...bloody...perfect.

Okay, it's okay, she assured herself. At least she had kept her undies on. Except...

She glanced down and sure enough, thin nylon turned completely see-through when it was wet.

And he didn't even have the courtesy to turn away. He just stood there watching the chilly rivulets of lake water drip from the ends of her hair and roll down her chest, down her stomach and into the soaked hip-band of her panties.

Abruptly releasing her, Jon-Michael reached over his back and grabbed his T-shirt, dragging it off over his head. He extended it to her. "Here, put this on."

She pulled the soft cotton garment over her head and thrust her arms through the appropriate holes, tugging the shirt down until it covered her to mid-thigh. The retained body heat sent a reactive shiver of appreciation skittering down her spine.

"Listen, Hayley, I'm sorry," he said.

Her head jerking up, she stared at him, skeptical to the bone. "Sure you are."

He blew out a breath and looked out over the lake. "Believe it or not, I didn't come out here to hassle you. And it was not my intention to scare you like that either." He hesitated but then turned to look at her and added grudgingly, "The truth is, I heard you had left Bluey's upset and I was concerned. I felt bad about what I said earlier and I, uh, just wanted to make sure you were all right."

Her exercise-induced fatigue had already disappeared beneath a rush of adrenaline. Now her hard-earned equanimity was destroyed as well—and all by a few kindly spoken words from the last person she expected to be kind.

Jon-Michael's general motto was "don't apologize, don't explain," yet he had just done both. And if his explanation was reluctantly given, he had extended it all the same with devastating sincerity.

She stared at him in confusion, then to her complete and utter horror, felt her lower lip begin to tremble and hot tears rise in her eyes. Dear God, not again. Did her supply of these damn things have no limit?

Apparently not, for just when she thought she had finally exhausted her quota for the night, here came more, cresting her lower lids to slide silently down her cheeks.

"Heyyyy," Jon-Michael crooned in alarm. "Hey, now, I didn't mean to make you cry. Shhh." He regarded her with consternation. "Ah, come on, Hayley, don't cry. Please. Oh man, do not do this."

His earnest entreaty only made her tears roll faster.

"Oh, hell." Reaching for her, he sank to sit cross-legged on the dock.

Hayley didn't worry about her awkward sprawl across his lap. She did not expend any energy thinking, period. Wrapping her arms in a death grip around his neck, she pressed her face into the warm, bare hollow just below his collarbone.

And bawled.

It was quite a while before she regained awareness of Jon-Michael as an entity separate from herself. All she knew at first was that he was solid and warm and something she could hold onto. She gradually took comfort from the strength of the arms that held her, the soothing voice that murmured reassurances and his fingers tunneling through her damp hair, stroking her back.

Eventually, her body quit shaking and her tears dried up. She lay limply, her face hot where it pressed against his chest. In fits and starts she grew aware of matters beyond her own flayed emotions. First it was Jon-Michael's scent: the man-smell of his skin, the barest trace of left-over cologne, a hint of sweat. Then it was the rustle of some night creature making its way through the woods edging the property.

Ultimately, however, what gained her complete attention was the breeze on her all but naked butt where the borrowed T-shirt had ridden up. With a sound of distress, she untangled an arm from around his neck, reaching back to pull ineffectually at the bunched material.

"I'll get it," Jon-Michael said, and she both heard the words he spoke and felt their resonance vibrating through the chest beneath her ear. Tough-skinned hands untangled the T-shirt and gently smoothed it over her hip.

Bringing her own hands to his chest, she stiff-armed herself away from his upper body and peered up at his face. A minute ago she had acquired comfort from him. Now she was beginning to feel like a first class fool, an unfortunately familiar sensation this evening. Her gaze slid away as she slipped off his lap.

"My purse is around here somewhere," she said hoarsely. "Could you find it for me?"

"Sure." There was a moment of rustling. Then he

extended it to her.

She took it, dumped the contents out onto the dock, then pawed through the pile until she located a tissue. She blew her nose, stuffed everything back in the bag, and then reached for her small stack of clothing. Her panties had mostly dried and she donned her jeans. Her vulnerability decreasing in direct proportion to the amount of skin she covered, she speared her fingers through her hair to hold it off her face, expelled a deep breath, and finally looked up to meet Jon-Michael's level gaze.

"I'm sorry." The words were beginning to feel like her personal theme song.

"Hell, don't apologize. I feel like it's my fault."

She made a rude sound. "You always did flatter yourself you were the center of the universe," she said, but the statement lacked ire and she gave him a small, wry smile.

Jon-Michael did not dispute her, but neither did he engage her in their usual verbal wrangling. She didn't know what to think when he merely stroked a fingertip down her cheek.

"Between your husband's murder, the trials and the upcoming execution, you have had a mountain of shit to deal with the past year or two. Having people remind you of it regularly must make for some damn difficult moments." He contemplated her quietly for a moment. "You used to have some pretty strong convictions about capital punishment."

She went very still beneath his stroking finger.

His hand also stilled, then dropped away. "Holy shit. You still do, don't you?"

"Don't be ridiculous," she said coldly. "That was a long time ago."

"You used to be dead-set against it," he remembered aloud. Then his dark eyes pinned her in place. "But as you said, that was a long time ago. What does Hayley Prescott, widow of the victim, think about the death penalty now?

They say the staunchest conservative is a liberal who has been mugged. So what is your opinion? Does Lawrence Wilson deserve to die?"

"Read my lips, Johnny. I do not want to talk about it."

Calling him a name he had always detested for sounding juvenile did not deter him nearly as well as it used to. The sheer force of his gaze kept her eyes locked on his, and his tone became downright authoritarian. *"Does Lawrence Wilson deserve to die?"*

Hayley looked at him sitting beneath the faint illumination of the waning moon, his feet and chest and the hard abs that stopped women in their tracks bare, his dirty-blond hair flopping over his forehead, his eyes and facial stubble more inky than the surrounding shadows. How on earth could a gaze that appeared so sleepy look so commanding at the same time?

"When did you stop drinking?" She counter-demanded. When in doubt, attack. That had always been her philosophy when dealing with Jon-Michael, and the issue of his sobriety was the one question she deemed most likely to get him off her back. Raising her chin, she drove the point home. "When did Jon-Michael Olivet, the lush of Lincoln High, trade in his ever-present bottle of Black Velvet for a club soda?"

But he answered without hesitation or the least sign of embarrassment. "The day after I rolled around on a blanket with you," he retorted readily, "then woke up to discover I could not remember a single thing about what must have been the best damn night of my life if I am to believe even half of what the soccer team told me."

Jon-Michael could see the possibility had not occurred to her. He watched with interest as it stole her composure. She blushed, she opened and closed her mouth several times and could not quite hold his gaze. He had witnessed a lot of uncharacteristic behavior from her tonight and wished in a way he could pursue this particular response, but that wasn't his primary objective at the moment. He didn't want to give her time to recover her equanimity before he moved in for the kill. "Does Lawrence Wilson deserve to die?" he demanded for the third time.

"*Yes.* Okay? What do you want from me, Jon-Michael? Lawrence Wilson is an animal." She didn't have the least problem meeting his gaze now and what he saw in it made him ache in ways he did not care to acknowledge.

"He made himself a sandwich in my kitchen and sat down to eat it while Dennis damn near bled to death on the floor!" Rising to her knees to face him, her posture unnaturally rigid, she demanded, "They put down mad dogs, don't they?"

He was pretty sure she intended the remark to be offhand, perhaps even a little flip. But her tone was too defensive and her hands were fisted at her sides. "That's what Wilson is," she continued. "A rabid dog." She shook her head. "No, he is worse. He gives whole new meaning to violent. It's only fitting that he, too, should be put down."

Jon-Michael pushed up from his sprawl and knee-walked the old planks until the distance separating them dwindled to mere inches. Reaching out, he ran his hands up and down the arms she held so stiffly at her sides. She flinched at his touch but he did not let go. Instead, he rubbed more firmly. "But?" he prompted gently.

"But nothing. There is no but." Trembling, she avoided his gaze.

"Yes there is," he whispered and eased her into his arms. "You never could lie worth a damn. Not to mention if you were any stiffer we could paddle you across the lake."

She grew even more rigid in his embrace and Jon-Michael smiled into her hair. But he knew she had about reached her limit for the evening, and ignoring the number of questions he still harbored he said lightly, "But not to worry, baby; you don't have to tell me if you don't want to." He held her a little tighter. One hand slid up between her shoulder blades while the other stroked down over her hip, and he buried his nose behind her ear in flyaway hair just beginning to dry. "At least not tonight," he amended, closing his eyes and inhaling. "You don't have to tell me anything else tonight."

"I do not have to tell you anything, ever, if I don't want to," she said firmly.

"Ah, now that is where you're wrong," he disagreed. "We will be talking about it again, all right, and probably a lot sooner than you think. It's obvious you have a serious conflict going on with yourself. Clearly, I need to take you in hand and get you straightened out."

"Why, you fat-headed, arrogant, son of a—" Straining away from him, Hayley saw the self-satisfied smile curling up one side of his mouth and swallowed the rest of the words clogging her throat. Oh, the bastard. He had pissed her off on purpose.

"That's more like it," he said. "I hardly recognize you when you go all sweet and pliable on me." His grin grew. "I could get used to it, though."

"In your dreams, bud."

"You want to hear about my dreams, Hayley?" Leaning his upper body away to gaze with heavy-lidded eyes down into hers, he rubbed his hands up and down the curve of her ass, nudged his pelvis a little more firmly into the notch between her thighs, letting her feel his erection. "You want to hear how I wake up all in a lather from dreams of the night when you opened your sweet thighs…"

"My God, you never let an opportunity pass you by, do you?" Reaching behind her she peeled his long hands off her butt, then climbed to her feet. "Have you actually ever gotten anywhere with a line like that?"

"Not too often."

"Well, there's a huge surprise, being it's so smooth and all." Yawning, she looked down at him and realized she was actually pretty relaxed again. And tired enough to sleep. "Jon-Michael?"

"Yeah?" He, too, had risen to his feet and stood with his hands in his front pockets, staring down at her.

"I am sorry about the crack I made earlier."

"Which one, petunia? You always poke so many holes in my ego it's hard to keep up."

"About you picking a fight just to make your father angry."

"Forget it. You were right. The old man hauled me up in front of him this afternoon to ream me out for being an embarrassment to the family name. I hadn't actually thought as far ahead as getting my name in the Chronicle to rub his nose in it, but I was looking to take it out on someone. So, when Brian was too stoned to play, I picked you."

Hayley ignored the apology that was implicit in his words and went straight to the heart of what she found really interesting. "What is the story with you and your dad? It sure surprised the hell outta me when Kurstin told me you had gone to work in the family biz."

Jon-Michael laughed. "It is an unlikely fit, all right. And as you can see, it was an experiment that didn't work for shit. Some day you and I just might have to sit down and swap stories." He cocked an insinuating eyebrow at her. "You show me yours, honey, and I'll show you mine."

"Absolutely. We'll have to do that." Her tone was sarcastic, but as they rounded the trees and walked side by side up the sloping expanse of manicured grass, she privately acknowledged her fierce curiosity.

And wondered just how long she would be able to hold onto her own secrets if divulging them was the only means of discovering his.

Chapter 9

"Thanks for fitting me in on the 4th of July," says the prospective client as he takes the seat facing my desk.

"It was good timing on your part—I just dropped by to pick up a contract for a client." And with everything I need to do today, I should have put him off. But I took one look at the man and decided I could spare twenty minutes.

He is in his mid-thirties, handsome in a clean-cut, upwardly mobile sort of way with his dark hair and light eyes, and wearing clothing whose casualness comes at a deceptively expensive price. Urbane is the word that pops to mind. "You said on the phone you think you would like to rent rather than buy?"

"Yes. I have a feeling I'd like to settle in Gravers Bend. It's beautiful here and has the advantage of being away from the city while still retaining reasonable access to it if I crave a sudden fix of urban culture." He shrugged his elegantly clad while. Because when all is said and done I'm a city boy at heart. I want to be sure I can adapt to small town life before I tie myself down to something as permanent as a mortgage."

"That is probably wise." I pull a listing book off the shelf, then glance back at him. "If you could give me an idea of what you are looking for?"

"I'd like something on the lake."

So he has the income to go with the clothing. It is with genuine regret I meet his gaze across the desk. "I am sorry. The lake is all privately owned and the few homes that are summer rentals are not available this late in the season."

Which was a damn shame. As much as this guy would have loved the lake, I would have loved the commission more. Still, it gives me an idea of what kind of money he is willing to spend. "Do you prefer a house or an apartment?"

"If a house on the lake is out of the question, I would prefer an apartment. Somewhere quiet for my work." He leaned forward. "I have a passion for tennis, though." The smile he flashes is all white teeth and self-deprecating charm. "Perhaps you have something near a club? I trust there is a club that caters to tennis?"

"Of course, our country club." I, too, lean forward. "And there's a nice two-bedroom townhouse on the green I think would be perfect for you. It is private, quiet and very elegant. They only rent to members, of course, but the requirements are not exceptionally stringent and as it happens, I'm a member. I head the Fourth of July bash every year and I would be pleased to sponsor you as my guest. That would give you a chance to look around, get a feel for the people and check out the facilities." Then I recall my professional decorum. "Or I could simply run you out there now to take a look around. Forgive me, I have a tendency to forget myself when it comes to this event. You must think I'm crazy for suggesting you spend your Friday night stuck at some social affair where you won't even know anyone."

"Actually, I was just thinking what an exceptional woman you are to go out of your way to make me feel welcome like this." He rises to his feet and sticks out a hand. "I would be honored to be your guest. Shall I meet you there?"

I also stand and shake his hand. "Yes. Friday night at eight-thirty. Do you need directions?"

"If you write down the address my GPS will do the rest."

"Then I will leave your name at the desk and make sure you are included at our table. Or better yet, come at eight and I will see that you get the grand tour before the dance begins. Here is my card, Mr. Holloway."

"Please, Patsy," he says charmingly as he tucks the little rectangle of embossed card stock into his breast pocket. "Call me Ty."

I am still riding the wave of my success an hour and a half later when I turn into the driveway and shut off the engine. I climb out of the car and go around to the back to pop the hatch. Reaching in, I pull out the new compound bow I stopped to purchase on the way home.

It is a surprise for Joe, one I intend to give him at the conclusion of a small, private celebration I have planned, a minor festivity I consider well-earned. The price of the weapon is a drop in the bucket compared to the commission I will be getting from the Ty Holloway rental.

Okay, so it is not official yet. As far as I am concerned, however, it is already money in the bank. I have been in real estate long enough to have developed a sixth sense for successful closings. And the vibrations this one sent out has me practically dancing up the driveway.

The house is quiet when I let myself into the kitchen and I open the door to the garage to see if Joe's car is there.

It is, so he is home.

Smiling to myself, I silently climb the stairs, thinking to surprise him in the bedroom. But it, too, is empty and I come to a halt in the middle of the room and simply stand there frowning as I look around. Then I shrug. So he's out back, tending to the yard. And that is just as well, actually, for it gives me a moment to put a big frilly bow on my gift and stash it away to be brought out later. Yes, much better to stick to the original plan. I have already decided the presentation of the compound bow he has been eyeing for the past six months at Gaard's Sportsman should be the evening's coup de gras. Giving it to him immediately would merely slow the momentum of the celebration. I lean the bow against the wall next to the closet so I can pull the box of ribbons off the shelf.

A faint bump from the third floor filters through the silence. Frowning, I pause in the midst of tying my bow to glance up at the ceiling. Is Joe upstairs? I finish fastening the red ribbon and rise slowly to my feet.

I am quiet as I climb the stairs to the third floor. The door to the little-used storeroom at the end of the hall is open a crack, and I approach it cautiously.

Reaching out, I ease the door more fully open and look into the room.

I can see Joe's head and shoulders over a stack of boxes, and the look on his face makes my heart pound. Entering the room, I round the stack and stop dead at the sight that greets me.

The closet door is wide open, and I stare at the clippings and photos that line the interior, the video that plays silently on the television screen. I press my hand against my mouth, my knuckles mashing my lips to my teeth as sickness crawls up my throat.

Then my husband's head suddenly snaps around and his nostrils flare. His eyes, as they meet mine, are wild. My hand drops to my side.

"Joe," I moan in agonized disbelief.

* * *

"Haul out those glamour duds, girlfriend," Hayley said. "I wanna see what you're wearing to the big bash Friday night." She dropped onto her back atop the plush coverlet on Kurstin's bed.

Pushing up on her elbows, she shook her hair out of her eyes and watched her friend disappear into the walk-in closet.

"I can't work up any enthusiasm for this party," Kurstin said from the other side of the wall.

"Why not?"

"Well, it's just more of the same ol', same old, isn't it? Deja vu all over again. I've lost count of the number of Fourth of July dances I have attended at the club." Kurstin emerged from the closet holding several gowns. "There won't be a soul there I haven't known my entire life, Dad and Jon-Michael will snipe at each other all night, and I'll be stuck in the middle as usual."

"So, blow it off. Come to Bluey's and I'll put a reserved sign on a stool at the bar. We have a good band playing this weekend."

"Don't think I'm not tempted. Except then I would have to make up a raft of excuses for both Father and the stockholders expecting to see me at the club, and in the end it would turn out to be more trouble than it's worth."

"Plus, you're a social creature by nature. You will probably have a great time once you're there."

"Yeah, maybe. What do you think, this one?" Kurstin held up a white floor-length gown. "Want to know what I would do this weekend, given the choice?"

"Too bland," Hayley decided, eyeing the dress. "What would you do?"

"Get laid. This one?" She held up a pale green strapless number.

"Oh, God, you too?" Hayley sat up and impatiently waved away the dress. "Forget the wardrobe for a minute. How long has it been for you? I bet it hasn't been nearly as long as it's been for me."

"Don't wager your hard earned paycheck on it." Kurstin draped the gowns over a slipper chair and crossed the room to join Hayley on the bed, bracing her spine against the tall footboard. "It might turn out to be the biggest sucker bet you ever made."

"You think so? Well, tell me this, then," Hayley said. "Have you had sex more than twice in the past two-and-a-half years?"

"Well...yes."

"Not me."

"Yeah, but you've had some turbulent years. At least that is an excuse of sorts. I don't have an excuse, aside from the fact that I know every man in town."

"Ooh. In the biblical sense?"

"No. Try to stay on track here, Hayles. If I knew them all in the biblical sense, we would not be having this conversation."

Kurstin tapped her foot against the Aubusson rug. "I know their families, their histories—hell, I bet if push came to shove I could even quote you their childhood illnesses."

Hayley scooted to an upright position. Sitting cross-legged, she grasped her ankles and pressed her knees toward the mattress, then allowed them to relax, lazily working them up and down like fairy wings opening and closing. She looked up from the contemplation of her bare calves to meet her friend's gaze. "If you could have just one evening of uncomplicated, guilt-free, fantasy sex, what kind of man would you pick?"

"A construction worker," Kurstin promptly replied. "With a hard hat, hard hands, and a great big, hard..."

"...to resist smile." Hayley grinned.

"That, too. It is definitely up there, right after really hard working hips. What about you? Who would you pick?"

"Remember 'Ranch' romances?"

"Please," Kurstin said with pained loftiness. "You know I only read enlightening fiction." But she could not prevent herself from squirming beneath the get-real look Hayley gave her. "Okay, okay, I might have read one. Possibly two." Her foot stilled on the carpet as she leaned forward. "And man, was I enlightened," she admitted enthusiastically. "This gorgeous rancher had the little blonde heroine every which way there was. It was great. Inspiring, really."

"Exactly," Hayley agreed. "That's who I would pick. Some big ole rancher with ten gallon shoulders and a stallion-sized dick he has to strap down with the thingamajig on his holster just to prevent himself from ravishing me on the spot every time I come on the scene." She laughed but then immediately sobered. "Instead I get real life. How lowering. I got my period this morning, I have a zit starting next to my nose, and you know how I get when it comes to the opposite sex. I can talk trash with the best of 'em, provided it's only you and me. I don't have a problem holding my own with the barflies who hit on me at work, because that's business. But when it comes to doing the Up Close and Personal with a regular guy, all that introversion I have worked like a slave to overcome rears its ugly head. Every stinkin' time."

"And the closest I'm bound to get to a construction worker in this lifetime is an ancient Coke ad on TV that I, um, may have recorded back when," Kurstin admitted, climbing off the bed and reaching for the topmost evening gown draped over the dainty slipper chair. She held it up in front of her. "So, back to real life. What do you think? Should I wear this red number to wow the local boys at the country club dance? Or do you like the pale green better?"

* * *

"Joe," I say again and my heart pounds in my breast as I take in my husband's wild-eyed gaze. "What are you doing up here?"

Only slowly does he turn entirely away from the closet with its damning contents. His fists clench and unclench as he stares at me and I take a cautious step backward, frightened of him for the first time ever. That one step forward strikes me as threatening.

"What am *I* doing here?" he demands with quiet fury. "Don't you think that's a question better asked of you?" He takes another step toward me, waving a stiff hand toward the closet "What the hell is this, Patsy? It looks like a fucking shrine to Hayley."

You're stupid, Patsy. I hear the echo of my mother in his

tone and raise my chin, stepping past him to inspect the destruction done to the closet door. Relief flows through me when I get close enough to inspect it, for the damage is minimal, really. The lock has simply been drilled out and the door opened. I turn back to Joe. "Why did you remove the deadbolt?"

"Because I don't like stumbling across locked doors in my own goddamn house. Are you going to answer my question, Patsy? What is all this shit?"

"Just a few articles I have gathered over the years about her poor husband's death and the trials and stuff."

"A few articles, my ass. This looks like every fucking word that has ever been written, not to mention every sound bite ever recorded. How did you get all this shit? This is sick, Patsy."

"It is not sick!" I disagree furiously while Mother's voice in my mind sneers, *ignorant, unnatural girl.* "Hayley Prescott is one of my oldest, dearest friends. It is only natural I am interested in what has been going on in her life."

"Oldest, dearest... For Christ's sake, Patsy, up until this summer you hadn't seen her in twelve damn years!"

"So what? We have a bond that will endure until the day I die."

"You have a bond," Joe repeated flatly. Jesus. He had known for several months now that their marriage was falling apart, but this! This was just plain crazy. He started to demand what kind of bond she thought she had with Hayley but then shook his head. No. *I don't want to know.* Looking inside the closet, he thought of all the nights he had found her missing from their bed, and took a step back, distancing himself. "I'm leaving, Patsy."

"No!" She rushed forward. "You cannot." Grasping his arm in both hands, she stared up at him, her expression beseeching. "Joe, please. This is insane. Let us talk about it...we can work this out."

"Not today we can't. I gotta get out of here."

"But where will you go?" she demanded plaintively.

"I don't know. I'll get a room at the Inn for tonight. I'll worry about something more permanent tomorrow."

"You come home tomorrow, Joseph Beal. We will talk about this."

"Yeah, okay." But Joe could not envision moving back in. Not when he felt so much relief at the prospect of moving out. She followed him down to their room and he felt her watching his every move as he threw a few things in a bag. She trailed him again as he hauled the small duffel down the stairs and through the kitchen to the door to the garage. Standing in the open doorway, she wrung her hands as he tossed his bag on the passenger seat of his Buick. He climbed into the sedan, hit the garage door opener clipped to the visor and fired up the ignition. Then he backed out of the garage and hit the remote again to close its door.

Without another glance in her direction.

I watch until there is nothing to see but the inside of the firmly closed garage door. Then slowly, I back into the kitchen and shut the door.

It is not until later in the evening that I remember the compound bow I bought Joe. It falls out of its hiding place when I slide some hangers aside to hang up my suit.

I catch it before it hits the floor and stand looking down at it for several moments, stroking its red satin ribbon. I had such high hopes for this evening and now my dreams have been trampled to dust.

Then I straighten my shoulders. None of that now. Negative thoughts are not allowed. They are counterproductive at best and self-defeating at worst.

Joe will be back. And until he is—?

Well, I will simply console myself watching a few of my favorite taped news segment from my Hayley file.

Chapter 10

"Whataya you suppose the name of this orchestra is?" Jon-Michael muttered in Kurstin's ear as he came up behind her in the country club ballroom. "Maestro Muzak and The Dull Notes?" He winced as the musicians launched into a lively rendition of *Tie a Yellow Ribbon 'Round the Ole Oak Tree.* The song had been popular before he or his sister was born.

She smiled at him over her shoulder. "Behave yourself."

He circled her to stand face to face. "Damn, Kurstie, it's Friday night and we're a couple of hot-blooded mammals. A veritable stud and studette, you and I are. So what the hell are we doing in a room full of colorless, small town civic-minded citizens?"

"Fulfilling our Olivet duty."

He winced. "I was afraid you'd say something like that." Finding a handy post, he propped his shoulders and the flat of one foot against it and gave her a slow once-over. "You're lookin' mighty fine this evening," he said, eyeing her red dress. She stood out in the sea of pastels surrounding them. "I salute your gutsy fashion statement. Might I fetch you a small libation from the bar?"

Kurstin grinned at his choice of words, squirreling the noun away to use herself someday. "I would love a double bourbon on the rocks," she admitted. "But I think I'll stick with 7-up for the present. At least until I've finished chatting up the board of directors. Then just watch my dust, Jon-Boy, because I am sneaking out early to go get roaring drunk at Bluey's. Hayley can take me home."

Foot sliding to the floor, Jon-Michael straightened away from the post. At last, an opportunity to find out how Hayley was faring after the other night's unexplained swim and crying jag. She had managed to ignore him completely at the bar last night. "And how *is* our little—"

"Kurstin, Jon-Michael," a voice interrupted and impatiently he turned to see Patsy Beal sail up with a dark-haired stranger in tow. "I would like you to meet Ty Holloway," she said, drawing the man forward. "I am sponsoring him as a new member of the club. Ty, this is Kurstin McAlvey and her brother Jon-Michael Olivet."

"Hi, how y'doin'." Jon-Michael offered his hand readily enough but his attention was perfunctory and he immediately turned back to Kurstin, only to find her studying the newcomer with interest. Well, shit. Fact-finding mission terminated before it got off the ground.

He allowed her to be dragged away following the exchange of pleasantries. Lounging back against the pole once again, he watched as the new guy—what had Patsy said his name was again, Halliday?—deftly extracted Kurstin from Patsy's company as well. Huh. Smooth operator.

Jon-Michael shrugged irritably. What the hell, no sense in being a dog in the manger. Yeah, he was bored and would rather be anywhere besides the country club. Didn't mean he had to begrudge his sister a good time. He went into the bar and ordered himself a club soda.

"Jon-Michael."

The tone of disapproval was enough to alert him to the speaker's identity. Suppressing a sigh, he turned, drink in hand, to face his father. "Dad."

Richard looked him over. "When the hell are you going to learn to wear appropriate attire," he demanded coldly, taking in Jon-Michael's white T-shirt, impeccably tailored tuxedo jacket and slacks, and the burgundy cummerbund that matched his high top Converse sneakers.

Jon-Michael snapped the turquoise bow-tie he had

borrowed from Bluey. "Well, I admit my color coordination skills could stand a little work. Yet I slid past the club's dress-code police, so what do you care?" Aside from the fact that he had once again violated the sanctity of the precious Olivet name, that is.

"Christ," Richard said in disgust. "And you consider yourself fit to run the company." He turned and walked away.

Jon-Michael shrugged and carried his drink back into the main ballroom. He knew he was in serious trouble, however, when within the space of twenty-five minutes he had passed on two separate opportunities for a little flirtation. Either woman would have helped kill the time until he could escape, and ordinarily he would have been all over them like airbrush strokes on a centerfold. Both the women who had approached him were attractive and willing. Hell, face it, they were *female*, and that alone had been sufficient for him in the past.

Not tonight.

For as long as he could remember, he had bantered with and teased women. Pretty women, ugly women, grandmas or young girls, it made no difference to him. Flirting was as inherent to him as breathing. Ladies were one portion of the population he could always garner approval from, and after his mother's death their unconditional admiration spread balm on a spot perpetually rubbed raw by his inability to attain anything close to that from his remaining parent.

Not that he did it merely for that reason, at least not since college. He just enjoyed flirting with the double X chromosome gender and they seemed to enjoy returning the favor. It was a fun and harmless form of entertainment.

Tonight, the ghost of Hayley ruined even that. He complimented Mrs. Rivers on her gown, then moved on. He danced with Francine Johnson, but when she stood close at the number's conclusion and batted her eyelashes up at him while tracing a languid finger up and down his jacket lapel, he excused himself and went off to invite eighty-year-old, four-foot-ten Gertrude Brown to dance. Staring off into the distance over the top of her blue-white hair as he navigated them in a slow foxtrot around the floor, he tried to figure out what the hell Hayley was doing to him.

And he had...nothing. His only certainty was that the situation was rapidly losing its amusement value. Hayley was the one female in Gravers Bend with whom his fail-proof flirtation methods consistently failed. And surprisingly, that had always been okay with him, because her staunch refusal to be impressed and her snide digs at his technique had freed him to simply be himself around her. Aside from his sister, there had been damn few people about whom he could say that.

Then one night he had finally done something right with her. Too bad he could not recall what it was. All he knew was everything changed and he regretted, as a consequence, that she hated his guts. Regretted it big time. But eventually, he had learned to live with what he'd done.

As a result of that night—or, more to the point, of how he had shot off his big mouth afterward—he had sat up and taken a good hard look at the direction he was letting his life be led. Then he'd wrestled control of it before it could become firmly entrenched in the downward spiral it had been racing toward. For that alone he owed her.

When Kurstin told him Hayley was coming back to town, it had never occurred to him that his life might change as a result. He had simply expected to fall into the same old pattern of him flirting and her resisting. Except this time he would be sober.

And at first that was exactly the way it had worked. But something had shifted the other night when she'd cried all over his chest and he had watched his damn T-shirt slip-sliding up over her naked hip.

Something that prevented him flirting tonight.

The music came to an end and Jon-Michael smiled down at Gertrude, pouring on the charm as he escorted her back to her table. That it took conscious effort gave him tight teeth. But it also strengthened his determination.

Because tonight was a fluke, and he would do well to keep that in mind. He *would* get his life back to the way it was supposed to be.

If it was the last damn thing he did.

Ty didn't release Kurstin when the music came to an end. "One more dance," he said and tightened his grip on her while he waited for the music to resume.

She tipped her head back to look up at him. "Oh, but I really should be getting back to—"

"One more."

Her head settled back on his shoulder and she smiled as they began to move to the new tune.

When the song came to an end and the combo immediately launched into *The Girl From Ipanema,* Kurstin and Ty looked at each other, grimaced, and walked off the floor. At the edge where sprung hardwood met carpeting, he turned her toward the linen-covered tables lining the wide bank of windows overlooking the pool. "Join me at my table."

Kurstin reluctantly disengaged her arm from his grip. "I would truly like that, but I cannot."

"Okay. I'll join you at yours."

"Ty, I have business to attend to."

"Private business or the glad-handing variety?"

"A little corporate social mingling."

He gave her a lopsided smile. "So take me with you. I wouldn't mind meeting some of Gravers Bend's movers and shakers."

"Fine," she agreed. "But when you're trying to stay awake over aperitifs I want you to remember it was your idea ."

Kurstin was surprised to see Jon-Michael deep in conversation with Mildred Bayerman, the only female to sit on the board of directors at Olivet Manufacturing. Curious, but unwilling to interrupt, she steered Ty to a table on the opposite side of the dance floor where her father sat with three other board members and their wives. Reaching it, she performed introductions.

Ty watched as Kurstin systematically charmed everyone at the table with a vivacity that appeared to be as natural to her as breathing. Her vibrant red dress brushed his pant's leg as she turned to the man on her other side.

"How is your granddaughter doing, Mr. Thompson? Is she still taking ballet?"

The guy's face lit up and he pulled out his wallet. Kurstin moved closer in order to admire the photographs the older man showed her of a small, freckle-faced kid in a pink tutu. Then she turned her attention on the three people seated on the other side of Thompson. "Hello, Mr. Roley, Mrs. Roley. How is the golf game going? And how are you doing, Mr. Lorenz? Are you saving a dance for me this evening? I haven't had a chance to do the Twist since you and I won the contest at the St. Paddy's Day dance."

The man hopped up with an enthusiastic offer right on the spot, and Kurstin turned to Ty. "Excuse me a moment, won't you?" she murmured and allowed the board member to lead her to the floor. Ty observed her animated dance with the older man for several moments before turning back to the people at the table to exchange small talk.

Patsy Beal had just joined him when Kurstin and the Lorenz guy returned to the table. Kurstin gave her a warm smile.

"Congratulations," she complimented the realtor. "You have pulled off another outstanding party." Then hooking an arm through his and flashing a mischievous smile his way, she added, "And thank you so much for introducing me to Ty."

"It was my pleasure." Pasty glanced around. "I have not seen Hayley this evening. She could not make it?"

"No, I'm afraid she had to work. And speaking of missing persons, where is that husband of yours? I haven't seen him tonight either."

"Oh, he's around somewhere," Patsy replied vaguely. "I have been so busy it is hard to keep track."

Kurstin laughed. "Given the amount of work you put in, I suppose he might as well have stayed at home for all he'll see of you tonight."

Patsy murmured something noncommittal and then glanced at her watch. "You will have to excuse me. I just wanted to stop by for a moment to check on Ty and make sure he did not feel neglected. Now that I know he is in good hands, I really must have a few words with the pyrotechnics expert." She hurried off.

Standing with Kurstin by the pool a short while later, Ty found himself paying more attention to her expressive face than the fireworks exploding against the dark bank of clouds in the sky. He paid only the scarcest notice as the pyrotechnics tinted those clouds an ever-changing palette of jewel tones. The photos of her he had found online had not done her justice. They hadn't conveyed a fraction of her enthusiasm or charm. Seducing her would definitely not be a hardship.

Resisting the impulse to rush the seduction might prove to be the difficult part.

Kurstin leaned into the mirror in the ladies' room a short while later and smiled with unabashed good humor at her high color. Small wonder she was flushed: her heart was dancing, her pulses fluttered, and excitement skittered along her nerve endings. And to think she had not wanted to come tonight.

She blotted the sheen from her T-zone and reapplied her lipstick. Standing back, she fluffed her hair with her fingertips, tugged the bodice of her scarlet dress more firmly into place, and surveyed the overall result.

Not bad. And who knew...

If she played her cards right, she just might get lucky tonight.

Looking up from the series of sketches he had drawn on the tablecloth when the wine list card would not hold them all, Jon-Michael's voice trailed off in mid-explanation. "Oh, hell, Mildred, I'm sorry," he said, recalling where they were for the first time in fifteen minutes. "I must be boring you to tears."

"Not at all." She gave him the smile reputed in company circles to make sharks clear a path for her out of professional courtesy. "I like your enthusiasm."

He was embarrassed by it. Mildred Bayerman was a tough old broad from the days when the description was considered a compliment. When she had cornered him demanding to know why he had quit Olivet's, he'd found himself bluntly informing her of his differences of opinion with his father. And when she asked how he would do things differently, he had told her.

Ad nauseam.

Face growing hot, he stood and forced his trademark charm-your-pants-off smile. "How about a spin around the dance floor?"

"Thank you, no." She looked up at him without bothering to return his smile. "What I would really like is to see a formal presentation of all these ideas for expansion. Present it at one of the board meetings."

"Yeah, I will have to work one up," he agreed and did not, by so much as a flicker of an eyelash, allow his expression to show his knee-jerk reaction, which was *Don't hold your breath.*

His father would have the proposal quashed before the minutes were even read and Jon-Michael was tired to the bone of having his expertise mocked as if he were a boy playing at being a grown-up.

Still, if Jon-Michael had Mildred's backing Richard might find that tougher going—

"Make it soon," she commanded, and he smiled noncommittally then gave her a formal bow as he bid her good night.

The instant he left her table he strode straight out the door. Trying not to get too attached to the tiny kernel of hope unfurling in his chest.

* * *

Hayley looked up when the lounge's door opened. It was late and the bar was closed but she hadn't gotten around to locking up. Sliding her hand below the bar so the money she had been counting wasn't the first thing the after hours visitor spotted, she flashed a quick look at the sawed-off oar handle to make sure it was in easy reach before turning her full attention to the newcomer ambling toward her out of the shadows. Then the breath she had not even known she was holding eased out of her lungs.

Jon-Michael.

His formal clothes were rumpled and his hair was windblown. She slanted him a sardonic look. "Slumming after the big dance, Johnny?"

He did not reply, just kept on coming. Rounding the end of the bar, he strode right up to her, slid his hands into her hair and gripped her skull. Tilting her head back, he stared into her eyes for a heartbeat, then slammed his mouth down on hers.

It was an angry kiss, fast, rough and carnal. The heat of his tongue against hers, the nip of his teeth sinking into her lower lip, knocked her off balance. Then, before she could orient herself to either accept or reject the unasked for kiss, it was finished and he was slamming out again as silently as he had entered.

Hayley sagged against the counter at her back, scrubbing her lips with the back of her hand, her gaze blindly fixed on the bills she held clutched in her fist. She tried to summon up a little righteous indignation, but instead felt an oddly exciting thrill of fear. If she had half a brain she would be demanding just who the hell he thought he was.

Instead, she stood there with her lips throbbing beneath the pressure of her knuckles, reliving the hint of neediness she had sensed beneath his anger.

And feeling as if her days of holding herself aloof from him were seriously numbered.

You dumb shit. You stupid, sorry-ass dumb shit. The words were a mantra chanting in Jon-Michael's brain the entire ride home.

He let himself into his second floor loft in the brick warehouse on Davis Drive, tossing the keys to the Harley in an abalone shell on the Stickley console table by the door. It should have been dead quiet this time of night in the heart of the industrial area, but the artist next door was entertaining again. Her headboard thumped rhythmically against their adjoining wall as she exhorted someone named Oh Baby to greater, deeper, harder efforts.

Seemed like everyone in the world was making time tonight except him. Jon-Michael walked straight across the room, and opening the window to the tiny fire escape landing, climbed out. He pulled his sax case out after him.

Flipping open the latches, he lifted the instrument out of its dense molded foam, fit the reed to its throat and raised it to his mouth to wet the reed. Then he lowered it to his lap again. And groaned.

Fuck. Why had he gone and kissed her? Not that he could bring himself to regret it. Still it was a tactical error.

One he could not afford. He had merely been bored and lonely earlier this evening.

Now he was bored, lonely, and more than likely screwed.

Chapter 11

When Ragged Edge retook the stage after their break the following Wednesday, business tapered off at the bar. Even as Hayley cleaned up the counter below the bar, she could not help watching Jon-Michael. He had ignored her for the past several days.

Which, fine, was just as well. But if she lived to be a hundred and six she swore she would never understand what went through that man's teeny-tiny brain.

Lucy came up and slid her tray onto the bar and her rear onto a vacated stool. The pink had washed out of her hair and she had substituted a couple packages of Berry Blue Kool-Aid for the black portion in honor of Independence Day. Her nose stud was a ruby and her satin push-up bra white. The look had gone over big ever since its debut Friday night. Everyone loved a patriot.

She gave her order then blew out a breath. "Man, I am whupped."

Hayley assembled and delivered the tray of drinks. As she was washing odds and ends a while later, she heard a familiar voice call her name. Kurstin stood with an attractive man down the bar.

Hayley grinned. "Hey there, stranger. Give me a minute to finish up here and I will be with you. Grab a stool." She rinsed the last of the glasses she had washed by hand because the dishwasher was still in operation when they had run out, then turned it upside down in the tiny drainer.

Wiping her hands on a towel, she walked down the bar

to where Kurstin and her escort sat. She flipped the towel over her shoulder. "We've been ships in the night lately, girl," she said. "I'm glad to see you." Extremely glad, for with their different schedules they had hardly seen each other at all for the past several days. She dropped coasters on the bar. "You must be Ty," she said to Kurstin's companion. "I'm Hayley Prescott." Flashing a big smile, she reached over to shake his hand. "What can I get you?"

The story of my career, sweetheart. Exultation rushed like champagne bubbles through Ty's veins. *This* was the reason he was here. This woman with the rich brown hair and the hundred-dollar smile was responsible for wooing him from the civilized side of the contiguous United States to this little backwater burg on the Other Coast.

Not her damn BFF. He wasn't sure how it had happened, but somehow he had gotten so hung up on maneuvering the luscious blonde toward her seduction these past few days that he had damn near forgotten his goal.

But it—*she*—was standing right across the bar from him and seeing her in the flesh affected him like a thump upside the head. He hauled his shit together in a red hot hurry. So, no, thinking with his dick was a mistake he would not repeat. Kurstin was a means to an end. That was all she was.

Hayley was his goal.

Hayley glanced down the bar a while later to see Kurstin momentarily alone and joined her. "Where is New McHottie?"

"Men's room." Kurstin cocked a golden eyebrow. "And you do know your cultural reference is woefully out of date, right?"

"Yes, well, not all of us are blessed with your facile knowledge of up-to-date television entertainment," she retorted cheerfully. "Or, oh, give a rip." She gifted her friend with a toothy smile. "But speaking of blessed, I'm tickled to see one of us having her wish fulfilled." She hesitated, then admitted, "Okay, maybe I'm just the teensiest bit envious as well. But still, I am happy for you."

When Kurstin gave her a blank look, Hayley snorted and said, "How soon we forget." She leaned closer to elaborate in a low voice, "To get laid? Wasn't it just— what?—Monday   we had that conversation? Now, granted, your Ty isn't a construction worker, but still, not a bad night's work for someone who thought she knew every man in town."

Kurstin laughed but then confessed in equally low tones, "It wouldn't have been a bad night's work…if I had had that particular wish granted. But it hasn't happened yet. The chemistry is definitely right. But for some reason he is being depressingly gentlemanly about the whole thing."

Hayley's head went back. "That rat bastard!" she said in faux shocked undertones. Slapping the bar with the flat of her hand, she leaned closer to her friend. "Where have all the bad boys gone? There are sure as hell none to be found when you really need one. I tell you, this never would have happened to the heroine in a Ranch Romance."

"I know. Reality bites."

"Whoa." She blinked. "You *must* be distressed if you're reduced to using vulgar slang. Still and all," she offered as she straightened up and busied herself neatening items both on and below the bar. "If the way he watches you is anything to go by, it is only a matter of time. At least you have strong probability on your side. That's nothing to sneeze at." She shot Kurstin a hopeful look from beneath her lashes. "I don't suppose he has a brother, does he? One with a yen for adventuresome sex?"

"Is that what you're into, adventuresome sex?"

"I'm sure I could be, given half a chance. Problem is, no one has ever offered me the opportunity to find out."

Ty returned from the men's room as the band was breaking for their second intermission. Jon-Michael joined them and Hayley watched through narrowed eyes as he draped himself over the corner of the bar and managed to carry on a conversation with his sister and her date while ignoring her presence entirely, except for a curt order for a club soda. She slammed it down in front of him and took herself off to attend to the break rush.

The two barmaids had borne their loaded trays off to their respective tables and the crowd around the bar had thinned when Hayley was hailed by a masculine voice. She looked up to see Joe Beal standing on the other side of the bar. His hands thrust in his pant's pockets and his dark eyebrows drawn together in a frown, he regarded her soberly across the space separating them.

"Hey," she said with guarded congeniality. She actually liked the guy but was scrupulously careful not to encourage what was surely a temporary infatuation on his part. "Want your usual?"

"Please."

She felt his gaze on her as she poured a jigger of rum over ice and filled the glass to the top with Coke from the soda gun. Wiping off the bottom of the glass, she handed him his drink and accepted his money.

Joe crowded close to the bar as she turned back from the cash register and leaned in to eliminate even more distance between them. "Hayley," he said in a low, earnest voice. "I heard something tonight I think I should pass on to you."

"Yeah? And what is that, Joe?" Since he often hung around initiating conversations, Hayley only attended to this one with half an ear. She gave him a vague, distracted smile as she restocked her supply of cocktail napkins.

"The night clerk over at the Inn told me the day clerk took eight new reservations this afternoon within the space of an hour and a half."

"Uh huh. That's good, isn't it?" She wondered if her

supply of limes would last through the evening or if she should cut another one.

"No, it's not good at all. Hayley, pay attention."

She looked up. "I am paying attention," she insisted and gave him another polite smile. "You said the motel took a good number of reservations today. It's their peak season and they are the only game in town. What is so unusual about that?" *Yes, one more.* She picked a lime from the fruit basket.

"The clerk said two of the reservations were for a Senator Jarvis from New Hampshire and staff. Three more were from journalists from different east coast newspapers. Another three were reserved in the name of eastern seaboard television stations."

The lime dropped from her suddenly nerveless fingers to roll silently across the floor.

If Ty had not happened to have Jon-Michael in his sights the moment the other man's head suddenly snapped up and his entire body tautened like a hunting dog on point, he never would have known something was up. Almost as quickly as Kurstin's brother went on alert, he relaxed back into his sprawl across the bar's countertop, leaving Ty to question the validity of his own instincts. All the same, he casually turned his head to follow the sight-line Jon-Michael's gaze had taken.

And saw Hayley down at the far end of the bar. Staring at the man across from her as if she might puke her guts up at any minute.

Ty glanced back at Jon-Michael, but the sax player had propped his head in the palm of his hand and was teasing his sister with lazy good humor as if nothing out of the ordinary had just taken place. Hell. For all Ty knew, nothing had.

Except...he didn't believe it. Something was in the wind.

And if he wanted to be in a position to find out exactly

what it was, he had better quit messing around and step up his plans for Kurstin McAlvey.

Jesus, she had turned white as a sheet. Jon-Michael took the curve too fast then eased up slightly on the throttle as he leaned into the turn. The Harley's headlight cut a swath through the star-studded darkness and wind roared in his ears.

It was as if every drop of blood had left her face. One minute she had been paying a distracted sort of attention as Joe Beal leaned forward to yammer something in her ear, and the next her head had snapped up while every bit of her natural color drained from her cheeks.

He cut the bike's engine and coasted down the drive to the old man's estate. He gave Hayley's window in the darkened mansion little more than a passing glance. He was pretty sure he knew where he would find her.

And, sure enough, she was sitting on the dock right where he thought she would be. Knees drawn up to her chest, ankles crossed, she hugged her shins as she stared out into the darkness shrouding the peripheries of the lake. The invisible chorus of frogs and crickets went abruptly silent at his approach, making the creak of the dock as he stepped onto it sharp as a gunshot.

"Go away," she ordered without turning around.

"No."

"Dammit, Jon." She sighed wearily, staring out into the night. "I am in no mood for your motherless-chile-don't-know-right-from-wrong routine right now."

"You're in luck, then—I didn't plan on running it by you."

"Go. Away."

"Not gonna happen, petunia." He listened to the soft slap of water against the pilings for several seconds, then sat down behind her. Sliding his legs along either side of her hips, he crowded his chest up against her back. When she leaned forward, holding herself stiffly away from him;

his upper body followed.

He did not push his luck, however, by trying to wrap his arms around her as well; he would probably just gain himself a sharp elbow in the gut for his trouble. Forcing his fingers to relax, he rested his wrists atop his bent knees and let his hands dangle.

"You okay?" he asked quietly when the silence had stretched on awhile. One by one, the crickets resumed their nocturnal chorus, joined occasionally by the amphibian rhythm and bass section.

"Oh, sure." The little huff of air she exhaled said otherwise. "I am just super-dandy." But her spine relaxed a bit against his stomach and chest and her shoulders lost some of their stiffness.

"The carrion-eaters are coming to town, huh?"

"To pick this carcass clean." Her back settling a little more firmly against him, she shot him a puzzled glance over her shoulder. "How did you find out?"

"Joe told me." Right after he had cornered the guy at the end of his break and demanded to know what the fuck he had said to make Hayley go whiter than Mother Voodoo's bleached bones. After hearing the explanation, he had wondered when Beal had gotten so cozy with the staff at the Royal Inn. But since that was hardly his main consideration, he hadn't asked. Instead, he had kept a wary eye on Hayley, biding his time until closing. "Along with some Senator from New Hampshire?"

"Wonderful. He chatted up the entire bar."

"No, he told me. Period." Cautiously, Jon-Michael slid his arms around her, taking it as a good sign when she didn't immediately head-butt his teeth down his throat. "But Hayley, honey," he felt compelled to caution her, "I wouldn't go holding my breath if I were you. I doubt a motel full of vultures and a hot-shot senator will pass unnoticed. Not in this burg."

"No, I certainly mustn't hope for that," she agreed bitterly. It was the gravity-laden resignation in her voice, however, that had Jon-Michael tightening his hold on her.

"The official countdown has begun," she said, staring straight ahead. "It is now less than thirty days to the execution. You know what, Johnny?"

"Don't call me—"

"I sort of hoped if I wasn't available the media would move on to something else—or at least find another angle to pursue. Out of sight, out of mind, or some such optimistic bullshit." She sat quietly for a moment, then emitted a sound like a balloon leaking air. "No such luck, I guess. I'm a hot commodity."

He didn't know what to say to her, so he remained silent. What could he say? She had been living in a goldfish bowl for a couple years now and her hopes of escaping it had just been blown to hell. He rubbed her cool, bare arms with his warm hands.

"The television journalists are the worst," she said in a low voice. "Not that they aren't all equal opportunity hounders, but at least most of the newspaper people end up writing a fairly complete, factual account." She stared out over the water. "News on TV, though, has been reduced to nothing more than thirty second sound bites. And let's face it, even those are slanted in whatever direction will draw the most ratings."

Jon-Michael hated the resignation in her voice. Sure, she had a right to her distress. But the Hayley he knew had never simply rolled over to accept whatever bad luck came her way; she had fought back. She could be reserved at the oddest moments, but she sure as hell had a mouth on her when it counted most. That was an ironclad guarantee. The defeat he heard now made him crazy.

"We interrupt your local programming to bring you this special bulletin," he burst out and tightened his hold when she jerked in his arms. "A recess has been called in the latest Lawrence Wilson appeal after both lawyers were called to the bench. We take you live to the county courthouse for an in-depth interview with Hamm

Blowdry, our trial-watch specialist. Hamm?" Jon-Michael stuck his fist out, a mock microphone. "Can you tell us why the recess has been called?" He felt Hayley go very still within the cradle of his body.

"The lawyers consulted with the judge in a manner that can only be described as highly secretive," he replied in a deeper, smoother voice. "So all I can say is the recess could have been called for any number of reasons." He paused one beat and then two. "Hayley Prescott may well have broken down under cross examination and admitted to something nefarious. I was in the john at the time, but I always did think there was something just a *lit*-tle too goody-two-shoes about that woman. Or it is always possible there was evidence of jury-tampering. Odds are decent an ancestor of Wilson's changed his name at Ellis Island. He's probably connected clear back to Sicily."

He brought the fist-mike back to his lips. "Well! Whatever it turns out to be, you can rest easy knowing this Nose for News will stay on the job until the last rock has been overturned and its seamy underbelly thoroughly examined."

Hayley wanted to be insulted he was mocking her misery. She wanted to hang onto her sense of being misused.

But she couldn't help it; she laughed.

"It is not funny, you know," she said sternly...then ruined the effect by snickering. "You may think your little improvisation is a joke, Jon-Michael, but you are actually not that far off the mark."

"Yeah, I know. But you can't let the assholes get you down."

She twisted around to stare up at him. "Oh, easy for you to say. You haven't had them dogging your every footstep for the past too many years."

He did not reply, but rather stared down at her with those inscrutable chocolate brown eyes. Hayley felt his hard chest shift against her shoulder as he shrugged. She twisted back to face front. A few minutes later, his chin lowered to rest atop her head and they sat in silence, staring out at the dark, impenetrable lake, each thinking their separate thoughts.

Eventually, she made a subtle movement that caused Jon-Michael's legs to go lax on either side of her, his arms to drop away. She flipped over until she was on all fours, her knees between his thighs, her hands braced against the dock next to his hips. She craned her head back to stare up at him.

"Thanks," she said softly. And stretched to peck a soft kiss on his lips.

For an act intended to be merely friendly, the effect was dizzyingly electric. Her head froze in the act of pulling back. Her gaze snapped up to meet his.

Jon-Michael sucked in a sharp breath.

Then he wrapped his fingers around a fistful of her thick, warm hair and tugged to tilt her head back further yet, exposing the vulnerable arch of her throat. He lowered his head to kiss her.

He fully expected to control it, thought he could just kiss her socks off for a few red-hot minutes, then stroll away, unaffected.

Funny how it didn't work that way.

Not when her lips were incredibly soft and the inside of her mouth hotter than a crucible. The instant her lips parted and he slid his tongue into a humid cavern that felt like home, he realized he was in deep, deep trouble.

Too damn late to do him a bit of good.

With an involuntary rumble deep in his throat that sounded suspiciously like a growl, he lay back, pulling Hayley atop his chest. Immediately he rolled them until her backside kissed the dock's worn planks and he was propped on his side half beside and half over her. His kiss grew fiercely urgent against soft, receptive lips.

With forearms flat against the deck and his hands in her hair, he hemmed her in, not trusting her to stay with him all the way. Sure, she clung to him now, twisting to rub her breasts against him as she kissed him back with that furnace-hot mouth and supple tongue. But who was to say she wouldn't come to her senses any second now and kick his sorry butt right off the dock? Before that happened he intended to experience as much of her as possible.

He unbuttoned her vest one handedly and smoothed it open. He started to pull his mouth away but she made a sound of protest and thrust her hands in his hair to bring him back.

So he went back to kissing her. Hard, deep, wet kisses. Then he determinedly raised his head and looked down at her.

"Jesus." For all intents and purposes she was bare to the waist. Her vest, lying open against the wooden planks, and the once-perky little turquoise bow tie did not constitute much in the way of cover.

She was all light golden skin, creamy triangles of white flesh and pale pointed nipples. The boathouse light was on tonight and its softly diffused illumination coming through willow branches painted watercolor delicacy over what he had missed the last time they were here.

He slid down to angle his mouth beneath her jaw, pressing kisses into the sleek skin there and scraping his teeth along the warm column of her throat as he worked his way down its satiny length. His right hand, impatient with the pace, raced ahead to stroke the delicate curve of her left breast. It was warm. Soft. Silky. Plucking its tiny jutting nipple between his thumb and forefinger, he gently squeezed.

"Oh!" she breathed. Her back arched up off the dock. "Oh, my gawd!"

He watched her. "You are so pretty, Hayley. Just...so... damn...pretty."

Hayley looked up into Jon-Michael's Hershey-dark eyes, so heavy-lidded and absorbed as they studied his fingers working her breast, at his mouth, unsmiling within the framework of his omnipresent dark stubble. Then his gently compressing fingers pulled at her nipple again, and her eyes slid shut as she focused on the sensations telegraphing straight to the coil of tight, aching *want* pulsing deep between her thighs. "Jon-Michael, *please.*"

"What, do you want, Hayley? This?" And he moved lower, his gaze intent on her face as his mouth closed around her unattended nipple and sucked hard. His hand slid from her breast to work the fastenings to her jeans.

Lightning struck, a white-hot blistering bolt shooting from her breast to that needy, aching spot deep between her thighs. Hips arching, she shuddered, her hands coming up to clutch fistfuls of his hair, holding his head to her breast. "Oh, God, oh, please."

Her sweet responsiveness brought Jon-Michael up onto his knees, his back hunched to keep his lips anchored to her breast. But he had to release it to pull off his shirt and fling it aside. Then he tore at her jeans, pushing them down to her calves. Hayley bicycled her feet, kicking free of the restriction. Dropping back over her, he positioned himself between her legs.

Gently recapturing her nipple, he gave it a single suck, drinking in her sharp gasp of arousal. Releasing it with a final pull of his lips, he moved up to kiss her again, his hands scooping beneath her head to cradle her skull. Reveling in the soft fullness of her wild hair twisting between and around his fingers, he looked down at her.

"Touch me," he demanded and closed his eyes in unmitigated pleasure when her hands rose to stroke the hair-roughened muscles of his chest. When they trailed to his diaphragm and slowly caressed his abs on a downward trajectory, he shuddered all over and eased down until he was lying on his stomach between her thighs.

Running his hands along her smooth shins to her ankles, he strung kisses from her diaphragm to her navel. Her knees were bent on either side of him, the soles of her feel flat against the dock, and he circled her narrow ankles with his fingers, raising her legs and pushing them back until she was spread open beneath him, her knees brushing her breasts. The feel of her lace covered mound, damp and warm beneath his chest, had him gritting his teeth and pressing his erection against the old weathered boards. He dipped his head to tongue her navel.

"Oh, God, Johnny. Please."

His fingers slid down her calves to the backs of her knees, then to her thighs, and he raised himself to look down at her. Inexpensive synthetic lace covered her, but it clung damply, revealing more than it hid, as it outlined plump, feminine lips. "I will please you," he assured her hoarsely and lowered his open mouth to that beckoning lace.

He exhaled a long, hot breath over her cleft and felt her writhe, heard her breath catch. Using his tongue on her, he felt the soft lips part, the lace tucking into her silky little furrow. He scraped his teeth over the round pearl of her clitoris, then grew impatient with the cloth separating his mouth from her naked flesh.

Sliding his hands into the panties, he rent them in two with one fierce yank.

Hayley shot up onto her elbows. "Jon-Michael!" It was clear she was shocked by his action, perhaps even outraged.

"I'll buy you new ones, Hayley," he promised and lowered his head to lick at her, fascinated by the smoothness of the plump lips beneath his tongue. He tore his gaze away from the pretty, pretty sight and raised his head to meet her eyes. "I swear, I will buy you new ones, but, please, first let me…"

Her elbows melted out from under her and he lowered

his head once again.

Lust rode him hard, but there was something even stronger at play, something expanding like a helium balloon in his chest as he brought her nearer and nearer to orgasm. The emotion built as she clutched at his hair and pleaded for release. It exploded like a bomb when she cried out and clamped her thighs over his ears. When she gradually went limp beneath him he raised his head to press a gentle kiss against the inside curve of her sprawled thigh. "Jesus," he said wonderingly, "I love you."

He could hardly credit it, but that was exactly what he had felt growing inside him. Not pride in his prowess, not male satisfaction that he could make her come. Love. Holy shit. "I love you, Hayley," he repeated. Raising up on his knees, he reached for his zipper.

The next thing he knew, the bottom of her feet hit him squarely in the chest and she gave a mighty thrust, sending him flying.

He landed on his ass on the end of the dock. Feeling himself going over, he threw out an arm to catch himself, but he was too damn close to the edge and, stomach plunging like a Tilt a Whirl, he toppled over.

The cold water felt shockingly cold as it closed over his head before he could regain control of his reflexes. Then he gave a strong kick and surfaced with a roar, flinging his hair from his eyes. Hayley was scrambling into her pants on the dock above him, tears trickling down her cheeks.

"What the hell, Hayley! Why did you do that?" Furious, he reached for the dock to hoist himself up.

She stomped on his fingers with her bare feet. "You bastard," she sobbed. "You dirty rotten bastard!"

"Ouch! Sweet Baby Jesus on the B train!" Snatching his hands back, he treaded water at the end of the dock. "What the hell is the matter with you?"

She dashed the backs of her wrists against her cheeks and quit fumbling with the buttons on her vest to pin him in place with her glare. "Do not talk to me about love, you stinking two-bit Casanova," she said fiercely. "Don't you *ever* talk to me about that! The last time I heard those words from your lying lips, I found myself the reigning slut of Lincoln High!"

Shock ran through Jon-Michael. Oh, God, he had told her he loved her that night, too? Was there *no* stone he had left unturned before he had gone straight from her to inform the entire—

But sexual frustration, for the moment stronger than guilt, cut short his journey into self recrimination. Jon-Michael refused to show so much as a hint of his astonishment. He flashed her a nasty smile. "You liked my lips just fine a minute ago, sweetheart," he said coolly, eyeing her up and down as she bent to snatch her tattered panties off the dock and stuff them in her pants pocket. "And your principles were not nearly so high and mighty. Note they didn't rear their sanctimonious little heads until *after* I got you off."

Her hands stilled and slowly she straightened. There was not a tear in sight when she approached the edge of the dock to look down at him.

Causing atavistic short hairs on the back of Jon-Michael's neck to stand on end.

"That is true," she acknowledged and uttered a low, throaty laugh that drew his attention from the look in her eyes. "And for that I really must thank you, Jon-Michael. It has been an age for me." Squeezing her thighs together as if in remembrance, she peeled her vest open to once again display her naked breasts. Licking a finger, she rubbed it over her nipple, and his cock, which had shriveled like a leaky balloon when he hit the cold water, reared to full attention once again.

"Take a good look, Johnny," she invited, still rubbing that finger back and forth, back and forth, across her erect little nipple.

He lunged for the dock.

But she was ready for him and, planting her toes on his

shoulder, she shoved him back in the water. Her voice was flat when it reached his ears.

"Take a good, long look," she reiterated, closing and buttoning her vest. "Then think of me when you die of hairy palms. Because you will never see these babies again."

Chapter 12

Where on earth is Joe? I stop pacing at the living room window every few minutes to look out. He was supposed to be here ten minutes ago.

Three times now we have made plans to get together to discuss our marriage, and three times he has called at the last minute to say he can't make it. But he promised he would be here today, no excuses.

I do not understand why he doesn't just move back home where he belongs. So I saved a few newspaper clippings and a handful of television sound bites about an old schoolmate. Big deal. What is so problematic about that? Hayley is an old friend—it is only natural I am interested in the extraordinary events surrounding my chum the past few years.

You're a stupid, unnatural girl.

No. No, *dammit, I am not. Hayley told you so, Mama!*

I will *never*, as long as I live, forget the day Hayley did so. *No* one ever championed me to my mother before. As long as I can remember, Mama told me I would never amount to anything. She said I would never be as smart or as pretty as my friends.

I will admit the old bitch did not mention the shortage-of-beauty part the day Hayley stood up to her. *That* particular day her harangue focused entirely on my supposed lack of intelligence.

Man. I can still feel the heat of the late August afternoon, can still hear the drone of the blades on the old-fashioned overhead fan as it lazily moved the stagnant air.

Mama gives me a look of utter contempt when I fumble straightening the stack of towels she just informed me are not folded correctly. "How can one person be so blessed stupid?"

It is not the first time she has attacked my competence. Unfortunately, repetition does not prevent me from feeling helpless and clumsy every time I hear it.

"Will you get on with it!" she snaps impatiently, the intense scorn in her pale blue eyes skewering me. "It's not a complicated task, Patsy Ann. I swear, if you graduate this year it will be by the grace of God and nothing else. It is a mystery to me how you managed to make it this far."

Someone taps on the wood-framed screen door and I turn to see Hayley Granger standing on the other side. Oh, God, just let me die now. *The door hinges creak as Hayley pulls it open and her voice is quiet and contained when she inquires if I am ready to go. All I can do is stare at my feet in numb misery as she pulls the wadded towel out of my hands, efficiently folds it and adds it to the stack. I watch her make short work of folding the remaining towels and then follow her to the door.*

But once we have pushed through it, Hayley pauses and looks back at Mama. "You know, Mrs. Dutton," she says with even-voiced politeness, "perhaps if you weren't always riding Patsy so hard you would see, far from being stupid, she is actually one of the smartest kids in our graduating class."

Of *course* from that moment our lives were indelibly entwined. *No* one had spoken up for me like that before. Not one single, solitary soul had ever bothered to insert herself between me and Mama—let alone to tell the old bitch, without actually uttering the words, that she was full of shit . God in heaven—I never felt such joy!

So why would I give a great goddamn when Hayley became the scandal of Lincoln High a short while afterward? Mama gloated unmercifully, of course. And in my heart of hearts, I know that ordinarily I would have gone with the flow of popular opinion and dropped

Hayley like a red-hot spud. Instead I stood firm and refused to let anyone utter innuendoes about her in my presence.

A car pulling up to the curb out front now jerks my attention back to the present. Looking out the window, I see Joe climb out of the car, and everything else is immediately forgotten.

I reach the door before he makes it halfway up the front walk. Opening it wide, I hold it ajar as he approaches, then stand back. "Please," I say when he hesitates on the threshold. "Come in."

He does and with disappointment I notice his hands are empty. "I hoped to see your bag."

"I'm not moving home, Patsy."

I have never understood what men want, Joe least of all, but this is too much. "Why not?" I demand hotly, then immediately adjust my tone of voice. "I have done my best by this marriage, Joe."

"I'm sure you have, but—"

"Don't I keep an immaculate house?"

"Yes."

"Don't I always have a hot meal waiting on the table when you get home from the office?" At his tight-lipped nod, I say in a carefully non-confrontational tone, "It is not always easy, you know. I have responsibilities and stresses in my job, too. But I have done it all the same. I have been here to grant your every wish."

"Maybe I don't want my every wish granted," he interrupts. "Did you ever think about that? Did you ever consider just once I would rather have a partner than a personal servant?"

Rage, thick and black as crude oil, bubbles inside me. I open my mouth to unleash a few home truths but then snap it shut, the words left unsaid.

"What?" he demands.

"Nothing," I say calmly, refusing to acknowledge negative feelings, never mind express them.

"Dammit, Pats! If you have something to say, just come on out and say it. Get it the hell off your chest."

"There is nothing on my chest, Joe."

He spits something obscene and rams his fingers through his hair. Controlling himself with a visible effort, he draws a deep breath and slowly lets it out. "No," he agrees flatly. "I can't imagine you ever cutting loose to the extent where you might actually allow yourself a reaction like anger or hurt. That would be way too messy, too human. Or hell, it would be socially incorrect, which would be even worse, wouldn't it? At least according to your interpretation."

"There is no need to mock me, Joseph."

Joe blows out a gusty sigh. "You know something? I'm not. I am honest-to-God not mocking you. I'm just…tired. I can't live like this any longer. Do you hear what I'm saying? I cannot live in dread of upsetting your carefully structured world. I am sick to death of constantly fearing this will be the one change I suggest that upsets all your rules and routines."

He looks into my eyes as if searching for something, but I do not have the first idea what he wants. I hear his words clearly enough. I just cannot absorb their meaning. My tense shoulders slump when he suddenly sighs again, because this one sounds scarily resigned.

"I'm going upstairs to get some things," he says flatly. "Then I am going back to the Inn. But tomorrow I'm gonna start looking for a more permanent place to live."

For a long time after Joe departs with two fully packed suitcases and a box, I wander the house. By the time I end up in the master bedroom dusk has cast shadows across the floor. Minutes tick away as I stand in the middle of the room staring vacantly at the wall I had personally given a faux antique leather finish.

Then I shake myself free of the funk that has me in its grip, cross the room to the closet, and pull out the compound bow I bought to surprise Joe that night.

The night he first walked out.

I look at it gripped in my white-knuckled fist while a host of suppressed emotions clamor inside me. The red bow, faintly dusty but still festive, taunts me. Oh, God. My inclination is to rip and to rend and to shred the damn thing until it is nothing but a smear of red threads on the carpet.

Of course I do not. Mature women do not throw tantrums like spoiled children. I gently untie the ribbon and set it aside. Holding the compound bow by its smooth fiberglass grip, I raise it into the approved shooting stance.

Joe will be back. He has to be. I only learned to handle a bow in the first place because he has a passion for hunting with them. He will not forsake me now. Not after everything I have gone through for him.

I nock an arrow and struggle to pull the bow string back. The draw weight is geared for Joe's strength, of course, and I cannot get it to move more than obstinate fractions of an inch at a time. Stubbornly, I renew my efforts. Arms quivering, I am about to give up when I suddenly muscle it to a place where the cables kick in, making it draw back more easily. From there I pull the bow string back in a steady, smooth motion. I twist to take mock aim first at my reflection in the mirrored closet door, then at the framed wedding photo of me and Joe that sits on his highboy.

I have actually become uncommonly proficient on the compound bow. Wouldn't mama have been amazed? Too bad the old biddy up and died before I could prove to her I am good at something. As for Joe...well. Did *he* appreciate his wife's proficiency, even a little? Perhaps at one time. But he sure as hell does not seem to any more.

Well, never mind. He will be back. It is not as if he thinks I am stupid or anything. He is simply going through a midlife crisis, that is all this is. One hears all the time about men suddenly doing crazy stuff to prove to the world they are not getting old. I just have to be patient. I have to keep my mind occupied until he comes to his senses.

He will be back.

Stupid, unnatural girl. You just keep telling yourself stories. You never did have the brains God gave a peanut.

"Damn you, Mama. Shut...the hell...*up!*" Whipping around, I release the bowstring and watch dispassionately as the arrow shoots across the room to enter the wall with a resounding thunk. Plaster explodes and the arrow quivers where it buried itself a good two inches into the lath.

"Close but no cigar," I mutter. Plaster dust, trickling in a lethargic stream from the hole in the wall, piles upon the framed photograph of Mama, and I turn away. Clearly I need to get back to regular practice; my arrow missed by a good inch. Because, face it.

With no cigar, close isn't worth shit.

Chapter 13

Jon-Michael lay on his back on the couch, staring up at the high ceiling and brooding. When it got him goddamn nowhere, he rolled off the couch and prowled barefoot around his loft apartment. Three times he passed by his office, an area set apart from the open space by a wall of stair-stepped glass bricks. After the fourth pass-by, he went in and dropped into his chair. Gripping the edge of the desk in both hands, he looked down at the piles of notes and sheets of graph paper cluttering the desk top. And blew out a long, weary breath of exasperation.

What the hell. Mildred Bayerman had been pressuring him with phone calls about it ever since the Fourth of July dance. He might as well draft a formal proposal of his ideas for expanding Olivet Manufacturing. At least then he could tell her he was working on it.

It turned out applying himself to the project felt good—even if he could not visualize giving an actual presentation to the board of directors. But searching for the most viable way to convince a group of technological dinosaurs of the need to enter the twenty-first century helped focus his mind on something other than Hayley Prescott for longer than five minutes running. And that was a welcome break.

He managed to lose himself in the intricacies of the presentation for well over an hour. Little by little, however, pieces of his Wednesday night, no, Thursday morning encounter with the maddening brunette began to intrude on his concentration. He tossed his pencil down in disgust and gathered his papers together. Wrestling them into a rough sort of order, he leaned back in his chair, knowing damn well he wouldn't accomplish another thing today.

When she had first walked off and left him treading water in the cold, black, pre-dawn lake, all he had felt was a shitload of fury. He told himself she was nothing but a vicious cock-tease and any thoughts of love he had harbored were strictly borne of the moment, fathered by a surfeit of male-patterned horniness. If he were smart, he'd concluded, he would chalk it up to a date, or encounter, or sex or whatever gone wrong and write her off. Once and for all. Because who the hell needed the aggravation?

Once his sexual frustration had worn off, however, he'd conceded he was kidding himself. What was more, if he ever hoped to get back in Hayley's good graces he would have to work for it, because no way the first move would originate with her.

He needed to do something. He had no idea what, but he had to come up with a way to make amends. And it had better be now, too, if he didn't want her staring right through him as if he didn't exist the way she'd been doing damn near exclusively since she had first rolled into town.

Because while his anger had been fueled by surging testosterone and as quickly forgotten, Hayley's was all too real. And unfortunately all too justified. Her fury was fed by the memory of an actual injustice. The true miracle here was that she had managed to act with any civility toward him at all.

He could hardly believe he had told her he loved her that long ago night by the lake.

At the same time part of him could envision it all too easily.

There had always been something about her that drew him like a fish to the lure. Something deeper than her killer smile or round butt. Perhaps it was her refusal to be impressed by his wealth or his charm. Or maybe it was her way of saying what she thought, instead of paying lip-service to what she thought he wanted to hear as so many had done. He wished he could remember the emotions of that night. If they were anything like last night—

Then, yeah, he could envision saying the words.

Problem was, he had failed to live up to his pretty declaration. Had not behaved like a man in love. He had acted like the eighteen-year-old self-indulgent rich-kid budding alcoholic he had been at the time.

It was a little late in the game to beat himself up over it, however. All this had happened a long time ago and he was a different person than he had been back then. Not to mention the Catch-22 aspect scratching in the back of his brain. Yes, he had thrown away the opportunity for something special that night.

He couldn't help but wonder, though, how long it would have been before his drinking managed to destroy whatever had begun to grow between them. When he had awakened with a pounding head, a roiling stomach, and an absolute black hole where the previous night's memory should have been, it had changed him irrevocably. Shaken to the core, he had heard his sexual exploits repeated back to him by the friends he had told in unforgivable detail and knew he needed to make a serious change in his life.

He had felt apologetic for years afterwards, but he didn't have a thing to apologize for now. He had been sober for more than a decade. When he told her he loved her last night, she could not have been any more surprised to hear the words than he had been. But he acknowledged the truth of them…and knew it hadn't been Black Velvet talking. Neither had it been his dick.

He had to wonder, though, why she'd surrendered up her virginity to him all those years ago. Because he had told her he loved her? Or had the words been said in the heat of the moment or even later after the orgasmic bliss had faded?

Had she said them back?

Part of him wanted in the worst way to back off, to retreat behind the protection of the social mask he had perfected before he hit puberty. Its practiced charm had shielded him from rejection over the years, and now with only the smallest effort on his part it could continue to do so.

Another part urged him to rear up on his back legs, beat his chest and drag Hayley off by a fistful of her thick hair. *That* part wanted to hold her prisoner until she understood just who was boss around here. Until he convinced her he had grown up and was no longer the self absorbed ass he had been back when.

An infinitely more mature part of him put on his shoes and socks, collected his wallet and let himself out of the loft.

* * *

Son of a bitch! Ty Holloway wanted to put his fist through the nearest wall when Kurstin walked through his doorway and told him the news. He stared at her incredulously. "Are you fucking kidding me?" he said. "How did the media manage to track her down so quickly?"

Kurstin gave him a puzzled look and he scrambled to cover himself. "I mean, you'd think their first inclination would be to search for her in New England, wouldn't you?" *Get a grip, man*, he cautioned himself. *It will be all right. You still have the inside track.* It didn't stop him, however, from muttering, "Fucking vultures."

And saw nothing ironic in the sentiment coming from him.

"You sound like Jon-Michael." Kurstin kicked off her shoes. "And not to sound insensitive or anything because Hayley is my best friend in the world, but I skipped lunch today and it's catching up with me. You have anything to nibble on?"

"Come on," he invited and led her to a seat at the breakfast bar of the digs Patsy found him. He watched Kurstin kick off her strappy heels before he rounded the counter to see what he had to offer.

She had come straight from work to his townhouse and he eyed her in appreciation as he put together a snack and poured her a glass of wine. She was so elegant with her impeccably groomed blonde hair, tasteful makeup and long demure skirt, underneath which she had crossed her legs in a manner that struck him as anything but demure. At the same time, she was approachable and warm as she sat there with the top two buttons of her silk blouse undone, swinging a bare foot and smiling at him whenever he looked her way.

He slid a plate in front of her and came around to sit with her as she ate. It was time to kick his proposed seduction into high gear.

He told himself it was strictly business when he leaned over to kiss her the instant she swallowed the last bite. He removed her wine glass from her fingers, set it aside, and moved in closer.

For the story, he reminded himself moments later as he dropped the whisper-thin silk onto the bedroom carpet and peeled her bra away.

She was his ticket to moving up the food chain, and he was not about to forget it. But when her head thrashed from side to side on the pillow and he slid deep inside the slippery clasp of her body with a powerful thrust of his hips, potential for a Pulitzer prize-winning story was not the uppermost thought on his mind.

* * *

Bluey's was a three ring circus, and Hayley feared she was the dancing bear. She struggled to stay calm while a flood of out-of-town media jockeys jostled for space at the bar, yelling drink orders and attempting, many of them at the top of their lungs, to elicit her life story. They were rude and pushy and showed not the least compunction about elbowing the regular patrons out of their way. Even Marsha and Lucy had a difficult time getting close enough to the bar to place their orders.

"Hey, Hayley!"

She looked up and a strobe went off in her face for the third time in as many minutes. The current contender for her attention called, "Have you talked to Senator Jarvis yet?"

She blinked against the blue spots floating in front of her eyes. But to answer the question, yes. She had taken the senator's call but told the woman she was not putting herself even more firmly in the paparazzi's crosshairs to further the senator's agenda. Jarvis was well known in New Hampshire for trying to get the death penalty back in play.

Not that she was sharing that conversation with the press.

A brief, now-you-see-it-now-you-don't flood of sunlight washed and retreated across the lounge floor, alerting her that the front door had opened to admit someone new. *Oh, goody.*

She really needed yet another journalist in her face right now. Then Jon-Michael's voice, stringing obscenities together with rare creativity, cut through the din as another flash went off in her eyes.

"Get that the fuck out of her face!" Striding into the throng, he ripped the camera out of the hands of the most recent contender for the Hayley Prescott photo-of-the-night award and turned to look for the nearest bar maid.

"Lucy!" He tossed her his sax case and a small, exquisitely wrapped package. "Get Bluey out here." Twisting to fend off the photographer who jumped at his side making grabs for the camera, Jon-Michael held it aloft and fumbled to pull up the right menu. Then he found it and the photographer howled in outrage when Jon-

Michael hit the delete-all button with one satisfying, economical tap of his finger. "Am I sure?" he murmured, clearly responding to the digital security prompt. "Damn straight." He hit a button and the photographer moaned.

Jon-Michael looked down at him. "Oh, that was small spuds, chief. You wanna see this expensive little camera stay in one piece, I advise you to back off. I am feeling just the tiniest bit clumsy tonight."

The roar of voices rose to deafening proportions. Then the unmistakable sound of a twelve-gauge shotgun being cocked sliced through the high decibel babble like a chainsaw through butter, and the lounge went very still.

"What the hell is going on out here?" Harve 'Bluey' Moser stood outside his office door, a cigarette illegally glued to his lower lip and a shotgun cradled in his arms, the fully primed barrels pointed at the floor. "Hayley," he said into the sudden silence, "you okay?"

She drew a shaky breath and pulled herself together. "Yeah. I'm fine."

"Uh huh." He looked less than convinced. "And I suppose these fine people howling your name are just a bunch of blues lovers, huh?"

"They're media trash," Marsha snapped, elbowing a network reporter out of her way and slapping her tray down on the bar. She straightened the waistband on her polyester slacks, yanked down the points of her vest and reached across the bar to give Hayley's forearm a comforting squeeze. Then she turned to address Bluey. "These lowlifes have been shoving our customers out of their way, yelling questions I would blush to answer to my father confessor, let alone tell the world, and shoving cameras in Hayley's face ever since they barreled through the door."

"Who, exactly, took her picture?"

"This joker here for one," Marsha retorted with a jerk of her thumb at the culprit. "But Jon-Michael deleted it."

"Yes, and I'll have you know—" the agitated

photographer started to say, only to have Bluey step on his words.

"Shut up," the old man advised. He did not so much as twitch the shotgun in his arms but the photographer looked at his set face, shot a nervous glance at the weapon, and shut up.

"The guy with the white shirt took one," Lucy contributed, pointing out the individual in question. "And the babe with the bad haircut over there snapped off a couple."

The woman she had indicated shot her a look brimming with incredulity that anyone with two-toned hair could possibly disparage a perfectly acceptable spiked buzz-cut.

One of the customers pointed out yet another photographer who had shot off a frame and Bluey ordered them all to delete their images.

"Forget it," one photographer snapped, and all the others hesitated when he demanded belligerently, "What is this, a police state? You don't have the authority to make us delete our work."

"This is the state of the blues, boy—and I own it. I have the authority to do whatever I damn well please."

"I'll call the sheriff. I know my rights."

"You're not too bright, are you, son?" Bluey gave him a pitying look. "Hayley, pass this sorry sumbitch the phone. Punch 911, boy, just like you were still in the big city. And don't you believe a word you hear about police brutality in small town cops. Who says they would just as soon lock you up and throw away the key as look at you? Our Brutus isn't like that at all."

Paulette Benson, Gravers Bend sheriff, would have been surprised to hear her new name, and she was *not* like that at all. Bluey, however, was a better judge of human nature than the photographers. They deleted their memory cards or, in the case of one photographer who still worked old school, handed over his exposed film.

"Now the way I see it, you have a choice," he informed them. "You can stay and listen to some finest-kind blues, or you can go. Bother my bartender again and you get bounced. One more flashbulb goes off in her face and your camera gets smashed. It is all strictly up to you."

No one left.

Hayley discovered her hands were less than steady as she poured the first drink in the wake of the brouhaha. One might expect she would be accustomed by now to this sensation of having her skin peeled back so the fourth estate could get a good gander at her inner workings, but that simply was not something a sane person grew used to. Feeling the spotlight of attention focused on her made her feel naked, exposed, and alone. The only revenge at her disposal was to water down the journalist's drinks. And a feeble reprisal that was.

Her heart pounded and her temper simmered, and Jon-Michael was the last person in the world she wanted to deal with. But there he was anyhow, sliding his handsome muscular butt onto a newly freed barstool, propping his head up with one hand, and pushing an exquisitely wrapped package across the bar at her with his other.

"Hey, sweet thang," he murmured. "I got you something."

It had been a rough night and she was in no mood. Regarding the beautiful package as if were both reptilian and venomous, she said shortly, "Not now, Olivet."

He flashed that big ole charming grin at her. "Yes, now, Prescott," he insisted with an underlying hint of steel that told her he would not go away quietly.

Damn him. Damn him straight to hell. She knew what was in that package, and the last thing she needed tonight was to open it in front of an audience. In her mind's eye she could see her cheap, synthetic lace panties in pieces in his big hands. She heard again the intensity in his voice when he had said, *I'll buy you new ones, Hayley. I will; I'll buy you new ones, only you gotta let me*—and felt her face flame. It was payback time for knocking him off of the dock and into the water last night. He was going to publicly present her with a pair of rich-boy hundred dollar undies and there was not a damn thing she could do to prevent it. Several people were already hanging around the bar just waiting to see what was in the package. More than one was a reporter.

She tore off the ribbons, shredded the wrapping paper, and ripped open the box. Then she simply stood there for a moment, staring at its contents.

She uttered an abrupt bark of incredulous laughter and reached inside the box. Pulling out a pair of Groucho Marx glasses, complete with nose, bushy eyebrows and bristly mustache, she whipped them on, hooking the ear pieces in place and smoothing the brows. She looked up at Jon-Michael and gave him a mega-watt smile, feeling clothed again. "Thank you."

"My pleasure, darlin'. Pour me a club soda, will you?"

"You got it." A moment later she set it down in front of him. "This one is on the house."

"Mighty big of you, sweetpea." Considering band members' soft drinks were gratis every night of the week. Picking it up, he saluted her with it, then took it with him as he sauntered off toward the stage.

She watched him go, and the stress knotting her stomach since last night slowly began to unravel. Maybe, just maybe, she would some day allow him to see her breasts again after all.

"Interesting look," a woman's voice murmured a couple of hours later and Hayley turned to find Kurstin seated on a bar stool, her upper body draped across the top of the bar every bit as bonelessly as her brother had ever managed. Chin atop her stacked hands, she gazed up at Hayley, a crooked little smile tilting up one corner of her mouth. "Didn't anybody ever tell you the early Brooke Shields look is passé?"

"You're kidding me." Hayley licked her thumb and smoothed a synthetic brow. "And here I thought I looked so hip." She gave Kurstin a small smile. "So, what can I get you?"

"White wine." Kurstin was silent a moment as Hayley selected a glass and filled it. She looked up when Hayley tossed a cocktail napkin on the bar and set the drink in front of her. "I just stopped by to lend my moral support," she said, lethargically pushing herself upright. "But it looks as though my concern was premature. Here I was expecting it to be a zoo but it is actually rather civilized in here." Sipping her wine, she looked around. "Well, civilized if one doesn't mind being the undisputed center of attention. That's gotta be a bit wearing."

"You don't know the half of it. And if zoos are your thing, you should have been here earlier, before Bluey whipped out his shotgun."

"Yeah, right. Pull the other one. You must think I was born yesterday."

She just raised her eyebrows and Kurstin sat a few degrees straighter. "You're serious?" At Hayley's nod, she said with mild indignation, "Well, crap. I always miss out on all the good stuff." But then her expression dissolved into a dreamy little smile and Hayley had a sudden flash of what Kurstin must have been doing while she had been busy fending off reporters and their intrusive flashbulbs.

For a brief moment raw jealousy bloomed, tough and tenacious as a broadleaf dandelion in the height of summer. Then she ruthlessly weeded it out and cast it aside. All these years she had managed not to let bitterness consume her. Damned if she'd allow it entry now because her best friend achieved something she wished she could find for herself. Something, moreover, Kurstin richly deserved.

She leaned close on the pretext of wiping the bar and murmured low, "Kurstin Olivet, you little slut. You got lucky tonight, didn't you?"

Kurstin gave her a dreamy smile.

Hayley's loneliness deepened and her gaze sought out Jon-Michael up on the stage. He stood with his head down and his shoulders rolled in, his lips locked around the sax's reed and cheeks bulged as he blew out the melody. His eyes were closed, but they slit open as he brought the instrument up, tilting his head back a little bit more with each spiraling note. His gaze slid across hers, then snagged, locking on her face.

Hayley felt its impact low in her stomach.

Jesus, she heard his hoarse whisper, *I love you.*

The voice might be in her head, but she could hear the wonder and surprise in his voice as if he were standing right next to her, speaking in her ear. *I love you, Hayley.*

He had not been loaded to the gills last night. And it had been she who had been caught up in the throes of the moment, not Jon-Michael. So why had he said it?

Staring at him now, she could almost believe for a moment he had meant it. As their gazes locked, she thought she heard him blow a note off-key, as if he, too, were experiencing whatever it was holding her in its grip. But she must have been mistaken for when she concentrated on the melody it was as seamless, as smooth, as ever.

Then a journalist down the bar demanded a refill on his drink and the spell was broken. *For God's sake, Hayley, what a fool you are. What a blind, pitiful fool.*

Letting go of the gossamer spell, she tore her gaze away from the man up on the stage and went back to work.

What the hell was that all about? Jon-Michael's gaze followed Hayley's progress up and down the bar as she filled orders, wiped off the countertop, talked to his sister. His heart banged against the wall of his chest, sweat rolled down his temples, and while both could be attributed to the hot blue lights overhead or the normal every-night exertion he expended, he knew better. It was that look they'd exchanged.

His eyes had developed this habit lately of tracking her movements during the odd moments he surfaced from the lure of the music. Never, however, had he looked up to find her already watching him with eyes made big and needy by some suppressed emotion so potent it threatened to blow the top of his head off.

By rights, she ought to look ridiculous with her fly-away hair back-lit by the bar lights and that silly disguise he had given her perched on her nose. But she didn't. Instead, all he could see tonight were her big eyes behind those clear plastic lenses, burning with emotions that reached across the space separating them to grab him by the throat. Her gaze had locked on him and made him play a flat instead of a sharp, and it was a damn rare event that could distract him from the music. But there were secrets in those hazel green depths, secrets and maybe even a vagrant promise or two.

Well, she couldn't just give him a look like that, then expect him to politely back off. Maybe it meant nothing more than she was stressed from a hellaciously bad night. But maybe it meant something more.

Either way, he *would* get to the bottom of it if it was the last damn thing he did.

* * *

Kurstin left Ty's townhouse in the wake of a call from her brother. When she didn't return within forty-five minutes, he began pacing, too restless to stay in one spot for more than a minute at a time. She had been gone a good two hours now.

He peered out the window at the lighted greens of the golf course, strode over to the kitchen area and picked up the bottle of wine, then set it down without pouring himself a glass. He went over and snapped on the television, only to immediately turn it off again. Beneath every restless action, he cursed his self-imposed exile from Bluey's.

He wanted to be where the action was, but the place was bound to be crawling with East Coast journalists tonight, at least a few of whom could be counted on to recognize his byline photo. That was all he needed at this point, to be identified as a reporter. If it became known, Kurstin would kick him to the curb so fast his head would swim. And he needed to be in her life.

His shoulders hitched uneasily, but he quickly squared them.

For the *story*. His restiveness had nothing to do with the thought of being cut off from the woman herself. He could find sex anywhere. Maybe not as sweet, maybe not as hot. But hell, when it came right down to it, one woman was basically the same as the next. Professionally, however, he needed an inside source if he hoped to get the jump on all the other yahoos pouring into this little backwater burg.

That was the *only* reason he was so unsettled as he waited for Kurstin to come back.

* * *

Tempers were growing short in Bluey's. Or may have been short all night, for all Hayley knew. The first she noticed it, however, was during the band's last break. There was always a rush for drinks when the live music stopped, and in the sudden crush at the bar she noticed that little arguments were breaking out all over the lounge like brush fires in an arid field. Everyone had an opinion they wanted to express. Emotions were riled.

"You don't report the news," she overheard a long-time patron accuse a journalist when she was called down the bar to refill a drink. "You create it."

"That's ludicrous!"

"The hell it is. Look at O.J. Simpson."

"That was a hundred years ago, for God's sake."

"Maybe. But it was pretty much the turning point when celebrity media events became more news worthy than actual news. Simpson wasn't accused of anything that doesn't happen pretty much daily in a thousand similar cases. But because he was a known name, from day one the networks turned it into a goddamn circus."

"It was news!"

"Yeah, worth maybe a week's worth of thirty second sound bites. Hell, there was another case going on in Sacramento at the same time that was virtually ignored, and *it* involved a serial killer, for cri'sake. At least the print journalists got around to mentioning it, even if they gave it hardly any column space. That's more than so-called television reporters managed to do."

"Capital punishment is wrong," she heard someone else say. The speaker banged her glass down on the bar for emphasis.

"The hell you say!" came a hot defense. "What is *wrong* is spending hundreds of thousands of the taxpayers' hard-earned dollars to house, clothe, feed, and then try to rehabilitate one of these jokers, only to have the prisoner eventually released so he can immediately kill again. Hayley! I need another beer, please."

She silently filled the order and set it down in front of the man, collecting his money and putting it in the till.

"What do you think?" he asked her when she handed him his change. "What's your opinion on the death penalty issue?"

Every reporter within hearing distance immediately quieted and waited to hear her reply. Hayley simply looked at the man.

He grimaced. "Sorry. I guess you're not the best person to ask right now, are ya? You're probably a bit biased."

Oh, for pity's sake. She walked away, but no matter which way she turned there were similar conversations going on.

"This night cannot end soon enough to suit me," she

muttered to Kurstin at one point. But it dragged on endlessly until she felt as if she were caught up in one of those old Twilight Zone episodes they watched back in the day on Nickelodeon. "On second thought, I should probably be careful what I wish for."

"Why is that?" her friend inquired in an equally low voice, pushing her glass across the bar for a refill.

"Well, we're just delaying the inevitable, are we not? Bluey can control what happens in here because it's private property and he retains the right to evict anyone who gets out of line." Putting the soiled glass aside, she filled a new one with wine. "The minute I step outside that door, though, I'm gonna be fair game." She set the fresh drink in front of her friend. "And don't think the vultures don't know it."

She had relocated from the eastern seaboard to the western, had crossed an entire country in an attempt to get away from this very situation. She'd hoped if she removed herself from the heart of the turmoil the furor would die a natural death.

It should have. Yet here she was in a predicament too similar to the one she thought she had left behind. It dogged her footsteps as surely as it would have had she simply stayed in New Hampshire in the first place. She could try to ignore it; she could refuse to respond. But it was right here in her own back yard just the same.

Leaving her nowhere left to run.

Chapter 14

"Give me your keys," Kurstin said a short while later, her voice pitched low to prevent anyone from overhearing.

"Why?" Hayley pulled her purse out from under the bar even as she asked.

"Because Jon-Michael and I are going to see if we can do something about helping you avoid the jackals when the bar shuts down."

Hayley, who had far more experience with media persistence than she cared to think about, bit her tongue to keep from blurting, *I won't hold my breath then.*

Good thing she did, too, for she had seriously underestimated the Olivet siblings' ingenuity. After the bar closed and the till was balanced, Kurstin exchanged tops with Hayley. Bending from the waist, her friend brushed her hair briskly upside down, then straightened, tossing it back and fluffing it out to get an approximation of Hayley's volume. She bound it loosely in a scarf and slipped on a pair of dark glasses. Then she eased out the back door.

Jon-Michael and Hayley waited by the front door. Faintly, from around the corner, they heard someone yell, "There she is!"

The media who had been hanging around the parking lot waiting for her to come out stampeded in a mass exodus from the front parking lot. Jon-Michael snagged her by the wrist and dashed for his Harley. Strapping his sax case to the back of the Soft Tail with one hand, he pulled his World War II German leather helmet free with the other. He tossed it to her and swung a long leg over the gas tank, straddling the bike. "Get on."

The engine turned over with its distinctive, deep throated growl and they peeled out of the lot. Hayley clutched his waistband with one hand while slapping the helmet to her head with the other and awkwardly manipulating the strap beneath her chin.

They roared through the quiet streets, flashed past the blink-and-you've-missed-it downtown district, then continued on to the only slightly more substantial industrial sector. Jon-Michael killed the engine and coasted down an alleyway, rolling to a stop behind a brick warehouse. They dismounted and he unlocked a door set deep in the brick wall.

"Come on." He pushed his bike inside and kicked the door closed behind them. After rocking the motorcycle back on its kickstand, he accepted the helmet Hayley silently held out to him and hooked it over the handlebars. Then he collected his sax case and ushered her to the freight elevator.

They did not speak until they had stepped inside and he'd tugged down the top half of a steel-mesh door. Its bottom glided up to meet it and the sound of heavy metal gates clanging together shook Hayley from her silent introspection. She turned to him as the elevator jerked and groaned its slow way up one floor. "Where are we?"

"My place."

"What about Kurstin? Are we abandoning her to the ravening hordes?"

"Yep. If she can shake free of the journalists, she'll meet us here. Otherwise she will go home or to the new boyfriend's place." He gave an indifferent roll of his shoulders. "Wherever she intends to spend the night."

The elevator ground to a halt and he manipulated the doors again. He ushered her out, then preceded her to a door a few feet away. Unlocking it, he stood back and waved her inside.

It was dark and Hayley took only a few hesitant steps over the threshold before she halted. In a distant part of the vast warehouse she could hear a rhythmic thumping and the muffled tones of a woman's voice. Behind her, she heard the door close and the ping of Jon-Michael's key landing in something. Then she felt his fingers, warm and rough-skinned, slide along her skin to cup her elbow. He steered her around a glass brick partition and deep into the gloom of a cavernous room whose ceiling soared into invisibility high overhead.

"Wait here a sec," he commanded and left her. In the stygian darkness, over the sound of his retreating footsteps, the rhythmic thumping was more pronounced and the woman's voice clearer.

"Oh! Baaby," the voice crooned. "Yes, right there. Harder, baby. *Harder!*" The rhythmic thump grew louder, more persistent. "Oh, God, yes. *Yes!* Just like that."

A lamp flicked on across the loft, illuminating Jon-Michael's left profile while casting his right side in shadow. One lean cheek was highlighted by the play of light as he straightened. He looked at her across the room and smiled wryly, accentuating the soft groove that framed his mouth. His way-beyond five o'clock shadow, where it curved down from his upper lip just inside that raised groove, was a dark slash that dissolved into shadow on the side farthest from the lamplight.

"Sorry about the sound effects," he said. "Carol-Anne has a new boyfriend, and they have been going at it hammer and tongs for three weeks now."

"Oh, bay-bee," Carol Anne growled. "OH. Bay-bee. Uh-huh. Uh-huh." The headboard pounded against the adjoining wall. "Oh, God, baby, yes. Yes, yes, *yes!*"

Jon-Michael cleared his throat. "I'd, uh, like to tell you it will be over any minute now, but the guy has prodigious stamina." Carol-Anne's enthusiasm rose yet another decibel higher and Jon-Michael, stared across the room at

Hayley.

She had no doubt the heat she felt spreading upward from the scooped neckline of her borrowed top stained her chest, her throat, her cheeks a brilliant red, even in this low lighting. A fear she felt justified when he said a little desperately, "Music! I'll, uh, just put on some music. Make yourself at home."

A week ago, she might have cracked a joke and then pulled up a chair to critique the show. Well, with Kurstin she would have. Maybe not with Jon-Michael. At the moment she did not find all the rampant sexuality coming through the walls particularly amusing. It was too hard on the heels of the other night's debacle on the dock, and it made her feel flushed and uncomfortable. Edgy.

"Mind if I look around?" she asked as Jon-Michael toyed with a stack of CDs.

"Go ahead." More lights sprang on and the sound of John Coltrane's saxophone drifted out of speakers mounted overhead. Jon-Michael turned up the volume in an attempt to drown out his neighbor. He succeeded in submerging Carol-Anne's voice beneath the wailing sax, but the rhythmic pounding was not as easily ignored. It lent a carnal counterpoint to the music no amount of volume could alter. The knowledge of a whole lot of unleashed pleasure transpiring on the other side of the wall suffused the loft like a lush, musky perfume.

Hayley tried her best to ignore it. Sexual awareness was the last thing she needed tonight, and she determinedly shoved it aside as she wandered Jon-Michael's condo, checking everything out.

The floor plan was mostly open concept, with pockets of privacy provided by glass brick dividers. The floors were planked hardwood, the perimeter walls brick broken up by tall, multi-paned windows, and the interior walls rough-textured plaster painted a warm, creamy café au lait. At the far end a curved granite breakfast bar delineated the kitchen area. Wide oak-plank stairs midway down the long interior wall rose three steps to a landing before it turned right to hug the interior wall and climb to a loft overlooking the main room.

Knowing without being told Jon-Michael's bedroom was up there, she confined her curiosity to the lower floor.

"You want a cola or a club soda, Hayley?"

She glanced at him over her shoulder. "No. Thanks." What she wanted was to keep him as far away from her as possible until the atmosphere became a little less volatile. "You have a nice place here." She squatted down to study an old leather steamer trunk on the stairway landing.

"Thanks." He had kicked off his shoes and socks and, looking down, seemed to be studying his long, narrow feet. She, too, watched as he flexed his toes.

Then he looked up at her again, smiling slightly when he caught her crouched down to poke through his stuff. "I'm gonna have a beer. You sure you don't want something?" Without awaiting an answer, he padded barefoot to the kitchen.

Hayley went very still. "I thought you quit drinking," she said, rising to her feet and coming down the stairs. She took a few steps toward the kitchen.

"I did. Oh, the beer, you mean?" He pulled opened the refrigerator door and withdrew a bottle. Twisting the top off, he held it up for her to read the label. "It's non-alcoholic."

She rolled her shoulders. "I knew that."

"Uh huh." His smile grew more crooked.

The sexual activity on the other side of the wall was louder down at this end of the loft and it seemed to be reaching a crescendo. Hayley ducked behind a glass brick divider in hopes of putting some space between it and herself. She found herself in Jon-Michael's office.

It was very businesslike and looked well used, immediately intriguing her. Who would expect a saxophone player to give space to such corporate and workroom looking paraphernalia? Hayley stared at a shelf that held some kind of mechanical stuff with what looked like movable parts. Having no idea what they might be, she started sifting through a black wire 'In' basket.

"Find what you're looking for?" Jon-Michael inquired.

She glanced up to see him leaning as usual against the nearest convenient surface—in this case the glass brick divider. He had crossed his legs at the ankle, one hand loosely cradled his beer, and the thumb of his other was hooked in his front pocket.

She shot him an unrepentant smile. "Dunno. I just got started." Picking up a thick report that was clipped together, she flopped down in the chair behind the desk. She turned on the green-shaded light and sat back to read, her feet propped atop the mahogany desk.

She had only read a couple of paragraphs before she realized she'd hit pay dirt. Her feet slid off the desk and she sat up straight. After skimming through the rest of the report, she looked up at him.

His current pose was not nearly as indolent as he stared back at her.

"This is a proposal for the expansion of Olivet's," she said slowly.

"I know."

"*Your* proposal."

He cocked an eyebrow and remained silent.

She blew out a frustrated breath. "If you have all these ideas for expanding your family business, Jon-Michael, why are you working at Bluey's?"

"You have a Masters degree in psychotherapy, honeychile. I am sure you can figure it out."

She studied him for a moment and then nodded. "Ah. Richard doesn't like your ideas, huh?"

"*Richard* would rather run the business into receivership than take advice from his punk kid."

"Is Olivet's in trouble?"

"It's headed there, but the old man cannot see past the current quarter's financial statement." He came into the room and opened a file drawer. Pulling out a folder, he tossed it on the desk in front of Hayley, then dragged over a chair and sat, bending over to point out aspects of the financial report. "See, here and here," he said, indicating the areas he was most concerned with. "Right now it looks good, at least on paper. But—" He proceeded to explain what the problems were and what needed to be done to ensure continued profits.

Hayley was fascinated by his enthusiasm. "So, you're going to submit this report to who? The board? The stockholders? Well, good for—"

"No," he said flatly and sat back, his expression suddenly blank.

"—you," she trailed off lamely. Her eyes narrowed on his impassive face. "What do you mean, no?"

"Just what I said." Spine growing rigid, Jon-Michael stared at her. "What part of the word do you not understand?"

"They've already turned you down? Is that why you left the business?"

"I left because Dad wouldn't even consider my ideas."

"Well, Richard doesn't have total autonomy, does he? He has to account to his stock holders. What did the rest of the board have to say?"

"I didn't bother showing it to them. They're in Dad's pocket anyhow."

Shoving her chair back, Hayley snapped ramrod erect, her arms crossed under her breasts. Her toe tapped an impatient tattoo against the floor as she studied him through narrowed eyes. "You didn't bother to show it to them," she repeated flatly.

"Well, actually, I didn't have anything *to* show them. I talked up a few of my ideas to Mildred Bayerman at the Fourth of July function at the club, and she ordered me to work up a proposal."

Hayley smiled. "Okay, so you are *going* to—"

"No. I just developed the thing to get my mind off other matters." *Namely you.*

She thumbed through the pages of drawings, charts, and text. Then she arranged them in careful stacks on the desk and looked up at him. "I don't know a blessed thing about business, Jon-Michael, but even I can see you have some very workable ideas here. Why on earth would you go to all this effort simply to let it collect dust on your desk?"

"I told you," he said without heat. "It is a waste of time. My old man has the board all sewn up."

"So that's it? You just accept defeat without making a single attempt to change their minds?"

"Yep."

"My God." Her head drew back. "I do not *believe* you."

His jaw tightened at the hint of contempt in her voice. He could tell her about the part he had developed. He knew he could sell it to any number of people in their client base in a nanosecond, because he was pretty damn sure it was going to be a game changer in the industry. He would give it to Olivet's for free if his father would just give him one second of respect. But he had lived with years of having to sell himself—to no real effect—and he was sick of it. So he merely said, "Yeah, well, believe it."

She shoved to her feet, the chair rolling across the floor with the force of her movement. She looked down at him with undisguised disdain. "You keep telling me you are not the same man you used to be. Well, that's a crock. You haven't changed a damn bit."

He watched as she turned and stormed from the office. Then he surged to his feet. "The hell you say!"

* * *

Ty had temporarily forsaken pacing to stand at the bedroom window overlooking the carport. He had been there for a solid fifteen minutes.

Bluey's was closed; it had *been* closed for a while now. So where the hell was Kurstin?

Headlights swept the trees lining the green as a car rounded the curve down by the driving range. Straightening, Ty smoothed his hair but then slumped again when the vehicle turned off before reaching the complex containing his townhouse.

Dammit, she had said she'd be back to spend the night, so why wasn't she here? He wanted to find out what happened at the bar tonight. Besides, it was late and the roads were dark and deserted at this hour of the morning.

What the hell was keeping her?

* * *

Jon-Michael caught up with Hayley in the living area. She stood at the window leading to the fire escape, her back to the room as she stared out at the dim pools of illumination cast by the street lights stretching down Davis Drive. Her spine was rigid and her face without expression when he caught her by the elbow and spun her around. "What the hell is that supposed to mean, I haven't changed a bit?" he demanded.

She twisted her elbow free of his grip. "It means you still run away the minute you're faced with a problem. God forbid Jon-Michael Olivet should ever stick around long enough to deal with one of his messes."

He reared up, fury driving him several steps closer until he towered over her. "That's bullshit."

"If you say so."

"Damn straight I say so. It is *total* bullshit. You don't have the first idea how I have handled the problems that arose at work between Dad and me, so where the hell do you get off telling me I've dealt with them by running away?" He looked her up and down. Then he nodded. "Oh. I get it. We aren't talking about the proposal any longer, are we, Hayley? You're referring to the way I handled that whole fuck-up I made of our night by the lake." She merely looked at him and he said furiously, "I tried to talk to you about it! For years I tried, every damn time I saw you."

"You came to my house once!" Stabbing her fingers into his chest, she gave a shove, but he didn't budge. "One lousy time you tried, and then you took off for college and never looked back."

"The *hell* you say!"

"No, the hell *you* say, Jon-Michael! If we happened to be thrown together, if we had to be in the same room after that night, you would put on that Mr. Personality dog-and-pony show you're so good at and offer up some slick, facile apology. But you never once made a serious attempt to get me to listen—"

"What was I supposed to do, tie you up and gag you so I could say my piece without you screaming me down or slamming the door in my face?"

"Oh, hell no. That would have taken too much effort."

"Jesus!" Frustrated and furious, he smacked his palm against the window's wooden casing beside Hayley's head. He glared down at her, breathing heavily.

She barely even flinched. "The *only* time you attempted an apology was if I was already somewhere you were and it was convenient," she continued implacably and with a bitterness she had honestly believed long forgotten. "Then—and I will give you this, Johnny—you could certainly blather on with the best of them. But I have news for you, bud. Charm only goes so far when you don't back it up with any real effort. And not once did you exert yourself to make me comprehend *why* you had done what you did."

Whipping her hair back with her forearm, she blew out a ragged breath. "You *never* went out of your way to do that. You never explained how you could have made love to me, how you could have told me you *loved* me, only to turn around and give the entire soccer team a blow by blow description of me losing my cherry."

"I was ashamed!" he yelled, moving as if to slap the casement again. Pulling his hand back before it made contact, he scrubbed both palms across his face until his cheeks stretched. Then, hands dropping to his side, he stared down at her. "Christ," he said hoarsely. "I was all but *paralyzed* by shame, okay? I didn't know what to say to set things right."

"So you took the easy way out and didn't say anything at all. And you are still taking the easy way."

"You don't know the first damn thing about it."

"I know that when you're in doubt, you walk away. I know you haven't had to fight for a thing in your life."

"*I haven't had to...?*" He heard himself parroting her words and broke off, swearing roundly. Then he braced both hands on the casement, caging her in and bending over her until they were eyeball to eyeball. "Let me tell you something, sister," he said between his teeth. "I have fought every single day of the past thirteen years to stay sober. I have fought not to be the irresponsible little shit I was then. I was a self-absorbed eighteen-year-old budding alcoholic who messed up your life in a big way, and for that I am sorrier than you will ever know. And when it came to making a choice between straightening things out with you or getting myself clean and sober, I freely admit I chose to fix *me*.

"Do you think you're the only person in the world to have trouble come knocking at your door, Hayley? Maybe we have never had a killer turn our lives upside down, but you were there with Kurstie and me after Mom died, and you know damn well being rich did not guarantee us a charmed existence. Your old man may have taken off, but at least your mother was there to cheer you on in any endeavor you were involved in. We had a father who was too fucking busy to just *once* watch his son play sports or see his daughter act in a school play." He stood over her, sucking in and expelling ragged breaths. "So I drank and generally acted like an asshole, and Kurstin married the first sweet-talker who offered to take her away from it all. Neither was a winning solution."

Hayley blinked warily when Jon-Michael calmed down as abruptly as he had erupted, speculation gathering in his dark eyes. He studied her closely. His right hand slid away from the window casing to fiddle with a lock of her hair. He wrapped it around his middle finger, stretched it out and rubbed his thumb over the shiny strands.

"What about you?" he asked in a voice so smooth it made the hair on her nape stand on end in alarm. "Since you're so hot to exorcise private demons, why don't we sit down and get cozy while you tell me all about your feelings on the death penalty."

Her heart gave a tremendous thump. Simultaneously, the doorbell pealed, and with a growl of frustration rumbling low in his throat, Jon-Michael unwound the curl from his finger, pushed back and went to answer the summons.

She blew out a soft breath of relief. Saved by the bell might be a cliché but she would grab her reprieves where she could.

Kurstin breezed into the main room of the loft, pumped up on success and adrenaline. "I can't think of any other creatures quite so easy to bamboozle as city folks convinced they're dealing with a country rube," she said with a grin, tossing her purse on the coffee table. Shoulders rocking, she punched the air overhead with pointing index fingers and wiggled her hips in a little victory dance. Brought up short, however, by the palpable wall of tension hovering between Hayley and her brother, she dropped her arms back to her side.

"Whoa," she said, looking back and forth between the two. "What have I interrupted here?"

Hayley opened her mouth to say *not a blessed thing*, but Jon-Michael was faster. "Have a seat," he invited, flopping down on the couch. "Hayley was just about to share her feelings on the death penalty issue."

"No, I wasn't."

"Oh, yeah. You were." His eyes hardened. "Or maybe you would rather *run away*."

She glared at him and Kurstin blew out a breath. "Hoo boy. I really did miss something, didn't I?"

"Only an analysis of my character by the resident expert here," Jon-Michael said. "Hayley thinks I don't deal with my problems very well, that I prefer to run away instead of sticking around to face them head on. She, on the other hand, is a much more evolved individual than I am, aren't you, sweetpea?"

"Go to hell, Johnny."

His hand flashed out to grip her wrist and he gave her a yank, causing her to stumble forward and tumble onto the couch. She sprawled half on, half off, his lap. "I have told you more than once not to call me Johnny."

She pushed herself off his lap and onto the cushion at the far end of the couch. Taking a furious swipe at her flyaway hair to shove it off her face, she wrapped her arms around her shins, hugged her knees to her chest, and glowered at him. She didn't say a word.

Her best friend did. "Jon-Michael!" Kurstin remonstrated indignantly and was gearing up to say more when he cut her off.

"Stay out of it, Kurstie," he said without taking his gaze off Hayley. "You and I both know she has a shitload of conflicted feelings when it comes to this issue. If she's going to be Ninja quick to assassinate my character, she should damn well be prepared to put her money where her mouth is." He drilled Hayley with his narrow-eyed gaze. "How about it, hot shot? Care to expound for a change on something that is difficult for you to talk about?"

"Fine," she spat. "You want to know how I feel about capital punishment? I will tell you exactly how I feel."

Then her bravado stalled out like a bad spark plug, because this was an issue she had a tough time acknowledging even to herself. "I-I-I..." She swallowed hard, took in a deep breath, and tried again. "I have mixed feelings about it, okay?"

"You used to be vehemently opposed to it," Kurstin said softly. She sat down on the coffee table, which sent Jon-Michael rolling to his feet to fetch her a chair.

"Yeah. I did," Hayley agreed, watching them move back the table and drag forward a leather sling chair. "It seemed so simple then. Taking a life as reparation for another was wrong. Period. End of discussion." She emitted a little huff of derision. "Well, you know what? It is a whole lot easier to take the moral high ground when you have not had to personally view the result of New Hampshire's rehabilitation program." She lowered her forehead to her knees for a moment. Then she turned her head and looked at Kurstin, ignoring Jon-Michael entirely. She wasn't ready to forgive him for forcing the issue. "Lawrence Wilson is an animal," she said flatly.

"Nobody disagrees with that," Jon-Michael said.

A fine tremor shimmied down her frame. "He deserves to die," she whispered fiercely to Kurstin.

"I agree," her friend said gently. "Jon-Michael agrees. But neither of us shared your convictions when it came to the death penalty in the first place." She reached forward to brush a wayward lock of Hayley's hair behind her ear. "The question is not what we believe. I think the problem stems from the fact that way down deep inside *you* do not fully agree."

"No," Hayley protested. "Huh-uh, not true. I do agree."

"Do you? Or do you have a conflict between what you know he deserves and some gut-registering basic value you have held your entire life?"

Her tremors escalated into sturdier shakes. "Oh, God," she said. "I get this horrible queasy feeling every time I remember it is my testimony that is going to trip the trap door or depress the plunger on the needle." She gripped her knees tighter and began to rock. "Why do I feel so guilty, Kurst? I didn't commit the atrocity—he did. I only testified to what I saw."

Jon-Michael's hand wrapped around her ankle, staying her and spreading warmth up her leg. "Would you change your testimony if you could?"

For the first time since he had started her down this path, she turned her head to look at him. "I cannot shake the feeling that Wilson's execution will be nothing more than state sanctioned murder. You don't kill the killers to teach them not to kill."

"But if you had a last minute opportunity to do so, would you change your testimony?"

"No," she said flatly. "I told the truth. Finding him guilty was just." Then she rubbed her temples. "God. Listen to me. First I am on this side of the issue, then I'm on that side of it. I don't know where the hell I stand."

"You did what you had to do. The verdict was up to the jury and sentencing was mandated by the judge. You don't have to love the outcome, darlin'. You told the truth, so you have nothing to feel guilty about."

She glared at him. "Well, thank you for pointing that out, Jon-Michael. Now I can rest easy."

"Hayley, I'm only trying to help."

"Well, do you suppose you could try to be a just little less insulting about it?"

His hand tightened around her ankle. "Jesus. What'd I say?"

"'You told the truth, so you have nothing to feel guilty about'," Kurstin supplied. Seeing her brother's blank look, she said gently, "You think she doesn't know that?"

"I am not completely lacking in intelligence," Hayley agreed. "I have not been sitting around this past year just waiting for some big, strong man to come along and point out the error of my feeble feminine reasoning powers. 'Don't feel guilty, Hayley,'" she mimicked in a voice she deepened to approximate a man's. She made the face of an airhead who finally gets the connection. "Oh! Okay."

"Dammit, I hate it when you two start in on that 'insensitive male boob' routine," he growled. "I do not produce estrogen so I can't possibly understand a woman's anguish, is that it?"

"But you do not seem to understand, Jon-Michael." Hayley realized she had stopped trembling and felt a surge of affection for him. "I appreciate that you would like to solve my problems for me. But I *know* my guilt is misplaced, and you know what? I feel guilty anyway." Bracing her elbows on her knee caps, she scooped her hair back off her face and stared at him. "Maybe if I had allowed my beliefs to be known from the beginning I'd have an easier time letting myself off the hook now."

It sounded like psycho-babble bullshit to him, but nobody had to hit this kid over the head before he learned his lesson. Jon-Michael kept his mouth shut.

"What?" Hayley demanded.

"*What*, what? I didn't say a word."

"Yeah, and you look as if you're ready to explode, too. What thoughts are boiling around in that fertile little brain of yours?"

"Well, if you are so all-fired hot to set the record straight, Hayley, it seems to me you have a golden opportunity right at your fingertips. The town is lousy with journalists."

She looked at him as if he had suggested she shuck out of her clothes for a stroll down Front Street. "Sacrifice the tiny bit of privacy I've managed to hang on to?" she said incredulously. "Let my private-most dilemma be turned into a thirty second sound bite?"

"Actually," Kurstin interposed, "it's not a bad idea. No, think about it, chickie," she said when Hayley's astounded gaze swung to pin her in place. "Not a sound bite, a half hour or an in-depth show. You could pick one person to talk to—maybe Barbara Walters would come out of retirement. Or a journalist whose work you admire. The point is to sit down with someone and explain how not only the murder, trial and appeals, but the constant bombardment by the press as well, has kept you on the ragged edge of your emotions for a couple of very long years. Talk about your feelings regarding capital punishment. Who knows? Maybe it will assuage the guilt or, failing that, start a national dialog on the subject. And as an added bonus, once you have given an exclusive, the rest of the carrion-eaters might actually leave you alone." She peered at her friend's still face. It was a viable idea. It made sense.

Except, Hayley was private. It had taken a great deal of pushing and shoving on Jon-Michael's part just to get her to open up to *them*. And she sure as hell had no history of airing her feelings for public consumption. "What do you think?" she asked when Hayley remained silent. "Hayley? Say something."

Hayley looked up at her, and Kurstin knew what a butterfly must feel like, pinned to a entomologist's board.

"It will be a cold effin' day in hell."

* * *

"Where the hell have you been?"

Kurstin turned from disengaging her key from the lock in time to see Ty bearing down on her. "Well, hi!" she said in surprise. Her lips curved in a spontaneous smile. "I thought you would be fast asleep by now—"

He pushed her up against the closed door, hands tight on her shoulders. "Asleep? Bluey's closed down more than an hour ago. Where the fuck have you been?"

He could feel the facade he had spent so many years perfecting melt away. At this moment, however, pressing her up against the door, his labored breath blasting her in the face, he didn't give a shit. His usual slightly detached amusement was nowhere to be found. And the last thing he felt like was the scion of old school-tie wealth he'd been portraying ever since he had hit town. He felt like who he really was, the son of a long line of West Virginia miners that had worked hard, aged early and died young.

"The media clowns were hassling Hayley," Kurstin explained breathlessly, not even attempting to stop him when he began roughly removing her clothing. "So Jon-Michael and I set up a false trail for them to follow." He pushed her panties down to her ankles and dropped to his knees to remove them. "I led them round town while Jon took her back to his place. Then I joined them for awhile. We had quite a talk." She was uncertain if he was listening or not; his mouth had found itself an occupation. "Oh, my God." Her head thunked back against the door.

He pulled back and looked up at her. He had heard her, all right. For once, he just didn't care. He had been scrambling up the ladder for as long as he could remember, clawing his way toward the top. Now, for the first time since he had set his course as a scholarship student back in college, he didn't race to take advantage of the golden opportunity she had just offered him. He rose to his feet, freed himself from his fly, and thrust into her.

"What?" he demanded, his fingers gripping the backs of her thighs, pulling them high to make her take him deeper. "You never learned to use your goddamn cell phone?"

Chapter 15

I twist the ornate Adams bell-pull next to the front door and listen as the bell peals in the depths of the Olivet mansion. I pick a speck of lint from my skirt then straighten, shoulders back, hands calm, a pleasant smile on my lips. Several days have gone by since I've seen Hayley. We have both been busy, but it is important to make time for close friends. Which is why I have squeezed forty-five minutes out of my schedule for a quick visit before heading to work this afternoon.

I wait expectantly but no one answers the summons, so I give the bell latch another twist. Taking a step back I take a discreet peek through the leaded glass side light. The view is distorted, but I can make out most of the entry. It looks cool, dim, and empty of inhabitants. No one appears from the kitchen located at the far end of the hallway. No one comes down the sweeping staircase.

An irritated sigh escapes me. Because, really. How inconsiderate. I specifically timed my visit for after the noon hour in order not to interrupt Hayley's rest. I know my friend sleeps later than most, given her late-night schedule. But honestly, it is high time she gets out of bed. It doesn't do for her to sleep the entire day away.

Unfortunately, inconvenienced as I feel, there is nothing I can do about it. Suppressing another sigh, I turn away. Pounding on the door until Hayley awakens is not a dignified solution. And clearly Ruth, the Olivet's cook, has not arrived yet and Richard and Kurstin are already at work, so no one is available to let me in. I consult my watch, then march back to the top of the circular drive where I left my car.

There is no use bemoaning what I cannot change and time spent unproductively is time wasted. I still have forty-one minutes left of my allotted time. There is dry cleaning to be picked up and groceries and personal items that need restocking. I will accomplish what I can during this unexpected block of time, then sit down with my day-planner when I get to the office.

And schedule Hayley into another time slot.

Hayley jumped at the heat spreading across her back from the male chest suddenly snugged up against it. Before she had quite recovered from that, warm lips nuzzled her neck.

"Mornin' petunia," murmured a sleep-husky voice. Hard hands reached around her to lightly grip her bare thighs.

Desire tugged deep and she jabbed her elbow half-heartedly behind her. Her lips curled in a tiny smile when it actually connected with a vulnerable spot below Jon-Michael's ribcage and air *oofed* out of his lungs. His hands slid away as he stepped back.

"And a good morning to you," she murmured congenially. Shutting off the water she had been running for a drink, she turned to face him.

He gave her a wounded look and made a production of rubbing his injured side. "You didn't have to slug me," he muttered.

Right. The muscles in his stomach were so lean and defined bullets probably bounced off them, but she was supposed to believe her puny little jab had done him grievous harm? It was all she could do not to grin at him.

And that would never do. Damn. Where had all of last night's anger gone?

She had been so angry with him and Kurstin, first for

insisting she explore feelings better left unexamined, then suggesting spilling her guts for the delectation of a nation of TV viewers might somehow help matters. They had compounded their treachery by leaving her stranded here at Jon-Michael's for the remainder of the night. Kurstin could easily have dropped her off at her car when she had left, but oh, no. Both she and Jon-Michael insisted the journalists would have the car staked out for her eventual return.

And, fine, that was likely true. It did not mean she was thrilled being stuck here.

At least she had been smart enough to draw the line at Jon-Michael's invitation to occupy his bed. Not that he had suggested she sleep in it *with* him, but he had tried to insist she take it. He must think she had STUPID tattooed on her forehead in an ornate red-ink font. As if she would get any sleep wrapped in sheets that smelled of him.

She had slept on the couch.

Yes sir, some of that anger would come in handy right about now. She stood in nothing but a pair of panties and a T-shirt of his she had been forced to borrow, with Jon-Michael naked except for a pair of raggedy-ass jeans he hadn't even bothered to zip up. Unfortunately, anger was not in her morning makeup. Instead, she was one of those intelligence-impaired individuals who generally woke up sort of vague and happy. She yawned, still sleepy. It was simply too much effort to pretend belligerence. "Keep your distance," she said without a hint of teeth to what should have been a stern warning.

"You're the boss." Jon-Michael stepped back and dropped onto one of the kitchen chairs behind him. Hooking one elbow around the doweling of the chair's ladder-back, he stretched out his legs and studied her affable expression.

He was bemused by her lack of ire. Her usual tendency was to fight him tooth and nail.

Then he shrugged it off and allowed his gaze one quick trip across her topography. It was far from Sofia Vergara lush, but it sure got the job done for him. "How did you sleep?"

"Fine."

"Good. I've always found that couch sort of short."

"You are six feet tall, Jon-Michael. I'm five-six." She yawned again. "I had plenty of room."

"I suppose." He watched the slow, lazy blink of her heavy-lidded eyes, took in the flush across her cheekbones, the dark hair crazy-curling around her face, and had to clear his throat. "So. Uh, how about some breakfast?"

"'Kay," she agreed amiably and turned to the refrigerator. She opened the door, bent to look inside, and then pulled out a carton of eggs and a quart of milk. "Scrambled okay?"

Jon-Michael laughed and climbed out of his chair to remove the items from her hands. He set them on the counter behind her. "No, I meant how would you like *me* to make breakfast."

"Oh." She gave him a sleepy, dulcet smile. "That's even better."

"Ah, man," he murmured. "I can't take this." Wrapping his hands around her hips, he lifted her onto the counter next to the breakfast ingredients. He stroked his fingers down her legs, spread her knees and stepped between them, rubbing his hands lightly up and down her thighs. "Are you always this sweet in the morning?"

She blinked at him. Hitched a shoulder. "Beats me. I wake up pretty happy."

"It's nice. *Killer* nice." He brought his hands up to cup her face, then leaned forward and kissed her. Gently. Sweetly.

She made a humming sound low in her throat and draped her arms over his shoulders. Her lips were soft beneath his and appreciation rumbled in Jon-Michael's throat. He opened his mouth a little over hers, but strove to keep the kiss light and friendly.

Then Hayley slid the tip of her tongue into his mouth, shooting his intentions all to hell.

Groaning, he plunged his hands into her hair, wrapping fistfuls of the bobbing curls around his knuckles and pulling her head back until her throat arched. Rocking his mouth even more firmly over hers, his kiss lost all semblance of its sweet intent and became hard, demanding. And still she made that little humming noise as her lips clung faithfully to his.

What might have been minutes or his entire lifetime later, he pulled back. Staring down at Hayley's kiss-reddened, swollen lips, he could not smooth out his ragged breaths as he took in that offered mouth, those closed eyes and flushed cheeks.

Sweet Squalling Baby Jesus, the way she made him feel! He wanted to dominate her and use her hard; he wanted to worship her tenderly from the top of her head right down to her toes. With the tip of his tongue he toyed with her mouth, probing at the soft lining of her lips and watching as they opened yet wider to accept a deeper penetration. He obliged her with one slow, gliding plunge, but when she sucked on his tongue he damn near lost it. He pulled back and bent his head to kiss the baby-soft skin beneath the point of her chin. It felt so amazing he got hung up stringing a line of kisses long on heat and suction down the length of her throat.

Loosening his unyielding grip in her hair allowed her to lift her head until it was once more upright. He untangled his fingers from curls he could swear fought to maintain possession of them. Once free, he smoothed his hands over her shoulders and down the long line of her back. At her waist he gathered the loose folds of his T-shirt and pulled it tight against her body until it clearly revealed the pert outline of her breasts. Lowering his head, he opened his mouth over her right nipple.

"Oh!" Hayley didn't hesitate to thrust her breasts forward and her head promptly dropped back once again. He alternated between sucking on and catching the sharp little point between his teeth and tugging at it. She made helpless sounds of arousal and clamped her thighs around his hips. As the cloth over her right breast grew wet her fingers speared through his hair to hold him in place.

By the time he lifted his head, her hips had instigated a slow bump and grind against the countertop. Staring at the impudent thrust of her nipple beneath the soaked cloth, he reached out and pinched its unattended mate. Squeezing and gently tugging, he raised his gaze to look into her eyes. "I want to see you naked. Now."

Luckily she seemed to have forgotten her vow he would never see her breasts again, for she actually obeyed his command and peeled the T-shirt off over her head. It fluttered to the floor and she scooped her hands beneath her breasts, pressing them up in offering. "Oh, gawd, Johnny," she said hoarsely. "Please."

A short, succinct curse escaped him and his hands clenched her hips as he lowered his head and wrapped his lips around the sweet protuberance of her left nipple. Pressing it to the roof of his mouth with his tongue, he drew on her strongly.

A keening sound purled out of Hayley's throat and he switched to her other breast, giving it equal attention. His hands slid over her hips to stroke her inner thighs. He smiled to himself when her legs spread wider with each successive brush of his fingers. She was so responsive. So, damn—his fingers brushed the damp satin between her thighs—*hot*.

With an inarticulate sound of encouragement, she raised her hips, pushing into his touch.

He pulled his fingers away and went back to smoothing them down her thighs. Needing to kiss her again, he raised his mouth from her breast. Before he could reach her lips, however, Hayley pressed an open-mouthed kiss into the damp contour of his neck and flattened her palms down his back.

Shuddering, he leaned into her touch. Even as he tilted his jaw first one way then the other in order to offer her the greatest access to his throat, he worked her panties down her hips with deft hands. *Love you.* The words drifted like smoke through his brain, but this time he was smart enough not to say them aloud.

Hayley's hands moved around to his chest. She stroked it, whispered her fingers through its light fan of hair and tugged. Then she rubbed her hands down his abs. Leaning forward, she kissed his mouth as she slipped her fingers from ridge to ridge in a downward trajectory. A moment later her hand delved into the open fly of his cutoffs.

Every muscle in Jon-Michael's stomach clenched and he fought the urge to push his cock into her palm and finally feel her fingers curl around him.

He wanted that. Wanted it bad.

Wrapping his hand around the back of her neck, he kissed her with unbridled passion, then stepped back. "Let's see about you," he whispered and bent to kiss her stomach. Gradually his head lowered until it was buried between her thighs. His tongue slipped out to part soft, plump folds.

Hayley sucked in a sharp breath and pulled her heels up onto the counter, opening herself up to him. In an almost immediate reversal, she gripped his hair and pulled his head back, letting her legs drop back over the side. She looked down at him and shivered at the heavy-lidded dark eyes returning her gaze. "You sure like to kiss me there, don't you?"

The smile he gave her was slow, one-sided, and carnal. His tongue slid over his bottom lip. "Uh huh." He rubbed the side of his face against her inner thigh, his morning stubble a rasp against her skin. His eyes never left hers. "Let go of my hair, darlin', and I'll show you how much."

She didn't relinquish her grip. "I   don't want to come that way, Jon-Michael. I want you inside me."

His jeans dropped to his ankles almost before the last word was spoken. He kicked them aside and reached for her.

"Wait." Hayley jerked erect at the sight of his hard-on. "Wait a sec. I wanna look." And she did precisely that, at length, while he stood in front of her looking as though he were trying not to fidget. His penis stood out from its nest of dark hair, pointing at her like an accusing...well, finger was not the word she was looking for. No, this was more a club, and screw the simile. This baby was thick and long and so damn masculine. And it pulsed crazily beneath her unabashed scrutiny. "Oh my," she finally murmured.

"Just your standard model, ma'am. But let me show you what it can do."

"In a minute." She hopped down off the counter. "I wanna touch it."

"God Almighty, Hayley. You're doing this on purpose, aren't you? You are trying to see if you can take me from zero to ninety in under twenty seconds." He threw up his hands in resignation. "Fine then. Go ahead."

He had not really expected her to take him at his word. So Jon-Michael's breath exploded out of his lungs when she did precisely that. His chin snapped down and he stared at the sight of his cock protruding from her fist.

Her very tight fist. He scowled at her.

"I'm running on a real lean mix here, so you remember you have got no one to blame but yourself if my engine blows." He was embarrassed to note he could barely push his words past the tightness of his vocal cords.

Holy crap, didn't she used to be *shy*? Okay, maybe never that, exactly, but... "I mean it, now. Do not come whining to me about being all revved up with nobody left in the race." Then he quit babbling like a fucking idiot and grit his teeth against the pleasure of her fist sliding up and down his dick. Not to mention the sight. Sweet Mother Mary, the sight.

"I love all the car references," she murmured and gave him a sleepy, sexy smile. "What does that make this then, your hot rod? That seems appropriate. *Hot*," she murmured, stooping to stroke his junk against the delicate inner curve of her breast. "*Rawd*." Holding him steady, she brushed her nipple back and forth against the very tip of his hard-on, transferring its minute drop of pre-cum. She smiled up at him as she spread it around, making her nipple glisten. Then she bent her head and pressed a kiss against the blunt head of his dick.

"Okay, that cuts it," he breathed. Pulling her to her feet, he slid his hands to her hips, and lifted her in the air. Hayley's legs separated to wrap around him. "That's my girl," he approved on a ragged breath. "Reach down and grab my cock, Hayley, honey. Guide me home."

Happy to oblige, she did as he said and held him steady, edgy excitement flooding her as he slowly lowered her. She felt so hot and swollen, so empty, yet she jerked skittishly when the broad head of his penis penetrated her.

Jon-Michael immediately stilled. He looked into her eyes. "You okay?"

"Um hmm. Sure." But she had tensed and they both knew it. She bit her lip. "Just give me a second. It's been a long time for me."

His fingers bit into her as his hands tightened on her butt. "Here, let me pull out."

"No!"

"Yeah. We'll try another position and—"

"No, I want to do it this way. Just give me a sec—"

He raised her off him. She was outraged at having her wishes summarily ignored, but before she could express her displeasure he was pressing kisses into her forehead. "I'm sorry, Hayley, I am so sorry. I forgot all about a condom." He swung her into his arms and headed for the stairs.

Up in the sleeping loft, he laid her on his king-sized bed, then bent to paw through the night stand drawer. By the time she struggled to her knees, impatiently swiping her hair from her eyes with the inside of her forearm, he had located a carton and turned with it in his hand.

She thrust a finger at it. "Put one on," she ordered. "And then I want you to do it the way you were going to do it down there."

He looked down at her, one corner of his mouth tugging up. "Bossy little thing, aren'tcha?" He donned the condom as directed but said seriously, "Look, darlin', that might not be the best position if it's been awhile." Then his gaze narrowed, turning intent. "How long has it been, anyway?"

"A while."

"Uh huh. How long a while, exactly?"

"A few months before Dennis died."

"Jeez Louise! Look, maybe we'd better—"

She narrowed her own eyes at him. "Do not even suggest the missionary position, Olivet." That was practically all Dennis had been interested in and she wanted to do it standing up like Jon-Michael had started to do before she had gone all tense on him. She had never had a man do her that way.

Jon-Michael looked at her all naked, determined and greedy-eyed, and wondered about her experience. He had a feeling it was not particularly extensive, but she sure as hell had killer instincts. It had taken her all of two minutes downstairs to reduce him to a randy, no-control teenager.

"No missionary," he agreed. "But I get to be in charge here, and the first thing we do is build back up the intensity."

She perked up. "By playing garage the hot rod again? I liked that."

"Of course you did. You were damn good at it."

She gave him the hundred-dollar smile that threatened to stop his heart every time. "No kidding?" She said it as if no one had ever complimented her sexual prowess before. "Thanks."

God, he wanted to eat her up. "Oh, honey, it was definitely my pleasure. Let's get you revved up again and then you can have it any way your little heart desires. Standing, sitting, sideways, doggy; you name it. Myself, I kinda like the missionary position."

"You would. Why stand when you can lie down, huh?"

"Damn straight." Jon-Michael gave her a slow once-over and a smile so smoldering if Hayley still wore panties she was pretty sure they would spontaneously combust. His voice was a sable brush stroking her nerve endings when he added, "Bet I could make you like it, too."

She did not doubt it for a moment. But having a reputation to maintain, she raised a skeptical brow. "So far all I'm hearing is a lot of talk. For all I know, that's all I'm going to get." She shook her hair behind her shoulders and sang softly, "I—can't—get—no-oh. Sat—is—fact—shun."

The next thing she knew, she was buried beneath a hundred and eighty-five pounds of naked male.

"Boy, you have a mouth on you." Jon-Michael pushed up on his elbows to look down at her. "Maybe I oughtta find a better use for it."

She must have looked as interested as she felt, for he barked out a laugh. "Then again, maybe not. It would keep you quiet for awhile it's true, but then—"

"We would have to listen to you holler and scream," she inserted smoothly.

The corner of his mouth crooked up but he didn't reply as he used a fingertip to hook a strand of hair out of her eyes. "You know what our problem was downstairs?" he asked her softly. His lips touched her hairline, her eyebrows. He moved her hair aside and kissed the side of her throat.

She angled her jaw to give him more room. "What?"

"We moved too fast. I think we have to slow things down."

Jon-Michael was a man of his word. He fed her slow, deep kisses, trailed his fingers over every inch of her body, used his lips on parts of her she never dreamed could be so erogenous. He took his own sweet time about it, too. Heat spread throughout Hayley's body, and her fingers curled to grip the bedspread on either side of her. With every brush of his fingers or his stubble-roughed jaw against her inner thighs, the spread of her legs widened. But he ignored the one place she most wanted touched.

"Oh, please," she finally begged. "Please." Her hips thrust high in an attempt to follow the hands that were sliding away as he rocked back on his heels between her feet. "Please-*please* Jon-Michael."

Sweat beaded his hairline and rolled down his temples and throat, but he gritted his teeth and ignored her plea. He rolled her onto her stomach.

For several moments he msssaged her back, settling her down. But soon his fingers started slipping over her sides, and with each firm upward knead her breasts rubbed against the spread. Hayley pushed up slightly and he reached under her to cup her breasts. He caught her nipples between his fingers and tugged, leaning forward to slide his erection between her legs. He rocked it back and forth along her slippery cleft.

"Oh, God, Jon-Mich..oh! God, please!"

He was tempted to simply pull her hips up and shove into her. But there was that long ago night he needed to make amends for, and he needed to be face to face with her when he did so, the better to see her every expression, to memorize her every emotion. He climbed off her and rolled from the bed.

Hayley turned over slowly and looked at him standing

at the side of the bed staring back down at her. She whispered his name enquiringly.

"Come on, darlin'," he said gently extending his hand to her. "We're gonna take care of that itch for you now."

She let him pull her off the bed and stumbled after him. Her knees were weak, and she felt the beat of her heart in that swollen place deep inside her.

It was a hot, empty, aching feeling.

He crossed the room and sprawled onto an armless Bentwood rocker. He looked up at her. "It's not standing up, Hayley honey, but neither is it the missionary position. Will it do?"

"Sure," she said, but then merely stared down at him for a moment, her mind blank.

He drew her forward and maneuvered her until she stood astride him. "Ease yourself down on me," he instructed. "Take it as slow as you want. We have all day."

Bracing her hands on his hard shoulders, she lowered her hips until she felt the head of his erection probing at her opening. His hands settled on her hips, but he did not try to hurry her along and she reached between them to wrap her hand around the base of his penis and hold him steady as she lowered herself inch by cautious inch.

She was burningly aware of the satin-covered rigidity in the U formed by her thumb and index finger, of the fullness of his shaft forging a trail through slippery tissues that had not been delved in far too long. Then her hand was in the way and she removed it, giving one last, firm push. She found herself fully impaled, his spread thighs hard beneath her butt, his sex hot and inflexible, stretching high inside her. Cautiously, she inched her legs forward and gave a slight push-off with her toes to set the rocker moving. His penis withdrew halfway then plunged back in, and her eyelids flew wide. "Whoa!"

"Jeez-us Louise," Jon-Michael said in a gritty voice. "You are so. Damn. *Tight.*" He planted his feet and took control of the rocking chair's rhythm, his hands on her butt easing her up his rigid shaft on the forward motion, then sliding her back down it as he rocked them back. He filled her with himself, almost withdrew, then filled her again.

Over and over again.

The slow, inexorable stroking set up a friction she knew would send her burning out of control in no time. She clutched his shoulders, trying desperately to hold back the inevitable, to draw it out and make it last. But it was like trying to fight wildfire with a cheap plastic water pistol. Her eyelids grew heavy, her head dropped back and her lips rounded as small, breathy "oh, oh, ohs" hiccupped up her throat. Each one more audible than the last. Her head felt too heavy for her neck and dropped back.

Jon-Michael's fingers tightened on her ass and his voice growled in her ear. "God. Yes. That's it, darlin', that's it. Come for me. You look so damn beautiful. Come for me."

"Jon-Michael?" Her eyes slit open to find him watching her. "It feels so good." She dug her fingers a little harder into the muscles of his shoulders. "You feel so good in me."

His hips lifted off the seat and his hands slammed her down on him with increasing force on each rock back. "Don't hold back on me, Hays. I wanna watch you come. I want to see your face when I make you climax." He sucked her nipple into his mouth, his gaze trained on her face.

Her ragged panting turned to low moans and she squeezed her eyes shut, concentrating on sensations gaining force within her. "Please," she pleaded frantically, drawing her knees back to feel him reach a little deeper. "Oh, God, Johnny, *please*. Oh. My. Gawwwd." She began to convulse in his lap. "Jon-*Michael!*"

"Look at me," he demanded. Releasing her nipple, he shoved himself deep and held her in place with hard hands. "Look at me, Hayley."

She opened her eyes to stare into his. He growled hot, dark words.

And her orgasm, which she already believed the finest thing she had ever experienced, ramped into overdrive.

"Yes!" Jon-Michael went berserk, watching her, feeling the sweet weight of her, the hot slick clasp as contractions clamped firmly around him over and over again. His feet slammed to the floor, stopping the rocker in the rocked back position, and he held her hard against him while his hips thrust up off the seat in a fierce rhythm that pounded him deep inside of her. "I love you, Hayley," he panted. "Jesus, God, I love you, love you, love you." Then his teeth snapped together and he groaned deep in his throat, hips jerking spasmodically to the beat of his hot, pulsating release.

Hayley collapsed on his chest, her face buried in the contour of his neck, her legs extended limply and her arms flopped over his shoulders. He clasped her nape beneath the wild tangle of hair even as he wrapped his other arm around her waist, thumb hooking over her hipbone, his fingers splayed down her hip. Sweat glued them together and the bedroom loft reverberated with the harsh rasp of their labored breathing.

"Sweet Baby Jesus," he finally murmured, rubbing his cheek against the top of her head. "I know it must have been good before," he said hoarsely between gulps for breath, "because my words have come back to haunt me more times than I can count. But it could not have been like this." His fingers squeezed her neck, tightened on her hip, holding her to him possessively. Stropping his cheek against her hair, he said quietly, almost to himself, "I don't care how loaded I was, I would have remembered this."

"It was not like this," Hayley agreed. She had never felt *anything* like this before and she had a sinking feeling she knew what made the difference. Even as she took comfort in Jon-Michael's arms, in the soap-and-water scent of his neck where her nose was buried and the heat and strength with which he surrounded her, she assured herself weakly that this was not *love*. No fricking way. It was simply good sex with a sober partner. And good sex was a dime a dozen, right? Well, maybe not for her, but that was only because circumstances had seen to it she didn't get around much. That could change, though, and when it did she probably wouldn't even remember what doing the rocking chair boogie with Jon-Michael had been like.

Really.

"Hayley?"

"Umm?"

"Why did you sleep with me that night by the lake?"

She stiffened all over and felt his shrinking penis slip out of her. "I have to get going," she said, struggling to sit up.

His arms tightened. "No! Listen, never mind, it doesn't matter. You do not have to talk about it if you don't want. Just ...don't go yet, okay? Stay with me for a while."

She subsided, but muttered uneasily, "Well, just for a little while. Then you have to take me to my car. I have stuff to do before I go to work." And she had to think.

She *really* needed some time alone to think.

Jon-Michael got Hayley to shower with him and he fed her, but although she talked to him with apparent ease, there was a reserve about her that kept her closed away from him at her most basic level. He seethed with frustration when he delivered her to her car an hour and a half later. It must have shown, too, for the two journalists who were sitting on the Pontiac's hood took one look at his face and unyielding posture and quietly removed themselves without attempting to interrogate her.

"Don't you ever put up the top?" he asked as he opened the car door for her. It creaked in protest.

"Occasionally. If it looks like it's going to rain."

He handed her behind the wheel and closed the car door. Then squatting down he propped his chin on the hands he had curled around the window opening. "Come home with me after work."

Hayley had been congratulating herself on the fact that this was Jon-Michael's night off and she would not have to face him. And, yet—

Slipping on a pair of sunglasses, she gazed at him through the protective shading of their lenses. "I don't know, Jon."

"I'll come pick you up so you don't have to run the gauntlet of reporters to your car."

"Then you would just have to drive me back to my car again tomorrow."

"I don't mind."

She started the Pontiac, staring straight ahead. "I have to think about it."

He rose and leaned over the door until his lips were a centimeter from her ear.

"Fine," he said in a gruff rasp that raised goosebumps down the entire side of her body. "You think about it. Think, too, about the fact that no way in hell was this a one-off deal. If you don't want to come to me, then I will come to you. I'll just wait until you're asleep to slip into the house, slip into your room. . .maybe even slip into you. 'Cause, baby, I know something about you now."

He trailed a rough fingertip over her temple, down her cheek and, catching at her hair, gently hooked it behind her ear. His breath was warm as it traveled the whorls leading to her auditory canal. "I know you are *eeeeasy*—" his voice went low and rough on the word, stretching it out "—when you first wake up."

Hayley could not stop the shiver that slicked down her spine any more than she could stop her next breath.

"And Hayley, honey," he continued in his everyday voice as he pushed to his feet and looked down at her with dark, intent eyes. "While you are busy doing all that thinking, think about this. I will not hesitate one second to use that to my advantage."

Chapter 16

Strongly held opinions had drawn a line in the sand between the citizens of Gravers Bend. Those who made money off the journalists overrunning their peaceful little town liked having them around. Everyone else found them a pain in the ass.

"Christ a'mighty," muttered one of the Blue Dolphin's regulars when he walked into the cafe and discovered someone had usurped the counter stool where he had sat to eat his breakfast and shoot the bull with his friends every Monday through Friday for the past seventeen years. If that was not insult enough, even the seats considered undesirable were all filled up; there was not an available spot in the joint. "When the hell are all these yahoos goin' home?"

It was a question many wanted answered. The media had booked all the available rooms at the Royal Inn and was busy crowding the town's restaurants and bars. Most were well mannered. There were enough behaving with arrogant big city condescension, however, to give them all a bad name. And their very reason for being in Gravers Bend sparked arguments over weightier matters than having one's usual place commandeered by an out-of-towner.

The Peninsula Women's Garden Club, comprised largely of genteel elderly ladies with discreet blue tints, nearly came to blows over the moral ramifications of capital punishment. Not since learning Bev Eldridge's granddaughter Molly had gone to Seattle for an abortion had the club seen such divisiveness over an issue. Acrimony was served up alongside tea, petit fours and watercress sandwiches.

The media's entrenched trend toward allowing speculation to take the place of good old-fashioned reportage of the facts and just the facts was debated over the dry-fly case at Gaard's Sportsman.

Differing opinions over the First Amendment's original intent nearly closed down the bar at the country club. Sides were swiftly drawn between those who believed the First Amendment offered blanket protection to all journalists, regardless of their behavior, and those who argued that a journalist's freedom to hound a body to death in search of a better rating was not what this nation's forefathers had in mind when they had penned the Bill of Rights. The membership, usually constrained by impeccable manners, grew so loud and irate that the hostess was forced to ask them to take the argument outside. When they did just that, she looked around to discover only two people left in the room.

Overnight, the sleepy little town of Gravers Bend had turned into a hotbed of controversy.

* * *

I am saddened by Joe's refusal to come home but not particularly worried by it. I go about my daily business, conducting my life as usual. Eventually he will be back. He is just going through a little early onset midlife crisis. He will get over it sooner or later and come home where he belongs.

Another aspect of my life has begun to bother me a great deal, however, because nothing about it has gone at all the way I expected. I have invited Hayley to meet me for lunch, for coffee and once for a glass of wine at the country club. Not once has she been able to make it.

Dammit, for years now I have yearned for her return. I

envisioned long talks in which my dear friend confided all her troubles, prepared myself for the day I could lend a sympathetic ear and a bracing shoulder. After all, that is what friends with special bonds do. They extend comfort and keep their counsel when secrets are divulged.

Yet Hayley shows not the slightest inclination to talk about hers.

I cannot help but feel a teensy bit resentful. I know Hayley has always been extremely private, but for God's sake. Such reticence is unnecessary between good friends. And, truly, in the greater scheme of things it is just plain rude. I bet Hayley talks to her oh-so-precious *Kurstin* about her problems. The bitch.

No. I must not allow myself slip into ire. Anger is wrong and granting oneself permission to give in to it inexcusable. Once parameters of social behavior are breached, civilization is left with nothing but chaos, pure and simple. The proper thing to do, of course, is go talk to Hayley yet once again.

And this time I will leave my friend in no doubt that I am at her disposal, a willing receptacle for all the garbage that has accrued in my darling Hayley's life.

It is several hours later when I finally approach Hayley in Bluey's bar. "Hello, dear."

"Patsy!" She shuts off the water where she has been washing something off her hand and gives me a smile that warms my heart. "Well, hello, stranger," she says. "I was wondering when you would finally accompany your husband to our fair lounge." She wipes her hands and sets aside the towel. "We see Joe in here all the time, but we never see you. And after all the times I asked where you were, wouldn't you think the bum would have mentioned you are here with him tonight?" She shrugs. "Men. I will never understand them."

I swing around to search the depths of the bar. Joe is here? I locate him talking to some men at a table in the lee of the stage and shake my head. Not only here, but a frequent patron from the sounds of it. I am beginning to think I never knew Joe Beal at all.

"What can I get you, Patsy?"

"Hmm?" I swing my stool back around and blink at the woman across the bar. "Oh! I will have a Riesling." A heartbeat goes by before I recall my manners. "Please." Then I cannot help but glance over my shoulder again. On the bright side, he obviously has not told anyone he moved out of our house. That can only mean he plans to come back home. Probably any day now.

"We have a nice Hoodsport Johannesburg Riesling. Made right here in Washington. How does that sound?"

"Fine."

"One Riesling, coming up."

I watch Hayley stoop to open the refrigerator beneath the counter. My old friend pulls out a bottle, rises and draws the cork. She pours a glass of wine and reseats the bung. Passing me the goblet, she asks me if I want to run a tab.

I decline and pay, then just sit there a moment, staring into the pale depths of my wine. I had a definite strategy when I walked through the door. I had known precisely what I intended to say and how I wanted to proceed. But finding Joe in the bar and learning he comes here all the time pisses me off—no!—throws me off my game. Straightening my spine, I force myself to concentrate. "Um, I have been wanting to get together with you, Hayley, to have lunch together or something. Just the two of us."

"I know. I'm sorry about canceling our coffee date last week. Things have been so hectic, but that's no excuse. I should have set aside the time." Hayley smiles apologetically. "The problem is more about scheduling than anything. My hours are different than practically everyone else's."

I nod. "As a realtor, I know all about erratic hours. I do not work as late into the evening as you, of course. But my hours are not exactly nine to five, either." I pull my cell phone out of my purse and bring up my calendar. "Let's schedule something right now while it is fresh in our minds. We need a chance to sit down and have a real heart to heart."

Hayley took a large mental step back, then felt guilty. It was so typically Patsy to want to organize everything right down to the nth degree. But the fact that her lack of spontaneity drove Hayley a little crazy was *her* problem, not Patsy's. Besides, she felt bad about putting her old schoolmate off for as long as she had. They used to be good friends. If Pats was a little too intense these days in her desire to hear Hayley's every secret and be let in on her every confidence, well, she should be able to circumvent the neediness while still making her old friend feel included.

Somehow.

Lucy came up to the bar. "I need a pitcher of the Brewhouse Blonde, Hayley," she said, slapping down her tray and scooping her hair behind her ear with impatient fingers. She had gone natural this week, which for her meant basic black and blonde. No theme colors. Her nose ring was a discrete onyx stud, her pushup bra was utilitarian black to match her Doc Martens and long skirt. "The stuff's starting to *move*! You should have heard these yahoos when Bluey first introduced it. Then they tasted it and they can't get enough." She shrugged at the vagaries of the small town man, then snapped her fingers. "Oh, and one Sex on the Beach." She included Patsy with a wry grin. "Don'tcha just love that name?"

"Sex on the Beach?" Patsy echoed faintly.

"You would probably like it," Hayley said, smiling at her friend as she swiftly assembled the order. "It's vodka and peach schnapps with OJ and cranberry juice. Pretty yummy stuff." She set the drink she assembled almost in the same breath she had recited its ingredients on the barmaid's tray, then drew a fresh pitcher of beer and added it to the tray as well. "Here you go, Luce."

"Thanks." Lucy swept the tray off the bar and walked away.

Hayley wiped down her work space, then turned her attention back to her old school chum. "You know what I'd like, Patsy?" It had come to her while she was putting together Lucy's order. "I would really like you to show me how to use a compound bow."

I stare at her in surprise. "You would?"

"Yeah. I think it would be fun to take your bow and arrows out to the woods and set up a target. Not only could you show me how it works, but it would give us a chance to be alone and talk. I am so impressed you know how to use something like that, and I would love the opportunity to see how it's done."

I find myself blinking rapidly. It was not what I had planned. My intention was to take Hayley someplace elegant for lunch and lend a sympathetic ear while Hayley poured out all her troubles. I do not like it when my plans get changed. I do not—

Do you hear what I'm saying, Patsy? Joe's voice grouses in my mind. *I can't live in dread of upsetting your carefully structured life. I can't constantly fear that this will be the change I suggest that upsets all your rules and routines.*

I look at Hayley across the bar and recall what she said about being alone to talk. "Well...okay. I suppose we could do that."

"Excellent. When is a good day for you?"

Patsy flipped through her calendar. "How about Tuesday?"

"Tuesday it is. Two o'clock okay?"

"Yes. I will pick you up."

"It'll be fun. I'm looking forward to it."

Yes. I straighten my shoulders. *Yes.* It will be fun.

* * *

Jon-Michael showed up while the Friday night guest band was playing their last set. Sitting down at the end of the bar, he ordered a club soda, accepted it with a level look, then swiveled around with his back to the bar to watch the band.

Hayley cast surreptitious glances his way as she filled orders. She had been considering what she should do about him ever since she left him standing in the parking lot this afternoon. Face it, what he had said to her was tantamount to a threat: come to me or I will show up in your room, with or without your consent.

She didn't like being threatened.

She did like the idea of making love with him again. Liked it a lot. Of course, it sounded as if she would get that whether she went home with him or not, so perhaps he had not been threatening so much as promising.

No! Her spine stiffened. What kind of bullshit rationalization was that? She didn't care how good the sex was, he could not just blackmail her into doing what he wanted. And frankly, if she put her faith in Jon-Michael Olivet and his questionable protestations of love she was a fool looking to get exactly what she deserved. She had believed him when he had said those words years before.

Look where that had gotten her.

By the end of her shift, as she cashed out the till while Lucy and Marsha went through the close-down procedures, then got ready to go home, she was leaning toward taking a stand on the firm ground of her righteous indignation. The lights clicked off one by one around the room until the bar was the only island of illumination in a dark sea of tables and tipped up chairs.

Jon-Michael moved down the bar and sat across from her, silently watching her end-of-shift routine. He was still sitting with his elbow on the countertop and his head propped in his palm when she came back from depositing the evening's take in the safe in Bluey's office. She retrieved her purse off the shelf beneath the bar and glared at him.

He attempted to neither touch her nor turn on the charm. "Will you come home with me?" he asked in a quiet voice.

"And if I don't, Johnny? You plan to sneak into my bedroom?"

"Don't call me—" *Oh, Johnny. Please.* Jon-Michael cleared his throat. "On second thought, call me whatever your little heart desires. And yes, I do."

"Well, come on, then," she snapped, stalking to the door. "Why are we just standing here? Let's go, I wanna get this over with."

He swallowed a smile. For all her martyred air, he knew his Hayley. If she were truly opposed to the idea of going home with him, there was no way in hell he would ever get her to his place *or* himself within a hundred yards of her room at the old man's house. But he wasn't born yesterday. He kept his amusement to himself. "I'll bring the bike around to the back. Give me a minute, then come out the back door when you hear me rev it up. We'll leave the city yahoos in the dust."

Feeling more than a little deflated by her woefully inadequate willpower, Hayley bolstered her flagging ego by assuring herself she was going to use Jon-Michael unmercifully. She was not looking for the complication of messy emotions or demands of commitment. All she wanted was straightforward, good old-fashioned sex. He had shown her what she'd been missing and then some this afternoon, but it was just sex.

She was merely going back for more.

Jon-Michael did not make her wait for it, either. They had barely cleared the front entry of his loft following a fast ride through the quiet town when he turned, slammed the door closed and crowded her up against it. "I have been waiting for this all day," he said hoarsely and rocked his mouth over hers.

Like every other time he had come within kissing range, she was immediately drawn in, lost to time and place, her senses given over to the taste and textures of him. Hands fisted in his hair, she kissed him back, and before she was quite aware what was happening, he had her vest unbuttoned and had lifted her against the door at her back. She wrapped her legs around his waist.

"God," he murmured, kissing his way down her throat to the rapidly beating pulse in the hollow at its base, "I have never known another woman with skin so soft or lips so sweet."

"You don't have to romance me with sweet talk," she panted. His mouth encircled her nipple and drew hard, and her head thumped back against the closed portal. "Don't...need it."

Releasing that nipple, he kissed a path to its mate. "Ah now, that is where you're wrong. I didn't exactly give you moonlight and roses when you were seventeen, and I think if ever there was someone who deserves a little romance in her life, it is you." He tugged his target into his mouth and smiled up at her. "Besides," he said around her nipple, "that isn't sweet talk, Hayley, honey. It is the God's-honest truth."

Crap. He got to her; she couldn't deny it. Even so, she managed to give him a cool smile. "Didn't anyone ever teach you not to talk with your mouth full, Olivet?"

He laughed and went back to giving her breasts his full attention.

A while later, when her pants and undies had been stripped away and he was easing high inside her, he whispered, "Is this the reason you came home with me?"

Her arms clung tighter around his neck as he slowly withdrew and thrust, withdrew and thrust. "Yes."

He adjusted his grip on the underside of her thighs and

drove himself into her a little harder. The action elicited a corresponding sound embarrassingly close to a sob from deep in her throat and he eased out, then drove in once more—almost as if he wanted to hear it again. He repeated the action. And repeated it again. "I suppose you expect me to believe it's the only reason."

She was lost to the sensations his body was busy eliciting from hers. But she blinked, pulled her thoughts together and focused on him. "You oughtta. It is the only reason."

"Liar."

She thought about that later, satiated, boneless and plastered against him skin to skin, her face in the curve of his neck. *Liar*, he had said. She longed to deny it categorically but...could she?

She had been mindless with pleasure but holding herself back as if waiting for something. Then he had started that low-voiced *I love you, Hayley; love you, love you, love you,* and she had promptly soared off a sharp-edged precipice in a red-misted, orgasmic freefall.

Is that what she had really come here for—not just screamingly good sex but the words as well? Had she come for the vows of love and the feeling of being wanted more than she had ever been wanted in her life?

No, it couldn't be. She would not *allow* it to be.

"Don't think about it so hard," Jon-Michael advised in a low, soothing voice as she began to tense in his arms. He held her with an arm beneath her bottom, his free hand stroking from the small of her back to where her shoulders were braced against the door. "Just accept that it's good, Hayley. It is so good between us."

"God, yes," she agreed. She tightened her grip around his neck. "It's even better than my favorite Ranch Romance fantasy."

"Your what?"

"My...never mind. It's kind of hard to explain. I just never knew it could be like this."

"Neither did I." Slipping out of her, he straightened away from the door, then scooped her up and carried her around the glass brick wall into the living area. He laid her down on the couch and joined her, reaching to pull a chenille throw from the back of the sofa and snap it out over them. Tucking her head into the hollow beneath his collarbone, he wrapped his arms tightly around her. Then he grinned up at the ceiling. "Ya know, we really ought to try this in a bed sometime."

Jon-Michael felt her lips curl up in a smile against his chest and knew she was sliding into the sweet and mellow pliancy she got when she was sleepy. It was too soon, but even acknowledging that timing was everything and this likely wasn't even close to being the right time, he raised his head anyway and tucked his chin in to peer down into her face. "Hayley?"

"Hmmm?"

"I think you should move in here with me."

"Yeah, right," she agreed with lazy good humor.

"I'm not joking, darlin'. Now don't go getting all stiff on me," he commanded, tightening his arms around her when she did exactly that. "Just think about it for a minute. It's a good idea."

"It's a horrible idea!"

"It beats the hell out of going home alone every night to the old man's mansion. Does Kurstin even sleep there anymore?"

"Sometimes."

"Uh huh. And most nights she doesn't. You know and I know she is spending most of her nights with Holloway, and that's fine and dandy—I'm not saying it's not. Except sooner or later the carrion eaters are bound to figure out you're alone out there on the lake, and then where will you be?"

She pushed herself up to look at him. "Same place I have always been. On my own."

"That's my point, though, you don't need to be. Listen, I know Kurst would be there for you in a minute if you needed her—she's just caught up right now in her new relationship. But I am right here all night, every night. I can give you whatever you need: another presence in a dark house, protection, a buffer between you and the media. Hell, we can even live like brother and sister if that's what you want, although it seems to me that pretty much dicks up my one real selling point."

"Which is?"

"Sex on demand, darlin'. Think about it. I am yours to command, whenever, wherever you say, anyway you want it."

Hayley struggled to a sitting position, staring at him with such interest that her nakedness beneath the blanket slithering to pool around her hips apparently didn't register. He admired her breasts in the diffused light that came through the windows. "*Any* way?" she demanded.

"Sure." Her expression was so arrested that it was all he could do not to laugh. "Well, within reason."

"No, you did not say within reason. You said any way."

"And never let it be said Jon-Michael Olivet is not a man of his word. Any way you want it," he agreed and studied her intently. "Just what did you have in mind? You planning on tying me up? Whipping me?"

"I could *do* that?"

"Sure. I guess. If you really wanted to."

"Wow, that is so cool. Dennis was strictly a meat-and-potatoes kind of guy when it came to sex. I had a more adventurous streak but he never let me exercise it. There must be a million ways of doing it I never got to do."

"So, do we have a deal then?"

"Any time, any *way*, right?"

"Right. You agree to move in here and I agree to become your sex toy."

"Oh, man." She gave him a big, sleepy smile. "You so have yourself a deal."

Seriously, Prescott? Have you finally lost what little is left of your mind? For two days now she had been asking the same question, but it did not stop her from doing so yet again as she drove out to the Olivet's mansion Tuesday afternoon to meet Patsy. Sweet Merciful Mother Mary, what had she gotten herself into?

It was the damn sex-on-demand thing that sealed her fate. If that made her a total sucker, well, c'mon, her old sex life had been so mundane. Sex with Jon-Michael was anything but, so how was she supposed to say no to the opportunity for more? Then he had proposed putting her in the catbird seat. One offer to control the when, the where and the how of it, and she was a goner.

That part of her life was great, too. They had made love in places and positions she had only ever fantasized about. It was the other stuff she was having a difficult time getting a handle on.

"He's subversive," she had complained to Kurstin just yesterday. "How am I supposed to fight all his sneaky, underhanded tactics?"

"What does he do that's so underhanded?"

"He makes me laugh. He tells me I'm beautiful, that I have the softest skin in the world. He tells me he *loves* me!"

"The lowdown rat!"

"No, you don't understand, Kurstie. How am I supposed to stay aloof when he is spouting stuff like that all the time? It's not fair." She gave her friend a hard stare. "And do not think I don't know exactly what he is doing."

"Expressing himself, maybe?"

"Yeah, right," she scoffed and shook her head. "No, ma'am. He is setting me up for a fall...that's what he is doing."

"Oh, get a grip!" Kirsten stared her down. "For God's sake, Hayley, are you even listening to yourself? He loves you. You love him. Frankly, I don't see the problem."

"No, he *says* he loves me. Trust me on this, that is not

what he really means."

"But you love him, right? And that *is* the problem in a nutshell."

"No! Yes! Well, maybe. Someday."

"Okay, so perhaps you love him—we are not going out on a limb and committing ourselves here. But—and I am thinking this is the biggie—you have heard Jon-Michael say the words before and–" She whirled her hand encouragingly.

"And it all blew up in my face! That's what I'm waiting to happen now, for it to all blow up in my face."

"I am going to be a good, sensitive friend and say I empathize with your concern. Only, what if this time he is all grown up and a sober, responsible man who really does know how love is supposed to behave? What if he actually, truly means it?"

"Stop it, Kurstin. You're scaring me."

"Think about it, chickie."

She snorted now. Like she had been able to think about anything else. Because she wanted that. More than anything in the world, she wanted that.

And trying to convince herself she didn't was wearing thin. She could tell herself they had not spent enough time together as adults to really know each other any more. But she did know him, and not just the good. She knew the bad and the ugly as well. Plus, what had she said to someone not that long ago, that she counseled teenagers to get in touch with their own truths, to learn to never lie to themselves no matter how many lies they felt compelled to tell others to get through their days? It was sound advice.

But there was always a flip side, and God knew experience had kicked her in the teeth often enough to make her a realist. So how realistic was it to blindly believe Jon-Michael had changed so dramatically from the boy she had once known? Because she *had* been up close and personal with the bad and the ugly and, face it, he still seemed to have a problem sticking when the going got tough. And if there was an issue that needed resolving? Fuggidaboudit. Things had not gone the way he wanted in his family business, so he had turned his back on it and walked away. It was clear Olivet Manufacturing was his first love, but instead of fighting for his vision of what he believed the business could be, he was playing his sax in a blues bar.

She swore softly and it was with relief that she turned into the drive to the Olivet estate. Just for this one afternoon it would be a relief to put the problem aside– hell, to put *all* her problems aside—and concentrate on something else.

She was unlocking the kitchen door with the key Kurstin had given her when a woman with a remote mike and a man with a videocam on his shoulder rushed at her out of nowhere. Hayley nearly dropped the backpack containing the lunch she had packed as the mike was thrust in her face.

"Mrs. Prescott!" the woman said peremptorily. "How do you feel now that the execution is only a few short weeks away?"

Hayley gathered her wits about her. "This is private property," she said coldly, shoving the mike away. She turned the key in the lock and opened the door, then turned back to them. "Go away or I *will* summon the police."

"Tell us your feelings on—"

"I am not bluffing. If you are not gone by the time I close this door, I will call the sheriff and have you arrested for trespassing. I think you will find small town courts to be much less tolerant of this sort of harassment than the slap on the wrist you're accustomed to receiving in metropolitan areas." She stepped inside and slammed the door closed behind her. Leaning back against it, she fought to catch her breath as she her heartbeat thumped in her ears.

When she looked out the window they were gone, but the small measure of relaxation she had gained was lost. Damn them. Damn them all to hell. She sat at the breakfast bar and waited for Patsy to arrive.

She hoped it said something about her resiliency that she had managed to forget this stomach-lurching sensation of being ambushed. It was like having a cockroach unexpectedly scuttle out of the woodwork and run across your foot, and to her utter horror her first inclination was to call Jon-Michael.

She did not, of course. But it made her realize how big a buffer Jon-Michael's presence had been between her and the Fourth Estate since the hounds from hell hit town. Journalists never crowded into her personal space or stuck their microphones in her face when she was with him. She was not sure why, really. Much as she liked his build, he hardly possessed one of those huge, pumped-up bodies that intimidated by sheer bulk alone. There was something about him, though, that gave the reporters pause. Perhaps it was his aggressiveness. Or the fact that he was heir to the town's richest man. If an Olivet broke their cameras or stomped them to a pulp, they could not be certain it wouldn't simply be swept under the carpet in good old-fashioned small-town tradition.

Blowing out a frustrated breath, she buried her face in her hands. And here she had thought pretending she still lived on the Olivet estate would be her big excitement of the day. She didn't have the energy to wade through a mess of explanations to Patsy when she barely understood the adventuresome-sex-is-a-good-enough-excuse for moving in with Jon-Michael herself. So she had taken the easy way out and arranged to meet her old schoolmate here.

It seemed like a good idea at the time.

Hearing another car pull into the drive, Hayley climbed off the stool. Patsy was early, and for once her predictability was welcome.

Backpack in hand, she met her old schoolmate at the front door. "Hi." She stepped out onto the steps and pulled the door closed behind her. "Ready to go?"

"Uh, yeah, I guess." Patsy looked over her shoulder. "Hayley, there are journalists at the end of the drive."

"I figured as much. I ran them off the property, but I cannot do a thing about public domain."

"God, it was awful. They practically climbed on the hood of my car and yelled all sorts of personal questions."

"They can be a pain," Hayley agreed dryly, thinking, *Welcome to my world.* "That is why I thought we would take the rowboat and go over to Mavis Point, rather than drive. That sound okay to you?"

"Sure. I guess so."

"Good. I've got lunch." Hayley hefted the backpack. "Do you need help with the bow and arrow stuff?"

Patsy did not and soon they were arranging their gear in the bow of the rowboat and pushing off from the dock. Hayley rowed while her old high school friend sat on the aft seat and talked excitedly about her experience with the press.

All too soon, however, Patsy turned the force of her attention on how Hayley felt about the journalists' constant intrusion in her life. And the afternoon began to head south.

For God's sake. I would think Hayley might at least try to put herself out a little for an old friend. Is that truly so much to ask? After all, I am merely attempting to make her life easier.

"It is extremely unsettling, watching all these journalists run around Gravers Bend, turning everything upside down." I watch Hayley pull on the oars with even strokes. The boat shoots across Lake Meredith's glass-like surface, rapidly approaching Mavis Point. "Don't you find it so?"

"Yes." Hayley raises her gaze for a moment, her

expression indecipherable. "I do."

Thinking of the way the media is disturbing Graver's Bend's placid routines sets my stomach churning. And that is *before* I was personally exposed to how distressing they can be. "I wish they would leave, but I don't suppose that is going to happen." Draping my wrist over the transom of the wooden boat, I trail my fingertips in the cool water.

"No, it is definitely not going to happen," Hayley agrees.

I hate them, I think with sudden bitter passion. But I immediately bring myself up short. Hate is such an unproductive emotion, not to mention just plain wrong. I must not hate.

Small wakes stream out from my fingers and I concentrate on them, noting how pretty they are, how serene. I take several deep, calming breaths until I have myself under control again, then chat with deliberate aimlessness as I fill Hayley in on the gossip of people with whom we had both gone to school.

We reach the shore, and I help Hayley pull the boat above the waterline. Several times I attempt to reintroduce the journalists into the conversation, but somehow Hayley always manages to deflect the subject onto something else. She does it throughout our picnic lunch and continues to do so as I show her how to use the bow and arrow.

"They are everywhere I turn," I complain at one point.

Hayley merely says, "Hmm," and her smile is maddeningly noncommittal.

I refuse to be discouraged. "It must be particularly aggravating for you," I say determinedly, "since you are the reason they are here. Do they always hang out at Bluey's the way they did the other night?"

"Pretty much." Hayley nocks her arrow and takes a bead on the target I had pinned to the tree. The arrow wobbles in her grasp and barely clears the bow when she looses the draw string. "Damn. Show me again how you're supposed to balance the thing on this little doohickey."

I demonstrate the technique once more. Then I draw a deep breath, gird my loins and say with determined cheer, "I have just been struck by a brilliant idea."

There is an instant of dead silence and I narrow my eyes. Well, really. Hayley has not even bothered to glance in my direction. Would it kill her to demonstrate the tiniest bit of interest? I forged on despite the lukewarm reception to my opening volley. "I will be your new public relations liaison."

Hayley lowers the bow and turns to look at her. "Excuse me?"

"I will run interference between you and the media," I elaborate. The idea of dealing with all the outsiders responsible for disrupting my town's placid rhythms makes my stomach churn. At the same time, I know I can handle the responsibility brilliantly.

"No. Thank you."

"But Hayley..."

Without so much as a by-your-leave, Hayley raises the bow again and takes aim at the target. "No, Patsy," she says with calm finality. "I appreciate your offer, but please, just stay out of it. I have nothing to say to those people."

No, *let's hear your ideas, Patsy*, no *What a good and true friend you are, Patsy*. She doesn't even extend me the courtesy of giving the proposal a moment's consideration. Just a curt, *No, stay out of it*.

My admiration slips silently into something more rancorous.

Okay, that was not a resounding success. Hayley had hoped, when she suggested this outing, that she and Patsy would have a nice low-key hour or two, a chance to really get away and relax.

Well, she had enjoyed rowing the boat. And she had found learning a bit about the compound bow informative and her inept attempts to place arrows in the general vicinity of the target amusing. But Patsy seemed to have lost what little sense of humor she once possessed. There was an intensity about her now that was disturbingly close to repellent.

Pats had always lacked in the humor department. And God knew she had never been particularly spontaneous. But she had been a true friend in their senior year after Jon-Michael trashed her reputation. And once she had been sweet, which had always seemed miraculous all by itself, given the way her mother used to treat her.

Somewhere over the years the sweetness had faded. She had developed a sort of tunnel vision toward pursuing her objectives, and she was clearly oblivious to the fact that her methods trampled over other people's sensitivities. There were painful subjects Hayley simply did not care to discuss. Why could Patsy not accept the fact and move on to other topics of conversation?

Was that too damn much to ask?

Chapter 17

Kurstin walked up behind Ty and rubbed his shoulders. "What's bothering you?" she questioned softly. "You've been quiet all evening."

Oh, hey, what could possibly be the matter, he wondered sourly. Aside from the minor matter of the telephone call he'd received this afternoon, telling him to either produce or get his ass back to the newsroom if he wanted to have a job to come back to. He leaned into the hands kneading his neck. "Nothing."

Kurstin sighed. "Secrets," she said wryly. "I'm surrounded by people with secrets."

He tilted his head back to look up at her. "My day just turned out to be kind of frustrating," he said. "My muse deserted me, my characters refuse to speak. What can I say?"

He'd told Kurstin he was on a six-month sabbatical to write a book. "This is not exactly the stuff of earth shattering secrets." He bent his head forward again and growled a little when her fingers resumed their hypnotic massage. "Who do you know who's hoarding real ones?"

"Hayley."

"No fooling?" It took all his concentration not to tense up. "Huh. I would have thought her life was an open book, after all the publicity with her husband, the trials, the upcoming execution and all."

"It's the execution that has her all tied up in knots. She has such conflicted feelings about capital punishment."

Like a hound on the scent of an escapee, his every

journalistic instinct went on point. It was all he could do to say casually, "I would think she'd be for it."

"I know, right?" But then Kurstin explained Hayley's long-held stance on the death penalty and why it was tearing her apart her to still have strong leaning in that direction.

Ty stared down at the carpet beneath his feet as he listened. She had just handed him the story he'd come to Gravers Bend for. All tied up in silver ribbons. And...he didn't have the least desire to sing hosannas.

How dicked up was that?

* * *

Hayley followed Jon-Michael up to his bedroom in the early hours after the bar closed down and pulled a handful of scarves from her purse. She pointed to the bed. "Lie down."

"I'm beginning to think I've created a monster," he said as she straddled his chest to wrap strips of silk around his wrists. He watched as she then tied the bindings to the headboard, unsure if he cared for the look on her face. "Uh, Hayley, honey...about saying you could whip me if you wanted—?"

"No whips," Hayley tersely assured him.

"You have a bad day, sweetpea?"

"I really don't wanna discuss it right now, Jon-Michael." She gave the scarf a tug to test the strength of her knots.

"Oookay." He sucked in his stomach when she knelt beside him and bent forward, swinging her head from side to side in gentle sweeps that brushed her hair over his chest and down his abdomen. "It's not that I'm complaining about the sex, mind you," he said in a strained voice. "I mean, I hate to speak ill of the dead and all, but if you ask me your late husband had to be the worst kind of fool to try 'n curb your adventuresome streak. That's like having a concert pianist at your beck and call and only allowing her to play 'Chopsticks' on a Play Skool piano. But, Hayley, is this the only way we can communicate now?"

"Do you really care?" Her breath blew with humid warmth across the head of his cock, and lifting his head to watch it bob stiffly upright in direct response to the stimulation, Jon-Michael felt his lips twist in a wry smile.

"My dick doesn't seem to give a damn. But, yeah, I do care."

"Hmmm," was all she replied and then lowered her head to bestow a delicate lick.

"Wait," he panted. "Wait a sec. Let's talk about this."

"I don't feel like talking." She opened her mouth and sucked him inside.

Jon-Michael's hips came off the bed and his head pressed into the pillows, the need for conversation momentarily supplanted by need of another kind.

She eventually raised her head and knee-walked up the bed to settle herself astride him. Lowering herself until he was deep inside, she began to move. A breathless while later, they were both straining to hold back the inevitable.

"Untie me," he panted. "I want to hold you."

She didn't appear to hear him. "Saaay it," she moaned.

"Dammit, Hayley, untie me! Now!"

She moved harder on him. "Oh, please, Johnny, please. Say it." She reached for the scarves restraining him and fumbled to untie the knots. They had tightened with their movements. "Say it, say it, say it."

The knots came free.

His arms wrapped around her and he rolled them over. Digging his toes into the mattress, he surged into her. "I love you, Hayley. God! I love you. Come for me, baby. I love you so much."

She screamed his name and climaxed hard, locking her thighs around his waist and digging her nails into his back, triggering his own.

Breathing heavily, they collapsed in a tangle of arms and legs, bonded with sweat where their stomachs pressed and his chest flattened her breasts. Jon-Michael finger-combed her hair off her face and struggled to catch his breath. "You didn't put a condom on me," he panted.

Her breathing halted for a second, then slowly resumed. The infinitesimal shoulder movement she effected an instant later shifted her breasts against his chest. "Oh, well."

"*Oh, well*? What are the chances you could get pregnant?"

She thought about it for a moment. "Ninety-five percent nonexistent."

"Uh huh. Well, if it somehow happens anyhow, don't even think about getting rid of our baby."

She considered the autocratic order, considered as well her own strong feelings about the rights of a woman's body and men who thought they could dictate what a female could do with it. On the other hand, any potential child would be a result of her own negligence and neither did she believe in abortion as a substitute for birth control.

Not to mention the emotional impact of knowing any potential baby would be Jon-Michael's. She expelled a little sigh of capitulation. "Okay."

He stroked her hair, seemed to hesitate for a moment, but then said, "Hayley?"

"Um hmmm?"

"Why did you let me take your virginity that night by the lake?"

When she stiffened slightly in his arms, she felt him hold his breath as if waiting for her to shove him away.

Instead she relaxed again and released the breath she hadn't realized she had been holding. "Because I wanted to."

"Yeah, I figured that part out for myself. Why, though? Why then? I must have tried a dozen other times to get in your pants. You always laughed in my face."

She was quiet for several moments. Then she took another deep breath, expelled it and said quietly, "You were—I don't know—*real* that night." She shook her head, afraid she was not articulating what she had felt. "You were hurt because your dad hadn't come to your soccer game and for once in your life you were not trying to disguise your feelings with that Mr. Life of the Party facade you're so fond of hiding behind."

"So you thought you would reward me by letting me take your cherry?"

Shoving her head deep into the pillow, she gave him a level-eyed look. "You want to let me tell this my way, Jon-Michael, or would you prefer I play straight man to your sarcastic one-liners?"

"Sorry." A frown pulling his eyebrows together, he stared down at her. "At least tell me it wasn't a mercy fuck."

"Excuse me?"

"Dammit, Hayley, it's bad enough knowing I was drunk and probably careless. And you know perfectly well I'm still ashamed of the way I shot off my mouth afterwards. If you tell me you let me fuck you that night out of pity, I'm going to stick my tongue in the nearest electrical socket."

"Oh, for God's sake, Jon. You got me all hot and bothered. Pity had nothing to do with it."

"Good," he murmured and eased off her and onto the mattress, where he promptly reached to pull her into his arms. She rested her cheek against the swell of his pec and smoothed a hand down his torso, tracing the definition of his abs with her fingertips.

He crushed a fistful of her hair in his hand and she felt him raise his head to inhale its scent. "I remember that game, you know," he murmured. "I don't remember who we played, but I remember playing the best game of my life. I scored two goals."

"Yeah. I think that was what made it so hard for you to dissemble that night. You played one *hell* of a game and it just wasn't enough that Kurstie and I were there to cheer you on. You wanted your dad to see, too."

"If I ever have kids, I will be different than him," Jon-Michael said with low-voiced vehemence.

She pressed herself closer. "Yes, you will. I don't doubt for a minute you'll be a dedicated, attentive father." And it hurt to think about, because she couldn't picture who the mother of his children would be. She didn't visualize it being herself—not unless her fertility this morning hit a homer from the five percent probability base. There was just too much water over that bridge. Yet the idea it might be someone else was surprisingly painful to contemplate.

"So we talked?" he prompted.

"Yes. We talked a lot. Kurstin pointed out a while back you and I used to do that quite a bit, but with all the shit that happened following your share with the team, I'd forgotten. Anyhow, after the game you, your sister and I took a blanket into the woods. We laid there and watched the wind in the trees, and we talked. Both Kurstie and I tried to get you to stop drinking but you had a pint of Black Velvet you were determined to kill off. Eventually Kurstin left to find the kegger going on at the lake, but you and I stayed. We talked some more, then you kissed me, and one thing led to another. The rest, as they say, is history."

"When did I tell you I loved you?"

"After. You were sort of euphoric about what we had done and quite insistent I was not your average, every day roll in the hay."

"See? Even loaded I had extraordinary discernment. I obviously knew a good thing when it bopped me on the head. Did I hurt you? Physically, I mean?"

"Not really. Well, a little." One of her shoulders twitched. "No more than it would have hurt with any one else, I daresay."

He combed his fingers through her hair, holding it off

her face. He stared down at her. "Did you tell me you loved me back?"

For the first time she displayed a measure of discomfort. She stirred restlessly, pushing away from him. "I have to get up."

"Why? Where you gonna go? You live here now, remember?"

She said the first thing she figured Jon-Michael could not debate. "I have to pee."

It worked like a champ.

But he was waiting for her when she got back. Standing outside the bathroom door, he handed her a lightweight kimono when she walked out. He had donned his boxer-briefs. "So, did you?"

"Did I what?" She tied the robe and slid her hand along her nape to lift her hair from under the collar.

"Did you tell me you loved me back that night?"

Hayley simply looked at him for a moment. Then she sighed and nodded. "Yes. Yes, I did, all right?"

He reached for her but she circumvented the move by placing her palm flat against his chest. "But, Jon-Michael?" she said with soft-voiced finality. "I was wrong."

***

What the hell happened? Ty wondered. It was supposed to be so simple. Get in, get next to Kurstin, get the story, get out. Hit and run; it had been his MO his entire life and he had never given a good goddamn who got hurt in the process. Bottom line, he would do whatever was necessary to get the goods to move him that next beckoning rung up the ladder. Because he might have begun his life on the bottom.

But he had every intention of ending up on top.

So why hesitate now?

Ty sat in his deserted living room, staring at the telephone, willing himself to pick it up and make his move. He had what he had come for: he was in sole possession of one of the year's hottest stories. He should be burning up the lines getting it to his editor, because it was not a done deal until it was printed.

Hell, it wasn't a done deal until the paper with his byline hit the streets and went live online. He could be scooped right up to the instant it released. And before this baby was in the readers' hands, he had places to go, people to interview.

Bridges to burn.

That was the kicker. Because what about Kurstin, left on the other side when he burned that particular bridge to the ground? Ty blew out a gusty breath and shoved his hands through his hair, grinding the heels of his hands against his headache in an attempt to prevent it from pounding right through his forehead. He rested his head against the back of the couch and stared up at the ceiling. As if *that* held the answers.

What about Kurstin? It was the sixty-four-thousand-dollar question.

He'd never expected what he had with her. Women were for use. Recreation. They weren't for getting under your skin like a rash that can't be scratched. They sure as hell weren't for...ever.

If he ran with this story, he was going to lose her. That was a simple truth. If he didn't run with it, he would be flushing his entire career down the crapper. And what the hell would he have to offer her then?

Zip, brother, nada. He would be just one more loser in a world already overcrowded with the species.

His mouth twisted bitterly. Hell, he could visualize the whole thing now. He could see himself, the coal miner's spawn, coming to call, cap in hand, on the oh, so elegant blonde daughter of Gravers Bend's richest man. The chitchat over brandy played through his head. *What do you do for a living, young man?*

I'm unemployed at the moment.

Do you have any prospects?

Not really, sir. At least, none currently.

Her daddy would probably run his West Virginian ass out of town on a rail.

When it came right down to it he had two choices, only one of which was viable. The other was a fucking pipe dream that had been sweet while it lasted.

Ty reached for the phone.

***

Blinking against the glare of the tungsten lights blinding her the following evening, Hayley thought dully that the speed with which her life could change between one moment and the next should no longer have the power to catch her by surprise.

Yet it never failed to do so.

The bar was dim and mellow two minutes ago. She had been filling a desultory trickle of orders and listening to the band. Watching Jon-Michael.

Then the front door banged open and reporters and camera people poured through with their lights and their microphones, yelling questions at her that drowned out the Muddy Waters cover Ragged Edge was performing.

At first the words themselves were incomprehensible. All she heard was a babble of voices, chaos coming not only from the journalists with their lights and mics and avid expressions, but from patrons voicing their confusion as they looked on. Then little by little the meaning of the shouted questions sank in.

And her heart began to pound.

"Hayley!" They surged nearer, squeezing customers out of the way until only the width of the bar stood between her and their ravening curiosity. "Is it true you strongly oppose the death penalty? How does it feel to know you could be directly responsible for sending a man to his death? Hayley! Look over here! What is your opinion of capital punishment?"

Oh God, Oh God. The pitcher she was filling hit the counter with a thud, and the beer tap snapped back as her fingers went lax. Her vision grew white and a harsh buzzing sounded in her ears, as if she had suddenly stepped into a swarm of angry bees.

Only vaguely aware of someone issuing terse threats of bodily harm, she registered without real interest the agitation of a crowd being jostled. The journalists directly in front of her were shoved roughly aside and Jon-Michael appeared.

"Take a deep breath," he ordered the minute she focused on him. With a hard elbow to the ribs, he fended off the reporter jockeying for position next to him. "Back off!"

Vaulting over the bar, he wrapped his long-fingered hand around the base of her skull and pressed. "Head between your knees, darlin'." He pushed it there himself when she did not immediately comply. "Dammit, Hayley, breathe!"

She sucked in air and the buzzing faded from her ears and color slowly reemerged in her vision. She tried to order her thoughts.

Jon-Michael's intervention had momentarily diverted the journalists. But they were sharks whipped to a feeding frenzy and she was the hemorrhaging chum. Hayley didn't fool herself his presence would be enough to divert them for long. Not this time.

Is it true you are strongly opposed to the death penalty? She felt naked, exposed, and she remained seated on the floor behind the bar, her forehead resting on her kneecaps. Logically, she understood her violent, gut-felt opposition to the death penalty was not of monumental import. At least not in a sane world.

But this was the world of New Age media, where a senator from the other side of the country traveled all this way to confer with the victim's wife about the same man's execution. Where a woman's beliefs—in lurid juxtaposition to the testimony responsible for convicting a killer—would be reduced to a thirty second sound bite and accorded the same sensationalism one might expect had she sold national security-sensitive secrets.

Hayley knew exactly how it would work. The journalists would examine and reexamine her convictions on the five o'clock, six o'clock and eleven o'clock news. Newpapers would do likewise, if not as often, in more depth. Until not a single nuance escaped their combined scrutiny.

She was so damn tired of her every thought being afforded its own notoriety. And emotionally, this public airing of privately held views felt like the worst sort of violation.

How on earth did they even *know* this?

She was aware of Bluey emerging from his office, demanding to know what the hell was going on. The babble of voices increased.

"I've told you folks before not to bring it in here," he rumbled in his deep, bad-tempered, cigarette-raspy voice. "Now, get out or I will call the sheriff."

"Would that be Sheriff Brutus, Mr. Moser?" one of the journalists demanded snidely and several snickered. They had obviously learned Bluey had snowed them the last time he'd wanted to rid himself of their presence.

"No, son, that would be Sheriff Benson," Bluey snarled right back. "And it's a funny thing about our Paulette: she is a real stickler for the law. For instance, she upholds my right to deny service to anyone I deem a disruptive influence in my establishment." The false jocularity in Bluey's voice dropped away. "Now take it away from my property, or be arrested for trespassing," he said flatly. "Your choice."

The journalists grumbled, but they went. Hayley knew the reprieve was temporary at best, but at this point she was grateful for whatever she could get. She had to pull herself together. She held up her hand for Jon-Michael to pull her to her feet and immediately turned to her employer. "I am so sorry, Bluey. I know you didn't anticipate anything like this when you hired me. Do you want my resignation?"

"Don't be an ass, girl," he snapped and went back into his office.

"How did they figure it out?" Dazed, she turned to look up at Jon-Michael. "How the *hell* did they figure it out?" She felt raw and bruised and thought she had surely hit a personal low point.

Mercifully clueless how much lower it could get.

Fighting her way through the gamut of reporters outside the bar at closing time was like wading upstream through a river of molasses. She felt surrounded by an omnipresent malevolence determined to attach itself to her. To feed on and suck out every ounce of energy she had left.

Which was pitifully little.

Jon-Michael shoved and pushed, trying to clear a path for the two of them to his Harley. But for every journalist he displaced, two more immediately filled the void, each and every one of which was loud and intrusive, buffeting her with the press of their bodies and their glaring lights and cameras, demanding answers to their questions.

She was shaking by the time the bike roared to life. Jon-Michael gave the throttle some gas and wheeled the Harley out of its slot. She buried her face against his damp back and clung to his waist as he swore and shoved encroaching reporters away with his feet, ruthlessly keeping the bike moving forward, daring all comers to stand in its path.

When they reached the alley behind his loft, he helped her off the bike and held her by the elbow for a moment to steady her until the strength returned to her knees. "Come on," he said gruffly. "We need to get inside. I doubt the vultures are far behind."

Her head snapped up. "You think they know where we are?" she asked in a panic.

"Do you doubt it?"

"Oh, God. It never occurred to me. They haven't staked out your place before."

"I don't pretend to understand it. I just know there are damn few secrets in a town this size and odds are decent by now someone's discovered you're living with me. Once they have that, finding my place is probably child play." He pushed the bike into the hallway and rocked it back on its stand.

"Of course." She followed him inside, then checked and rechecked the door she had closed behind them to make sure it was locked. "I'm naive not to have thought of it myself."

He looked up at her from where he crouched next to the bike. "No reason you should. I don't know why they never bothered us here before. Dad's got clout in this town. Maybe they think I wield similar power." His shoulders moved in a negligent shrug. "Whatever their reason for leaving us alone, all bets are clearly off. Something set them off and it's a whole lot stronger than fear of retaliation by the so-called heir to the Olivet fortune could ever be. If that's even what gave us breathing room in the first place."

He watched small tremors wrack her slender frame and surged to his feet, frustrated by the entire damn situation. He wanted to put his fist through the nearest wall and roar obscenities. "Come on," he said gently instead, wrapping an arm around her shoulders and hugging her to his side. "Let's get you upstairs."

They reached the second floor a moment later and he opened the freight doors on the elevator. Stepping into the hallway, the first thing they saw was Kurstin sitting with her knees drawn up to her chest on the floor outside Jon-Michael's door. She struggled to her feet.

"You look nearly as stressed out as Hayley," Jon-Michael greeted her. "You've heard the news, I take it." Releasing Hayley long enough to unlock his door, he ushered both women inside. His eyes narrowed on his sister. "How the hell did you get in here, anyhow?" If there was a gap in the warehouse's security, he needed to know so he could plug it before the vultures descended en mass.

Kurstin cleared her throat twice before she said, huskily, "Your neighbor recognized me and let me in."

Hayley left Jon-Michael's side and crossed over to his sister. She felt shell-shocked and in need of the comfort of her oldest friend's embrace. Wrapping her arms around Kurstin, she bowed her forehead into the curve of her neck. "God, I am so glad you're here. Thanks for coming." Another tremor shook her. "I don't understand how they found out, Kurstie."

Kurstin, who had stood stiffly within her embrace, pulled away. She pulled her iPad from her purse and walked over to perch on the arm of an overstuffed chair. She turned on the tablet and brought up a page. Standing, she shoved the iPad into Hayley's hands.

Then took a step back.

Hayley was aware of Jon-Michael coming up behind her as she stared blankly at the headline for an online newspaper. It screamed to the world a pithy version of her dueling views on the death penalty. She grew increasingly cold as she read the article.

It was as if someone had climbed into her head. Climbed in and scraped down to the bottom of her brain to mine her barely-acknowledged-to-herself thoughts. The article exposed her inability to reconcile her long-held belief that the death penalty was wrong with her current ping-ponging between being sorry she was the one whose testimony was responsible for Wilson being on death row and not being sorry at all.

Jon-Michael swore with soft-voiced viciousness just as

she glanced at the byline photo.

"But, that's Ty," she said numbly. "What is he—"

"Apparently he works for a newspaper in Rhode Island and has all along," Kurstin replied in a monotone. "He lied, Hayley. About everything. All the stations have been talking about his exclusive."

"Exclusive?" Hayley echoed in confusion. "My life is his *exclusive*?" She went back to the article. Ty actually presented her story with a gentle, sympathetic touch, but still she bled a little harder with each word she read. "How does he *know* all these things?" She felt as if he had reached inside her soul and exposed her innermost feelings.

Which would have been awful enough.

But he then thrust it forward with bloody hands as if it were so many entrails offered up to the carnivorous masses. Her pain was lion-and-the-gladiator style entertainment. Glancing over at her best friend, she saw that Kurstin's face was chalky.

And she saw the guilt written there.

No. Hayley's lips formed the word but no sound emerged from her throat, which felt lacerated and raw, as if she had swallowed a rusty razor.

"I didn't know I was talking to a journalist, Hayley," Kurstin said in a voice that begged understanding.

No! Hayley kept trying to swallow, but her throat felt pulpy, closed, destroyed by the dull-edged blade of betrayal. How could Kurstin have done this to her? Oh, God, how could she have *done* this?

"I thought I was talking to the man I was falling in love with, the man who loved me." To speak aloud of Ty's betrayal sent needles of pain stabbing along Kurstin's nerve endings, but she swallowed hard and forged past them in an attempt to make Hayley understand. "I didn't even set out to do it. I said the word 'secrets' and he said he didn't have secrets, who did? And somehow it just...came out." She extended a beseeching hand. "Hayley, please…"

"*No!*" Hayley twisted sideways, stepping back before Kurstin's hand made contact. She truly feared the touch would eat like acid through her flesh to burn a destructive path to the bone. "No, don't touch me."

She could not stop staring in horror at her best friend, the one person in the world she had believed she could count on until the end of time. Her eyes shut with the pain, but she immediately forced them open again. She parted her lips to speak, but no words emerged.

So she simply turned away in silence and forced her weary muscles to carry her up the stairs to Jon-Michael's bedroom.

CHAPTER 18

Ty was packing to leave when the phone rang. Even as he rose to answer it, he cursed himself for hoping it was Kurstin.

He knew it wouldn't be. She had too much style to give him the time of day, especially after the way he handled the termination of their relationship.

He hadn't had the balls to tell her face to face he had lied to her, used her. He sure as hell hadn't attempted any sort of explanation to try to make her understand why. Taking the coward's way out, unable to face having to see the betrayal on her face, he had allowed her to find out for herself. For that alone, he knew she would never forgive him.

He'd had a shot at a once-in-a-lifetime relationship and hadn't tumbled to the fucked up choice he'd made until it was too late to do him any good. But life went on, right? The decision had been made and couldn't be changed. He would just have to learn to live with it.

Snatching up the phone, he snarled a hello. The caller turned out to be a head hunter from the New York Times, confirming their appointment in New York Monday afternoon. Hanging up moments later, Ty stood at the window and assured himself this made up for everything.

Hell, yeah. He was on his way. The upcoming interview would be the first vital step he had been waiting to take for*ever*. Straight into the big-time. Ty Holloway, son of a dirt-poor miner, was mere days away from reaching the fast track and the realization of all his dreams. Rubbing his chest over the hollow spot in his heart, he stared moodily out at the green.

Life did not get any fucking better than this.

***

I listen to my co-workers talk about the newest bit of media hype surrounding Hayley Prescott. *See,* I think as I methodically work my way through the paperwork on my desk. *If you had listened to me, you would not be in this situation. But, no. You had to put your faith in your fucking precious Kurstin. Look where* that *got you.*

Well, never send a girl to do a woman's work, I always say. *I* will take care of this mess, tidy up all the sordid loose ends, just the way Hayley should have trusted me to do in the first place. I bet she is damn sorry now she did not.

The moment the office finally empties for the day, I reach for my cell phone and make a call. Tapping a quick little rhythm on the desk top with the eraser end of my pencil, I listen to the phone ring on the other end of the line. When it's picked up on the other end, I toss the pencil aside and straighten my posture.

"Hello," I say with brisk efficiency. "This is Patsy Beal. You and I need to talk."

Jon-Michael stood in the doorway staring down at his sister. "I'm sorry, Kurst," he said and smoothed his thumb and index finger down the creases on either side of his mouth, feeling helpless. "She refuses to talk to you and I just can't get her to budge."

There were shadows beneath Kurstin's eyes as she looked back up at him. Her face was haggard and her expression haunted but she didn't utter a single word of protest.

She simply turned and walked away.

Ty picked his way carefully through the woods. As dumbass places for a meet went, this one ranked right up there with the dumbest. But when he'd objected and suggested the cafe was a more reasonable alternative, Patsy Beal had simply laughed incredulously.

"If you think I am going to be seen anywhere in Gravers Bend with you, my friend, you are out of your mind," she had replied coolly. "You, sir, are persona non grata around here, and I am not about to have my name linked to yours."

"So why the hell you wanna meet me at all?" he had demanded churlishly. "I thought you were Prescott's good and great friend."

"I am more of a friend than you can possibly imagine," she'd retorted coolly. "And as it happens, I know the complete story, not just the portion you weaseled out of Kurstin." She had fallen into silence for a moment, before adding flatly, "It will play well above the fold, Holloway, but the choice is yours. Take it or leave it. It makes no difference to me."

So, he had taken it. Why the hell not? It wasn't as if he had anything left to lose at this point.

And maybe it would prove to be that one perfect column to add the final luster to his resume.

Jon-Michael climbed the stairs to the loft. This really wasn't a good idea and he knew it. What he ought to do was remove himself for a while, because he was upset and not feeling a hundred percent sympathetic.

He found Hayley in the bentwood rocker, using her toes to rock herself, her arms wrapped around her middle. She hadn't bothered to dress in two days and was still wearing one of his T-shirts, wrinkled now and sporting a stain by the hem where she had sloshed her tea. He was losing patience with her apathy. It was unlike her to simply give up. When things went wrong for the Hayley he knew, she came out fighting.

Every damn time.

She looked at him with haunted eyes. "Is she gone?"

"Yeah. She's gone." Jon-Michael went to the dresser and picked up his wallet. He stuffed it in his back pocket and rummaged around for his keys. Locating them, he turned and watched her rock back and forth, back and forth, staring off into space. "Listen," he said gently, "I know you're feeling betrayed in the worst way. And Kurstie messed up big-time, no doubt about it. But it wasn't deliberate, darlin', and she's been hurt by it too. When are you going to let her off the hook?"

Hayley tensed all over and the rocking came to an abrupt halt. "Excuse me?" She slowly turned her head to regard him with dull eyes. She hugged herself harder. "She threw me to the dogs and you're *defending* her?"

"I'm her brother, dammit! And you of all people should know this wasn't a result she anticipated when she talked to Holloway. Not in a million years would Kurstin hurt you this way. And while you haven't bothered looking at her since you learned what happened, I've seen what knowing what she triggered is doing to her."

He scraped his hair off his forehead with both hands and stared down at her in bafflement. "I don't get it, Hayley. Time and again, you have managed to forgive the unforgivable. Why are you being so implacable now?"

"Maybe I am sick to death of you Olivets turning my life into a goldfish bowl. I don't want to live center-stage any more."

"How many times do I have to apologize for what I did more than a dozen years ago? And let me remind you, petunia, all those journalists came to town without Kurstin's help."

"Right. She only made it worth their while."

Jon-Michael saw the spark of temper flickering in her eyes and tried to be encouraged. Anger beat hell out of her god-awful lethargy. He wanted to haul her into his arms and hold her safe. Another part of him wanted to shake her for her refusal to cut his sister any slack. He did neither. Instead, he swore under his breath and took a large step back.

He tried to distance himself not only physically but emotionally. "Listen, I've gotta get out of here before I say something I regret."

"Fine," she said flatly. "Run away. You are good at—"

He was suddenly there, with hard hands on her shoulders, pushing her back and holding her chair in the far rocked-back position while thrusting his face close to hers. "Don't. Say it," he warned through gritted teeth. "*I'm* not the one in this relationship who keeps dancing away from the truth. You can't even get off anymore unless I tell you I love you, but I have yet to hear those words in return."

Seeing the rage, the fear, that flashed in her eyes, he inhaled a deep breath and slowly expelled it. "I'm sorry. I shouldn't have said that. Dammit, I didn't want to let this degenerate into the two of us saying things we don't really mean." He let her go and straightened, watching the set of her pointed little chin as she stubbornly refused to curb the furious rocking, which his release of the chair set in motion. He walked away, but paused at the top of the stairs.

"Please," he urged quietly, looking across the room at her and hoping like hell that if she would not return his gaze she would at least hear him with more than just her flayed emotions. "Try to look past your pain at this. Don't throw away a lifelong friendship because of one mistake. Be a better friend than that."

He was downstairs with the front door open when he stopped to stare at his office space. *Ah, hell.*

Slowly, reluctantly, he closed the door again and walked back to the space. He flipped through the old-fashioned rolodex he kept his little-used phone numbers in until he came to the one he sought. *If I want her to do something painfully difficult, I guess I better pony up the same.*

He pulled his cell phone out of his pocket and thumbed in the number.

"Mildred?" he said a moment later. "When is the next board meeting? Tomorrow?" He wrote a notation on his calendar, assuring himself it wasn't too soon. What the hell. Might as well get it over with. "Pencil me in, will you? I'm ready to make my presentation."

I had prepared for every eventuality with my usual attention to detail. Until Ty Holloway actually walked into the small clearing not far from the train trestle that crossed Big Bear Gap, however, I had not been entirely convinced I would be able to carry out my plan.

I do not look around at him, keeping my concentration focused on my bow's sight and the target. Still, I am fully aware of him standing at the clearing's edge, jiggling the change in his pockets and shifting his weight from one foot to the other. I let the arrow fly, then frown when it buries itself in the target slightly above the bulls-eye. I nock another arrow, certain I can do better. Even with these cheap-ass store-bought wooden ones.

Ty's patience with my slow, deliberate movements lasts maybe ten seconds beyond that. "Did you call me all the way out here to watch archery practice or do you have something you actually want to tell me?" he finally demands.

"Have a seat, Ty." I indicate a fallen log to my right.

He blows out a bad-tempered sigh but does as directed.

"Hayley likes archery practice," I inform him, sparing him a brief glance.

"Yeah? Well, hey. That certainly oughtta wow 'em on the five o'clock news."

I fire off another arrow but am unhappy to see it, too, go high. *Damn.* I am still letting the bow pull up when I release the arrow. Or maybe it is the cheap wood target arrows themselves. I only bought them because they are generic, with none of the identifying characteristics of arrows I fletch myself. Reaching into my quiver, I pull out another and nock it again. Finally, I look over at Ty. "Does that type of sarcasm pass for wit where you come from?" I inquire mildly. "Because I have to tell you it does not play all that well here." I shrug. "Then again, perhaps Kurstin enjoyed it."

His expression closes. "I am not discussing Kurstin with you."

I arch a brow. "No? Given the way you used, then dumped her, I did not realize you harbored soft feelings for her. But forgive me if I am mistaken. Love is undoubtedly treated as differently back east as humor is."

He shoots me a thunderous glare, but I turn my attention back to the target. "Rumor has it she is crushed. Hayley will not have anything to do with her and Kurstin is trailing around town looking like a whipped puppy." I had rather enjoyed that when I saw her on the street yesterday. Served her right for betraying Hayley the way she did.

"I suggest you tell me whatever the hell it is you called me out here for," Ty says through gritted teeth. "Otherwise I'm out of here. I've still got some packing to do."

"Leaving town?"

"Yes."

"And going where?"

"New York. I have a job interview at the NYT."

"Why, how nice for you. And you only had to destroy two women to get it, too."

"That's it." He rises to his feet but then freezes when I swing to face him, my steel-tipped arrow pointing straight at his heart. "Jesus. Put that down."

"I do not care you messed up Kurstin's life," I say in a conversational tone. "Serves her right for breaking Hayley's confidence." Then my voice goes hard. "You made a huge mistake, however, when you went public with Hayley's private pain. Yes, she has inconsistent feelings when it comes to the death penalty. But you should not have made them public, Ty. She *never* wanted to talk about her conflicted feelings over capital punishment, but you went and told the world."

"And what bothers you most, Patsy? That I aired her conflict—or that she didn't confide it to you?"

My bow dips slightly. "What?"

"She never talked to you about them, either, did she? What happened, did you learn her feelings right along with everyone else who read the news?"

"Do not be ridiculous." Okay, that sounds defensive and I hurry to add, "Of course not."

He knows I am lying. "Kurstin is her best friend and Hayley didn't want to tell *her,* but Jon-Michael dragged it out of her. I don't think she told you at all."

"In a pig's eye she would tell Jon-Michael anything," I scoff. For a second there he had me going. Clearly, however, it was just a ploy to distract me.

"Why wouldn't she?" Ty looks at me as if I am a simpleton and my fingers tighten on the bow. *Stupid, unnatural girl*, Mother's voice whispers.

Yet it is Ty's voice that says, "They have been living together ever since the first reporters blew into town."

"Liar!" Rage at the very idea fills me and it is all I can do to stand still. Look calm.

I do not think I am doing a great job of it because he raises his hands in a gesture of mollification. "Yeah, yeah, okay. You are absolutely right." The jerk takes a step back, but his calves bump against the log he has been sitting on, bringing him up short. "Hey, I'm just blowing smoke." But his expression is pitying.

He *pities* me.

He probably thinks I'm *stupid*.

I release the line, letting the arrow fly.

For an action so fast, so explosive and violent, it is conducted with surprising quietness. The arrow strikes him, its velocity lifting him off his feet. Then his heels smack against the log behind him and he tumbles over onto his back. Breathing heavily, heart thundering, I creep up to the fallen log and peer over.

He has fallen almost squarely into the tarp-lined shallow depression I dug with the little camp shovel I found in the garage. Looking down at him I whimper a little.

It is not at all like killing a deer. There is very little blood, which is good since it means I hit him squarely in the heart as I had intended. I lean over, grip the arrow just above his chest and yank it out.

Now there is blood and I look around until I see a patch of moss. I gather up a handful and press it against the wound to stop the flow. His heart is no longer pumping and he is lying on his back, so what I disturbed removing the arrow is bound to be all there is. Gravity will take care of it.

Still, it is imperative fresh blood be kept to a minimum. The last thing I need is to attract wild animals before I can get back to dig a deeper grave. Then, flipping the edge of the tarp over him so I do not have to look at my handiwork, I squat on my heels and tug, dragging him the couple essential inches to bring him fully into the depression. "Oh my God. *Oh* my God," I croon and grab for the shovel.

Moments later his body is covered and I have gathered up armfuls of needles and leaves to scatter over the raw mound. I am sweaty and disheveled when I finally straighten and I slap at the bits of leaves and needles clinging to my hands, my clothing, my arms and legs.

After climbing back over the log I pry the target from the tree and stuff it into my backpack. Then I pull out the canteen and dribble water over my fingers. I scrub the dirt free of my hands and scrape it from beneath my immaculate manicure, pouring more water over each hand to rinse away the mess. I wet a handkerchief and scrub at the spots that dot my arms, my legs. Then I carefully rinse the shovel and pack it away. I pick up the backpack and swing it onto my back, retrieve my bow and quiver of arrows, then take another look around the clearing. My breathing is rapid and jerky and I am trembling like an aspen in a high wind.

OhGod, ohGod, what have I done? I feel so—Oh, God, I feel so...

Powerful.

In command of the situation.

I draw myself erect and my breathing evens out. I run a final organized, assessing gaze over the clearing to make sure I have left nothing behind.

I killed a man today. Me, the woman who abhors socially incorrect behavior, *killed* a man. And, oh, God help me.

I liked it.

***

Hayley sat and simmered in the rocking chair long after Jon-Michael left. How dare he berate her for feeling betrayed by her ex-best-friend's failure to keep her secrets. "Don't hold it against her, Hayley," she mimicked bitterly. "She is hurting, too, Hayley."

Blood certainly was thicker than water.

Fine. She did not give a great big rip. Let him defend his darling sister, attack *her,* then walk away. Talk about typical. Once again Hayley Granger Prescott was left to face her screwed up life all on her own. Jon-Michael didn't stick around when the going got rough.

Like *that* was a big surprise. She'd known going in this relationship was based on one thing and one thing only. When it came to the bottom line it was about the sex. Good sex, *great* sex even, but when all was said and done, theirs was merely a physical connection.

I am not the one in this relationship who has been dancing around the truth.

Okay, the past two nights their physical connection had been nonexistent. They hadn't made love. Jon-Michael had simply wrapped her in his arms and held her. He'd called Bluey and told him she couldn't come in when she had shown no inclination to get dressed and face the outside world. And the only time he'd left her side was to go to work himself. Even then he had come straight back home again.

Yeah, well, big deal. He was probably softening her up for the big pitch about poor, pitiful Kurstin. Kurstin, who had always been Hayley's one reliable haven when she desperately needed her. Kurstin who had ripped Hayley's heart out and handed it to her sleazy, lowlife boyfriend to feed to the wolves. Her sleazy, lowlife boyfriend who—

Ripped Kurstie's heart out, too.

She caught sight of herself in the mirror across the room as she slowly climbed to her feet. "Good God."

She studied the reflection of her dull skin, looked down at her wrinkled shirt. She was a mess. Running a hand through her stringy hair, she crossed to the phone to call Bluey.

Then she went to take a shower.

Kurstin sat on the dock and stared blindly out at the lake. The sun was hot on her shoulders but she felt frozen inside. Thighs hugged to her chest, her arms wrapped around her shins, she rocked in silent misery.

She had messed up in the worst way and was afraid she would never be allowed to atone for her abysmal lack of judgment. How had everything fallen apart so damn fast? One minute she'd it all. Then the next...*poof!* Everything was gone.

She'd fallen for Ty like Lucifer from heaven—and had been exposed for the dumb shit she was before the entire town. He'd left her with nothing: no pride, no faith in her own judgment and certainly no love. The public nature of her humiliation hurt; she didn't deny it. It was nothing, however, next to the very real fear haunting her every waking moment.

Since her mom's death, only her brother and Hayley had loved her unconditionally. It was their good opinion she valued. She knew Jon-Michael already forgave her. But what if Hayley wouldn't? If she couldn't?

What if she left town and never talked to her again?

Seriously? She infused a touch of steel back in her spine. *If your guilt doesn't kill you first, your melodramatic, overwrought what-ifs probably will.*

But if Hayley *didn't* forgive her, if she did pack up and leave rather than remain in the same town with her, then damn Ty Holloway's black soul to everlasting hell.

For he truly would have taken from her one of the few things of value she had left.

Hayley ran the gauntlet of journalists to reach her car. They were as pushy, loud, and intrusive as ever, but taking a page from Jon-Michael's book, she stripped off the kid gloves in her dealings with them. She kept her head up, her mouth shut, and looked neither right nor left as she plowed a path through the crowd to the Pontiac. She used her elbows when they did not move quickly enough and slammed her fist down on the fingers of the opportunist who curled his hand over the driver's door to detain her. Ripping a microphone out of another's hands when it was shoved in her face, she aimed for maximum damage when she hurled the sensitive piece of electronics to the ground.

The Pontiac, cranky from its lack of use the past several days, groaned and complained when she turned the ignition. Finally, and with grudging ill will, the engine turned over, coughed, then caught. Hayley reached for the radio dial and cranked up the volume. The Shins helped drown out the cacophony of voices yelling questions at her. Questions echoing Hayley's most deeply held doubts.

"Hayley, I need to talk to you!"

How she picked up on one voice when so many were

competing for her attention, she didn't know, but her head swung around and she scanned the street. "Patsy?"

Then she spotted her friend parked down the block waving a beckoning arm at her. The other woman leaned out her car window and Hayley reached for the volume knob on the radio to turn it down.

The moment Patsy saw she had her attention, she called again, "I need to talk to you!"

For crying out loud, Patsy, now? Right here? Her old schoolmate's obliviousness to anything unconnected to her own agenda astounded her. It shouldn't, she supposed; it was the new Patsy's standard operating procedure. Hey, Pats wanted a tete a tete? Why let a little thing like a dozen glory-hungry reporters get in the way?

Swallowing her exasperation, she yelled, "Go to the Devil," and put the car in gear, moving it inexorably forward through the crowd surrounding her.

Her determination must have shown, for the journalists fell back. *See me work my magic on the Red Sea*, she thought with self-deprecating humor. *Moses's got nothing on this girl.*

After all, *he* did not have a deteriorating drop-top Pontiac.

It was the first small tug of amusement she had experienced in what felt like eons.

She pulled onto the outlook at Devil's Outcrop ten minutes later. When Patsy pulled her car to a stop alongside her moments later Hayley was perched on the car's hood, her feet on the front bumper.

She watched Patsy climb out of the car and slam the door. *She looks different.* There was a glow to Patsy's cheeks, a brightness to her eyes, Hayley had never noticed before. "You look like you have a secret, Pats," she said and then winced. That was not her favorite word of the moment. But a marvelous thought occurred to her and it perked her right up. "Omigawd, are you *pregnant*?"

"Pregnant?" the other woman blinked, clearly

blindsided by the question. "Why would you think that?"

"Because you look so, I don't know, radiant or something."

Patsy's fingers came up to brush her hair away from her temple. "I do?"

"You definitely do. I noticed it right away."

I can not help myself, I preen a little. Lately, it has seemed almost as if Hayley does not really want to be my friend anymore. Yet here she is telling me I look radiant. Maybe I should re-think some of the dark thoughts I have been entertaining.

"So are you?" Palms pressed flat against the hood, her heels lightly drumming the grill, Hayley narrows her eyes, subjecting me to a closer inspection. "You have that glow about you, which means you have either spent the afternoon with your husband screwing your brains out, or you're pregnant." She smiled. "It's gotta be one or the other."

There actually is a third possibility. I enjoy my secret but keep the identity of that possibility to myself. "I do not think I am pregnant," is all I reply. It is sure as hell true.

Hayley shoots me a crooked smile. "The other is always good, too."

I stare at her expectantly. Any moment now Hayley will apologize for choosing the wrong friend to confide her secrets to. She will tell me I am a much better friend than Kurstin could ever dream of being.

But Hayley simply sits there, staring out at the lake and maintaining her silence. My feeling of well-being starts to fade, replaced by a surge of dissatisfaction spreading like ink spilled upon a blotter. Until it ultimately absorbs every last vestige of light-heartedness. The sun has not really dimmed, has it? I try to drag a calming breath past the tightness in my chest. No, surely not. It is simply an illusion that things are suddenly darker.

"What did you want to talk to me about?" Hayley asks.

I have to clear my throat twice to speak past the lump in it. "Ty Holloway," I finally manage to say.

The small, half-smile disappears from Hayley's face and her clear hazel eyes go cold and flat. "I don't want to talk about that bastard."

"I just wanted to let you know I took care of him for you. You do not have to worry about him ever again."

"Well, that is very thoughtful of you," Hayley replies flatly. "But what did you do, escort him to the airport and personally put him on a plane out of town?"

"No, uh…"

"Because you'll have to excuse me if I don't derive a lot of comfort from the thought. It's a free country, after all, and there isn't a damn thing we can do to prevent that asshole from coming back to wreak more havoc in my life if he wants to."

"He will never bother you again, Hayley."

"So you say." She slides off the hood. "Listen, I appreciate your efforts. You've been real sweet—"

I can *feel* my spine lengthening and growing erect. *Now* I will finally hear those innermost thoughts from which I have thus far been excluded.

"But I have to take off. I need to talk to Kurstin before I go to work."

What? So unprepared am I for a betrayal of such magnitude, I can only mouth the word. And as usual Hayley is not paying me the least bit of attention as she rounds the Pontiac, opens the driver's door and slides behind the wheel without another word of explanation. I cannot *believe* it. Hayley is leaving me here to cool my jets while she hares off to her goddamn precious Kurstin?

That *bitch*! That fucking bitch!

"Listen, I will talk to you real soon," Hayley promises, starting the engine. "Maybe we can go bow-and-arrow shooting again one of these days."

And practically before I know what's what, my old friend puts the car into reverse and backs out onto the lake road. With a casual wave of her hand, she shifts into drive and roars off down the road.

I call her a couple filthy female-anatomy-centric words as I pace back and forth in front of my car. God, I am a fool. Worse, a *sap*. I realized the moment I saw Hayley exit Jon-Michael's building that Holloway was right about that much at least. I had proof Hayley is whoring around with Jon-Michael, a man she professed to despise, and *still* I gave her the benefit of the doubt.

Well, it is time I face facts. Hayley does not give two hoots about our friendship, and she is never going to confide in me. She probably would not even notice—let alone care—if I never got in touch again.

Hell, she probably would not notice if I dropped *dead*.

This is wrong. I gave her everything and got zip-all in return. What is so damn special about her that she can treat me this way? Nothing, that's what. There is not one special thing about her at all.

You stupid, unnatural girl.

I freeze mid-stride. Then hug myself. Oh, God. Maybe that is it. Maybe Hayley, too, thinks I am stupid. Maybe all those times she said we were friends were nothing but a big pack of lies.

Well, screw her! I explode into action, whirling toward my car and yanking the door open. I climb in and slam it closed behind me. Who the hell needs her? Jerking the safety shoulder harness across my body, I snap it into place. I am going straight home to dissemble that stupid closet-shrine I erected to my so-called good and great friend. Then I will go drag my husband back home, because I am tired of his shit, too.

And *fuck* Hayley Granger Prescott!

CHAPTER 19

It was blacker than the bowels of a West Virginia mine shaft, except for an infinitesimal red-hot core. Not that Ty could actually see that core. But damned if he questioned its existence. It pulsated somewhere just beyond his line of vision and he felt it for what it was: epicenter to the agony abrading his nerve ends like broken glass with every sluggish beat of his heart.

Instinctively he understood it held the potential for his destruction. Breathing was sheer agony and a debilitating weight threatened to crush his chest, his face, his legs. He shifted his body with the utmost caution.

The walls pressing down around him rumbled a warning and the canvas that covered his face parted. Dirt trickled into his eyes, his nose, his mouth. It slithered down his open collar. He immediately stilled.

Oh Christ, oh Christ! He was buried alive. There must have been a cave-in. It was every miner's nightmare.

Except—

He wasn't a miner, was he? He had only been down in the mines two or three times in his life. Just enough to know he would do anything, anything at all, to avoid following his father's footsteps into that employment hell. But if he wasn't a miner, he didn't get it. How the hell had he come to be trapped in a cave-in?

Once again he pushed against the weight pinning him down and more dirt slid through the canvas to trickle over his face. Panicking, he kicked and bucked frantically in an attempt to fight his way free.

The red pinprick at the nucleus of his blackout exploded in a crimson blaze of agony, rapidly expanding to the size of the sun. Ty froze, his body rigid, his teeth clenched to bite back an anguished scream.

What happened? What the *hell* had happened to him?

Kurstin's face flashed into his mind. Then Hayley Prescott's. Almost immediately both were superseded by Patsy Beal's.

Holy shit, the crazy bitch shot him! She had shot him with a fucking bow and arrow, and the arrow must still be in him. Then she had...what? Buried him alive? She must have.

Oh, God. Was he buried shallow? Buried deep? It could not be too deep, could it? Surely he would have noticed an open grave if one had been dug in the vicinity.

A small sound of derision escaped his lungs. Yeah, right. He being such an observant guy and all so far.

He took as deep a breath as his messed up chest would allow and determinedly pushed upward with his hands.

It hurt. Jesus, God, it hurt, and the canvas he appeared to be wrapped in gaped wider with each successive struggle, allowing more dirt to dribble in. Pretty damn sure he was going to suffocate before he reached the surface, he started hyperventilating.

Then his right hand suddenly broke through the earth and was bathed in warm air. His left hand and arm were weak, but gritting his teeth, he forced strength into them. What seemed like a lifetime, but was likely mere moments later, he was sitting up in a shallow grave, dirt and bits of the forest floor scattered around him.

Greedily, he sucked in lungsful of pure, sweet air.

***

Jon-Michael tossed his key ring into the abalone shell on the Stickley table. Two days ago he would have sung out at the top of his lungs, "Lucy, I'm hooome," ala Desi

Arnez. Then again, two days ago everybody's lives had not been turned inside out. He held his silence and took the stairs to the loft two at a time.

"Petunia?" he said softly, cresting the top stair. "I'm back."

The room was empty.

"Hayley?" Anxiety clutched at the pit of his stomach. It was too quiet; he knew without checking further she wasn't here.

Swearing softly, he strode to the closet. Ripping the door open, he stood listening to his own breath saw in and out of his lungs as he stared in numb surprise at her clothing. He had expected the rod to be empty, but her stuff was right where it had been this afternoon.

He found her panties and the T-shirt of his she'd worn for the past two days in the bathroom hamper. Her make-up was still scattered across the counter. He sank down onto the closed toilet seat and rubbed his fingers across his forehead. Okay, good. She wasn't gone forever. She had merely gone out for a while.

He blew out a breath. She'd be back. If not by the time he had to go to work, then surely by the time he got home again.

* * *

When Hayley found Kurstin's car in the garage but no Kurstin in the mansion, she walked down to the lake. She saw her friend, still in her upscale work clothes, sitting on the end of the dock.

Hayley stepped onto the boards then stopped, staring uncertainly at her friend's back. Overwhelmed by a barrage of turbulent emotion, she stood for a moment trying to figure out how to deal with them. Nothing helpful sprang to mind and conceding defeat, she pressed two fingers to her throat and softly cleared it.

Kurstin's head snapped around. Seeing Hayley, she scrambled to her feet. "Uh, hi," she said, then hummed a kind of non-word. It made her feel like an ass and self-consciously she tucked her blouse into the waistband of her linen skirt, smoothed out the wrinkles creasing the fabric over her lap. Unable to sustain eye contact, she looked away to gaze blindly out at the lake. She felt disheveled and—for the first time in her life—awkward in Hayley's presence. She bent to pluck her suit jacket off the dock, but after straightening once again she simply folded it over her arm and hugged it to her stomach. She took a deep breath, softly expelled it and stiffened her spine. Then turned back to face her best friend once again.

For a moment they simply looked at each other. Then Hayley gestured awkwardly toward the mansion. "Um, no one was home up there."

"No," Kurstin agreed. "Ruth left for the day and Dad— well, who knows where he is?"

"I am so mad at you," Hayley said in a rush, her voice low and fierce.

She nodded. "I know."

"I don't have the first idea how to deal with all this fury. It wasn't supposed to be like this. You're the one person I thought I could count on forever and you...dammit, you—"

"Betrayed you."

"*Yes*." Hayley held herself so rigidly she looked like a stiff breeze could snap her up and sent her scudding across the lake. "You turned my innermost insecurities into a public spectacle. I'm open game now, Kurstie, vulture bait. I cannot *sneeze* without someone wanting to report it on the news. God, how could you *do* that to me?"

"I don't know. I—" Kurstin looked at her friend standing in front of her with her fists clenched and anguish in her eyes. Tears welled in her own but she blinked them back. "It just happened, Hayley—I didn't plan it. If I could take those few minutes back, I'd do it in a heartbeat. I swear I would."

"I think I knew that all along." Hayley blew out an obviously frustrated breath but lost a little of the rigidity keeping her spine rebar-straight. She subjected Kurstin to an intense once-over. "And I truly am sorry about Ty. What he did to you... Well, that just stinks."

Dammit! Kurstin could deal with Hayley's anger. It might break her heart but she could handle it. Her friend's sympathy, however, just did her in. Forcing composure in her voice, she said, "Yes, well, shit happens."

To her dismay her control failed her in the middle of the last word and her voice cracked like a thirteen-year-old boy's. The tears she had been holding back by will alone rose in a rush, cresting her eyelids and overflowing. She whirled away, presenting Hayley with her back.

"Oh, sweetie." Hayley's warm hands turned her back around and pulled her into a hug. "Don't go thinking this means my mad-on at you is over," she warned gruffly. But she hugged Kurstin tightly and stroked her hair with a gentle hand. "Still, the guy is an idiot," she growled. "You deserve so much better."

Kurstin sobs grew audible. "I don't *want* better," she protested disconsolately. "I w-want Ty." She stiffened. "No! I do *not* mean that," she protested, pulling out of Hayley's arms. She sniffed inelegantly and knuckled her eyes. Her chin went up, wobbly but proud. "I wouldn't take him back on a bet."

"Uh-huh. Who are you hoping to convince here, Blondie, me or you? If Patsy hadn't gotten Bigmouth Holloway out of town, you'd probably take him back in a heartbeat."

Kurstin's heart clenched in anguish at the knowledge that he was well and truly gone, but she nevertheless protested, "I really wouldn't. I have more pride than that."

Hayley made a rude noise. She dug a folded tissue out of her jeans pocket and handed it over. "Here. Blow your nose. And face facts, Kurst. Life isn't a Ranch romance where the spunky heroine gets to do the cool thing that brings the hero to his knees. We are idiots for men. I hate to say it, but it's true. They make our lives a misery, but do we boot their sorry butts to the curb?"

Kurstin was pretty sure the despondency on her face said she couldn't disagree, but Hayley went on as if she had. "No, we do not. Admit it. We welcome them back with open arms so the misery can live on. I think the best we can hope for is to make 'em pay a little first." She kicked off her sandals, unsnapped her jeans, and slid down the zipper.

"Look at you!" she fussed, kicking off her pants. "You look like Bernice the Bag Lady. Slide out of those nylons, girl. There must be a half dozen runs in them. Hasn't anyone told you pantyhose are passé?"

"Dad insists I wear them at the office," she mumbled.

"And since when have you taken Richard's fashion advice? Rip 'em off. You have a certain image for elegance in this little backwater burg, which, I gotta tell you, at the moment you're doing a piss poor job of upholding."

Hayley sat down on the edge of the dock and dangled her bare legs over the side, lazily swishing her feet back and forth in the cool water of the lake. When a moment passed without activity from her friend, she glanced over her shoulder. "Well, come on, hop to it," she said briskly. "Jeesh. You'd think nobody ever taught you to change out of your good clothes before going outside to play."

Kurstin ripped off her pantyhose, hiked up her skirt, and sat down next to Hayley on the end of the dock. She swiped both cheeks with her hands, wiping away her tears. "Why are you being so nice to me? I thought you were supposed to be furious."

"Yeah, well, I am. I didn't say all is forgiven, Kurstin Elise, so don't go believing it is. But it occurred to me that if I write you off totally as my very best friend, that leaves me with...Patsy."

An involuntary snort of laughter escaped Kurstin. It

was the first spark of amusement she had felt in what seemed like a dog year. "Put like that," she said, "I guess you truly are stuck with me. Warts, bad judgment, and all. At least I have a sense of humor."

"Not to mention how difficult it is to get Patsy across the trestle."

Kurstin sighed and tilted her head to rest against Hayley's shoulder. "I truly am so very, very sorry. I screwed up majestically."

"Yes, you did." Hayley slipped her arm around her waist and gave her a comforting squeeze. "But I wasn't much of a friend to you, either. I'm not proud that when you needed my support the most, all I could think of were my own problems."

Kurstin's lips formed a moue as she expelled an exasperated breath. "You always were a perfectionist."

"Yeah, and you're conceited. You don't just screw up like the rest of us peons, you screw up...how did you put it... magnificently?"

"Majestically."

"Yeah, yeah, whatever." Hayley nudged her shoulder into Kurstin's. "Let's just agree everything wrong in the world truly is all your fault and leave it at that."

Leaning against each other, they lazily swished their feet back and forth in the cool water and stared out over the lake for several silent moments. Then Kurstin nodded.

"Good plan," she agreed with a tiny smile. "I believe it's a healthy thing, giving credit where credit is due."

* * *

I park in the lot at the Royal Inn, but make no move to climb out. A light wind ruffles the leaves of the birch trees, dappling the motel's stucco exterior with shifting shade patterns. I watch three crows hop through the finely ground beauty bark beneath the rhododendrons. And draw a deep, cleansing breath for luck.

Expelling it, I climb from the car and lock up. Staring at the building, I straighten my suit jacket. Brush nonexistent lint from my skirt. Then I square my shoulders and head for the building.

Outside room 203 I pause for yet another calming breath. I have no idea why. It is not as if I am actually nervous or anything. I simply have not seen Joe for a while and want a moment to collect myself. Nothing more.

I knock on the door.

The volume on the television inside the room lowers and a moment later the door opens. Joe's face registers surprise when he sees me on his doorstep. "Oh...hey, Pats," he says and shifts awkwardly.

"Hello, Joe. May I come in?"

"Huh? Oh! Sure. Come on in." He steps back to allow me entrance. "Uh, sorry about the mess." He sweeps some Jockey shorts and dirty socks off the carpet and tosses them in the closet. Then he shifts awkwardly from foot to foot. "I wasn't expecting company."

The room is not at all the neatly kept space I demanded and came to expect when he lived at home. I perch on the edge of a chair and gingerly push aside several dirty glasses and fast food containers on the table next to me to clear a place for my purse.

"Can I get you a glass of water? A soft drink, maybe?"

"No, thank you. I will come directly to the point. I want you to come home."

He stilled. "Uh-huh. Patsy—"

"Before you say anything, please hear me out," I interrupt, sitting straighter on the edge of my seat. Is that pity on his face? I cannot abide pity—there is absolutely nothing pitiful about me. *Stupid, ungrateful girl,* mother's voice whispers in my brain. *You will never amount to anything.*

"Dammit, Mama, shut up!" I mutter.

Joe does an odd double take. "What?"

"Hmm?"

"What did you say?"

"Nothing. It was not important. A slip of the tongue." I shake off the specter of my mother. "I dismantled the closet," I inform him a bit stiffly when he continues to stare at me as if I said something freakish. For heaven's sake, what was the matter with him? "I threw away all my clippings and tapes of Hayley. You were right, Joe, it was a dumb thing to have collected. She is not the friend I believed her to be and certainly not worth jeopardizing our marriage over."

"Pats—"

"Come home where you belong."

He sits on the edge of the bed facing me. Leaning forward he plucks my hands from my lap and chafes them between his own. "That's not going to happen, Patsy," he says gently.

"Of course it is."

"No. It's not. Our marriage is over."

I tug my hands free. "Do not be ridiculous. Of *course* it is not over. I have done precisely what you said I should do: I got rid of my Hayley things. Now you have to do your part. Come home."

"Patsy, I've seen a lawyer. I want a divorce."

"No!" I surge to my feet. "That is *wrong*. What will people say?"

Joe's expression hardened. "Who gives a shit what people say?"

"I do. Oh, my God, I should have seen this coming. It is all *HER* fault, you know."

"What? Whose fault? What the hell are you talking about?"

"Hayley! If it were not for her, we would still be together. We would still be *happy*." I snatch up my handbag.

"This has nothing to do with Hayley."

"Like hell it doesn't! Well, she is not going to get away with it. She has to pay."

"Dammit, Patsy, this is not about any friggin' third party." Gripping my arms, he holds me in place while staring into my eyes. "This is about you and me, and I won't let you put the blame onto someone who has absolutely nothing to do with us."

I peer up at him. Is that true? Does this awful decision he made truly have nothing to do with Hayley? It seems as if she is involved in *every* facet of my life these days, but maybe I am mistaken. "Then why can't you come home?" I demand. "I got rid of the closet."

"Jesus! Will you forget the fucking closet? You are not a stupid woman, Patsy, so why do you insist on talking like an idiot? *Listen* to me. This. Is. Not. About—Shit!"

Barely hearing anything beyond "stupid" and "idiot", I see no reason to stick around to listen to the rest of his harangue. I stalk on stiff legs out of room 203 and slam its door closed behind me.

***

"Where the *hell* have you been all day?"

Hayley closed the little-used rear door to Bluey's and leaned back against it. Adrenaline surged through her system from running the gauntlet of journalists outside, and she looked up at Jon-Michael, her smile probably coming across like defective neon as it flashed on and flickered out.

"Hey," she said breathlessly. "Didn't expect to see you here this early." Exhaling noisily, she blotted perspiration from her brow with her forearm. "Holy shit. Can you believe there are even more reporters out there tonight? Where do they all come from, you suppose—I wouldn't have thought there were enough rocks for them to crawl out from under." She pushed away from the door, too wired to stand still. "Did you see the six o'clock news this evening? I was the Top Story...except it wasn't a story, exactly, since there wasn't an ounce of factual-type, um, facts reported." Her brow pleated, then she laughed low in her throat. "Oh. I guess that's what a story is, huh, something made up? What I meant was, it wasn't news. It was more Top Speculation." A little chortle of laughter purled up from her throat.

Jon-Michael bent over her until they stood nose to nose and gripped her upper arms. Pulling her up onto her tiptoes, he demanded through gritted teeth, "Where. The. *Hell*. Have you. Been?"

"Out mending fences with your sister just like you said I should," she replied, straightening up smartly as it belatedly sank in he was angry. Furiously, icily, angry. *Dandy. Just what I need.* She thrust her chin up at him. "What?" she demanded of the unspoken accusation in his chocolate brown eyes.

"What, she says. It never occurred to you to leave me a note? To take one minute to leave a lousy message on my cell?"

"My messages are never lousy. I—"

His grip tightened. "Don't get cute with me. I'm in no mood. You have been the next best thing to catatonic for the past two days, then you just up and disappear on me without a word, but I'm not supposed to worry? I oughtta shake you 'til your damn teeth rattle."

She had seen him angry more times than she could count, but thinking back she realized that in all the years they had known each other, she had never seen his rage directed at her. It shook her to realize how badly she wanted to placate him.

That, in turn, made her defensive. She didn't owe him an explanation and she fiercely resented the quickness with which her adrenaline high had drained away, leaving her limp and weary beyond belief.

All the same..."I'm sorry," she heard herself whisper and strained forward to press up against him. His hands immediately released her to clasp her in his arms. He held her with a tightness that compressed her bones, but she simply stroked her cheek against his collarbone and wound her arms around his waist to hold him tightly in return. "I am sorry," she reiterated. "It never occurred to me you would worry. I didn't think."

"I didn't know where you were, when you'd be back."

"I got to thinking about what you said and went out to talk to Kurstin."

"So you've forgiven her?"

"Yes." She released him and pulled back. Reaching up, she smoothed a strand of dirty-blond hair away from his forehead. "I need to get to work. Bluey's expecting me in the office."

"I know. Who do you think told me you called in to say you'd be late?" He started to tense up all over again.

"Don't be mad at me. I told you I wasn't thinking straight." She raised up on her toes to give him a quick peck on the lips. Then she settled back on her heels. "I have to get to work, Johnny. Bluey's been so great about my being gone and I want to give him a full night's work."

"Okay. But you and I are gonna talk when we get home tonight."

Hayley bit back a grimace. Oh, goody, another heart-to-heart. *Because there hasn't been enough emotion packed into this day already.* "Ummm," she managed noncommittally, knowing darn well he would take it as an agreement when she didn't mean it as anything of the kind. Still, she didn't want him all riled up again.

At least not right now. She could not deal with his temper right now.

Maybe later.

The evening was every bit as draining as she'd anticipated, and then some. At least Bluey had trained the journalists to know they would be expelled from the bar if they bothered her while she worked. Unfortunately, there was no controlling the patrons.

"So, hey," one of them asked after ordering a drink, "Is it true what I heard on TV? You really against the death penalty?"

Hayley could practically see the ears of every journalist within hearing distance perk up. She set the drink she'd prepared in front of the inquisitive patron. "That will be eight-fifty, please."

The man forked over the money. "I figured they musta got it wrong, cuz that don't make no sense. Why would anyone be against the death penalty when it'd take care of the guy who did her old man?"

"Would you care for a basket of pretzels to go with that?"

And so it went.

"You feeling like the head exhibit at the zoo yet?" Lucy asked when she overheard a similar line of questioning. Two-tone hair belling out, she swung around to deflect the most recent contender attempting a debate on capital punishment with Hayley.

Hayley was wrung out by the end of her shift. The last thing she wanted was to embroil herself in a serious conversation with Jon-Michael.

Mindless sex was what she needed tonight, something to take her mind off her problems and leave her limp and relaxed instead of tied up in knots.

She set out to seduce Jon-Michael the moment they cleared the door to his loft, hoping not only to fulfill her own needs but to postpone the inevitable discussion. Turning, she raised onto her toes and kissed him, threading her fingers through his hair to hold him in place, stroking her breasts against his chest. Her lips were avid as they coaxed his apart, and she kissed him hotly.

Jon-Michael wasn't averse to being seduced and fell in with the program immediately. He kissed her back with matching heat and enthusiasm. Then he tried to pull back. "Wait. Hayley, honey. Wait a minute."

She didn't slow down and he groaned deep in his throat. His hands slid down the curve of her butt, where he sank his fingers in to pull her nearer. His mouth on hers turned fierce, hungry.

Then, summoning all the willpower at his disposal, he pulled away. Transferring his hands to her upper arms, he shoved her back and held her at arm's length. He vaguely registered the sound of his own breathing as he stared down at her. "Wait," he panted. "We can't do this—we've gotta talk."

"I don't want to talk. Love me, Jon-Michael."

"I will. I will, darlin'. In a minute. But first we need to talk."

She jerked herself away. Ramming her fingers through her hair, she glared up at him. "Why, because you say we should? Why can't we talk later? What's the point in busting the mood right when things are getting good?"

"For crissake, Hayley!" He, too, thrust his fingers through his hair as he stared at her in frustration. When she merely glowered back at him, he exerted enough pressure to put severe strain on his roots. "Do we even *have* a relationship beyond sex?" When she remained stubbornly silent, he continued grimly, "I would really like to know what you consider my role in your life, Hayley. For instance, if we subtracted the sex, where, in your estimation, would that leave us?" It was imperative, suddenly, that he know.

She looked startled, then conciliatory. "Oh, Jon--"

"If I weren't the owner of the cock scratching your itch," he implacably overrode her, "would you still be here, living with me?"

"How the hell do I know?" Hayley's urge to appease sank without a trace, belligerence rising to take its place. Clenching her hands into fists at her sides, she angled her chin up at him.

"What's not to know? It's a simple enough question."

"It's a *pointless* question. I mean, you *do* have the equipment, Jon-Michael, and we *do* have a sexual relationship. One, I would like to add, you seem to want every bit as much as I. So I don't understand the—"

"Do I mean *anything* to you beyond my ability to provide you with a good, hard fuck?"

She glared at him. "Of course you do!"

"She said in such loving tones," he mocked bitterly. Watching her begin to shake, he nodded in comprehension. "Ah. I get it. The dreaded 'L' word rears its ugly head. Well, let's make this real interesting, then, darlin'. Here is the million-dollar question. Do you love me?"

"Do I...?" Her voice faltered.

"Love me. Jesus, you can't even look at me, let alone say the word. I'll take that as a no then. I love you, you know."

Hayley stilled. Then she did meet his gaze. "You love me," she finally repeated flatly. "Yes, so I have heard you say." Her spine stiffened, her posture growing erect. "But, tell me, Jon-Michael, what does that *mean*, exactly? You said you loved me when I was seventeen, too—but then you broadcast the most private evening of my life to the entire school and left me to face the snickers and sneers all by myself while you skipped town."

She hugged herself to ward off the sudden chill settling in her bones. Given her sudden light-headedness, she deduced her face likely had drained of color, and her shakes increased. "Dad said he loved me, but it sure didn't stop him from taking off. And Dennis?" A bitter laugh escaped her. "Well, good ole Dennis was supposed to love me until death did us part. But his idea of love was screwing around with anyone sufficiently impressed with his newfound fame to have him."

She saw shock cross Jon-Michael's face and hated him in that moment for not allowing her to keep at least that part of her life a secret. "You will just have to excuse me," she said stiffly, "if the word doesn't mean much to me anymore."

Except...it did. Deep down, it still did. As he had so

rudely pointed out this morning, she could not even have an orgasm these days unless he first professed his love. She could only pray he wouldn't throw that in her face again because she didn't think she could bear it tonight. Too many emotions had stormed her senses in the past few days.

He didn't say a word.

Eyeing him warily, she said, "I'm tired. I think I'll go up now."

"Yeah, okay," he agreed quietly. "I'm going to lock up. I'll be up in a bit."

She could have sworn the earth's gravity had multiplied a hundredfold as she dragged herself up the stairs to the loft.

Chapter 20

Hayley was vaguely aware of the alarm going off. Hampered by the black wave of fatigue threatening to pull her under, she kicked toward consciousness. Jon-Michael's arm slid away from the dip of her waist and she felt the loss of his body heat along every inch of the skin he had spooned.

He rolled away and the clock's alarm went silent.

Turning over, she blinked at him through foggy layers of exhaustion. His back was to her as he sat at the side of the bed, his long spine angled over hard, widespread thighs. He scrubbed his hands over his face, the only sound in the dim loft the sandpaper rasp of calloused fingers meeting morning stubble.

She reached to scratch her nails down his back. It took every scrap of energy she possessed and her hand dropped to the mattress in the wake of a single pass, her fingertips barely grazing his naked buttock. It got his attention, however, for he turned to look at her.

"Hey," she murmured in a froggy voice.

"Hey, yourself, baby."

She gave him a drowsy, contented smile and heard him rumble a non-word deep in his throat.

"Ah, damn, Hayley," he whispered. "What am I going to do with you?" Dropping onto his forearm over her, he sifted his long-fingered free hand through her hair. "Just when I'm on the verge of thinking maybe I should give up the damn dream, you go and turn sweet on me."

Too exhausted to make sense of his words, she simply

gave him another smile.

Jon-Michael returned a crooked one of his own and traced a fingertip along her lips. "I love the way you wake up. I wish you'd forget to worry more often." Then he kissed her softly and adjusted the blanket over her shoulders. "It's early. Go back to sleep."

"'Kay." Her heavy-lidded eyes slid closed. Deep, drugging fatigue immediately sucked her back into the depths.

The next time she forced her eyes open, he was standing in front of the dresser mirror, his head cocked to one side as he watched his hands' reflection adjust the knot of his tie. His hair, still damp from the shower, looked almost as dark as her own. Even more uncharacteristic, his cheeks and jaw shone with the smooth sheen of a newly applied razor.

The blankets pooled around her hips as she pushed herself upright. Yawning, she knuckled her hair from her eyes, and meeting his gaze in the mirror, felt a grin tug the corners of her mouth. "Who died, Olivet? I haven't seen you shave or voluntarily put on a tie since I came back." He did not respond and the reason for it struck her. "Oh. *Duh.*" She smacked herself on the temple. "Sure I have. Bluey's bow tie on the Fourth, right? Forgot about that."

Still he didn't speak, and her eyebrows furrowed. His dark-eyed gaze in the mirror was steady on her, but why was it so wary and his mouth so unsmiling? Her warm fuzzies dissipated as memories of last night's argument and its tense aftermath suddenly resurfaced. The smile wobbled off her face.

They had been painfully polite to each other when Jon-Michael joined her in bed after securing the apartment. Conversation had been nearly nonexistent and what there was of it had been stilted and carefully polite. Not at all in keeping with their usual verbal skirmishes.

They had also maintained a physical distance between them. Failing to pick up where their lovemaking had left off downstairs, they had eventually fallen asleep, each hugging their own side of the bed. As if they were strangers forced to share the last hotel room in town. The only thing missing was a meridian of pillows down the middle of the mattress.

Awakening to the knowledge he'd gravitated to spoon with her during the night had temporarily stolen the memory.

She cleared her throat. "Um, where are you going so early?" Glancing at the clock on the dresser, she saw it was eleven-thirty, which wasn't early at all if one kept regular business hours.

"Olivet's." He jerked the knot of his tie into place and smoothed down the points of his collar. "I have a one o'clock presentation to make to the board."

She sat up straighter. "A presentation? You're going to present your ideas to the board of directors after all?" *Hello! Did he not just say so?* Her heart commenced pounding with brutal force.

He scrutinized her via the mirror. "Yes. I was going to tell you about it last night but other stuff got in the way."

She should have been happy about it. It was precisely what she had been urging him to do. Instead it scared her.

Her gaze on him faltered.

As if he had anticipated that exact reaction, Jon-Michael nodded. Picking an old-fashioned watch fob off the dresser, he attached it across his vest as he turned to face her. After studying her a moment, he shook his head as if in commiseration. "Poor Hayley. I'm about to eliminate your favorite excuse for holding me at arm's length. Ain't life a bitch?"

Fierce heat scalded her chest and throat, climbed her face to the hairline. Surging up onto her knees, her chin thrust out to a belligerent angle, she once again locked her gaze unflinchingly on his.

"How dare you mock me?" she demanded with low-voiced fury. "You don't have any idea what it's like to live without a vestige of privacy. Until I came back to Gravers Bend I might have been notorious, but at least I had a thought or two I could call my own. Not now, by God. Every time I turn around some ratty new detail of my life is revealed. It never ends. Just when I think there can't possibly be anything left to publicly humiliate me, something turns up. I feel like I've been stripped naked so the world can critique my body." A bitter smile twisted her lips. "Knowing damn well it will be found wanting."

"And just what the hell does that have to do with us?" Jon-Michael demanded furiously, stalking to the bed to loom over her. "With you and me? I'm not the one stealing your secrets."

"Yes, yes you are! You won't let me keep anything to myself!"

He sat on the side of the bed and reached to stroke the rigid fist nearest him. "Does this have to do with what you let slip last night?" he asked gently. "About Dennis cheating on you?"

She went very still. Then she batted furiously at the long fingers fondling the back of her hand. "No!"

Jon-Michael pulled back, both hands spread in an I-come-in-peace gesture. But he looked her squarely in the eye. "Because if it does, I've said it before and I will say it again. Your husband was a fool. But, Hayley honey—" he leaned in to grasp her chin firmly, their eyes mere inches apart "—I am not. I know exactly what I have in you. I'm also aware I screwed the pooch once before." Releasing her, he rose to his feet and stared down at her. "But know this. The woman has not been born who could tempt me to screw it up again by being unfaithful."

It terrified her how badly she wanted to believe him. But if she did and he let her down, it would kill her; she knew it on a visceral level. *Protect yourself,* a shrill inner voice warned. *Protect yourself, or this time he could destroy you.*

So she did. Taking a deep, calming breath, she

straightened her shoulders, raised her chin, and said very distinctly, "Nobody asked for your fidelity, Olivet. All I ever wanted from you is sex." Then hated herself for the baseborn liar she was.

It was too late to take her words back, however, even if she wanted to. Once spoken, words could not be recalled and Jon-Michael visibly withdrew. He stood looking her up and down, and there was something in his dark eyes that caused Hayley to hastily reach for the sheet that had drifted forgotten onto the mattress. She tugged it up and tucked it under her armpits, clamping her arms to her sides to hold it in place.

"Drop it," he immediately ordered with soft-voiced menace.

"What?"

"All you want is sex? Then drop the sheet. A little nudity between fuck buddies shouldn't bother a free-wheelin' sex pistol like you." He reached for his belt. "How do you want it, honey? Truth is, I'm a little pressed for time, so it will have to be quick. Quick 'n rough, maybe— I know that appeals to me at the moment. C'mon." He had his pants undone. "Why are you still covered up? I said drop it. Let's fuck."

Pressing her arms to her sides more tightly, she assured herself it was merely offended masculine pride that made him such a dick. So why, then, did tears rise with such scalding ease in her eyes?

Jon-Michael made a sound of disgust. Whether it was aimed at her or himself was anyone's guess, but he turned away, redoing his fly with none of his usual grace. He crossed to the bureau and picked up his wallet, checked the contents, and stuffed it in his back pocket. Then he turned to face her again.

"I apologize," he said stiffly. "That was crude and…" He rolled his shoulders impatiently. "I'm not going to say uncalled for, Hayley, because frankly I think I had a huge dose of provocation. Still, you have my apology."

She merely stared at him, hating the fact her lower lip was quivering. She could really use a little screw you bravado right about now.

Jon-Michael looked down at his hands. "I always thought you were about the gutsiest woman I knew," he said in a low voice. "I admired that, you know." He studied his fingers as if they had turned into the most fascinating objects he'd ever clapped eyes on. Then his hands abruptly dropped to his sides and he looked up at her. "I was wrong, though, wasn't I, Hayley? You're an emotional coward. And this push-me/pull-me shit we keep engaging in is not doing either of us a damn bit of good."

He stared at her as if waiting for some kind of argument. When she didn't immediately give him one, he shrugged.

Then turned and walked away.

Scaredy cat, scaredy cat. Hayley kicked the shower stall wall and thrust her head back beneath the pounding jets of water as if she could rinse the mocking words out of her head as easily as she rid her hair of shampoo. *Emotional coward, my ass,* she thought testily. Jon-Michael was full of shit. She was cautious—with cause. That did not make her a coward.

She twisted the water off and wrung out her hair. Okay, so maybe these days she was the slightest bit *fainthearted* when it came to making any sort of commitment. Big deal. Once upon a time she had trusted her feelings, had freely offered up her heart right, left, and sideways. Look where that had gotten her. A deadbeat dad, a red-hot reputation, a philandering husband and life in a goldfish bowl. So if she erred on the side of caution, she'd say it made her smart, not an emotional coward.

And just what did that last thing he'd said even mean? If he thought they weren't doing each other any good did it mean he wanted her to pack her stuff, which had began accumulating in his place, and move out of his life?

"Oh, God," she muttered, "this is a total waste of time." She dried off, slapped on lotion and pulled on her bra and panties. With less than four hours sleep, her head felt as if the high school marching band was holding practice in it. She hadn't done laundry in too long and really needed to go back to the estate to get something clean to wear. Bet your ass, though, she could look forward to a pack of reporters hanging around outside the Olivet gate, all geared up to stick their microphones in her face, blind her in the glare of their lights and demand answers to intimate questions she had hesitated to discuss with her best friend.

She had to get out of here. The walls were closing in on her.

Actually, talking to her best friend sounded like a plan, but when she called the Olivet house no one answered. Kurstin was either in the shower where she wouldn't hear the phone, using a hair dryer or—crap, of course—at work.

Hayley donned a pair of shorts and a sleeveless T-shirt, then pulled a comb through the wet tangle of her hair. She went through Jon-Michael's medicine cabinet and found a bottle of ibuprofen.

She took three, put the bottle back and shut the mirrored door. Catching the reflection of her blank stare, she blinked and shook her head impatiently. One thing was for certain. She could not spend the entire day staring at these walls or she would be a raving lunatic before the morning was gone. She located her bathing suit. Might as well do what had worked for her in the past. She would head out to the Olivet estate, grab her stuff and take a swim until she quieted the thoughts scurrying through her mind like so many rats in a maze.

She had opened Jon-Michael's front door when her conscience kicked in. Hesitating on the threshold, restlessly tossing the keys in her hand into the air then snatching them back, only to immediately send them aloft again, she debated herself.

The verdict was still out on whether she had won or

lost the dispute when she closed the front door again. But she tried Jon-Michael's cell phone.

It went to voicemail.

So she went into his home office, where she located the appropriate number, picked up the phone, and dialed.

"Good morning, Olivet Manufacturing."

Hayley's fingers tightened around the receiver. "May I speak with Jon-Michael Olivet, please?"

"I'm sorry, ma'am, Mr. Olivet is unavailable."

"Oh." She had not planned for that. "Um, how about Kurstin McAlvey then? Is she available?"

"Yes, she is. One moment please."

The connection closed and then opened again and her best friend's voice said, "This is Kurstin."

"Hey."

"Hayley? Is that you?"

"Oh, Kurstie. Everything is so screwed up."

"Tell me about it." Kurstin's voice, although dry, contained a hint of bitterness. But it gentled when she asked, "How did it get all screwed up for you, though, sweetie? Aside from the usual, I mean. The press finally manage to stage a successful raid on the last of your closely guarded secrets?"

"I don't think I have any left to guard," Hayley replied glumly. "No, this is worse. Jon-Michael and I had a big fight this morning. So big I am not even sure I'm supposed to *be* here when he gets back."

"Don't be absurd. Jon-Michael loves you madly."

"He says I'm an emotional coward, Kurst."

"Well, you are."

"Kurstin!"

"Girl, please. As far as committing to Jon-Michael is concerned, you have a yellow streak up your back a yard wide." Call Waiting blipped for Hayley's phone, but Kurstin ignored it. "On the other hand," she continued gently, "you've been given more reason to be cautious than any woman should ever have to contend with, not the least of which came from Jon. He'll remember that as soon as he cools down from whatever set him off this morning." The Call Waiting signal blipped for the third time and Kurstin said impatiently, "You want to get that damn thing? It's very annoying."

"Yeah, hang on a second." Hayley pressed the flash button to access a second line. "Hello."

"Hayley?"

"Patsy, hi. Can I call you back in a minute? I'm on the other line."

"I just wanted to see if you would like to go out and shoot some arrows with me this afternoon. I don't have to be to work until six."

"Okay, sure." It was exactly what Hayley needed. Something mindless and physical to take her mind off the continuing soap opera that was her life. "Where do you wanna meet? That clearing above Mavis Point?"

Patsy laughed and her voice was laced with an amusement Hayley didn't understand. "Yeah, sure, why not. Meet you there around two?"

"Okay, see you then."

Patsy hung up on her.

"Bye," Hayley murmured and clicked the flash button again. "Kurstie? You still there?"

"Yes. Who was that?"

"Patsy. We're going to meet in a while to do some target practice with her bow and arrow."

"Whooped-dee-do."

"Don't start. I don't know why you're so hard on her lately." Then she made an erasing gesture. Realizing her friend couldn't see it over the telephone, she rushed on, "But that's not important right now. What am I going to do about Jon-Michael? I need to tell him something before he goes into that meeting, but the receptionist says he's not available."

"Yeah, he's been locked in with dad since he got here. Man, wouldn't you just *love* to be a fly on the wall to catch a snatch of that conversation?"

Hayley wasn't sure if the choked expulsion of air that caught in her throat was a laugh or a sob. "The mind boggles. Will you give him a message for me?"

"Sure."

"Before the board meeting? It's gotta be before the meeting, Kurstie."

"No problem. I'm going down in about ten minutes. What do you want me to say?"

"Just tell him...good luck, okay? That right is might. And I know he's going to kick butt."

* * *

"God. She's driving me crazy." Jon-Michael hooked a finger in the knot of his tie and yanked it loose. He craned his neck in the opposite direction and looked down at his sister. Shit. He didn't need this after the frustrating session he'd just had with his father.

He and Kurstin stood in a corner he had commandeered in the boardroom, and after a single glance over her shoulder at the people entering the room he turned the full force of his attention back on her. "One minute I'm sure she loves me, the next she is virtually telling me not to hold my breath. I don't know up from effing down anymore. I wish she would make up her damn mind."

"Yes, don't you simply abhor inconsistent behavior?" Kurstin commiserated. "It is high time she got over herself. Why, the way she acts, you would think every man she's ever loved turned her life into a circus or something. How immature can one woman be?"

Jon-Michael pulled at his tie again in frustration. "I've tried to show her how much I've changed. And I have told her until I'm blue in the face how much I love her."

"And I'm sure you are just patience personified when she shies away from believing you."

That pulled a wry smile out of him. Then he sobered. "She told me flat out this morning all she wants from me is sex."

Kurstin gave him a pitying how-stupid-can-one-guy-be look. "Oh, please. And you believed that?"

"Hell, yeah, I believed it. It's the reason she moved in with me in the first place."

"I cannot believe you are that dense, Jon-Michael."

"I prefer to call it realistic."

"Prefer anything you want. It doesn't change the fact you're a bonehead."

"Thanks, Kurstin. One appreciates knowing his family is firmly on his side in his direst hour." Remembering the rest of Hayley's message, however, he felt a corner of his mouth reluctantly tug up. He looked at his sister. "Right is might, huh?"

"That is what she said."

He pushed away from the wall he'd been leaning against, reaching up simultaneously to re-tighten the knot of his tie. "Then I suppose it's time to do what she said, isn't it?" He looked at the stack of papers she held. "Is that my proposal?"

"All twelve copies of it."

"Okay." He looked at the board members who had been slowly filtering in and taking their places at the long rectangular table. Drawing a deep breath, he held it a moment, then blew it out, deliberately pushing all the anger and hurt boiling through him to the back of his mind. "Let's go kick some ass."

***

The woods were dim and quiet and Hayley found herself dawdling on her way to the rendezvous point with Patsy. Dust motes filled shafts of sunshine filtering through overhead gaps in the trees to mantle her hair and shoulders in warmth. The deep breaths she inhaled were scented by a fecund aroma that soothed on a fundamental level. Tension eased out of her knotted neck muscles even as frazzled nerves began slowly knitting themselves back together.

Listening to the rhythms of the forest: the birds ceasing their songs at her approach only to start up again as soon as she passed, the breeze riffling the treetops, it struck her that many of her life's more perfect moments had happened in these woods. Given how rife with anxiety her current life was she found comfort in the memories.

She beat Patsy to the clearing above Mavis Point and appreciated simply sitting quietly on a fallen log, angling her face to feel the dappled sunshine on her skin. Closing her eyes, she leaned back on her palms and breathed in a measure of peace with every evergreen-scented lungful of air she inhaled.

Her eyes refused to open again until she heard Patsy's approach through the woods. Watching her friend step into the clearing, she greeted her with a spontaneous smile. "Hi," she called softly. "I am so glad you called. This is the most relaxed I've felt in days."

Stopping, I blink at Hayley in bemusement. The friendliness of her greeting jolts me. It confuses me and makes me want to fall back on the seductive yearning to be included in her confidences I have nurtured for so long. Maybe I should give it another try. Maybe Joe was right when he said our problems have nothing to do with an outside party. Maybe…

No. Seductive is the word for this home wrecking twat. Hayley Prescott is not my friend. The absolute truth of that was driven home by my conversation with Joe. Hayley is like one of those Pre-Raphaelite sorceresses, long-necked and wild-haired, with a reserved poise and a surface prettiness that fools the uninformed into believing she would never do anything underhanded. Inside, though, lives a fucking bitch scheming to beguile and ensnare.

And I have made up my mind. I know what needs to be done if I am ever to get Joe back.

Looking at her poised there like butter wouldn't melt in her mouth, I notice the log my erstwhile friend sits on is the one from which I shot Ty Holloway right off his feet. Amusement unfurling, I feel my lips curve up.

I am not the stupid one here. I am the powerful one, the one who knows where the bodies are buried. I laugh out loud, for in this case that isn't just an expression, is it?

"What's so funny?"

I like this feeling, this possessing a juicy secret no one else knows. I hug it to my breast. "It is just all so... deliciously perfect," I murmur.

"True, that." Hayley rises to her feet, twisting to brush needles and bark dust from the seat of her pants. "We just don't get enough of these fabulous days, do we?"

I am tempted to demonstrate my contempt at how wrong her interpretation is, but I control myself. It just sank in I do not have a plan. I, who am always prepared for every contingency, stand here planless for perhaps the first time in my life. I have no idea what I'm going to do next.

Okay, that is not precisely true.

I do know I am going to kill Hayley Granger Prescott.

Chapter 21

Hayley stretched. For the first time since Holloway's shit-fest of an article hit the fan she felt as though she could catch an honest-to-god deep-to-the-bottom-of-her-lungs breath. The hike up from Mavis Point trailhead had left her pleasantly tired, sunshine lay soft as a benediction upon her shoulders and the evergreen trees surrounding the open space she and Patsy occupied smelled divine. Smelled like *home*. Hands on her hips, elbows out and feet planted wide, she twisted from her waist to the right, enjoying the stretch along her upper body.

When she reversed to twist to the left she saw something behind the log from the corner of her eye. She pivoted her left foot back to get a better view.

And felt something whiz past her chest to *thunk* into a tree ten feet beyond the log.

Startled, she jumped back. Her foot rolled over a baseball-sized rock and without a scrap of dignity she performed a crazed but mercifully brief dance before landing on her butt. Right on top of another rock.

Wincing, she fished it out from beneath her hip. Before she could toss it aside, motion caught her eye. She looked up. And gawked, the hand holding the rock dropping limply to her lap.

Because an arrow, still quivering, was buried a good inch deep in the tree trunk. She whipped around to stare at her friend. "What the *hell*? You damn near shot me!"

To her amazement, Patsy merely shrugged. "Yes, it is clear I've let my practice slide a bit too much lately," she said in a cool voice. "My aim is too consistently off true...even if only a smidge."

"You *meant* to shoot me?" But, no. She must have misunderstood.

Patsy's prompt don't-be-an-idiot look strengthened the belief and she sucked in a relieved breath.

Only to have it catch in her throat when her old schoolmate said, "*Duh.* Of course I did."

"What?" Hayley shook her head. "I mean, I heard you. But... *why?*"

"Oh, do not play coy!" Patsy spat. "God! I idolized you! You stood up to my bitch of a mother for me. I would have done *anything* for you."

"I did?" Hayley frantically shuffled through old memories.

"You remember. You came to our house that day and heard her call me stupid."

"She did that way too often."

"No shit. But I am talking about the day you told her off but good. And you said I was one of the smartest people you knew."

"You are."

"Yeah, right," Patsy scorched her with a look. "Because when I gave you every opportunity to get your horrible experience off your chest by talking to me about it, you were *sooo* open to taking advantage of my intellect."

"Patsy, I haven't talked to *any*one about it." Or no more than she could help, anyway.

"Don't give me that. I bet you talked to your oh-so-beloved Kurstin about it."

"No. I have not." She resisted the urge to cross her fingers as she lied without a qualm. "Nor to Jon-Michael either."

Patsy glared at her. "Which does not change the fact you should have talked to *me*." Then she barked out a laugh.

The sound was so dark, so chilling...and an exact

match to the cold, cold eyes Hayley couldn't believe belonged to the Patsy she knew. She shuddered and would have sworn under oath she felt her gut take the Polar Plunge. Glancing covertly around the clearing, she looked for the best route—*any* route—out of here. Patsy had lowered the bow and, oh, crap, another arrow she must have nocked into the bowstring while Hayley was busy falling on her ass. But she didn't need her psychology degree to see the other woman was not in her right mind.

And far beyond what her knowledge of the field could reach. Hayley feared it would take years on a psychiatrist's couch to get Patsy back on track. And *she* did not have years.

Surreptitiously, with the old adage about not bringing a knife to a gunfight singing through her head, she wrapped her hand around the rock she'd dropped in her lap. And fervently hoped something was better than nothing.

She climbed to her feet to be ready to take advantage of the tiniest opportunity to get away from Psycho Patsy.

"You know what?" the other woman said. "I *did* do something for you. *I* am still a good friend." Her look made it clear Hayley didn't deserve such dedicated friendship. "Even after you blew me off time after time, even after you constantly shoved me aside so you could go do stuff with your precious *Kurstin*, I still did you a giant favor." She waved a hand in the direction of the fallen log Hayley had been sitting on. "I told you this before but I don't think you really got it. I took care of the Ty problem."

No, no, no, no, NO! For the first time in her life, Hayley realized a person's blood truly could run cold. God knew hers had turned to ice. Because now the churned up forest floor on the other side of the log made sense. It was a grave.

Except, wait. If Ty had been in the ditch-like hole, she was pretty sure he was no longer. She shot it a sideways glance.

"No body." Dammit, she could not believe she'd said that out loud!

"Well, of course there is not, *stupid*." The satisfaction on Patsy's face at calling someone else the hated word told Hayley she was already dead to the crazed woman. "I buried him and made sure the ground didn't look as if it had been disturbed."

"Oh, the ground has definitely been disturbed," Hayley goaded. After years of working with a bow, Patsy's upper body strength beat hers all to hell, so no way would she take the other woman in a physical fight. Her only hope was to shake Patsy up enough to create an opportunity to get away. "There's a shallow grave there. But no body."

"What?" Patsy took a step toward her. "Bullshit."

"Dead bodies are hardly something I would lie about, Pats." *Please, please, let the nickname reach her.*

The other woman's face didn't soften an iota, but she did stride over to the log. And—oh, God!—actually turned her back on Hayley.

Who hesitated only a nanosecond before striking the back of Patsy's head with her rock.

Unfortunately, she pulled her punch at the last second. It wasn't smart, but, dammit, until this moment she had never struck another soul. Too bad her squeamishness cost her the chance to knock out Patsy the way she'd intended.

It did cause the other woman to stagger and fall over the log. Patsy bobbled her bow and with her feet still on this side of the log and her forearms slapping flat in the dirt on the other side, it tipped her quiver almost upside down. The arrows scattered on the ground in front of her.

Hayley lunged, reaching over her former friend's back. The bow had skittered too far away to grab, but she swept up all but two of the arrows before Patsy recovered. Something she did too damn swiftly, jabbing back an elbow.

Since Hayley was all but plastered against the other

woman's back the intended jab mostly slid off her side. It did, however, drive home the fact she was out of time and had better do something to up her odds if she wanted to escape this nightmare alive. She smashed her rock down on the hand Patsy had planted in the dirt to push herself up.

Patsy howled and cradled her fingers in her other palm. "You fucking *bitch*!"

"Really? That's supposed to hurt my feelings? You just admitted you're a stone-cold killer." She made a grab for the arrow still within her reach, but missed it. Knowing it was time to use her one and only advantage, she shoved upright.

And ran like hell.

She stuck to the paths. Some were overgrown, as if the current crop of school kids didn't mess around in the woods the way they used to. Even partially obstructed tracks were faster than breaking trail through the bush and trees, however. And the farthest from Patsy she could get, the happier she would be.

She knew these woods a lot better than her former pal did but not with a wide enough margin to allow herself to get cocky. Patsy had never liked tramping through the wilds the way she and Kurstin had, but neither was she dead clueless. Hell, for all Hayley knew her old high school chum had spent the past decade hunting and target practicing in this very spot.

Pushing her body harder than she'd ever done, Hayley felt her left butt cheek throb like a rotten tooth and her traitorous heart pound so hard she could barely breathe. She wouldn't be kicking up the burners any time soon to disappear down the trail in a blur of spinning legs like a cartoon roadrunner.

Still, if she could get to the train trestle without being nailed to a tree by Patsy's remaining arrows, she had a decent chance of getting away. Patsy had always hated crossing the trestle. How many times had they teased her about making turtles look speedy as she inched her way across it?

Hayley rounded a curve in the path and was only a few additional twists and turns in the path from reaching the rails leading to the trestle when a mound of rags piled against one of the massive Douglas firs suddenly stirred. Slapping a hand to her chest, she skidded to a halt as something besides the need to escape penetrated her brain. Wait...what? Was that—?

Off in the distance she could hear Patsy hot on her trail. Okay, not quite hot. But sure as hell too close for comfort.

"Help. Me." The voice was faint, hoarse.

Hayley jumped as if a skeletal finger had scratched down her spine. "What the f—"

The bundle of dirty clothing moved again. A man lifted his head.

She took her first really good look. And said flatly, "You."

Because, of course it was Ty Holloway. Who else would it be? As if things were not bad enough, she suddenly felt thrust into the middle of a new-age morality tale. He was clearly in rough shape, gravely injured and weak. And a really big part of her wanted nothing more than to save herself by sacrificing him to Patsy's madness. She didn't owe this guy a damn thing.

And yet—

That nasty, bloody hole in his chest was because of her. Because he had had the temerity to broadcast the story of her moral dilemma in a way that brought her national attention. Having already thrown aside her nonviolence policy in order to strike Patsy with a rock—*twice*—she kind of wouldn't mind beating the shit out of Ty for the public spectacle he had made of her life.

But did he deserve to *die* for telling a truth she had not wanted told? Kurstie seemed to see something in the guy—something *she* sure as hell could not. Or at least her friend had before he'd screwed her over as well.

She swore and squatted to get a shoulder under his armpit. Seeing the arrows still clutched in her hand, she said, "Here," and shoved them into Ty's. "Don't drop these, we do not want Patsy finding them." Then she wrestled him to his feet.

"Come on. I know you're injured and, given how hot you feel, are probably running a fever. But you have to move your ass if you don't want us dying here. Patsy isn't far behind and she still has two arrows left." And hopefully a hand too crippled to shoot straight.

But she wasn't betting their lives on it. "Move it, Holloway!"

He groaned but did his best to comply.

His best wasn't very good, and it promptly became apparent she needed to change her strategy. She had no idea how much blood the man had lost, but he was clearly too weak or in too much pain to do more than force one foot in front of the other.

She would give him this: he was not a whiner. But what had been a race between her and Patsy now became a game of hide and seek.

She kept them going toward the trestle but managed to get Ty off the trail and out of sight when she heard Patsy getting too close. Putting a hand over his mouth, she muffled his harsh breathing as Patsy stormed by muttering less than sane-sounding threats.

Hayley dredged up every hidey-hole she could remember between here and the trestle and hoped to hell they still existed. But her plan for her and Ty to follow as soon the Patsy was far enough ahead, hide out when the other woman backtracked, then try to get farther ahead of her again wasn't feasible. Ty was in no shape for a game of Hide and Seek. A short while later, when Hayley heard Patsy headed back this way, she could do little more than hope a new plan occurred to her. And fast.

Patsy had once again moved some distance past them before she figured out what Hayley was doing. And, oh shit, demonstrated she could still adjust when she suddenly sang out, "Come out, come out, wherever you are!"

Hayley felt Ty shiver next to her. She didn't blame him; she had goosebumps-on-goosebumps of her own. If Patsy's voice was anything to go by, the woman had tripped straight into crazy town. She had always been so logical-minded. But the chaotic manner in which she was chasing them through the woods was purely reactive. She'd certainly shown no sign of working through the logistics.

So far it had worked in their favor, but the woman was a hunter. Hayley feared Patsy would take a deep breath and start applying not only logical thinking to the problem of tracking them, but her hunting experience as well. And if Pats started looking for signs of where they had been, she would find their current hiding spot.

It was a good spot, but Hayley didn't fool herself into thinking they had left no clues for someone carefully searching. Ty wasn't bleeding at the moment, but his shirt sported still-damp bloodstains that may have transferred to the overgrowth they'd plowed through. And the two of them must have flattened their fair share of grasses and moss and bent all kinds of branches and twigs.

"How far are we from where we need to be?" Ty breathed the question directly in her ear, making her start.

She shifted to reply in the same method. "Not far from the trestle. But the moment we start to cross it we will be out in the open."

"Fuck." He slumped. Looking her in the eye, he said softly. "You have to leave me. I'll only slow you down."

She had thought it herself, of course. Yet to her surprise her knee-jerk reaction was a categorical, "No."

"Look, I'm not good at heights at the best of times. Right now I doubt I have the strength to even crawl the trestle. Kurstin told me you two were gazelles on the thing. Cover me up as best you can and go find help. Send someone back for me."

She hesitated, then nodded. She spent the next few minutes getting him comfortable on his back and carefully patting moss over the wound in his chest to hopefully keep any more dirt from getting in. Then she covered him in downed leaves and branches. As she started to cover his face, he said a quiet, "Wait."

She stopped with the final camouflage hovering above him.

He looked her in the eye. "If something happens to me, tell Kurstin I'm sorry. Tell her I really did care for her...more than I have ever cared for anyone in my life. Please stress that I know I made the wrong damn decision when I chose my career over her."

"Nothing is going to happen to you."

"But if it does—"

"I will tell her. Exactly as you said it."

"Thanks. For what it's worth, I'm sorry I screwed up your life as well."

"You know what? I thought you did. But right this minute it doesn't seem all that important."

His mouth curved up on one side and the sheer rueful humor in the midst of all this madness gave Hayley an unexpected glimpse of what had drawn Kurstin to him. "Nothing like being chased through the woods by a bat-shit crazy homicidal bitch to straighten out your priorities," he murmured dryly.

"I know, right?" She gestured with her full hands. "Ready?"

He gave a slight dip of his chin.

She started covering his face. His skin was dirty from clawing his way out of his grave, but it shone around his nose and mouth where she wanted to leave breathing holes. He had no doubt scrubbed at them to clear his air passages. Setting the camouflage aside, she dug beneath layers of dead vegetation to scoop up damp dirt. Carefully, she streaked it over the clean areas, then tried the flora covering again.

This time he blended in.

"I'm covering our tracks," she whispered and set about restoring their hiding place. When it looked as undisturbed as she could make it, she climbed to her feet. "I'm going to leave while she's still a decent distance away. Move as little as possible and I'll get help to you the instant I can."

A near-inaudible grunt was her only reply.

"Okay, then. Hang in there, Ty." She turned and carefully made her way back to the trail. She looked around to mark the spot in her mind. Then she broke into a run, trying to move as quietly as possible.

But in her head she screamed Jon-Michael's name with every stride she took.

Chapter 22

Jon-Michael had to bite back the urge to crow as he strode out of Olivet Manufacturing's boardroom. He did not attempt to prevent the big grin spreading across his face as well. He was still trying to wrap his head around the fact that, with the exception of his dad and Richard's favorite stooge, Jorge Jensen, the board had voted unanimously to adopt his proposal. Or that the legal department was already preparing an offer to lease the part he had developed. It was a big-damn-deal gold letter day.

His old man and Jensen might not have stuck around to congratulate him but everyone else wanted to. The minute he could break away from the back slaps, and Mildred's brisk handshake, he pulled his phone out of his pocket and called Hayley. It went straight to voice mail. Disappointment itched in his gut, but glancing at the time he saw it was almost five-thirty. Maybe Bluey called her into work early. He'd go grab a club soda at the bar and if she wasn't there, he'd hang with the regulars until she arrived.

Before he left, however, he leaned into Kurstin's office. "Hey."

"Hey, yourself!" She hopped up from her desk and came around to give him a big hug. Pulling back, she grinned up at him. "I'm sorry I ran out on you. O'Hurley's is on central time and I needed to catch them before they closed up for the night." Waving the subject aside with a whip of her hand, she squeezed him again.

"Congratulations—you did it!"

"I did!" It would not surprise him to hear his big-ass grin   bordered on maniacal. "Hayley and Mildred and everyone else who tried to talk me into presenting my proposal sooner were right. I let personal issues with Dad get in my way."   Laughing, he picked up his sister and swung her around. "But the board loved me!" With a final squeeze, he set her back on her feet. "Have you talked to Hailey since the meeting?"

"No. Too busy."

"My call went straight to voicemail, but I thought I would drop by Bluey's to celebrate with a club soda. Maybe she'll be there."

After an additional minute or two of rehashing the high points of his presentation, he headed out. He walked into the blues bar less than ten minutes later. His gaze went straight to Hayley's usual workspace, but Bluey was behind the bar. Jon-Michael walked over. "Club soda on the rocks, barkeep! In fact, let's go crazy and add a lime."

Bluey looked up from an American Blues Scene magazine spread open on the bar. "You're in a good mood." He reached for a glass with one hand and the soda spigot with the other.

"Had a really good day at work. Hayley around?"

"You ever known her to be here this early, boy?"

Jon-Michael's mood took a dip. "No, but I was hoping. I tried calling to tell her my news but she didn't answer." His cell phone rang and pulling it from his pocket, he saw it was Kurstin. "Excuse me, Harve. I have to get this." He thumbed the phone icon. "What's up?"

"I forgot that Hayley got a call from Patsy when I talked to her before the meeting. She said they were gonna do some bow and arrow practice."

"She should be back any minute to get ready for work then. Thanks, sis. I wondered where she'd gotten off to."

There was dead air for a moment, then she said, "Bluey plays the best music."

"Doesn't he? Why don't you join me."

"Lovely idea! I'm almost to my car. I'll see you in a few."

He'd barely shoved the cell back in his hip pocket when Joe Beal materialized at his side.

The other man ordered a drink from Bluey, then turned to him. "Hey."

"How's it goin', Joe?"

Joe shrugged. "Can't complain. You?"

"I had an *excellent* day." Jon-Michael looked around. "Patsy with you?" The words had barely left his mouth before he emitted a *Wrong answer!* buzzer noise. "Sorry, stupid question. She's out showing Hayley how to use her compound bow."

Joe's hand froze in midair, the glass halfway to his mouth. "What?"

Jon-Michael frowned warily at Joe's intensity. "What part did you not understand?"

"Patsy and Hayley together! That's not good." Joe reached out to grip his arm. "There is something really wrong with Patsy—and it's centered around Hayley."

Frostbite raced up Jon-Michael's spine. "Define wrong."

The chill spread when Joe described his wife's obsession—especially when he got to the part where Patsy's hero worship turned to blame. "Why the hell didn't you warn Hayley?" Jon-Michael snapped.

"I couldn't wrap my head around it. I have been married to Patsy for a long time and kept telling myself the hairs on the back of my neck did *not* stand on end the last time I talked to her. But when you said they were out together and Patsy has her bow...shit. I can't keep fooling myself. This is trouble, man. Big trouble."

Jon-Michael pulled out his phone and hit Kurstin's number.

She picked up after the second ring. "I'm almost there—"

"Where were Hayley and Patsy going?" he interrupted.

"She didn't say. But they went to Mavis Point last time and Hayley likes to shake things up. So I would bet on Big—"

Jon-Michael hung up before she finished. "Call the Sheriff's department and tell Paulette what's going on," he said over his shoulder, then pushed through the door before Joe or Bluey had time to reply or reach for the phone. Just before the heavy oak panel closed behind him, he called back, "Tell her they may have started from Big Bear."

Reaching his Harley, he slung a leg over and kick-started the machine. A moment later, as he thrust a foot to the ground to control his skid during a sharp turn onto the road, he saw Kurstie's car approaching. She made a U-turn and fell in behind him. He also noticed Joe's big Dually turning onto the road.

Then, emptying his mind of everything not relevant to his goal, Jon-Michael opened the throttle.

***

The train tracks appeared out of nowhere. Suddenly they were just there, seemingly headed straight toward the path Hayley trod before both railroad and trail gently curved west toward Big Bear Gap.

All she cared about was reaching the tracks without Patsy catching up with her. Realizing her luck could change any second, Hayley ran as fast alongside the rails as her poor pounding heart and abused lungs would endure.

A minute later she burst out into the clearing edging the cliffs. With the trees now at her back, the early evening sunshine lost its filter and struck her fully in the face. Blocking the glare as best she could with a shielding hand, Hayley stepped onto the tracks. She trod the rustic ties cautiously until her eyes adjusted. The instant they did, she took off like a cat with a starved fox on its tail.

Suddenly she was on the trestle over the water, the shades of blues and greens far below indicating the varying depths. And there was no turning back.

Hayley blew out a pithy *pfft*. Who was she kidding? Turning back had ceased to be an option the minute Patsy shot at her.

Her feet set up a rhythm against deck tie after deck tie, and before she knew it she had passed the trestle's halfway mark. The glimpses of lake through the gaps between the rough timbers settled her nerves and she began to believe she was almost home free.

"I am going to enjoy killing you, you hypocritical bitch!"

Patsy's strident voice nearly on top of Hayley convincing herself she had a chance to escape screwed up her rhythm. The toe of one shoe skidded into the gap between the ties, sending her sprawling.

She caught herself before she face-planted, abrading the heels of her hands. Looking at them, she snorted. Bloody scrapes sure as hell were not her biggest problem. She whipped a look over her shoulder as she shoved herself upright.

And strung together a mixed-up string of prayers, pleas and obscenities. Her former friend was farther across the trestle than she had expected. Being batshit crazy, as Ty had so aptly called her, seemed to have erased Patsy's lifelong fear of the trestle.

At the moment she was struggling with the bow. To Hayley's dismay, the rock with which she had struck her former friend had damaged the hand holding the bow rather than the one needed to draw back the arrow against killer tension. She had forgotten Patsy was a leftie.

Hayley barked out a laugh that sounded scarily close to hysteria. As if she'd had a plan for *anything* that had happened from the moment Patsy first shot at her. She launched off the tie like a runner from a starting block. By the time she hit the third timber, she was running flat out.

Damned if she planned to die today at the hands of a woman she once called friend.

As though Hayley's unamused laugh was the catalyst to set the other woman off once again, Patsy began raving nonstop, threatening all manner of chilling mayhem and torture. Hayley tuned it out as best she could and focused on hauling ass to the other side of the Gap.

She was within a yard of her goal, almost close enough to jump to solid ground, when an explosive blow to her upper arm sent her staggering. Her vision went red around the edges and she fell to her knees. Slowly she looked down. An arrow had stabbed through her triceps. The point and three inches of shaft stuck out in front of her arm. The feathered end stuck out the back. Blood oozed a viscous red trail to her elbow.

Her head went swoopy. Knowing Patsy would be on her to finish the job if she passed out, Hayley swallowed the saliva pooling in her mouth, breathed in deeply then slowly exhaled through her nose until the nausea retreated. Bracing her good hand on the track, she pushed herself up.

And screamed at the top of her lungs when agony seared her arm. Simultaneously, cold horror iced her gut.

The rail beneath her hand had begun to vibrate.

"Oh, shit." Gritting her teeth, she made herself climb to her feet. She found clutching her elbow to her side with her free hand stabilized the arrow and dialed back the pain from *This is fucking* killing *me* to a mere *Hurts, hurts, hurts!*

Somewhere in the distance a male voice called her name and her heart slammed against the wall of her chest. Recognizing the precious voice, she screamed Jon-Michael's name. With Patsy growing closer, moving *now* was imperative. At least the other woman had yet to nock a second arrow. It gave Hayley some hope she could make it off the tracks without being shot again.

Fiercely focused on placing her feet, she entered the

shade of the woods before she realized solid ground supported the ties she navigated. Stepping onto a rail preparatory to getting the hell off the tracks, she could feel how much its vibration had intensified.

And, dammit to hell, knew she had to warn Patsy.

It was without a doubt the stupidest, most reckless idea she had ever had. Yet no matter how crazy her old schoolmate had become, despite Patsy doing her damnedest to kill her, Hayley didn't have the stomach to leave her to be mowed down by a train. Not without at least attempting to save her.

She turned back toward the sunny cliff.

I am within a reachable distance of the solid cliffs on the other side of the Gap when Hayley, who should be fairly far ahead of me by now, suddenly emerges from the woods. "Patsy!" she yells. "Hurry up. The train is coming!"

What the—? She wants to help me? I did not see *that* coming. Not after watching my arrow knock her on her face. So why the hell is she out in the open, warning me of some stupid train?

The big compound bow hangs limply from my left hand, my broken right hand throbs like a bitch, and I blink at her. "What?" Is this some kind of trick?

"Patsy, *please*, move your ass!"

I stare at the arrow sticking out of my one-time friend's arm and feel a savage sort of satisfaction. And yet...

"You know, Mrs. Dutton," I hear her voice say to Mother in such polite but firm tones, *"perhaps if you weren't always riding Patsy so hard you'd see that, far from being stupid, she's actually one of the smartest kids in our graduating class."*

I stare at the arm she hugs to her side. At the arrow through her flesh. And the *blood*. "Oh, God, I did that," I say. I am simultaneously proud I hit my mark under less than ideal conditions—even if it was a body shot I was after—and horrified right down to my socks. "And—shit on a shingle!—I killed Ty!"

"Ty is not dead, Pats. He's badly hurt, but last I saw of him he was alive."

"He was?" Not really sure how I feel about that. Part of me supposes the fact I am not the stone cold killer Hayley called me earlier is a good thing. And yet— "I liked it when I thought I'd killed him," I murmur. Then I shake my head, because let's be honest. "No, I *loved* it."

I am momentarily swamped with self-loathing. "Who *does* that?" I stare again at the bloody arrow through Hayley's arm. "Who shoots one of her oldest friends?"

"Someone who needs help. Come with me and I'll see you get it."

I stand there, curiously indecisive. But it is hard to hear over the roaring noise in my head.

Until, over it, Hayley yells, "Move it, dammit! The four-forty's gonna be here any minute."

Confused, I frown down at the face of my watch. "But... it's almost five forty-five."

"For pity's sake," Hayley says, "Didn't you learn *any*thing hanging with Kurstie and me?"

And, snap! My remorse disappears. Christ. I never learn, do I? Because, for Hayley, Kurstin will always, but always, come first. And I will forever be nothing but a pathetic, poor-ass second. I fumble for my last arrow. It nocks surprisingly smoothly and I bring up the bow, ignoring the pain in my right hand while I draw back the bowstring with my left.

Hayley seems clueless, although she does take a step back into the woods, making it a lot tougher to see her in the deep, textured shade beneath the trees. It doesn't matter. I know I have her. I savor the moment and ask if she has any last words.

To my surprise, she says, "You should have paid attention, Pats. Because if it's five-forty-five at the Big Bear Gap trestle, the four-forty is right—"

The train roars around the bend and heads straight for

me. "On time," I whisper even as I see Hayley's lips mouth the same words.

Engulfed by nameless dread and with only seconds to decide, I choose what strikes me as the easier of two deaths and step off the bridge. I immediately regret my choice as I plummet   toward the lake. And I scream and scream.

Knowing striking it will shatter me into oblivion.

Chapter 23

Not even when he played varsity soccer had Jon-Michael run this fast. He'd left everyone who followed him to Big Bear trailhead in the dust. It felt like a lifetime but likely wasn't more than four or five minutes between abandoning his Harley at a non-navigable protrusion of rocks in the path to bursting out onto the cliff.

He skidded to a halt.

It was empty, which sent his stomach plunging. Because, please, please! Do not let that scream have been Hayley dropping to the water or, worse, just before she was struck by the five o'clock.

"Jon."

The faint voice had him whirling. At first he saw nothing and feared his mind manufactured the sound. But adjusting his sights downward, he located Hayley sitting, legs sprawled out in front of her and her back propped against a tree. At least the right half of her back was. The left side wasn't because—bleeding Christ on a crutch—a fucking *arrow* stuck through her left arm.

Grateful to find her alive, he closed the distance between them in two huge strides and dropped to his knees by her right hip. He wanted to haul her into his arms but could only reach out and hover a hand above the arrow.

"It hurts like the fires of hell," she said calmly, "but I think it missed the main arteries." Then her face crumpled. "Oh, God, Jon-Michael, Patsy is d-dead. I tried to warn her the five o'clock was coming, but she wouldn't *listen*. She was so damn messed up and she scared the shit out of me.

I tried my best to knock her out when we were on the other side of the Gap, but I didn't want to *kill* her. She truly, desperately needed help. More than anything, she needed that." Tears flowed along paths that showed this was not her first cry. "Not to *d-die!*"

Joe tumbled out onto the cliff in time to hear her, and abruptly sat. "Dead? How do you know?"

Kurstin was next out of the woods. "Who's dead?"

"Patsy," Jon-Michael answered before Hayley had to repeat herself. He succinctly summarized what she had told him.

Hayley only corrected him once, when she said Patsy jumped off the bridge to avoid the train. "And I buried Ty on the other side of the Gap," she added.

Aw, dammit. Hayley knew even before Kurstin's face turned bone-white she should have prefaced her statement with *why* Ty was buried. "He's not dead!" she hastened to say. "I am so sorry, Kurst, this mother-freakin' pain is making me stupid. But he's alive." She explained the situation in as few words as possible.

"Tell me where!" Kurstin all but danced with impatience. "I need to find him."

"You can't get him across the trestle, Kurst. He will have to be taken out, preferably on a stretcher, through the Mavis Point trailhead, the way Pa—" She had to swallow hard. "The way we came in."

"But I can dig him out so he can breathe fresh air and know he's okay. I can sit with him until someone comes to take him to a hospital. *Right*?" She waved a hand. "I know you have good reason not to like him, Hayles, but—"

"I'm warming up to him a bit," Hayley interrupted. Then, starting from the point where the tracks disappeared into the woods on the other side of the trestle, she described the curves in the path as best as she remembered taking them. "I might be off by a bend or two, but look for a curved branch at the base of a fir tree. You can see it from either direction on the path. It's the only deadfall right next to the trail." She went on to describe how many trees beyond the fir on the other side of the path Kurstin should count before cutting into the woods. "Or, hell, just call out to him. He should hear you." Unless he was in a lot worse shape than when she'd left him.

Kurstie bounded off in her fancy ballet flats. When she barely slowed upon hitting the trestle, Joe murmured, "Jesus. If that was me, I would probably be crawling across the thing."

"Ty said the same thing when he told me to leave him behind." Hayley rested her head against the trunk. "I don't suppose either of you have an Aleve?"

They did not, but minutes later she heard Paulette call out from the woods. Joe rose and went to meet her.

A brief while after that, the sheriff squatted in front of Hayley.

"God love us," she said softly. "Joe said Patsy Beal did this to you? Where is she now?"

"Oh, God, Paulette." Hayley's eyes welled with tears once more. "If she's not dead I'll be amazed." She was thankful Jon-Michael once again took up the explanation.

Paulette called the search and rescue team to start looking for Patsy's body. Soon after, Ben Myers and Evie Bell, Gravers Bend's EMTs, showed up, Ben packing a backboard under his arm like a surfboard.

Looking at the narrow-headed target arrow sticking out of her arm, he squatted next to her and said, "I'm sorry, chickie, this is going to hurt." He snipped its point off with a pair of powerful clippers.

Hayley was still catching her breath when he suddenly yanked the projectile out. Red-hot pain exploded in what felt like her entire left side. "Seriously?" she panted.

"Sorry. There is just no good way to do that. On the bright side, it doesn't look like it struck anything vital." He pressed a thick gauze pad against the wound and taped it down, then leaned Hayley against his chest so Evie could do the same to the exit wound. They slid her onto the stretcher, strapped her to it and smoothly rose to their feet with her on the backboard between them.

Evie split a look between Jon-Michael and Joe. "Can one of you follow us to the Mavis Point trailhead? I want to get Hayley to the hospital and we could use an extra guy to help Ben pack out Holloway."

"I will." With a final look down at the water where his wife had disappeared, Joe came over to join them. They all set off for the Big Bear trailhead.

The journey was far from comfortable but every movement didn't explode pain through her arm as it had with the arrow still in it. She was nonetheless happy to be loaded onto the ambulance that doubled as Graver Bend's hearse.

And eternally grateful not to be on her way to Swanson's Funeral Parlor.

They made a stop at the other trailhead, leaving Joe and Ben with a second backboard to collect Ty. Evie drove Hayley to the little two-story hospital. She and Jon-Michael, who pulled in right behind them, carried Hayley into the ER. The EMT gave the doctor on call her report then left to drive back to the trailhead to pick up Ben, Joe and Ty.

The sun had long gone down by the time the ER doc finally cut her loose. Weary, sad and sore, Hayley wanted only to go home. But as Jon-Michael tied her shoes so she could leave in the wheelchair the staff insisted she *would* ride as far as the hospital entrance if she wanted out of there, Kurstin banged through the door.

"Ty is leaving me to take some big deal job on the New York Times. For my own *good*, he says!"

"Dammit, Kurstin, take care of your own problems," Jon-Michael snapped.

But Hayley spoke over him. "What? Oh, for God's sake." She waited until he finished tying the second shoe, then slid off the hospital bed and walked gingerly to the door. Stopping, she turned. "What room?"

"Follow me." Kurstin eased past her.

Hayley took exactly one step before Jon-Michael raced up behind her with the wheelchair. "Sit," he said in a you-don't–*even*-wanna-mess-with-me voice. She sat, and still he swore under his breath the entire short trip down the hall.

She, on the other hand, marveled over the drugs they had administered for her pain. They were suddenly damn effective. She was rejoicing over how they not only killed the pain but made her feel downright happy-happy, when Kurstin turned into a room. Jon-Michael wheeled her in behind his sister.

Getting her head out of La-La-Land, she said, "Move aside," and took control of her chair to roll up next to Ty's bed. "I hear you're trying the do the honorable thing," she said without preamble. "That's gotta be an uncomfortable fit. You and I both know what you would really do given half a chance, so why don't you just tell Kurstie what you told me when you thought you were going to die?"

Her friend whirled to gape at her, "What did he tell you?" she demanded at the same time Ty said, "Hooking up with me is the worst move she could make."

"You'll be an old man if you're waiting for me to say, No, no, you have it all wrong." A wave of wooziness had her weaving a little on her feet and she braced herself. "But you do not get to treat her like a child who doesn't know her own mind when you're the one who is too chickenshit to air a few honest emotions. So, tell her what you really want, let her tell you what *she* wants and take it from there. But just remember this, Ty. If you do hurt her, she has a brother who would be happy to beat the crap out of you with his bare hands."

Jon-Michael, bless him, studied the knuckles of the fist he'd clenched.

"Not to mention a bestie—" she bounced her thumb off her chest "—who will help her bury the body where no one will ever find it. So, man up and tell the truth for a change. I wanna go home."

"Fine," he said, a little sulky to be called out on his emotional dodge-'em. At the same time, he looked at Kurstin with a gleam in his eye.

"Don't think I won't compare conversations with Hayley in the morning," Kurstin interjected. "I will know if you wuss out."

"That's our cue to leave," Jon-Michael said and Hayley nodded. She doubted either Ty or Kurstin even noticed when they let themselves out.

Ty eyed Kurstin warily. Except for her double-take when Hayley outed him, the woman had not taken her eyes off him. She barely waited now for the door to close behind her brother and best friend before demanding, "Let's hear it."

He took a deep breath and slowly exhaled. He hadn't given his life expectancy great odds during the however-long he had been in the woods. And his biggest regret had been willfully refusing to tell Kurstin the truth. Well, that and thinking it was a *good* idea not even attempting to explain himself in the wake of imploding their relationship.

Yet here he sat, not only alive but with a second chance a fingertip away. And still he had no idea where to start.

How 'bout with an apology? his conscience whispered. *You can never go wrong with an apology.* "I'm sorry."

"How nice." Ok, her cool tone made it clear she wasn't impressed. "Is that what you told Hayley when you thought you were going to die?"

"Yes. But mostly I asked her to make sure you knew how much I really did care for you." He quit hiding behind an emotionless recitation and reached for her hand. Looked into her beautiful eyes. "God, Kurstin. I have felt more in the short time I've known you than I have for everyone else in my life, combined. I don't know squat about love. So I can't say for sure if that's what all this turmoil is going on in here." He rotated the heel of his hand against the spot where his diaphragm met his sternum. "But it has to be something close to it. I sure as hell never knew it was possible to feel the way I do—both happier than I've ever been and scared shitless."

"Yet not once did you say a word to *me* about it!"

"I wanted to. God, I cannot tell you how much I wanted to. But every time I started to, I just couldn't. Look." He gazed at her helplessly. "You're like some damn...princess or something, while I'm—well, I'm from a poverty-stricken little nowhere town in West Virginia. A town I clawed my way out of before it could suck me into the mines. I've been clawing my way ever since—for jobs, for better by-lines, for that next rung up the ladder." He blew out a breath. "Then I met you and had a proverbial smackdown between the angel on one shoulder and the devil on the other."

"And we both know who won that round," she muttered.

"I'm not proud of it. When I sent the Hayley article to my editor, I felt honest-to-Christ sick. I knew I'd betrayed your trust and made *you* betray your best friend in the process. But the damn tipping point wasn't me worrying over giving up my dreams. It was the idea of meeting your father. I thought about telling him I had intentions toward you—then having to admit I was unemployed when he asked what I did for a living."

"So, what's changed, Ty? This is all very angsty, but five minutes ago you were ready to toss me away for a job on some stupid newspaper."

"Some stupid—? On the *New York Times!*" He long considered himself shock-proof. But hearing the NYC referred to as *some stupid newspaper* scandalized him right down to his toenails.

Yet in truth? "I would give that job up in a red-hot minute if you'd forgive me. If you'd let me stick around to be your guy."

"*Would* you." *There* was the princess persona he had mentioned. Coolly, she looked him over from the top of his head to the toes of his big feet where they tented the hospital sheets. "I'll have to review my options and get back to you on that. Meanwhile—" She climbed onto the bed on his uninjured side and, smelling like a million bucks, snuggled against his far from pristine body. "Just hold me for a while."

He wanted her to agree to be his right *now*. Wanted to pin down an ironclad arrangement she could not wiggle out of. Make her agree he could stay here with her. Or that she'd go to New York with him. *Something*.

But it had been a fucking eventful day to say the least. Wrapping his good arm around her, he did as instructed. And received a world full of comfort in return.

"So," he said with studied casualness. "Did I ever tell you I have a political-opinion blog that is starting to attract some attention?"

Hayley gave Jon-Michael a self deprecatory smile as he helped her into the local taxi he'd called to take them home. "I know what you're thinking."

"Do you? Good trick, considering I don't have a clue."

"You're thinking I'm a big-ass talker, giving Ty grief about being an emotional coward. Considering you've called me on being the same thing." The cab driver turned left at the highway instead of right and she frowned out the window. "Hey, he's going the wrong way."

Jon-Michael ran his hand down her hair from her crown to her nape, which he squeezed to redirect her attention on him. "You said you wanted to go home."

"I do. To *your* place."

"Yeah?" His tired eyes brightened and the corners of his mouth curled up like burning paper.

"Yes. I just wanna go home."

He leaned forward. "Harold," he said to the cabbie.

"Change of plans."

Ten minutes later, Jon-Michael had Hayley settled on the couch with a glass of water. "How you feeling?"

She gave him a sweet, loopy smile. "Mighty fine."

"Good drugs, huh?"

"Extremely." She took a sip of her water and grimaced. "A glass of wine would be good, though."

"Yeah, that's not gonna happen. You're a couple sheets to the wind as it is."

"There is that," she agreed amiably. She handed him the water glass. As he took it, she said, "I love you, Johnny."

He bobbled the glass, righted it with only a small splash across the back of his hand, then very carefully set it on the coffee table. "You—?"

"Love you." She yawned. "I'm a real big proponent of never lying to oneself, yet I sure refused to acknowledge the way I feel for you. For way too long, I refused to do that. But it's a funny thing when someone tries to kill you. It points out in rolling neon arrows how absurd lying to yourself is."

He watched her wince at the mention of arrows.

Then she shook her head as if to dislodge the image. "Anyhow, after I injured Patsy enough to get away, I ran like the frickin' wind. And all I could think of, with every step I took, was you. About how much time I wasted playing the same emotional dodge-em game I accused Ty of tonight. I should have admitted a long time ago what you and I both know."

His heart pounding like a sonofabitch, he sat carefully on the edge of the couch next to her. "And we know...you're in love with me?"

"*Crazy* in love with you. Mow-down-anyone-who-gets–in-my-way in love with you." Her lips curled up. "You had me at the Groucho glasses, Olivet."

Then she looked him in the eye with complete

seriousness. "You have turned yourself into such a fine man, Jon-Michael."

It was as if she'd reached inside his chest and wrapped her warm, capable hand around his heart. "Aw, Hayley." Carefully, he scooped up her, sat down in the space she had occupied and rested her on his lap. He cradled her with her good shoulder tucked against his chest, her round butt nestled in his lap and her legs sprawled along the couch cushions. Pressing his chin against her cheek, he said in a low, rough voice directly into her ear, "I love you so much. I have for a long, long time. Soon as your meds wear off I'm going to ask you to repeat yourself, just to be sure we're really on the same page here."

She laughed. "Fair enough, but the answer will be the same. Hey!" She raised her head. "I'm so sorry, I never even asked. How did the board meeting go?"

"I aced it! Your Right-Is-Might turned out to be prophetic. Except for the old man and Jensen, they voted unanimously for my proposal. And the company is going to lease my part." He shook his head in wonder. "I planned to give it to them, but the old man has been such a pain in the ass I'm dead happy to take his money." Then he shrugged. "Knowing you love me, though? All that could have gone completely the other way and I'd still say life doesn't get any better than this."

"Adore the sentiment." She rubbed her smooth cheek against his beyond five o'clock shadow. "But I love this outcome even more. And Jon-Michael?"

"Yeah, darlin'?"

"I am so glad to know I'll have you by my side when, or if, they execute Lawrence Wilson. Knowing I have you to lean on, I can get through either outcome." She pressed her cheek more firmly against his. "God, my heart feels like a big old balloon o' bliss. And the best part? I can't help but believe our life will continue getting even better."

"If that's even possible."

"I know, right? But I'd wager everything I own on it,

which, okay, isn't much. But if I *had* a fortune I would bet it all on us. Because I know in my heart our love is just going to keep growing."

"Amen, sister." Tilting his head, he pressed a gentle kiss to her pretty lips, then moved to rest his forehead against hers. "But I still want to hear it from you when the opiates are all out of your system."

"Deal."

And the following morning, she told him the same thing all over again.

EPILOGUE

Late February

The lighting inside Bluey's was a shade less atmospheric than usual on this frigid Monday night. Then again, it was a far from typical evening at the blues club. Jon-Michael and Hayley had rented the space for their engagement party.

Sounds of celebration: the boisterous laughter of their guests, the rise and fall of conversations, the clink of glasses and murmurs of appreciation over the beautifully presented, tasty hors d'oeuvres being circulated by the high school kids she had hired for the night, made Hayley smile.

Yet even as she appreciated the way Janiva Magness's lament about some guy who was never hers poured from the speakers to weave its way through the joyous party noise, she found herself peeking out the window. For the umpteenth time.

A strong hand rubbed circles between her shoulder blades. "She'll be here," Jon-Michael assured her in a low voice.

"I know." She turned to smile at him. "She called to let me know her stinkin' flight finally touched down." Which was old news she promptly waved aside. "It's still a long drive."

"Kurstie drives like a maniac and will be here before you know it." Leaning down, Jon-Michael pressed his lips to the curve where her neck met her shoulder. "In the meantime, how about we relax and enjoy the party?" he murmured. "It's our night to crow."

Her love for this man filled every atom of her being, pushing aside her impatience to see her best friend sooner rather than later. She missed Kurstie, but the past seven months had been the happiest of Hayley's life. "You're right. She will get here when she gets here." She smoothed his black and gold Art Deco inspired tie over his shirt and gave him a peck on the lips. "Buy a girl a drink?"

"You got it." With his hand pressed lightly against the small of her back, he steered her toward the bar.

Hayley stopped halfway there to introduce Jon-Michael to two Lincoln High teachers she'd built a friendship with since joining the staff in September. She smiled as he charmed their pants off in his laid back, low-key way. When the women excused themselves to freshen their drinks, Jon-Michael's secretary intercepted them to shyly introduce her boyfriend and tell them they really knew how to throw a party.

The boyfriend heartily agreed. "I particularly liked the photo booth," he said, whipping out the strip the young couple had taken to show them.

The entire night just warmed Hayley's soul and she laughed when they reached the bar. "Best. Engagement party. Ever." She turned to Bluey, who was personally bartending tonight. "Vodka and cranberry, please."

"You got it." He assembled her drink and poured Jon-Michael a club soda on the rocks. "Nice turnout," he observed as he slid their drinks across the bar.

"It is. I was tickled when so many people RSVPed."

A board member pulled Jon-Michael aside to discuss something and Bluey left to wait on the group who hailed him from the other end of the bar. They had barely walked away when a male voice at her shoulder said, "Hey."

She swiveled to see Joe standing behind her with his arm draped over Lucy's shoulders. Hayley had been surprised when the two hooked up around Christmas. She never would have predicted the combination, but they worked as a couple. "Hey, yourselves," she said and gave them both a hug.

Stepping back from Lucy, she ran her gaze over the other woman's one-shouldered Ed Hardy dress and reached out to tweak its silky fabric. "This is so you! And I love the red in your hair, too. Very chic."

They visited for a few minutes before Lucy excused herself to discuss something business related with Bluey, who was still at the far end of the counter. She had barely walked away when Joe edged Hayley away from the bar. Next thing she knew, the two of them were the sole occupants of a temporarily empty space. She raised her eyebrows at him.

Joe gently touched the edge of his thumb to what she knew, despite careful makeup application, were faint shadows beneath her eyes. "Jon-Michael tells me you've had trouble sleeping since Patsy's death."

Her first inclination was to dodge the implicit question with a few facile platitudes. Instead she nodded. Because if anyone was likely to understand the emotions she'd been dealing with, it was Joe. "I can't shake the feeling I should have done more for Patsy while she was alive," she admitted in a low voice. "It kills me that not only did I not, I often went out of my way to avoid her."

"You're talking to the man who moved out once he saw how screwed up his wife was," he replied. "So I get the guilt. The difference here is I've had a little longer to process everything. I spent a lot of time, both before and after Pats died, trying to figure out what the hell drove her to want to *hurt* people for cri'sake."

"And did you reach any conclusions?" *Because I could really use a conclusion.*

"You ask me, if anyone is to blame for twisting Patsy's psyche, it was her bitch of a mother."

"Which makes me feel even guiltier for not trying harder with her."

"Hayley, she was damn good at hiding how messed up

she'd become. You could have devoted every damn day to her and I bet the end result would have been the same. Most of us have more than one friend and naturally you would've divided your attention between yours. Patsy was incapable of accepting that. As for not doing enough? Jesus, look at the huge favor you did her by calling out her mom. I'm sure Patsy's hero-worship started out as a harmless talisman against her mother's constant belittling. Yet, aside from a pathological need to know your every thought, did Patsy ever simply say she was sorry for your troubles and let it go at that?"

Hayley shook her head.

"Neither did I, and I am sorrier than I can say for my insensitivity. I think too damn many of us looked at the events turning your life upside down as if it was an exciting big-screen thriller. But the difference between the rest of the town and Patsy is in the end her hero worship morphed into something that damn near got you killed."

Reaching for her hands, Joe held her gaze with a keenly serious one of his own. "So, big deal, you didn't want to spend twenty-four/seven with her. Except for maybe Jon-Michael, is there *any*one you have a desire to spend such concentrated time with?"

No. Not even Jon-Michael, if truth be told—and she loved him like her next breath. But she had always needed private time that was hers alone. The guilt, which had robbed her of sleep on a near-nightly basis, suddenly felt lighter. A wispier burden a fresh new breeze might whisk away.

She leaned in to kiss Joe's cheek. As she stepped back she gave his hand a fierce squeeze. "*Thank* you. You didn't say anything I haven't tried telling myself—but it has more weight coming from you. I get the feeling you struggled with the guilt as much as I did."

"Yeah." He shot her a crooked smile. "But I've learned to let it go."

"I'm glad. And I thank you from the bottom of my heart

for giving me the tools to start doing the same. I plan to take my newly-gained awareness of Patsy's pain and self-imposed isolation to use with my own needy students."

"Then my work here is done." He grinned at her and stepped back. "I think I'll go find my date and rock this very fine party with her."

Hayley was headed across the room to where Jon-Michael was shooting the breeze with former band members when she heard his father's voice say from over at the bar, "...'ly saying this is a ridiculous venue for an engagement party when he belongs to a perfectly good country club. I can only imagine what people are saying. I assume this was his fiancé's idea. If I had had any idea my son would end up marrying her I would have put an end to the little charity-case spending so much time with Kurstin."

She spun around to tell Richard once and for all where he could shove his supercilious, smugly superior arrogance. But Mildred Bayerman beat her to the punch.

"Richard," the older woman said coolly, "Jon-Michael is smart, charming and a goddamn business asset. He's dragging Olivet's into the 21st century. More importantly, he is a fine man. If anyone is the charity case here it's...well." Shaking her head she cut herself off, but gave Richard a pitying look.

Hayley watched Mildred collect her purse from the bar and slide off the stool she'd occupied. The older woman turned away from Jon-Michael's dad.

And saw Hayley standing there.

To Hayley's surprise, Mildred's cheeks turned pink as if she, who according to Jon-Michael was one of the fiercest women in the business, were embarrassed. Touched, Hayley walked up to the board member and pulled her into a heartfelt hug. "Thank you," she said in Mildred's ear. "Richard has needed to hear that for a very long time. Maybe coming from someone he respects as much as Jon-Michael says he does you, it will even sink in." Setting

Mildred loose, she stepped back and gave the older woman a wry smile. "But I won't hold my breath."

"Hayleeeeey!"

Whipping around at the sound of her best friend's voice, she saw Kurstin bearing down on her from across the room, an unbuttoned Burberry wool and cashmere trench coat flapping behind her.

Hayley turned back to Mildred and squeezed the older woman's hand. "I am so sorry, I need to…I have to…" She shrugged helplessly. "Kurstie's here."

Mildred squeezed back. "Go."

With a hoot of pure joy, Hayley raced to meet her best friend.

Jon-Michael watched his sister and Hayley collide in the middle of the floor and grinned as they whooped with laughter. Hayley had missed Kurstin something fierce, regardless of all the hours they spent talking on the phone or texting since Kurst's move to New York with her reporter. But as though no time at all had passed, the two women hugged, pulled away to check each other out even as they chatted ninety miles an hour, then hugged again.

When they separated once more, Jon-Michael watched Kurstin lean back and use her hands to sketch a body silhouette over Hayley. He had lived with his sister long enough to know she was verbally high-fiving his girl's dress.

Not without good reason. Hayley looked *hot* in her smoky silk stockings, sky-high black heels and little heart attack of a dress. The body-skimming old-gold peek-a-boo lace snugged over a silky, skimpy black slip. He spared a moment of serious admiration for the way its uneven hem flirted with her firm thighs as he bee-lined toward the women.

He met up with them just as Halloway, who must have dropped Kurstin at the door and parked the rental, arrived. Ty clearly made his sister happy, so Jon-Michael exchanged polite greetings before giving his sister an enthusiastic lift-her-off-her-feet hug. While he was not quite ready to sing Kumbayah with the guy, he would admit Ty had done an excellent job writing the Patsy story. And Hayley trusted him enough to have given him an in-depth exclusive regarding her mixed emotions over capital punishment and the man who had killed her late husband. Which had had the added bonus of getting rid of the rest of the media crowding Gravers Bend last summer. That meant if Lawrence Wilson was eventually put to death, even after last August's final hour reprieve, Hayley would likely still be yesterday's news.

Plus, and Jon-Michael would stick a needle in his eye before admitting this to anyone but Hayley, he followed Halloway's *In One Man's Opinion* blog. It disseminated some of the most erudite takes on current events he had ever read.

"We miss you at Olivet's," he told his sister.

"Oh, God," she said, "I miss everyone there, too. Telecommuting is great. But it's not the same as being there."

"So how is the Big Apple treating you?"

"Not too shabby."

"She doesn't love it," Ty put in.

"But I love *you*," Kurstin assured the man.

"Which is why she puts up with it." The look of love Ty gave her went a long way in upping Jon-Michael's approval rating. Then Ty turned to him. "So I have an engagement present for you two...and a little something for my love, as well."

"Ooh." Kurstie wiggled. "I love presents."

"Me, too," Hayley agreed. She eyed Ty's empty hands. "I don't see any ribbon-festooned packages so I am guessing it's smaller than a bread box."

"It is. But I hope you'll consider the sentiment behind it big." Ty's mouth quirked up on one side. "Huge, even."

"The suspense—not to mention the hyperbole—is

killing me." Kurstin smacked Ty on the arm. "Show us already!"

"As you wish. I tendered my resignation to the New York Times. I thought we could move back here."

For an instant, the space surrounding the four of them was a vacuum in the midst of the party revelry. Then Kurstin, who looked ecstatic and horrified at one and the same time, said, "But...you *love* the Times."

"No, I love you and I am damn fond of my blog. I like the prestige of working at the Times but I'm a small cog in a very big wheel. It could be years before I'm promoted to a spot where I get to do even half of what I'm already doing on *One Man's* ." He ran a thumb down the pink flush on Kurstie's cheek. "So I thought, why not make that my focus? It's really taken off in the past few months and I can write anywhere." He gave a casual shrug, but watched Kurstin closely. "Gravers Bend seems like a good place."

"Omigawd!" She threw herself in his arms. Hayley bounced up and down on her stilettos, then hugged Ty herself when he set Kurstin free.

Jon-Michael decided maybe the guy was all right after all.

Later, as he and Hayley swayed together on the stage they had designated the dance floor, he heard her mumble something into his neck. He tipped his chin to see her face. "What's that, darlin'?"

"I am just so, so happy," she said. "I have you, a job I really like, a kick-ass engagement party—and my best friend is gonna be back in town soon. Does life *get* any better than this?"

"Depends. Wanna go rip off a piece in the restroom?"

"Um, no. But I will give you a rain check for the room of your choice when we get home." She kissed his neck. "And just to sweeten the deal I'll add an additional ten years of the same. Whataya say?"

"It's a start, lover girl." He pulled her closer yet. "It is a damn sweet start."

Susan Andersen

Is the bestselling author of a couple dozen books. The Proud mama of a grown son, she lives in the Pacific Northwest with her decades-long soulmate and "The Boys," her cats Boo Radley and Mojo. The inhabitants of her little piece of the world are weird and wonderful, and Susan attributes her attempts to stay one step ahead of them with keeping her young.

To be kept apprized of upcoming books, visit www.susanandersen.com and join Susan's email list. She keeps them to the bare minimum and never shares her readers' information.

CPSIA information can be obtained at www.ICGtesting.com
Printed in the USA
LVOW10s0009030816

498827LV00032B/1243/P